Northwoods
A Novel by
Cindy Koch-Krol

For: Jeff and Jake—my rock and my tree!

Special Thank you to John VanDreel, Katie Compton, and Rocko, for helping me with the Cover Art. Rocko and Woofy are soul brothers in my book!

C. Koch-Krol, July 13, 2014

Part One: Woofy

Chapter 1

http://tessagates.blogspot.com.

Tessa's Travels

Tessa Gates: Free Lance Travel Writer and Restaurant Reviewer. I hike around the country in search of unusual and unique cuisine.

Where am I heading?

I'm traveling at the moment in North West Lower Michigan. I will soon be hitting:

Manistee
Frankfort
Interlochen
Traverse City
Suttons Bay
Northport
Acme
Elk Rapids
Bellaire
Charlevoix
East Jordan
Petoskey
Pelston
Mackinaw City

Upper Peninsula (watch for the best Pasty in the U.P. contest.)

About Me

Hi, my name is Contessa Gates, but you can call me Tess. I am a graduate of the Chicago Institute of the Fine Arts. I have an MFA in Journalism. Upon graduating two years ago I tried to find a job in my field and could not, so I took matters into my own hands. With mounting debts I decided to take to the road to find unusual restaurants that were serving unique cuisine write about them and sell the reviews to newspapers. My father in Chicago is my Agent. Any newspapers interested in purchasing my reviews can contact me through him. His contact info is in the box at the left.

At first I was traveling with a friend who was taking a year off between high school and college. Harold Whitney took me in his beat up 50-year-old Volvo, which was an adventure by itself, and which got me in shape for the backpacking adventure I'm on now. More than once we became stranded because of that machine and had to hike, sometimes up to ten miles, to get to a phone or service station. My father insisted on the purchase of a cell phone when I lost my Harold to a college in Arizona. I now have a smart phone that gives me internet access on my laptop, so I can literally update my Blog in the woods at my campsite if I need to. Dad likes the feeling that he can contact me any time of the day or night and vice versa.

I'm mostly on foot now. I sometimes get rides with people that have been vouched for by restaurant personnel, but on average I walk at least ten miles a day, sometimes as much as 30. I'm in the best shape of my life. If I didn't have to carry a 50 pound pack with me everywhere I could run a marathon!

I always pay for my food, which I believe gives me the right to be fair in critiquing it. So food, my monthly phone/internet bill, and my not inconsiderable student loan are my only fiscal concerns, along with a motel room about twice a week so I can shower and get some proper rest. Sleeping on the ground is not always as comfortable as it sounds, but it's a sacrifice I'm willing to make for my art!

See the box above for places where I plan to be in the near future. Also sign up for my mailing list to get future updates

If you have a suggestion of someplace my readers should know about, please Email me directly, my contact information is under my father's at the left. If the cuisine is unique or unusual I will seek it out no matter how far off the beaten path.

See you soon, at a restaurant near you!

Tessa Gates

June 5

Lush Green North Woods

Hi Dad and other readers,

I'm in the lush green north woods of lower Michigan. Three nights in a row I've slept in deep forest. The summer nights have been warm and wonderfully rich with the sounds of nature. I think last night an owl came and landed on the peak of my tent. At least it sounded like that's where it was. Most of the time if I am awakened by animal noises in the forest it's a simple matter of turning on my flashlight and they flee, but this owl kept hooting into my ear for nearly an hour before it finally found a farther perch. Dad knows I'm a pretty hearty soul that doesn't scare easily, but the eerie sound of the owl so close was starting to creep me out. It went away about 3 am and I was able to get a little sleep. A quick wash in a stream the next morning and I felt ready to go.

Tonight I'll be in a medium small town called Manistee and I'll find a motel room, hopefully one with HBO, so I can catch up on sleep and shower. There is a little mom and pop restaurant here called the Glory Diner which is purported to have unusual dishes made partially of jerky. We shall see! I will be showing up there about three pm today, if the calculations and road signs are correct. There is a dive between here and there called Tony's that I plan to try for lunch. I fear that their deep fryer is used frequently for most of the dishes though.

Tomorrow I'll be heading toward Frankfort and then up toward Traverse City. A reader told me about a little place run by Native Americans in a town called Northport. I should arrive there in about a week's time. The report I got was that all the food they serve is mostly from wild game sources. I can't wait to try that.

More later,
Tessa Gates

Chapter 2

When Tess entered the little run down building that housed The Great Moose restaurant outside of Northport, Michigan, the line of patrons sitting at the bar all turned to look at her.

"Sorry guys, I know you were expecting Marilyn Monroe, but all you got was me!" she said. Every one of them either smiled or laughed outright. It was not until then that she noticed that they all had the swarthy dark skin of a Native American. In fact looking around the room, she noticed that she was only one of three white people in this establishment. And as a whole, there was only one woman to four men.

Now that the tension in the room had eased up she looked around. No ambiance to speak of. Décor was early cottage complete with taxidermy heads of things that someone had killed. It looked like a total dive but she had eaten in worse places and they had surprised her with good food, so she kept an open mind.

She stood by the door for a moment longer and a waitress came up to her.

"You can sit anywhere, miss, we don't have a hostess."

"Thanks," she said. She picked out a booth near a window and sat, pulling a greasy menu from behind the sugar container on the table.

"What can I get you to drink?" the waitress asked.

"Oh, I got a few more miles to go tonight, maybe just some water for now, and I'll order something else later after I eat."

"OK, I'll give you a few minutes."

Tess spread out the menu before her and looked. There didn't seem to be anything real unusual about it. Then she spotted it. There was a description of a fish dish that included a sauce: salmon in pepper sauce. She had no idea what that would be like but needed to try it.

The waitress came back with her water. "What can I get you?"

Tess waited overly long still looking through the selections. "Do you need a little more time?" the waitress asked.

"What's the pepper sauce like?" she asked absently.

"The what?"

"The pepper sauce, on the salmon, what kind of peppers?"

"Oh that. Bobby makes a great white sauce with hot chili peppers, green bell peppers and yellow sweet peppers. No one really likes it though. Lots of people ask for the salmon without the sauce."

"Is the white sauce milk based or cheese based?"

"Cheese, Munster, Provolone, and Parmesan, with a dash of cream for binding."

"Really," Tess looked up and took in the waitress for the first time. She had luminescent golden skin. Her eyes and hair were a matching shade of black. Her uniform had hide fringe that would have been more at home on a leather jacket.

"Yes, and a special ingredient, buffalo cheese, cheese made from buffalo milk. One of our tribal members has a big buffalo ranch down by Manistee. He supplies us with meat, cheese, milk, sausage, ground buffalo meat that goes into our burgers. Stuff like that."

"I didn't even know a buffalo could be milked."

"Oh, yeah," the young woman assured her. "We pretty much do everything to a buffalo that you white people would do to a cow."

"Are you an Indian?" Tess asked and then corrected, "I'm sorry, Native American?"

The lovely young woman smiled displaying a row of straight white teeth. "Yeah," she said. "This is my sister's place. My brother and I work here. She's the one behind the bar."

"Oh, how interesting." Tess said, looking over at the bartender. "Who is Bobby?"

"Bobby Flay?" She quipped. Tess laughed at the culinary joke. "Bobby is my sister's husband, he does all the cooking."

"And does Bobby have any other specialties that aren't on the menu? Now would be the time for him to trot them out. I'm a restaurant reviewer. Tessa Gates."

"Why hello, Tessa. I'm Mary Redwing and please no hockey jokes, OK?"

"I couldn't come up with one that fast anyway. I'm not a big hockey fan."

"Usually men ask to see my Stanley Cups. Yah, that one never gets old," Mary said. The roll of her eyes and the sarcastic tone said otherwise.

"Would you like to talk with him?"

"I'd love to." Tessa said with a smile and Mary Redwing walked back to the kitchen. Soon Mary was back with her brother-in-Law, Bobby, sister Ruth and her younger brother who looked to be about 19, who was introduced as David but in the course of the next conversation was referred to several times as Kicky.

Bobby described several dishes that he could make all of which contained some sort of wild game and locally gathered vegetation. In the end she ordered the salmon with the pepper sauce, the moose pemmican with blue berries, the venison steak with morel mushroom sauce and a bowl of the buffalo stew with barley. Kicky suggested she get an order of fry bread as well because it was made daily by their mother who did this task particularly well.

"Are you going to eat all of this?" Kicky asked her.

"I'm certainly going to taste it all," Tess said to him. "Why would you and a few others care to join me?"

Kicky turned toward the others and dismissed them with a gesture, "They've already eaten. But I just got off work. I'd love to join you."

Tess sized up the young man in one glance. He was tall and strong looking for a 19 year old. She thought that he might look young for his age he could be twenty or even twenty-one. His skin was the same luminescent golden as his sister's and his muscles seemed well formed from what she could see through the loose fitting t-shirt he was wearing.

He was too young for her. But then so was Harry. It had been over a year since Harry had stopped driving her around in his beat up Volvo.

Harry had been a lovable geek and a very good friend. He had taken a year off after High school to travel with her. But he had gone off to college last fall and stayed there for the summer semester. Tess had hoped he would take up driving her this summer as well, but she couldn't pay him so he had no incentive to quit his lucrative cooking job to come home to Chicago. Oh well, she thought. It's all good. She had found ways to keep herself safe while on the road. She never even felt the need to use the pepper spray her father had given her. She never felt that she was in danger of being raped. But many men had propositioned her over the last year that she had been without other male companionship. The type of people who propositioned her were not men that Tess would normally give the time of day, truck driver sorts and men over thirty or sometimes even over forty. It was easy to say no to them. Not her cup of tea. Tess was no prude, she'd had a boyfriend in college but it hadn't worked out. Harry was more than a friend, he was like her little brother, but sex was out of the question with him. She used to baby-sit for him, for goodness sakes. Besides she considered herself too good a Catholic to engage in casual sex. Her career needed nurturing right now. She didn't want to risk pregnancy. That would mean getting off the road for a while. Right now she had a good thing going. So no matter how enticing this young Native American sitting across from her seemed, sex was out of the question. Nevertheless, he watched her with an expression of puppy-like expectation. He seemed to want her approval above anything else.

"Sure, you can join me," she said, trying to hide her interested gaze behind a friendly smile. He slid into the booth opposite her. "Would you watch my stuff? I need to go, wash my hands," she said with a wink.

The fact was that she did have to wash her hands. She had been traveling up M22 to Northport all day. She could find no one to drive her up this side of the peninsula from Traverse City last night, so she had walked the entire 28 miles with her backpack. In the bathroom of the restaurant she unpacked her towel and washcloth and did a cursory wash of her hands face and upper body in the bathroom sink. She donned a fresh top and last of all changed her socks, washing the ones she had been wearing all day in the basin and then rolling them tightly into a plastic bag. Later, when she got to her campsite she would take them out and hang them on her tent line to dry for tomorrow. When she got back to her table she unpacked her camera, laptop and cell phone and laid them each out on the table in case she needed them.

"We don't have Wi-Fi here," Kicky said doubtfully.

"Don't need it. I can mount a hotspot with my cell phone." Then when she saw his confused look she added, "Dontcha just love technology?"

He let loose a short bark of laughter at that. From then on his approving smile did not leave his face.

As the food began to arrive Tess took pictures of each entrée with her digital camera.

One particularly nice leafy vegetable came in a small salad and Tess couldn't figure out what it was. "Those are ramps," Kicky told her. My Mom and my other older sister gather them out in the woods in this area. You're lucky you came at just the right time. The morels and the ramps are both in. By next month there won't be any of either. Well, I mean, we'll still have morels for a few months because mom collects them and dries them."

"Where does Bobby get the wild game, the venison and the moose and all that?"

"We hunt them," Kicky said. "We're all really great hunters in this family."

"Is that legal?"

"Long as no one finds out!"

"That's not true!" Mary said, walking up with a pitcher to refill her water glass. "Don't let him kid you, Tess. We have several hunters that give part of their game to us during hunting season. We have a huge deep freeze in the back and we take from those stores all year."

Tess shook her head at the young man, "Now why did you want to go and lie to me like that?"

"I'm not lying. I would never lie to you, Tess," he said.

All at once the air seemed to close in on her. Kicky stared intently into her eyes. He had a very strange look on his face. If Tess didn't know better she would say it was . . . adoration?

"Whoo," Tess said waving her hand in front of her face. "Is it hot in here?"

Tess got back to work. She tried each dish, one at a time, savoring the first bite of each in her mouth allowing it to swirl through her taste buds and getting a good feel for the flavors. After each bite she put down her fork and typed on the laptop keyboard for a few minutes, then took a drink of water and tried the next dish. Kicky watched all of this with interest. Tessa's enjoyment of the flavors was audible. Kicky's smile renewed itself whenever Tess made a noise of pleasure rolling her eyes heavenward.

After she had tried each dish and made notes of them, she dished out the parts of the four meals she wanted to finish. She was mostly taken with the venison steak topped by morel sauce. She wanted to eat more of that for certain. But she also took medium sized portions of the dried moose meat that had been re-hydrated in a buttery sauce with blueberries and small cooked pieces of what looked like rice but Kicky explained were grains of wheat. She took a few more spoonfuls of the Buffalo stew before pushing the rest of the bowl over in front of Kicky. But she kept all the ramp salad to herself. She tasted the fry bread. It was very similar to a fried donut only the size and shape of a largish pancake. A sprinkle of powdered sugar and it would almost be an elephant ear like at the carnival.

"Wow, Bobby is a master. I haven't been this full of great food in a while!" she exclaimed.

"Isn't this your job?" Kicky asked.

"Well, yeah, but I don't generally eat this much. I usually just try each dish and then set it aside, but I guess it's a testament to your brother-in-law's good cooking that I ate so much of his food."

"So are you going to give us a good review?"

"I'd say that's fairly well assured!" Tess got Mary's attention and asked for a glass of wine and the check.

"Bobby said that your meal is on the house tonight." Mary said.

"Um, no it's not." Tess said. "I always pay for my food, and that way I can be fair and honest about the review I write. So please make out a bill for me."

"You, um, also bought my dinner," Kicky said looking down at the table and the empty plates. "I can't allow that."

"My treat," Tess said. "It's a business expense. And besides, maybe I can figure out something for you to do to pay me back."

"Such as?" he asked, his brow arching.

"Do you have a car?"

"Sure, I got a car. Do you want to go for a ride?" he said leaning into the table closer to her and looking directly into her eyes. "I can take you for a ride." His double meaning was clear and Tess found, to her own astonishment that she was thinking of taking him up on it.

"That would be highly unprofessional of me," she said, mentally reminding herself to rein it in, girl!

Kicky looked down at the table. He seemed confused.

"I'm sorry," he said at last. "I didn't mean to make you feel uncomfortable. Do you need a ride?"

"I need to find a place to sleep tonight and then tomorrow I need to get back to Traverse City, or maybe a little farther if you know anyone going toward Elk Rapids."

"Elk Rapids? Do you need to get to Elk Rapids by tomorrow?"

"Yes, it would be good," she said.

"I know someone who can take you straight there tomorrow on his boat."

Tess smiled delightedly, a boat ride! That would be great and something unusual to write in her Blog. So it was agreed. Kicky left the table to bus the dirty dishes and when he came out he grabbed a glass from behind the bar and filled it with Pepsi from the fountain.

"I'll buy you a drink, if you like. Wine? Beer?"

"I can't drink," he said.

"Really?" It occurred to her that Alcoholism is traditionally a big problem with Native Americans, but she would never say that to him, that sounded racist even to her own Irish ears.

"No, I'm not old enough."

"You're not 21?"

"I'm . . . No I'm not 21." She looked at him with her head tilted again.

"Wait," she said and reached across the booth to squeeze his upper arm. His muscle was like iron. "You must really work out. Most guys only work out if they are getting on in years. They want to stay young, keep that 18 year old body."

"Well, I still have mine." He said with half a grin. So he was only 18. He was a good eight years younger than she was. She was on the verge of giving herself permission. He's of a consenting age. He would certainly give her a good time. She had a roll of condoms in her pack, why was she hesitating?

Then it occurred to her. It was that adoring stare that he gave her. He had not been able to take his eyes off of her. She thought about his childish effort to look lascivious, offering to take her for a ride. She couldn't get a read on him. First she thought that he had all the confidence of a young man comfortable with his sex appeal, but the next instant he seemed like a hopeful teenager half expecting to be rejected.

Love at first sight? Impossible. Lust maybe. She would be completely in the wrong to act on this lust. She didn't want to lead him on. That would be cruel. She was leaving tomorrow on his friend's boat. Why would she want to get herself entangled?

"Do you like it?" he asked her, that hopeful expression was back in his eyes. She couldn't remember where the conversation was.

"Do I like what?"

"My 18 year old body," he said.

This was very frank, too frank. She turned her face away from his.

"Hey, I'm really sorry," he said. "I've never done this before. I feel like such a fool. I don't know what to think. Sometimes it's like you want me to come on to you and other times you just want to keep things business-like. You are the most confusing person I've ever met."

"Are you reading my thoughts?" she asked.

"No, well, no, not really. It's," he stopped. He slumped in his seat. "It's too hard to explain." He had sputtered. He had actually sputtered!

"Listen, I have to go find a campsite. Would you like to help me find one and then once I get set up we can talk for a while."

He visibly brightened. "Yeah, I'd really like that." He jumped up and went over to his sister Ruth behind the bar. Ruth looked past him over to Tess. Tess felt the disapproval in this glance. Mary came to the table with the check.

"You're sure about this now?" she asked flipping the check down on the table.

"Yes," Tess answered distractedly. "Is there a reason why your brother should not take me to my campsite?"

"No," Mary said, and then sighed. "We're just a little concerned about him, that's all."

"I won't hurt him." I said smiling.

"I'm sure you mean well," Mary said cryptically as she walked off.

Tess got out her credit card and had Ruth run it through at the bar. She put a large tip on the card as well. Tess got her belongings all packed up in her backpack and Kicky grabbed it away from her and carried it out to the car. He loaded it in the trunk and then went to her side to open the car door for her. As he was walking around to the driver's side of the car she noticed that there was a woman's sweater in the back seat.

"Is this your car?" Tess asked him. She was on verge of getting jealous over the sweater of some unknown girl in his car when he spoke.

"No, this is Bobby's car. I don't have a car. Sorry."

Tess shook her head. What in the heck was she thinking? What did it matter if Kicky had another girlfriend? The most Tess could spend with him was one night. Why was she reacting as if she had a hold on him? This was so confusing.

"Do you know of a good place where I can camp? Somewhere where I can build a small fire maybe and set up my tent?"

"Would you prefer beach or woods?"

"Oh, beaches are nice to sleep on. I can form the sand around my body."

Kicky bit his lips. "I've never before actually wanted to be sand."

He started the car and drove. About four miles up Kicky took a turn and went down a two track. They ended up at a little cove facing East with forest all the way around. The spot was very secluded and she began pitching her tent at once before it got any darker. The sun had not yet set behind them. Kicky gathered some fallen branches from the forest and some dry reindeer moss for tinder. He had a small blaze going on the beach before she had her sleeping bag unfurled.

She came and sat next to him by the fire.

After a few minutes of silence the sky began to darken. Kicky put his arm around her shoulders and drew her in closer to him. She came into his embrace willingly enough.

"I can't stick around you know," Tess said, after he released her from a tender yet exciting kiss.

"I know," he answered simply. And he stopped her from saying anything more with a second kiss.

Chapter 3

Tess did not allow Kicky to spend the night with her. They made out for a while but Tess again made the point that she would be leaving in the morning and they would probably never see each other again after that. Kicky sat back on his elbows and said, "OK, then let's just talk."

They talked for another hour and just as Tess was about to tell him how tired she was, he stood and said, "You must be exhausted. I'll go now. What time do you want me to come and get you in the morning?"

"What time will your friend be ready to leave?"

"He gets out on the bay by 5:00 A.M. and is usually back by about 10 or 11. So he won't be able to take you out until at least noon unless you want to go out with him early."

She checked her watch. It was about 11:00 P.M. She would only get 5 hours of sleep if she went with him early.

"You're sure he won't mind?" Tess said again.

"Naw, he takes me out all the time."

"Well, why don't you come and get me at 4:30 A.M. and I'll be ready to go."

"OK," he said. He leaned in and gave her one last kiss before he got in the car and left.

On the road, there were times when Tess felt so lonesome that she thought she would go crazy. But she wasn't going to just fall in bed with a man because he was handy. She was too good a Catholic for that. Every time she was tempted in that direction she thought about what it would be like to kneel in a confessional and tell a priest her sins. She knew the sin in her heart was just as bad as if the sin where in her body. But, at least if she kept the sin in her heart she wouldn't be risking S.T.D.'s.

Besides, the men she met on the road were just not the sort that she would be willing to bed down with. Most were players. Too many men offered her sex in such a casual way that she thought up a joke to put them down and used it over and over.

"Sorry, I'm saving myself for Sylvester Stalone." The name didn't matter. Once she said she was saving herself for Dog the Bounty Hunter, the guy laughed but he also took it personally. Like he wasn't better than the Dog! After that she stuck with people who had more charisma. Lately the best results were the variation where she was saving herself for Brad Pitt. After all he was bound to get tired of Angelina some time soon.

So far she had not met anyone who was willing to risk the law in order to get into her pants. She went to great lengths to make sure of this too. Harry and her father had both voiced the fact that she was laying herself open to the risk of rape. She spent a good deal of her alone time talking with

God. One of the things she asked for: protection from evil people.

She only took rides from people with whom she felt comfortable, people who were trusted by the proprietors of the restaurants and people that bore her no ill will such as women, or men with children. She rarely got in a car or truck with someone that was not vouched for by another. If her intuition popped negative toward someone, she would take a pass.

Intuition and her faith in God had kept her safe so far. Dad had given her a can of pepper spray to have handy and when she was traveling she kept it on a clip on her belt loop. If somcone noticed it there at her hip, it was generally a good idea if she did not take a ride from him. It was almost as good as a loaded gun, only non-lethal.

It did not keep her from being overpowered, it only reduced the chances. In addition, she had taken combined Martial Arts in college as her Phys. Ed. Credit but that was 4 years ago. She didn't have anyone to practice with so she knew she was a little rusty.

Dad felt that she should have a traveling companion. He was retired now and on a fixed income. He couldn't afford to buy her a car and besides he had moral reserves against buying things of that nature for his child who had a job and responsibilities of her own. He had worked in the publishing industry, one of the long list of jobs on his resume. So now he was acting in the capacity of an agent for her. In addition to editing and submitting her articles for publication, he kept track of her finances. As soon as she was fiscally able he would let her know that she could start looking for a good used vehicle. Tess knew that she wasn't there yet. She still had too many student loans. She paid double on the loans when she could, in hopes of getting them paid off in less than the five years that were slated for the task.

As she lay in her sleeping bag that night waiting for sleep to overtake her, she wondered about her finances. She pulled out the computer and logged on checking the balances of her bank accounts. Her checking account showed sixteen recent payments from newspapers that ranged between $25 and $150 depending on the size of the paper. Her debit card transaction from tonight had not cleared yet, but yesterdays had and her balance was still good. Her savings account had a bit more in it but not enough to buy a car and insurance both. If she could sell about 25 to 30 columns per week instead of the 15-20 she now sold regularly, she would be able to afford a car, insurance, gas, and maybe even a more frequent motel room. Of course, more people would buy her columns if she could get to more populated places faster and a car would help with that. Tess had chosen the open spaces of the Midwest first so that she could camp to save money.

The only thing she could do was struggle on. She closed the laptop and laid her head back down.

She woke one time in the night. She couldn't tell what had awakened her. But as she laid there she heard a noise in the woods. It sounded like steps, but not really. Maybe it was Kicky sneaking back to her campsite to make sure she was OK.

"Kicky?" she said. The sounds outside went silent. "Kicky is that you?"

She listened again. Nothing. Not even a chirp from a grasshopper. Tess realized her heart was racing with a rush of adrenalin. Her ears were completely attuned to sounds outside the tent. But there were none. She thought about turning on the flashlight and going out.

In her mind she went through the options. If it was an animal it had probably been scared off by her voice. If it was a human being then he or she would probably have been as surprised by her presence as she was and likewise skulked off. If it had been Kicky, then he would have answered if he could hear her. Maybe he was moving away into the woods and didn't hear her. He would be back soon, she thought. She heard the movement again, this time closer and outside the flap of the tent.

"Kicky, is that you?" she asked in a normal sounding tone. There was no answer. The movement had again stopped. It seemed that whatever was out there was about five feet in front of the tent. "That does it," she said. She turned on the flashlight and pointed it out the flap of the tent. She pointed the beam of light out and swept back and forth until it landed on the bright orange of eyes shining back toward her. The animal gave a short yip and put his head back down on his folded front paws.

"You're a dog," she said to him. "Hey boy, do you know how bad you scared me?"

Head down on his forepaws he wagged his tail twice, no more. Then he closed his eyes again as if he wanted to sleep.

"OK, OK," she said. She closed the tent flap pulling the zipper down into place again. "I guess it's OK, I don't need to know where you came from."

She calmed herself as she lay back down. She was asleep again in minutes.

Next time she woke it was with the alarm. It was still dark outside. She closed her eyes after shutting off the alarm thinking how nice it would be to get two or three more hours of sleep, but they popped open again at the thought of being out on Grand Traverse Bay.

"What I do for my Blog readers!" she exclaimed and got up. She dressed and struck camp with her usual efficiency warming up some coffee she had stored in a thermos from yesterday's trip. Luckily there were still enough hot coals to do the job. Kicky showed up exactly at 4:30 in time to finish off the coffee.

"You got this camping thing down, girl," he beamed. He still wore that expectant grin.

"Where did you go last night?" Tess asked.

"Oh, I wasn't far off," Kicky said.

"Something strange happened. I heard a noise outside the tent and when I got my courage up to look, a dog was sleeping outside the tent like it was watching out for me."

"A dog?" he asked doubtfully. "What kind of dog?"

"I don't know. All I could really see of him was the reflection of his eyes. He looked like a big dog though, like maybe a German shepherd, and I think he had a light coat, maybe a Husky or Malamute. Why do ask?"

"No reason. Are you sure it wasn't a dream?"

"No, I had a rush of adrenalin that was very real. I did not dream it."

"But you saw a dog?" Again he sounded doubtful.

"Yes, I saw a dog."

"You're sure about that?"

"It was some sort of animal. It had the muzzle of a dog and a light grey coat. Mostly I saw the orange eyes shining back at me from the flashlight."

"Maybe it was the Dogman of Michigan!" he said and grabbed her teasingly.

When her laughter subsided she said, "What? What is that?"

"The Dogman of Michigan. It's a legend. Lots of people claim they've seen it or heard it. It's a Dog that stands on its hind legs and is over seven feet tall."

"Really?"

"So I've heard."

"Is this an Indian legend?"

"No, it's been seen mostly by white men. Are you going up to St. Ignace?"

"Yeah, I'll be there in a few weeks."

"Go to the wax museum up there. It's called the Strange Michigan wax museum. They know all about the Dogman."

"You have got to be kidding me."

"No really, I wouldn't lie to you. Not ever, Tessa."

Tess slapped his abs with her hand. He barely flinched, but his smile deepened. The use of her name linked with the guarantee of honesty touched her heart. If only he would travel with her. If only she could stay long enough to really get to know him. But he wouldn't and she couldn't and there was no time for wishing. She had to keep moving to gain more material to do her job.

"I could go with you," he said as if he had heard her thoughts.

"Go with me? Where?"

He suddenly looked down, away from her face. “To Elk Rapids. My friend Chucky lets me go with him all the time when I’m not working.”

“Do you have today off?” she asked.

“Yeah, I do,” he said. His voice sounded strange with that statement but she couldn’t tell why. It was almost as if he was lying to her but at the same time deciding right then and there that it would not be a lie even if he had to quit his job to make it into a truth. In any case it was not her problem.

Tess finished getting herself packed up and they headed back to toward the car which was parked exactly where they had left it the night before. Furthermore, it was a cool morning, one in which someone might turn on the heat or at least have turned off the Air Conditioning for the ride in. But the AC was still on high when they started up the car. Kicky turned it off at once after the car started.

Chapter 4

June 13

Hi Dad and other happy readers,

I just want to thank Cora Kearny of Suttons Bay for the tip about The Great Moose restaurant. It was certainly a wonderful place with a great chef and interesting cuisine. It's a family run business. Ruth and Bobby are the owners, Bobby does all the cooking, Ruth tends bar. Her sister Mary is the head waitress, her younger brother Kicky is the bus boy and dishwasher. Their oldest sister and mother are also involved in the gathering of local wild plants, mushrooms, and other edibles such as blue berries and wild onions a.k.a. ramps. And other friends and family members hunt and fish to supply the eatery with all the game they serve. If you happen to be in the Northport area, and you could be if you like to gamble since it's about 8 miles from the Leelanau Sands Casino, you definitely need to stop in and give it a taste.

OK, that was a sample of what the review will be like, only I've added more description of their delicious menu. Restaurants like this one are a wonderful surprise for me since I spend so much time on the road and eat from lots of deep fryers through out the countryside. When you go there, tell Mary and Kicky I said hi!

I had already covered Traverse City for several days before I went up the West side of the bay toward Northport. I walked the entire way, 28 miles. So I was not entirely enamored of the idea of walking all the way back and through Traverse City, to get to Elk Rapids where my next review would be. Kicky told me about a friend of his, a fisherman named Chuck who would take me across the bay in his fishing boat. It was quite an adventure.

Did you know that there are actually two peninsulas north of Traverse City? Yes, the first, Leelanau peninsula is where I started from. Another peninsula a bit shorter is called Old Mission peninsula and at the very North tip of this land finger is a light house. I couldn't see the lighthouse because the water is so shallow at the north tip that boats have to travel far out toward the lakeside to get around it. The light house is significant though because it is at the exact 45th parallel. This means that it's exactly half way between the Equator and the North Pole. There's a piece of trivia with which you can stump your friends.

The Grand Traverse Bay was wonderfully blue and smooth today. There was hardly a breeze to kick up froth. Chuck and Kicky spent a little time with fishing lines over the edge and asked if I wanted one too. I said sure. Kicky showed me how to cast the rod and soon I was old expert. Neither of the men caught anything and they told me that the whitefish that I caught was not nearly big enough and I should throw it back and let it mature a little more. Catching a fish was one of the most exciting things I've done in a while. It was like a battle between me and the fish. It's amazing how strong the little thing was. Kicky told me to get the camera and took a picture of me holding it. It seemed pretty big to me. It was about 9 inches long and had put up quite a fight. Chuck said that he never keeps whitefish unless they are least 25 inches long and he never keeps Salmon unless they are 30 inches long. He's a successful Native American commercial fisherman so I guess he knows what he's talking about. I think they had a good time laughing at the white city girl so proud of her dwarf whitefish! They told me some stories about Great Lakes Ghost ships and other Ship wreck stories. I also heard some interesting Ottawa stories. I'd love to write some of them down and share them with you but I only have a few minutes to finish this update before I have to start walking again.

They dropped me off at the pier in Elk Rapids and I got directions on how to get to the next restaurant which was called the Rainbow Inn. I had lunch in town at a little take out place, called the Stop and Eat (yeah you read that correctly) that served a heck of an Italian Pesto Salad with Tortellini. I ordered an extra lunch from there as well and both tasted delicious. I'll be writing a review for that place too.

There doesn't seem to be a shortage of good restaurants in this vicinity, so I'll keep my ears open.

After Elk Rapids, I plan to head east to Alden and Bellaire, then north to East Jordan and Charlevoix. I plan to spend the night in a motel in Charlevoix and then go on up to a bigger town called Petoskey which I'm told is named after their state stone, or vice versa. The Petoskey stone isn't actually a stone but the fossilized remains of large single celled organisms. I'm supposed to stop at a rock shop up there to pick up a souvenir. My pack is already weighing in at about 55 pounds so I'm not going to get too many more things. Maybe I'll ship some stuff home to you, Dad. My latest acquisition is a beaded necklace from Kicky. He gave it to me as we were parting at the pier. I've been wearing it all day for lack of anything better to do with it. It's either wear it or carry it. Might as well wear it.

Alden is a pretty long way from Elk Rapids so I'll walk tonight for a while and find a place to camp in the woods. I'll make the rest of the trip in the morning. I spent the night in a motel near downtown Traverse two nights ago, so I won't stay in another hotel until Charlevoix. I can be there in three days if I don't get a ride.

More later,
Tessa Gates.

Chapter 5

It took two days of walking to make it to Alden. She made it to a little place called Torch River Bridge that night. It boasted a fairly average fish fry place, she ate there but it was nothing special so she decided not to review it. Then she spent the night on a stretch of wooded road just past the bridge. She had set up camp in the dark but in the morning she realized she had camped in the front yard of a huge house. She thought about going up to the house to apologize for camping in their yard but when she did she realized the house was empty. She figured it must be owned by someone who lived down in the city and this was their summer residence. Many people didn't show up at their summer "cottage" until the Fourth of July Holiday.

The next night she spent on a piece of fallow farm land outside of Bellaire. When she got to her first stop, a tiny breakfast café in the town of Bellaire, she heard from some locals that there had been a very bad animal attack down by Torch River Bridge. This got her interest because she had just been there.

"Was anyone hurt?" she asked.

"Yes, someone was killed." The local man told her. He turned back to his friend sitting next to him. "You know that guy Wallerman, from Chicago? He's got that huge house there by Torch River."

"Yeah," the man said. "Jack Block does his caretaking. I been out there to help him once in a while."

"Well he came up last night late. No one expected him. Something attacked him. No one knew what kind of animal it was. A bear maybe, or a cougar. Had claw marks on him about six inches wide. Jack found him dead the next morning."

It sounded like the house where she had spent the night. "Are there a lot of big houses like that on Torch River?" Tess asked.

"A few," he said. "Why?"

"I spent the night camped near one of them. I was just wondering if it was the same one."

They didn't answer. Instead they went back to their breakfasts. Tess enjoyed her farmer's omelet, and the coffee at this place was better than any she'd had in Michigan so far, so she gave the place a good review, which she typed up quickly and sent it out to her father. Then she packed up and hit the road again.

Tess didn't just take a shower when she got to her hotel in Charlevoix. She took two showers. She sent all of her clothes except a night shirt and her bathing suit down to the laundry service and then went down to the pool to sit in their hot tub for an hour. Usually she opted for smaller motels with no pools or HBO or Jacuzzi's. But after spending nearly a week in the wild, fishing on a boat and bathing in the lakes and streams she found along the road, she decided she could splurge this one time.

She would certainly not make a habit of it though. No, this time she needed to get clean and relaxed and get rid of some of the thoughts that had been haunting her. She opened up the tent and spread it out on the floor to dry out. It had rained since the boat ride. The tent was water proof but it still had the capacity to get saturated if you just wiped it down with dirty laundry and rolled it up to hike onward. Maybe she would stay in the hotel room an extra night just to get completely dried out. She would watch the local news tonight and get a weather report. An extra day here might be nice. She could just hang out in the book store for a while and drink coffee. Rest, sleep in a bed two nights in a row. That should put her back to rights.

When she got back to her room after the Jacuzzi soak, she noticed there was an e-mail from her Dad.

"Tessy, you can indeed stay two nights at the hotel if you wish. You have plenty of money to get you through your next loan payment and you've lately been bringing in three times what you spend on travel and meals so it's working out. You nearly have enough for a down payment on a used car. You'll have to walk a little longer if you want a new car with on-star or some other type of security thing. Of course if you get a van you could use it for camping. Keep a look out. I've heard there are lots of people trying to sell used campers or RV's lately. Maybe you can pick one up for cheap. I'd feel much easier if you had reliable transportation and a safe place to sleep.

"Bad news, I talked with my old pal Jacob Galbreath at the Sun Times. He is dropping your column until you get to Wisconsin. He doesn't think Northern Michigan is a place his readership would be too interested in going for dinner. I even played the old pal card and still it was a no-go. That's nearly $250 a week lost. As soon as he dropped that bomb I got on the horn and signed six more papers in Northern Michigan and in the U.P. It doesn't make up for it entirely but they were glad to see that you were going to be reviewing restaurants up in their area and even made a few suggestions. Two of them I had to give a copy of your Traverse City review to get them to sign on. And they are only interested in their own area. Once you get to Wisconsin they will most likely drop you too. Seems like you can't get ahead, only keep an even keel!

"Oh yeah, I heard from Harry. He had a helavan idea. He thinks you should start to contact travel magazines and sell articles to them too. I've started to write queries to some of them. That Writer's Markets book you bought a while back has lots of regional magazines too, so after the first rights are sold to the papers, I can sell serial rights to the regional magazines as well. I'll see if I can't build up your fortune a bit more.

"Harry is doing great in Arizona and asks that you start heading west once you find a vehicle. He really wants to see you again. He misses you a lot. Doesn't he e-mail you any more? He didn't tell me much about school. I hope he's happy out there.

"Anyway, I love you, and keep safe, OK?"

"Yur Dad."

A tear dropped from Tessa's cheek as she hit the reply button. Harry had been out in Arizona for nearly a year. He hadn't e-mailed her in the entirety of that time. Maybe it was time she e-mailed him. There was something wrong that he wasn't saying.

She dropped a quick line to her dad about the hotel room and the fact that she was going to stay until her tent dried out. She thanked him for all his hard work on her behalf. She knew he considered it a fun pastime in comparison to the type of work he used to do. Tess felt pretty lucky to have him as an agent. He didn't take a percentage. She had often told him that he should but he just vaguely commented that maybe he would later on.

He had been an office worker most of his life. He had done some copy editing, which is how he became friendly with editors at Newspapers in Chicago. He had done nearly every type of office work, including cleaning them, over the course of fifty years in the job market. At one point he had a very lucrative position as an office manager for an insurance company. That was when he had met and married his second wife, Tessa's mother, who was twenty years his junior. She had left him when Tess was only five and then died the very next year in a drunk-driving accident. Dad had been fighting to gain custody of Tess at the time. It was a topic they tended to ignore since it was now in the past. He would never tell her if it had been her mother who was drunk or if she was innocent and was hit by another drunk driver. Did it really matter now? Dad had raised her and done the best he could for her, but the fact of the matter was that he just had no idea what to do with his girl child. By the time Tess was 8 she was taking care of him, cooking his meals, washing and ironing his clothing, and managing to hold down her own homework and keeping her grades up. Hard work was never a stranger to this pair.

Tess sighed. She pulled up a new e-mail and inserted Harry's address.

Harry Carry!

Long time no see bro! What's happenin' down there in the Grand Canyon? It's been too long my friend! I want some details. New girlfriend? Tough classes? Homesick? Or are you just too busy for old friends? Whatever!

No seriously, I love you Harry and I want to hear from you. Please drop me a line. Did you see my new Blog? "Tessagates.blogspot.com." Go look me up and see what all I've been up to. Please Harry, this silence is killing me.

Love you, as always, Tess.

She fired it off to him. She knew that he would both smile and answer this light-hearted appeal. Sudden weariness overtook her and she cuddled up in bed. She flipped through the channels and found very little of lasting interest. Finally 10 pm rolled around and she watched the local news on a Fox station. After sitting through a bunch of bad news about the area, a child molester being arrested in a place called Lake City, an attack by a rabid dog in Bellaire, and a robbery in Baldwin, among them she let out a sigh of relief when the weather finally came on. A storm would be plowing through the straights area tomorrow but there was a cold front behind it that would assure cooler dry weather for at least a week. Tess shut down the TV and snuggled down into the covers. She was asleep in less than no time and for a change no dreams bothered her.

Chapter 6

Tess woke early, before 7:00 A.M. The two-cup coffee pot and the little package of instant coffee did not look appealing so she opened her laptop to find a breakfast restaurant. A peak through the window shades let her know it wasn't raining, just overcast. She had no clothes to put on so she called the desk to see if they were ready. But even so, she could use a new sweatshirt. She had lost weight since she began her hike up the West coast of Michigan. She hadn't expected that since she regularly overate in the line of her job. She had told Kicky that she didn't normally eat as much as she did that night when they dined together at his sister's restaurant but, if she had to honest, that meal was fairly close to average for her.

No, no, NO! She had resolved not to think about Kicky again. She would not. OK, so what should she think about? Her clothes. Yes, that was it. She went to phone and picked up.

"Front desk," came a girl's voice.

"Hi this is Tess Gates in room 312, are my clothes ready?"

"Just a minute please." Tess could tell that she had not been put on hold, but the phone was muffled, voices in the background indiscernible. "Yes ma'am. They are here waiting. Would you like me to send them up?"

"Please. Oh and is there a place to get breakfast around here? Maybe someplace kind of unusual?"

"Unusual?"

"Yes, out of the ordinary. I'm very experimental."

"Oh, of course, well there is a little café on the South side of town on the hill, some call it a greasy spoon, but they have a cook there that really knows his stuff."

Tess got the name of the place. "I'll be staying another night, I hope that's not inconvenient."

"No ma'am, I'll take care of it."

"Great, I have a pup tent in the middle of the floor drying out, so warn the maid not to move it, in fact, tell the maid she can skip my room. I have everything I need."

"Yes, ma'am, you can also put the 'do not disturb' sign on your door and the maid won't come in."

"Thanks," Tess hung up and within ten minutes she had her clean clothes. She pulled out her messenger bag. There was no sense in hauling around the big pack, especially if she was planning on coming back here. She loaded her laptop, phone, camera and wallet into the messenger bag, made sure she had the room key card and left. She passed the mirror on the way out and fluffed her hair into a natural position. This was all the prep she ever made. Her sandy blonde hair was short enough to need nothing more. Easy beauty, that's how she thrived.

To find a hotel that had a Jacuzzi and HBO, she had gone through town and almost to the outskirts on the north side. So she walked back to town and up the hill to the little place that had been suggested. It was quiet at 8 am on a Wednesday and the place was nearly dead. She sat in a booth by the window, her favorite place to sit in any diner, and looked over the menu. The waitress was an older woman with a beehive. Tess had to look at her twice to believe her eyes. It was stiff with hairspray.

"I hope you don't mind my asking but are there still hair dressers that know how to do that style?"

"Honey, you'd be surprised! What can I get you?"

"Coffee for now. But is there anything your cook does that is particularly unusual?"

"For breakfast? Heck yes. He does something he called the Mexican omelet. It's kind of like a Western omelet, only he amps it up a bit."

"Really? With what?"

"Jalapeños instead of bell peppers, Jicama instead of hash browns, and red bean sauce over the entire top. He also lays in heavy with the pepper jack cheese."

"What's the red bean sauce like?" She was getting excited.

"It's kind of like Chili only thicker. Actually he calls it Texas Chili. It has bits of steak in it instead of hamburger and it's laced pretty heavily with red pepper and cumin."

"That sounds good. I'll have an order of that. Does he have something with Bacon that's different?"

"Yeah, he does something for the kids now and then. He takes a sausage link and wraps cheese and bacon around it. He calls it Pigs in a blanket, but he broils it and it gets all melty. You can't eat it with your fingers. It's usually served with potato skins. Actually this morning he would probably substitute hash browns for the potato skins."

"I'm a restaurant reviewer, I don't want the usual, I want unusual. Can he do a special potato skin thing for breakfast for me?"

"I'm sure he would love to. Oh and of course there's our signature homemade cinnamon bread made into French toast. That's a local flavorite." Tess smiled when the waitress overemphasized the "L" sound in FLAVORite. "But are you really planning on eating three whole breakfasts?"

"I'm going to taste them for sure and then eat what I want of them. I doubt I'll finish everything. Hey, tell him that if he wants me to try anything else, I'm certainly game. I will try anything he sends me. And I always pay my check. That way I can be fair in my reviews."

"Oh, hey, that's good. Cuz we frown on people walking out on their checks."

"I know but sometimes restaurant owners want to float me some free food in order to get a better review. That doesn't fly with me."

"Oh I see." She winked and left the table. A minute or so after the woman put in the order she heard the voice of an angry man with a Spanish accent from the back.

"What the hell kind of order is this?" he shouted. The waitress shouted back in Spanish and soon a very loud argument was happening through the order window.

Tess looked at the only other two customers in the place and shrugged. As the waitress made herself understood the man went quiet and soon he was shushing her and saying, "OK, OK, OK!"

The woman went silent too with this and then turned to the lunch counter and started rubbing it vigorously with a cloth. When she looked up and noticed that all three of her customers were staring at her, she nodded her head in the direction of the kitchen and said, "Men!" The other two patrons chuckled.

The coffee was like nectar, and Tess took out her laptop to do a little writing. When the food arrived she took pictures of everything and quietly tasted everything. Three extra dishes were set out in front of her. One looked like pasta carbonara with bacon and parmesan. Another was similar to egg foo yung only with a different flavor that she couldn't identify and another was a turkey concoction that might better have been served at lunch time but which was made more breakfast-like with addition of a waffle served under it. The sauce of this was both gingery and sweet and she found that she liked it best of all. The other two patrons in the diner, two older gentlemen who were simply sipping at coffee cups and chatting were interested when the food came out. She noticed them watching and asked them to join her. The three of them polished off the five meals and she paid the check. The two men were making motions of leaving after she explained that the food was a business expense and sent the waitress off with her credit card. When she came back they were lingering.

"Do you mind if I stay for a while and write up my review while it's still fresh in my mind?"

The waitress looked around. Not at all, you can see that we don't get busy in the mornings. Maybe you can do something about that.

"It might help!" Tess said. The two older gentlemen bid her goodbye again thanking her for breakfast.

"Oh, Thank God," the waitress said. "Those two always stay half the morning making mood eyes at me."

"Really?"

"Oh yeah, Thank you for getting rid of them for me. Sheesh, they are like dogs! You take one of them home and the rest all come sniffing, you know?"

Tess laughed and asked if there was an outlet nearby. The woman bent to look and located one under the booth behind Tess. She plugged in and started writing. It was good that she was able to do it there because she noticed that she had several questions about flavorings and cooking processes and she got the cook to come out of the kitchen long enough to answer them. She also got his name and found out where he learned how to cook like that. He gave two answers to that, from his mother and from the military. He had been a cook on an aircraft carrier during the Gulf war.

"How can you afford to buy all that food?" the waitress asked.

"Well, I just spent $40 on breakfast and hopefully the article I write about it will net me about $200 from all the different papers that pick it up. I'll do the same thing at lunch and again at dinner, or maybe, if the lunch place I find isn't very unusual I will just eat a sandwich and go on my way, and then at dinner time I will spend about $100 and net about $300 from papers. At least that's what I hope happens. Sometimes it's more or less."

"Good gig," the woman said. "What's the down side?"

"I do a lot of camping and hiking. I travel to find restaurants but I have no transportation. It seems to be working in my favor though. I walk off my huge meals."

"I could use a job like that." She bussed the table and later came to fill Tessa's coffee cup. About 11:30 the place started getting busy again and Tess decided that it might be time to free up her table.

She was in no way hungry yet. Walking north along US 31 through the downtown area, Tess stepped into a few shops. She browsed the bookstore even though she only bought books on-line these days. It was so much easier to read one she had downloaded onto the Kindle App on her computer than to haul a whole hard copy of a book from place to place. She also checked out a little boutique. She bought a light blue hoody with a light house that said Charlevoix. It also had a big pocket across the front that she thought would be handy to have while traveling. She could put snacks in there and her cell phone in case she needed to call 911 in a hurry. She also tried on some shorts and found that she had dropped two sizes. She bought three pairs of them all in the same color of light blue. She liked the style, they were long enough to be comfortable hiking and had lots of extra pockets including balloon pockets on the sides of the thighs, good for carrying a camera, extra food or even a water bottle. The best part was they fit her. She wouldn't have to synch down her belt any more.

Each time she asked for a place where she could get some unusual food for dinner. Several people directed her to a little restaurant on 31 toward the North end of town called Charlie's. She remembered seeing the sign for it and decided that she would try it.

On her way back to the hotel she passed a little IGA store. Even though she told the waitress otherwise, she was feeling a pang of guild at having spent $40 for breakfast. She bought a package of cream cheese, a small tube of liverwurst, and six English muffins. It would do for lunch today and breakfast tomorrow and get her out of town just that much faster. They also had a coffee bar so she got two large cups of good coffee and carried them back to the hotel. When she got back she immediately put the two large coffees into her thermos for the morning.

After another dip in the Jacuzzi, Tess took a nap with the TV on HBO playing a movie with Ryan Reynolds. When she woke four hours later she realized how tired she had been. The nap had done her a world of good. She turned the TV over to the news and listened to the description of a grizzly murder as she dressed in her new shorts and sweatshirt. The police were calling it an animal attack. She thought it might be the same one that she had heard about two days ago in Torch River, but this one took place in Bellaire. Tess fleetingly thought that was odd. She had been in Bellaire as well this past week. But she dismissed it in her mind as she shut off the TV. They were about to cut to video of the crime scene. This was Northern Michigan; there were probably animal attacks in the news up here on a weekly basis, especially with so many tourists in the woods hiking.

She grabbed her messenger bag and headed back to Charlie's.

Charlie's was a good old American restaurant. They had a fairly authentic style Pepper steak, and something called spring onion casserole. They had a stuffed baked potato and deep fried ravioli the likes of which she hadn't had since she was in St. Louis, Missouri. Dinner only cost her $78 and that included the slice of Chicago style pizza that she talked away from the couple in the next booth. She admitted to having had better Chicago style pizza, but then again, she was born and raised in the Windy City, it wasn't hard. But it was good. The sauce needed more Oregano, and she told the chef this. He said he would remember that.

The walk back to the hotel room was slow because of the rich food in her stomach but she made it. As she walked by the golf course she heard the cry of what she thought sounded like a wolf. It couldn't have been she decided, since there wouldn't be wolves this close to a city. It had to have been a dog, or a coyote. Her thoughts went straight toward the dog she had seen outside her tent that night in Northport. NO, NO, NO! Stop thinking about him. You are not going back there to get him, so just stop thinking about it! She told herself.

She calmed herself and decided that maybe another soak in the Jacuzzi was called for before bed.

When she got back up to her room she got undressed and packed. The tent was finally dry so she rolled it into its holder and stowed it in its place. She had the leftover cream cheese and liver concoction in the ice bucket on top of an inverted plastic glass so it wouldn't get wet, a trick she learned in her travels, and everything was packed except her clothes for the morning. She would just have to jump into clothes, stuff her night shirt into the pack, send the coffee through the coffee maker to heat it up, and be on her way. When she hit the next big town she would have to find a Laundromat so she could wash her night shirt, the only thing that didn't get washed this week.

Having made her plans, Tess climbed into bed and put herself though her nightly ritual of meditation and relaxation that always put her to sleep whether in a strange hotel bed, or in the depths of the forest in a sleeping bag with the odd twig poking her in the back. She was asleep within minutes.

Chapter 7

The next morning at 7:00 A.M. Tess finished off the last of the liver and cream cheese concoction on two English muffins and stuffed her night shirt into the pack. She finalized things at the front desk and then walked out toward the North. It would be nearly a half days walk to Petoskey. It was about 15 miles away, according to Google Maps, an easy walk, and she was ready for it having rested yesterday.

About a mile outside of town she came across a nature bike trail. Many cities were building these. She had walked along one going up from Traverse City to Sutton's Bay on her way to Northport. She loved these routes. They were much safer than walking on the road. She was on a great adventure and yet she was so concerned, maybe even overly concerned, with safety. Having an adventure was good but she didn't want so much of an adventure that it would scar her for life.

As she walked she noticed the beautiful scenery: woods, wild flowers. The trilliums were in bloom in the shade under the oak trees, and so were the swamp marigolds, little yellow flowers that grew in abundance in the wet lands. She saw signs of animals, muddy tracks crossing the paved path. In all the time she had been hiking she hadn't yet seen a deer. She hoped that it was not outside the realm of possibility to see a deer or a bear even, a fox, or coyote, or even a bobcat. She didn't think she'd like to see a cougar in the woods, but she had her pepper spray, it worked on animals as well as humans. Tess had seen dozens of squirrels, both alive and dead in the road. She'd seen dead raccoons, and porcupines. She had seen dead dear as well. Cats and Dogs for sure, too. She always tried to cross the road so she wouldn't have to look at the dead animals close up. She had seen chipmunks alive, and all kinds of birds. But never had she seen a large live wild animal. She had heard them at night around her tent and turned on the flashlight to scare them away but the only time she'd ever seen an animal larger than a squirrel was the dog she had seen outside her tent that night.

That's when it happened. She turned a corner and just ahead of her standing in the path was the biggest dog she had ever seen. It was all light grey and had the smile associated with a Labrador but it did not look at all like a Lab. It might have been a husky or a malamute or one of those other highly furred sled dogs. It had a rough of white fur around its head and grey and black markings all down its back. Its tongue lolled out the side of its mouth. It looked up at her as if it were expecting her. She stopped, unsure what to do. She touched the pepper spray on her belt but then thought that maybe that wouldn't be wise. Instead she spoke to it. "Hey boy," she said, trying to sound friendly. To her own ears she sounded nervous. Oh well. "Who are you?" she asked. The dog stood its ground and wagged its tail once. It put its head down a little as if it wasn't sure if it should come any closer. She put her left hand out to it and again touched the pepper spray with her right hand. The dog looked at her, wagged its tail again and then turned. When it turned she could clearly see that it was a boy dog. It ran off down the walkway in front of her about 20 yards and then stepped off into the woods. She walked slowly up to where the dog had disappeared and looked into the woods. She couldn't see him.

"Where did you go, boy?" she said out loud, but was not gratified with as much as a growl. She kept on and a bit further up, maybe another quarter mile, there he was again. "You live near here?" she asked him, not expecting an answer. The dog barked twice though as if in answer. "I see," she said. She again put her hand out to allow him to sniff if. He didn't, he just turned again and walked on ahead of her. She followed. From time to time as she got closer to Petoskey she caught glimpses of the dog in the brush. He seemed to be keeping with her but not too closely. At one point she hadn't seen him for several miles and then suddenly looked behind her to see him following her about ten yards behind her. "Curious," she thought out loud.

She made it to Petoskey and realized that it was a bigger town even then Charlevoix. She decided to spend two nights there as well and this time got a small motel room. After reading an e-mail from her father she realized that her reviews from this area were selling to six different papers that were new as well as some of the bigger papers in Chicago and Michigan. The more reviews she could write in this town the better she would do. So she gathered her info and managed to find her way around this small city.

The second night, as she was getting ready for bed, she heard a noise at the door of her motel room. The motel she had chosen was on top of a hill at the south end of town near the local Wal-Mart. Just below the motel was a forested valley. When she looked out the widow she saw nothing. But when she opened the door she saw a very large grey dog out in the field beyond the parking lot. It turned and yipped at her. She stood and gazed at it in silence. Was that what had made the noise at her door just now?

"Here boy," she called, trying to lure him to her. But the dog came no closer. She left the door to her room open while she packed. But he did not come back to her door.

She finished preparing for tomorrow's hike and turned on the news. After seeing that the weather was still going to be good, gradually getting hotter over the course of the next few days, she turned off the TV. The door had stood open through all of this so after turning off the TV she went to the door and looked one final time out to see if she could glimpse the dog. As she put her head out toward the back of the motel she thought she saw a tail going around the far corner of the building. Oh well, she thought as she locked herself in for the night. She gave a brief thought about Harry, who had still not e-mailed her, and then fell asleep with nagging thoughts of Kicky on her mind.

In the morning she walked through town and out past several interesting looking rock shops but they didn't open until ten and she wasn't going to wait that long. It was a full day's walk to Mackinaw City if she made no stops, but she anticipated at least one stop. She made reservations on line at the KOA just south of Mackinaw so she had a place to stay already. She wouldn't get a hotel now again until she got to Sault Ste. Marie.

She stopped for coffee at a nice looking restaurant in a little town next to a lake, but there was nothing unusual about the menu so she didn't eat there. A little further up the road, once she passed the lake and was back into the woods, she saw the dog again.

"Are you following me boy?" she asked him. She got one yip for her trouble.

"Oh really?" she said. "Then we had better be formally introduced. My name is Tessa, what's yours?" The dog yipped again.

"Woof? Your name is woof?"

The dog yipped. "Ok, Woofy it is." She said. This time she was ready for him. She had picked up some beef jerky at one of the little convenience stores and she broke off a piece for him. He sniffed the air and drew a little closer.

"Take it carefully, don't snap my fingers off," Tess said.

The dog moved a little closer and soon his nose was up against the end of the jerky. He opened his mouth and then gingerly took the piece carefully out of her hand. He then backed away several feet and made short work of chewing the hardened beef before he swallowed it. She sat down and broke off another piece. Again he took it out of her hand carefully. "Good boy," she said. He wagged his tail twice and stopped. She broke off another piece. "Are you hungry?" she said to him. He barked once.

"I'm going to take it that means yes." She said. The dog yipped again, just once.

"Smart one, huh?" The dog tilted his head and looked at her. Then he looked down at the jerky in her hand. "Ok, I get it," she said. She handed him the rest of the jerky and when it was gone he sniffed her hands to make sure.

"I'll get you some food at the next town." She said to him. She petted the white rough around his head and looked deep into his yellow eyes. That was when she realized that he looked very much like a wolf. He might have been a sled dog bred with a wolf, but there were definite wolf tendencies in this dog. "Maybe I should call you Wolfy?" she said to him. The dog closed his mouth and looked meaningfully into her eyes and then yipped once.

Chapter 8

June 20

Dear Dad and readers,

I have a new friend! I have made the acquaintance of a dog named Woofy. I don't know very much about dog breeds but he seems to be part malamute and I would say part wolf. He definitely has a wolfy appearance about him. His eyes are yellow and the majority of his fur is grey with black striations, and his head ruff is pure white. He's a handsome fellow and seems to have taken to me. He came to me first between Charlevoix and Petoskey and when I got up north of Petoskey circumnavigating all the lakes on my way to the Straights of Mackinaw he has been traveling with me very companionably.

I had breakfast this morning at a little place in a town called Alanson, I'm still not sure whether the accent is on the first or second syllable of that name, I heard it referred by both while I was in town. It was a little bakery/yarn shop. I have been knitting since college so I decided to pick up some yarn and needles while there and make you a pair of socks for Christmas, Dad, so be surprised when you open the box, OK?

One of my breakfast companions gave me and Woofy a lift up to Pelston where there was a little greasy spoon but it turned out to be entirely too greasy for me so I just got coffee and surfed the web for a while looking for knitting patterns. I downloaded one and started knitting the sock but then a crowd came in so I decided to free up the table. There was nothing past Pelston but woods for many miles and then we came to a lake where there was a little restaurant called "EAT". By that time I realized that I was hungry, having only had baked goods for breakfast with a coffee chaser around 11:00 A.M. Woofy and I stopped at this place. I thought about bringing Woofy inside and saying he was a service dog, but I still don't know him well enough to know if he would behave badly indoors. I hope some kid isn't pining away for his pet while this animal is chasing after me.

Anyway I found a few interesting things on the menu including a beef stew made with morel mushrooms. I think morel mushrooms are fast becoming my favorite food. I got a couple of burger patties for Woofy and an extra bowl of beef stew that I ate the morels out of before I gave it to him. I think the poor thing was hungry. It had been following me for several days. I stopped and got a can of dog food for him when I got to Mackinaw City but when I opened it I gasped. Man that stuff smells bad. I decided right then and there that no matter what else happened I would not feed Woofy anything that I would not eat myself. No dog food for this fur person!

Right now I'm camping in a KOA just south of Mackinaw City. Tomorrow there are about five restaurants I have to check out. That means I'll be staying here tomorrow night as well. One of the places is down in Cheboygan about six miles southeast of town. I have a ride. One of the bus boys from a restaurant that I ate at tonight will drive me down there. He has also offered to take me across the bridge when I'm ready to go. Woofy did OK in the car up to Pelston. He just sniffed the inside of the car once and jumped right in.

I don't want to alarm you Dad, but I have been hearing about a rash of animal attacks around here. Three people have been killed in the last week they say by a rabid dog. I checked on-line and my dog shows no signs of being rabid so it can't be him. It's strange though because they have all happened in or near places that I camped on the way up. I was kind of alarmed by that fact. I camped in Torch River that one night and that's where the first victim was found the day after I was there. Then the second was found just south of Bellaire on a road that I had walked down. The third was found south of Alanson very near where Woofy and I met up. I'm a little disturbed by this and told the camp attendant about it when I got here. He told me not to worry since they have regular patrols at night. Nothing can get me here.

It just seems strange.

So readers, this is a big area for tourism so if you'd like to buy any of my reviews from this area, please contact my Dad, his e-mail link is in the box at the right.

Next I will be hitching a ride up to the U.P. (Upper Peninsula) and taste-testing every pasty I run across to find the best pasty in the U.P. And no I did not spell that wrong. A pasty is a meat and potato pie wrapped up in a pie crust. It sometimes contains carrots, rutabaga, or onions. The word "pasty" rhymes with cast, not waste.

I hope Woofy likes pasties, I have a feeling we'll be eating a lot of them as we work our way across the north edge of upper Michigan.

On to the Soo! Talk with you soon Dad,

Love you,

Tess

Chapter 9

Tess crawled into the tent that night and invited Woofy to come in too. Woofy pushed his head inside but would not allow his entire body to come inside the tent.

"Come on, boy," Tess said. "You can sleep on my sleeping bag." He came in another step but seemed uncomfortable. So he backed out. "Why won't you come in?" she asked and got two yips as her reply. "Ok," she said after trying to lure him in with another piece of beef jerky. "Stay out there then, see if I care." Woofy barked twice as Tess zipped the tent flap. He then pawed at the closed flap and yipped twice again. Tess unzipped the zipper to shush him. This was a campsite and a barking dog would not be popular there. When the flap was unzipped the dog came into the tent fully and would not let Tess near the flap again. "You want me to leave the flap open all night so you can come and go as you please?"

The dog barked once. "Oh really?" she said.

Woofy sat down on the end of her sleeping bag as if guarding the tent flap against her zipping it closed again. "I can't have you coming and going all night with the flap open," she told the dog. "Too many mosquitoes will get in. But at the same time, I can't have you barking all night in the park here either." She thought for a moment, Woofy watched her as though he was aware of the problems and she would eventually find an answer. "Ok, how about this?" she asked. Woofy tilted his head as if to listen to her brilliant solution. "I will leave the bottom of the flap unzipped, but the mosquito netting zipped up fully." She did this as she explained it to him. Then said, "Since the mosquito net doesn't have a bottom zipper you will be able to get down on your belly and nose your way in and out of the tent. OK?"

Woofy barked once very quietly.

Tess shook her head. "You know," she said, "Sometimes I think you understand what I'm saying to you." He barked once very softly. "Also, you seem to only bark once when you agree with me and twice when you disagree." One bark came in response to this. "Really?" she asked. One small bark and then Woofy nosed his way out of the tent under the mosquito net and the outside flap.

Tess woke only once in the middle of the night. Woofy was there beside her stretched out in front of her. She put her arm over the dog and heard him whimper slightly as if acknowledging her affection. She fell back to sleep. In the morning the dog was gone from the tent. When she got out of the tent to walk down to the bath house Woofy came up to her and excitedly danced around her feet.

"Good morning to you too, Woofy," she said. She grabbed the canteens and realized she needed a water bowl for Woofy. Not a problem, she would get one in town today. It was probably a good idea to get two bowls, one for water and one for food. After the bathhouse she walked back up to her tent and took out the mini-pack. Toting the laptop, cell phone and camera in it she set out for the home of the young man who said he would drive her to Cheboygan this morning. She got there and knocked at the man's door.

When he came to the door he looked at her and the dog. Woofy started to growl immediately. The boy was put off.

"What's the matter with your dog?" he asked.

"I have no idea," she said, then added, "Woofy stop it."

Woofy barked twice and growled again. When the man came nearer to Tess Woofy stopped him snapping his jaws at the man's leg and getting between him and Tess.

"He must think you mean me harm," Tess said.

"Why would he think that?" the young man asked her.

"I don't know, do you mean me harm?" Tess said eyeing him.

The man frowned. He lashed out and kicked at Woofy. Tess then knew that she should not accept a ride from this man. If he could kick a dog then surely she wasn't safe with him either.

"Maybe I better find another ride down there," Tessa said and then turned to leave.

"You're loss," the man said. His voice had a decidedly nasty tinge to it.

Tess left his yard as fast as she could and when she was 20 yards down the road she turned and called Woofy to come to her. He obliged willingly. They walked back to the main drag where Tess knelt down to Woofy's level and praised him greatly by rubbing his ruff vigorously and calling him good dog, good Woofy!

"Well, boy, this kind of changes my plans." Tess stated. She stood and looked down at her dog. "I guess we're hoofing it," she said to him. Then the dog did something that made Tessa laugh. He shook his head and blew out a breath between his dog lips. He looked so much like a horse settling its harness that Tess rolled back her head and laughed out loud. Woofy tilted his head and gave her his best dog smile, tongue lolling out the lower side of his face.

"Come on," she said touching his head. They began walking toward the Lake Huron side of town and down the road that would take them to Cheboygan. "Maybe we can catch a ride back here after lunch."

The trip to Cheboygan was uneventful and the food at the restaurant very good. Woofy made himself scarce as they approached town. Tess didn't forget about him though. She asked for a take out box for the leftovers and just kind of shoveled them all in together for the dog. There was one dish that was kind of spicy and she wasn't sure if it would be good for Woofy to eat that much spice, so she ate all of that one herself and left the blander food that was rich in meat and sauces to the take-out box. After sitting for a while longer in the restaurant to complete her review, she paid her bill and packed up.

On her way out of town she saw a small grocery store and stopped in. After walking down the pet aisle she realized that all the dishes for a dog the size of Woofy would be too heavy to carry in her over-loaded pack. So instead she walked down the aisle with the lidded plastic containers and found one that might work out OK. But on her way past the deli meat section she noticed that some of the lunch meat companies were packing their product in the same containers that she was planning to purchase and they were nearly the same price. So she decided to buy two packages of lunch meat to get the packages and she would feed the lunch meat to Woofy as a snack on the way back to Mackinaw City. She walked down the pet aisle one more time wondering if she should buy a collar and leash for Woofy. After thinking it through she thought it a bad idea since Woofy was not really her dog. He might take it in his mind to go back to whom ever his true owner was. By collaring him she would be laying claim to him. This is the argument she used but it really boiled down to the fact that she didn't want to make him unhappy. She only wished to treat him the way she would want to be treated if the rolls were reversed. Why this thought struck her as right, she did not know. But it was.

When she got out of town and back on the road toward Mackinaw City, Woofy caught up with her again. "Where did you spend you're time?" she asked him. She got a whimper in return. "Do you smell the food? Are you hungry?" One bark and not a very loud one at that. "Ok, here you go," she said and opened the take out box. He ate heartily and left nothing in the box. He had even eaten what was left of her oil drenched salad. He looked up at her licking his chops when she finished. "You're going to get fat," she said. "Most well fed dog on the planet." For this she got two barks.

She opened one of the containers of lunch meat and gave him a few pieces of it, then ate one herself. She opened the other container and stuffed the rest of the meat into it, then poured some water from her canteen into the dish and set it down for the dog. He drank it all and licked the bottom of the container.

"Ready to go?" she asked him. His mouth lolled open in a smile and he turned to walk ahead of her.

They arrived back at the KOA just in time for Tess to take a quick shower in the bathhouse and dress for dinner. She had fed the last of the lunch meat to Woofy when they were nearly back to the straights. It had not even gone warm in her backpack. So she put water in both bowls from the drinking fountain in front of the bath house and left them on the ground outside the shower room. Woofy was laying contentedly in the shade next to the bowls when she emerged. He picked up one of the bowls and put it inside the other and then presented both to her.

"Neat trick," someone said. Tess turned to see a girl of about ten watching Woofy. "How did you teach him to do that?"

"I can't take credit for that. He seems to be a pretty smart dog though, doesn't he?"

"He's not a dog," the girl said.

"He's not?" Tess asked, then decided to play along, "Then what is he?"

"He's a wolf," the girl said.

"How do you know?"

"My dad is a zoologist and he taught me the difference. I once tried to walk up to a wolf and pet it because I thought it was a dog. But my dad told me that wolves are bigger and stronger, they have longer muscles and bigger heads than normal dogs. Later I saw a husky dog and I could really see the difference."

“This one is probably a wolf/husky mix,” Tessa said to the girl.

“Nope, he’s full wolf,” she said. “Does he bark?”

“Yes,” Tess said. Then she asked very politely if Woofy would bark for the girl. Woofy came forth with a quiet muffled bark that she was getting used to hearing and interpreting as an agreement sound.

“Yep, that’s a wolf bark. Dog’s bark differently. If you want to come over to our campsite tonight, my dad will tell you for sure, but I’m almost positive this guy is full wolf.”

Tess found out where the girls family was camping and said she would come over this evening after supper.

The restaurant where she was eating had an outdoor terrace which was easily accessible for the clever wolf, so Tess opted for a table out there. It was a mild night, and had been a fairly warm day, so it was quite comfortable. She ordered four entrées and a salad. One of the entrées was a huge rare steak. She tasted it and liked it but she sliced off only a small portion of it for herself and put the rest on the ground for Woofy. He agreed with a slight quiet bark that barely raised any attention at all that it was indeed a tasty steak. Woofy also finished off the skin of a baked potato, an over-cooked summer vegetable medley, three pieces of breaded codfish, and half of a pulled pork sandwich. Tess kept the Shrimp Scampi for herself but shared the chicken pasta Alfredo with him, first eating what she wanted of it and then setting the rest of the plate on the ground for him. He licked his chops and smiled at her. When the chocolate cake desert arrived she placed a bowl of water on the floor for him and enjoyed what she could of the cake. She was about to set the rest on the ground when a woman across from her spoke up.

"Dog's can't eat Chocolate, miss. It's poisonous to them."

"Really?" Tess said.

"It makes them very sick. Better not give it to him."

"Wow, thank you for telling me. I'll have to be careful about that."

"It's probably not a good idea to give him table scraps either," she persisted. "It teaches them the bad habit of begging at table. You should just feed him dog food in his own dish once a day."

"Oh, indeed, that makes sense," Tess said. "Thank you for the info."

Tess went back to her notes on the computer and tried very hard to not to look in the woman's direction again. She was not about to take that last piece of advice, but she had more questions for the zoologist tonight.

Tess left the restaurant as quickly as she could and they walked back to the KOA campground. Setting up her computer on her sleeping bag, she wrote the two reviews from the restaurants they had tried today. She also made notes about a pasty she had picked up at a little place near the other end of town. After a quick check of her e-mail and a short post to her father she packed up the computer.

As she walked toward the girl's campsite the girl saw her and called to her.

"I knew you would come over," the girl said. "I was telling my dad all about your wolf."

The girl said her name was Kit, and her brothers were Colt and Jamie. Kit grabbed Tessa's hand and led her over to her parents. She introduced herself and Woofy to the parents.

"I'm Rick Kraft and this is my wife Dawn." He said pleasantly as he held out his hand to shake. "And where did you get a domesticated wolf?" he asked not looking the beast in the eyes.

"I didn't really get him at all. He kind of acquired me." She explained how they had found each other traveling through the woods a few days ago.

"Do you know how extremely dangerous it is, what you just told me?" he asked her.

"Well, if he really is a wild animal than yes, I understand the danger but I really don't think he is. I mean he doesn't seem to be."

"Well, he is a full blooded wolf, I can tell that from here." Tessa looked down into the animal's eyes as it looked up at her. Rick's gasp drew Tessa's attention. "You look it in the eyes?" he asked.

"Yes. Shouldn't I?" Tess said.

"Most wolves interpret that as a challenge." He said. "I suppose if you and he look each other in the eyes it means that he was accepted you as his pack leader."

"Or his mate," Kit said.

"Probably not," Rick said putting a hand on his daughter's shoulder.

"No?" she asked.

"No, I don't think a Wolf would see a human being as a potential mate but he could see a taller, more intelligent creature than himself as a pack leader."

"So you think Woofy thinks I'm his pack leader?" Tess asked. Woofy got down on his haunches then and ducked his head. A short disapproving growl issued from him.

Rick was immediately on his guard. He looked around to see if one of his sons had gone too near the wolf.

"That's odd," Tess said. "I've never heard him make that sound before. What's the matter, boy?"

Two short muffled barks came from his throat followed by another growl.

"Hey stop that, Woofy, you're scaring people." Woofy stood at once and came to her side. She sat down on a log near the fire and petted his rough.

"You want s'mores?" Kit asked and held up a stick with a half burned marshmallow that her mother was trying to corral between two graham crackers and half a chocolate bar.

"I would love one," Tess said to her, "But I have to tell you, I can never get the right amount of burn on my marshmallow. Would you make one for me?"

"Sure!" Kit said between mouthfuls of the sticky delight. She stuffed the whole thing in her mouth and grabbed another marshmallow out of the bag.

Tess turned back to Rick. "I do have some questions for you. I heard today that Chocolate is bad for dogs, does that hold true for wolves as well?"

"Well, I would assume so. He should not be eating sweets at all. He can eat any sort of meat there is. A wolf's digestive track can handle swallowing the bones of small animals like mice and squirrels and such. I'd be careful giving him fish though. Sometimes fish bones can be tough on their stomachs, although there is evidence that wolves have eaten fish in the wild with no ill effects."

Tessa was nodding and interjecting an affirmative sound as he ticked off each point. "So in the wild," she asked when he came to a lull, "Do they only eat once a day like a dog?"

"No, they pretty much eat anytime they come across game. Game is pretty small, rodents, chipmunks, squirrels. Anytime they can trick one and get it they will general eat it down. If they hunt in a pack and get a deer or some bigger animal then the pack will stay by that kill until they've had their fill. Then they'll move on and let the ravens take what's left."

"So eating several times a day is natural for them?"

"Yeah, I'd say so. Why? Does he want food more than once a day?"

"He'll eat whenever and whatever I give him usually. I almost gave him a piece of chocolate cake tonight but a lady at the next table stopped me."

"They let him come into a restaurant?" Dawn asked.

"Well, we were eating outside on the terrace and he slipped in. The waiter didn't mind, and he stayed under my table the whole time."

"That's really unusual behavior for a wolf." Rick said.

"Yeah, well, I've seen some really interesting behavior from him. Like these little barks. At first they were pretty loud but I was worried about disturbing other people so I told him to be quiet. So now he only uses his inside voice."

Rick shook his head, "I think you may be anthropomorphizing this animal. He doesn't understand what you're saying."

"I think he does," Tess said. Kit was trying to get her attention. Tess looked and the girl was trying to hand her s'mores. Tess took the confection and held it while she finished making her point. "He seems to agree with me by using his barks. Maybe it's just me reading things into his noises but when he barks once quietly he seems to be agreeing with me, and then if he doesn't agree or is trying to warn me away from something he barks twice loudly, and growls."

"Like he did when I suggested you were his pack leader." Rick said watching the wolf's reaction. The wolf shook his head and barked twice quietly.

Tess looked at Woofy. "You don't like it when someone calls me your pack leader do you?" The wolf barked twice and whimpered. "I'm not your pack leader?" Tessa asked. Two more barks and a growl directed toward Rick.

"Then what am I," Tess asked. "Am I your friend?" The wolf took two sliding steps toward Tess while still sitting on his back haunches but did not make a sound.

Kit looked at the wolf and said, "Is she your mate?"

Woofy stood wagging his tail and barked once, then put forth a long howl.

"Really?" Rick exclaimed. "Well, if he could understand what we're talking about then that would prove it. Wolves howl as a means of communicating between them and their mates. What he just did would have proved he thought of you as a mate, except we could have been talking about African elephants for all he knows."

Woofy sat down and growled.

"I would take that to mean that he knows we weren't talking about African Elephants, but I do see your point."

"He did a neat trick today though Daddy," Kit said as she took two more marshmallows from the bag. She recounted the two water dishes and how Woofy stacked them inside each other before handing them to Tessa.

"Wow, that means he was very well trained, probably by a professional. Maybe he's escaped from a film set. He might be a professional performing wolf."

"If that's the case then, maybe someone is looking for him," Tess said. "Would that sort of thing be broadcast?"

"I don't know. I haven't heard about any missing animals on the news lately." Rick said.

"No, the only animal news has been those attacks down state." Dawn said.

"Oh, I know, that's very frightening. They all happened right around where I had been camping too," Tess said. Rick looked at her.

"Really?" he said. Then he looked at Woofy.

"No, it couldn't have been Woofy. For one thing, Woofy isn't rabid and they said this was probably the work of a rabid dog."

"There haven't been any rabid dogs in Northern Michigan for over a decade. It was no rabid dog. They did find that the bite marks and saliva were that of a wolf though. I was called in on the one attack near Charlevoix. It was one of the worst things I've ever seen. But I can tell you, it was definitely a Wolf attack." He again looked at Woofy, who turned his ears back and dropped his head. A short whimpering sound escaped him and Tess reflexively reached down and stroked his head.

"What did it look like Daddy," the younger boy asked. Dawn gave her husband a look.

"This latest attack though, the one down in Pelston, has people very upset. Big towns like Petoskey and Traverse City are used to having the occasional murder happen even if they aren't as used to it as Detroit or Grand Rapids, but Pelston has not had a murder in over three decades. People come through that town all the time because of the airport, but still, not a single murder. But now there is this animal attack."

"I hadn't heard about another one, does that make four now?" Tess asked.

"Yes," Rick looked grave. "They all happened in areas where you had camped?"

Tessa told her story about traveling from Traverse City up through the Chain-of-lakes district through Torch River Bridge and Bellaire to Charlevoix. It wasn't until after Charlevoix though that she met up with Woofy. "But Woofy has been spending nights with me since Charlevoix, so I'm pretty certain he's not the wolf they are looking for. We didn't camp in Pelston. We came up through there to the straights." Tessa said.

"Was he in your sight the whole time?"

"Well, no, of course not. He's been following me but no, he's not with me all the time."

"When does he leave you? At night?"

"I imagine so, when I'm asleep I know he comes and goes as he wishes. I can't really keep track of him, I don't have him on a collar and leash."

"Does he come into cities with you?" Rick asked.

"He didn't come through Petoskey with me but he met me on the other side. I was worried about him that he might have gotten hit by a car or something. All the other small towns that we've gone through he stayed with me and walked either beside me or ahead of me always checking to make sure I was still behind him. You know?"

"That means he doesn't see her as a pack leader, right dad?" Kit asked.

"It could mean lots of things," Rick told his daughter.

"He was with me all the time when we were in Pelston though, and he's been with me ever since, so that one can't be pinned on him," Tess said. "I'm sure of that."

"So it's your opinion that if he had nothing to do with that one, he is also innocent of the others?"

"Well, it fits. He's not a violent creature at all; in fact he's very gentle."

"For a wild animal," Rick stressed.

"What do you think I should do?" Tess asked him.

"What do you want to do?"

"I want him to stay with me." Tess said simply.

"Well, I suggest you get a collar and leash and make sure he's with you everywhere and at all times. I think most of the people you come in contact with would appreciate it too."

"He's really smart though, as your daughter pointed out and I don't think he would attack anyone." Tess remembered the man who had offered her a ride to Cheboygan. She told Rick that story as proof that Woofy wouldn't attach, he only warned the man off and then stayed in front of him long enough for Tessa to escape safely. Then he came to Tess when she called him.

"Yes but what would happen if someone did attack you? Would he come to your defense attacking the person who attacked you?"

"Well, yes, I think he would."

"And what if an old friend came toward you quickly to hug you and he thought that person was attacking you? I'm just saying, Tess, that things could get out of hand. The minute he attacks a human being he is at risk of being put down. You have to be very aware of these things and not allow things to get out of hand. If he does think of you as his mate then he might end up attacking someone who just wants a friendly hug from you."

"Ok, I get it." Tess said. And she did. She didn't want anything to happen that might harm other people or her pet. Woofy had been working at a spot in his fur where some melted marshmallow had fallen on him out of one of the s'mores. He looked up when Tess spoke though. He went over to Kit and nudged his nose under her hand, then jumped up on her for a hug. Kit obliged with a stroke down the wolf's back while Woofy licked graham cracker crumbs off her face and chin. But he did all of this in the friendliest manner he could with no sounds and no sudden moves.

"I'm not afraid of him Daddy," Kit said.

"I know honey and that's OK for this guy, because he's trained. But not all wolves are like this one." He explained.

Tess called Woofy to come over to her and he immediately stopped licking the struggling girl and came. “I think we should say goodnight.” Tess said. “I have some work to do in the morning.”

On hearing this Kit ran over to Tess and jumped into her arms giving her a big hug. Tess hugged back but only in order to turn the girl away from Woofy. Both parents were in the middle of shouting a warning not to do that, but it was already too late. Woofy stood up and looked at Tess hugging the little girl. He was smiling and wagging his tail. “Can I play with Woofy tomorrow?” Kit asked Tessa.

Tess turned toward Woofy who was swishing his tail in agreement. “I don’t know honey, I don’t know if we’ll be around much tomorrow.” She looked over the girl’s head toward Rick. But Dawn was the one that answered.

“If there is time,” Dawn said. “Maybe Tess and Woofy can come over again tomorrow night after supper.”

“We can have some more s’mores.” Kit said playfully petting the big wolf.

Tess walked back to her own site. But as they neared it Woofy started to growl. He walked in front of Tess barring her way.

“What is it?” she asked in a low voice and reached for her pepper spray. Something was ahead near her tent. “Stay here,” she told Woofy and she inched forward trying to get a better look at what it was. Woofy suddenly growled louder and bolted toward the object. “Woofy no,” Tess shouted. But the Wolf was heading full tilt toward the dark mass near the front of her tent. Soon she heard loud growls and a snuffling commotion as the wolf faced down whatever it was. Tess came closer and got through a few trees where she had a better view. In front of her tent was a huge fat raccoon and Woofy was facing it down. The raccoon was hissing at the wolf and it seemed to be holding onto part of the garbage bag that Tess was planning to throw out in the morning.

"Woofy, let him have it." Tess said. And then Woofy backed off enough to allow the hissing raccoon to gain his feet again and scurry off into the woods carrying the little garbage bag.

"Ok, so you are kind of handy to have around," she said to him. "But I'd feel better about it if they would catch whatever it is that's attacking people. I know it's not you!"

Woofy let out a howl and Tess let him get it out of his system. Then she said, "Ok enough Halloween stuff for one night. I want you to sleep inside with me tonight so go relieve yourself now, because I'm zipping the bottom of the tent tonight. Woofy wandered off into the woods and was back before Tess was finished getting on her jammy pants. He climbed into the tent and stretched out on top of her sleeping bag. She closed the tent flaps zipping up the bottom as well as the top and unless Woofy acquired opposable thumbs during the night he was effectively locked inside with her. She playfully pushed his big body aside so she could get into the sleeping bag herself. Then he came and lay down next to her. He lay down with his back toward her and she stroked the soft fur of his side. She kept stroking him as they lay and at one point he rolled onto his back so she could stroke his tummy. She admired his long soft underbelly fur and stroked it, letting it run through her fingers. She kept doing this until she realized that the animal was becoming aroused. "Oh, My God," Tess said. "You really do think I'm your mate, don't you?"

Woofy rolled the rest of the way over toward Tessa and put his head on her chest. There he nuzzled his face into her clothing, bending his head so that it was tucked into her body. She put her arm up on his massive head and petted the side of his face.

"I love you too," she told him. Soon they were asleep.

Chapter 10

They woke only once in the night. There were some noises outside the tent. Woofy was growling. Tess sat up and said, "What is it boy?" She got only the low growl in response. "I'm not letting you out tonight for you to chase raccoons. Is that what it is?" Woofy barked once very quietly and stopped growling.

"Go back to sleep, it's not going to hurt anything." Tess told the wolf. Woofy must have agreed because he lay back down and didn't stir when more noises were heard outside the tent.

As a rule Tess kept everything of value inside the tent with her or took it with her wherever she went. So it was a big shock to her in the morning when she realized that her camera was not in its pouch. She remembered that she had uploaded the pictures from yesterday's meals onto the hard drive in preparation for selling them with the reviews. But she was certain that she had put it back into the pouch before she went to the campfire over at the Kraft's campsite. She had left the camera in the tent inside the mini-pack with the laptop and her phone. She checked those two things again and yes they were there and just fine. So where was her camera?

"If someone came into the tent last night to steal things from me then why would they take my camera and not my laptop or phone?" she asked. Woofy whimpered. Maybe this was the sound he made when there was a more complicated thought in his mind that he couldn't express with a yes or no. Because Tess was pretty sure that Woofy barked once for yes and twice for no. She didn't want to test it though in case it proved to be untrue.

"Oh, shoot," she said. "That stupid raccoon last night! I wonder if the camera got caught up in that bag he hauled off."

Woofy jumped up and tore off into the woods. He returned about five minutes later with the shreds of the bag in his teeth. Apparently he had found where the raccoon had emptied her trash, finding anything edible in it. There was nothing edible in her trash, just an old safety razor she had used on her legs yesterday and an empty shampoo bottle. The shampoo was a fruit flavor which is probably what had attracted the poor animal.

"No camera?" she asked, not really expecting an answer, but the wolf whimpered and barked twice.

"Crap!" she said. He whimpered again.

"Well, maybe I put it in my pack." She said and dumped it out on top of her sleeping bag. A strong odor rose from the contents of the pack and Woofy whimpered again. "What is that?" she exclaimed. She sifted through the clothing until she found a small bundle made up of one of her t-shirts. It seemed to have been knotted up. As she untied the knots she realized that the smell was emanating from this garment.

She took it outside the tent to finish unknotting it. Inside was a dead chipmunk. It looked like it might have been bitten, but it was so decomposed that she couldn't tell.

She didn't know how it could possibly have gotten there but it must have been a prank of some kind. Maybe some boys had found it in the woods and put it in here to see her reaction. Only she hadn't noticed it in time and only now was discovering it.

"Well," she told her wolf. "There's only one thing to do. I'll go out and bury this poor creature and we won't say another word about it. Whoever pulled this prank is not going to get the satisfaction of seeing me scream!"

She wrapped up the rodent again in the same t-shirt and took it out into the woods, dug a hole with her hands and buried the whole package. "I wonder if they have my camera?" she said to the wolf as she wiped the dirt from her hands.

Tess went to a restaurant that had been recommended as a great breakfast place. They had a buffet but from experience she knew that the dishes on the buffet were not always the best the chef could do, so she asked for suggestions. It appeared that the waitress thought the chef's hollandaise was especially good, so she ordered the eggs benedict and followed it up with an order of poached eggs with hash. As a whim she ordered the steak and eggs as well and was well pleased with the sizable rib eye she got on that plate. But once again she cut off only a small portion of the meat for herself to try and put the rest in the wolf box, as she was starting to call it, instead of doggy bag.

It was a good meal and all the dishes looked appetizing, she took pictures of them all with the camera on her phone, but she really didn't like doing this. She would have to e-mail the photos to herself. It was just an extra step. She really wanted a camera. She asked the waitress if there was a Wal-Mart nearby or even a K-Mart. She could buy a fairly good camera for under $200, and she really needed one. The waitress told her the nearest one of either of those two stores was back in Petoskey or up in the Soo.

Tess believed she had enough money but she would check her financials before purchasing. It occurred to her that she hadn't done that in a while. She had her laptop out on the table so she pulled up her on-line banking site and looked over her shoulder before typing in the password.

"God, Tess, paranoid a little?" she asked herself.

Her balance had grown. There was nearly three times the amount of money in her checking account than she thought should be there. She checked her savings account too but that had remained the same. She went into the account and looked at the deposits. There were several from some magazine in the East called "Travel Destinations." They had purchased sixteen of her articles both recent and past for their onboard travel magazine that they put in airports and on planes. This had netted her about $4000. She was astounded. The automatic payment of her student loan had taken place and the bills from her last three hotel stays had gone through as well. She had no problem. She could easily afford a new camera as soon as she found a place to buy one.

But that was a problem for later. Now her problem was that she had to get over to Mackinaw Island before lunch. The last two restaurants that she needed to try were on the Island. It occurred to her that the reason she bought the steak was because she knew she would have to leave Woofy behind on the main land when she went to the Island which was populated by horse carriages and hundreds of thousands of tourists. This is when she got a brain storm.

She left the breakfast place after the cashier told her that there might be a little shop across in the mall that might have a camera. He was a type of pawn broker but he often had cameras that had been lost or stolen from tourists.

"Great," Tess told him. "Maybe I can buy back my own camera from him."

The cashier chuckled. "Stranger things have happened."

Crossing the street, Tess stepped into the shop. There were some good cameras there, and some mediocre ones, but not hers. She bought one of the better ones that had a card compatible to her laptop and asked if the man had any more cards to go with. He turned up three more and she bought them.

She hiked back up the hill to the KOA and Woofy was waiting for her on the outskirts of town. She patted his head and stroked his neck. "How would you like to play with the kids this afternoon?" she asked him. He tilted his head.

"I'm going across to the Mackinac Island and I can't take you with me," Tess said. She knew he didn't understand a word of this but it was making her feel better about it explaining it to him out loud. "If you stay here and play with the kids nicely I'll bring you back something special tonight. I'll be back at the campgrounds by 9 o'clock. I promise."

He stood up and wagged his tail a bit, then barked once louder than usual.

"Oh, you agree? Good. Kit will be very pleased to play with you all day. Don't hurt anyone!"

Woofy tilted his head again and whimpered.

She dropped him off at their campsite and Kit immediately sprang at the wolf hugging him tightly around the neck and shouting with glee that she would take very good care of him.

"You sure about this?" Tess asked Rick and Dawn before leaving.

"Well, I think, after seeing his reaction to my oldest daughter that he can be trusted around children. You fed him today?"

"He had some steak and eggs and leftover hash. He does like to eat though so if you have an extra burger or hot dog, I'd be happy to reimburse you."

"Not a problem," Dawn said.

Tess said goodbye to Woofy again and reminded him that she would be back tonight. She walked away and when she looked back he was watching her, despite the desperate attempts of Kit to distract him.

Things went very well at the Island. The only mishap was on the boat crossing when she felt someone watching her. She turned but saw no one. She decided that this feeling was something she should pay attention to though, in light of the theft of her camera. So she got out the new camera and took several shots of people on the deck of the ferry. No one seemed to stand out to her though. So she forgot about it. She went to a little restaurant downtown for lunch and then had several hours to kill before she headed to the second restaurant up the hill just before the Grand Hotel. She found herself stepping into all the little tourist shops in town. She found herself a new t-shirt to replace the one she had buried with the chipmunk. It was tan with the words "Mackinac Island" written across the front in white. After looking through several more shops she came across a true tourist trap with "authentic" Indian Moccasins and a huge bin of rocks and minerals that tourists could purchase for $5.00 per bag. She ran her fingers through one of the bins and then noticed something. There was a backpack for a dog. The advertising on the paper head-tag clearly showed a dog wearing this thing. It was shaped rather like a horse's saddlebag, but it had a strap that would attach around the neck and another that would buckle under his tummy. Two bags hung down on either side of the dogs back and could carry things like water bottles and remote controls, only two of the ideas on the advertising. It was supposed to be a joke gift for someone really lazy who would try to make his dog wear the thing to aid in fetching beer from the fridge. But Tess thought it might be just what she needed. She said she would bring back something special for Woofy. She wondered if he would take to wearing it.

Oh, so what if he didn't. She looked at the price, $9.95. She had spent more on stupider things. She also bought a metal insulated cup that looked like it would fit in this thing. The other side pocket looked like it would handle his plastic water dish made from the deli meat containers. He could carry his own snacks and water. He might like that. She also thought that eventually if they get into a big town that has leash laws and pooper scooper laws, he could carry his own plastic bags to clean up his poop. That is, if he would allow her to put the silly thing on him. She might be ending up carrying it herself. After all, it's possible, despite what Rick thought, that he was just a really smart wild animal. He might not want to carry things for his pack leader's convenience.

Tess reviewed the second restaurant making short notes so she could rush back to the pier and catch a ferry back to the mainland. She logged on to her computer on the ferry ride and had 20 minutes to write the review in relative peace. There were a lot of people crossing who had spent the day exploring the Island but they were tired and not very animated.

She took the card out of the camera and inserted it in the card reader on her laptop to upload the photos she's taken at the two restaurants. She browsed through them editing them in her photo editing software. Once the files were where she wanted them, she e-mailed her father with the attachments.

Out of curiosity she took out the other three cards and one by one inserted them into her card reader. She was gratified by the fact that two of them were empty. But the third one had photos on it. As she paged through them she realized that this was the card from her lost camera. It had photos of food from her last three towns. She wondered how that pawn broker could have gotten a hold of her card.

Tess almost stopped paging through but then realized there might be a clue on this card, as to who could have stolen her camera. She kept pushing the right arrow until she got to the end of the food pictures. There was only one other picture on the camera. It might have been taken by accident by her. It was almost a total blur. But then she blew it up and looked more closely. It was a picture of her t-shirt, the one that she had buried with the little chipmunk. Off to the side of frame barely noticeable was a foot. The claws on the foot were curled under as if atrophied. And the fur near the foot was matted with a dark brown shiny sheen. It was barely visible between the severe focus problem and the low lighting. The flash had not gone off properly on this frame.

It was clear that the thief and the prankster had been the same person. He had stolen her camera that night from the tent when he put the rotting corpse in her backpack. He had tried to commemorate the event by taking a photo but the flash hadn't gone off so he got this blurred mess. He then was afraid his actions might have caused some attention and fled. Tess had left the camera out in the open inside the tent and that's why he had taken it and not the other valuables. He then sold the camera to the pawn shop. The shop owner must have taken out the card to wipe it of images like he had done to the others he had sold her, and replaced it with a clean card. Then he probably sold it before she arrived. It was just chance that she happened in there to buy a camera and needed extra cards for it or she may never have found this.

She uploaded the image to her hard drive and then wondered what, if anything, law enforcement could get from this.

More to the point, should she take the time to report it? The thief was probably long gone from here by now. She doubted that it had been stolen by a local. And the added touch of the chipmunk was definitely the brain child of a deviant mind. Maybe she should tell the local authorities about it. She would take the card to the Sheriff station in the morning.

She got out of the ferry in Mackinaw City and practically ran through town and up the hill to the campground. As soon as she walked up the road toward the Kraft's campsite she could hear the pounding of paws on the dirt road and braced herself. The wolf launched himself at her, jumping up high, licking her face, and wagging his wiggling butt and tail all over the place. She got down on her knees to be more at his level and he ended up knocking her over with his exuberant kisses. She rolled down onto her back, hair in the hard packed dirt of the camp road and he straddled her body pressing down on her to keep his tongue licking her face.

"Stop," she said to him. "Stop!" But she was laughing too hard to make it sound convincing. They had caused some attention though and a woman screamed that there was an animal attacking a woman. Rick had come running and calmed the woman down. Then he came over and rescued Tess by pulling the wolf bodily off of her.

"I'm glad to see you too," she told Woofy, "But you got to calm down dude."

Woofy had indeed calmed down and was panting, to catch his breath.

"Did he hurt you?" Rick asked her.

"No, he wouldn't hurt anyone," she said. It occurred to her that this statement was not only wishful thinking but a pre-emptive strike aimed at defending him from anyone who was afraid of him just because he was wolf. Would she be saying this until Woofy himself proved her wrong?

"I believe that, but he's a big powerful animal and he knocked you down very easily. He could have hurt you without meaning to."

"He was just playing."

"I know, but," he dropped off. Obviously he wanted to warn her again about how dangerous he was but she wasn't hearing anymore of it.

"How did he do with the kids today?" she asked him instead.

"Just fine. He really is very gentle. I'm afraid he may have learned a few more tricks. Or maybe he knew them already and taught them to my daughter."

Tess looked over at Rick and smiled. The way Rick referred to his oldest child as his daughter, Tess could tell that he really loved and admired Kit. What must it be like to be a man who loves his daughter so much? Tess wondered. She could clearly see the pride he had for her.

"Kit is a smart girl. I think she will make a wonderful Zoologist someday."

"She does love animals. She's always bringing home pets, kittens, puppies, one time she captured a Chipmunk and wanted to make it into a pet."

They got back to the campsite and were greeted by the rest of the family. The kids were excited about showing off all the new tricks that Woofy could do. And only some of them were things that he had already known how to do. They had him stacking things, and telling him to sit and lay and roll over and play dead dog, which he did with utter conviction. Kit even poked him with her shoe and still he didn't move a muscle until she told said, "OK, Kicky not dead now."

He got up, shook his rough and licked her face.

"Back from the dead," Tess said. She then realized that Kit had called Woofy by the name of the boy she had met in Northport.

"Why did you call him Kicky?" she asked.

"That's his name." Kit said.

"His name is Woofy," Tess told her.

"I know but he said his name was Kicky so I called him that."

"He said?" Tess was flummoxed.

"My daughter has a vivid imagination." Dawn said. "All day long she's been talking about Kicky and everything he's been telling her. I don't know what she's been reading, but . . ."

"What else did he tell you?" Tess asked, now curious about this girl's creative mind.

"Oh lots of stuff," she said. "He told me about seeing you for the first time and knowing that you were his mate."

"Really," Tess said.

"Yeah, and he told me that you and him had dinner together at a restaurant and that's when he fell in love with you." Tess had told them yesterday about dinner on the terrace with the wolf under her table.

"He said that he printed on you, or something. Did he put his paw prints on you?"

"Paw prints?" Tess asked. "I don't think so."

Rick had been looking at his daughter thoughtfully.

"Do you mean imprinted?" he asked Kit.

Kit looked at the wolf and then nodded. "Yeah that's the word. He imprinted on Tess. What does that mean?"

Tess looked over at Rick. She had never heard of it either.

"Well, my dear, you know what it means, you should tell us," Rick said to Kit.

"I don't know what it means. I just know that Kicky thinks it's important."

"What does it mean to you Rick?" Tess asked.

"Well, it's something that happens with animals. Some animals have a bonding instinct with others of its own species. We called it imprinting. It's proven that most birds have it and that's why they flock together. When a bird hatches from an egg it imprints on the first thing it sees, usually its mother or in some cases one of its siblings. Birds have a strong imprinting instinct. Other animals have it but it's not so strong. There are some animals, like wolves, that mate for life. For lack of a better term they call this bond imprinting. We humans of course call it the love bond. But in an effort to not anthropomorphize animals we can't just let it be said that the most basic of human instincts, that of love, can be said of lower forms of life. So Woofy can't just love you, he has to imprint on you."

"Do you believe that Woofy loves me? Or is it this imprinting instinct?"

"Oh, he loves you all right. I don't hold with some scientists that say that animals don't have emotions. I'm absolutely sure they do. I've seen evidence that squirrels in the wild grieve for their lost companions. A duck whose mate has been hit by a car will cry out for hours next to the dead body before hunger drives it back to the pond to search out food. A swan that has lost her mate will kill the mate of a neighboring swan out of revenge and jealousy."

"So how does that differ from the imprinting instinct?" Tess wondered.

"Imprinting is a bond. It's rather like the bond that forms between a mother and child just after birth when she holds the baby and breast feeds her. Bonding gets all mixed up with love in humans. But in animals the instinct, some scientists suspect, comes from Darwin's law of nature, the survival of the fittest. A female will bond with the male that will give them the strongest genetic offspring. A male will bond with a female who will be most likely to give him offspring that will carry on his seed."

"Are you talking about sex?" the older of the two boys asked. Then looked at his brother and giggled.

"It's not called sex when animals are involved," Dawn told her sons, "it's called breeding." She glanced at her husband and Tess had to smile because the double meaning was starkly clear to all three adults. Tess glanced at Kit though wondering how much of this she was getting.

Kit had an extremely adult expression on her face. Smart kid, she probably understood most of this.

"When animals are left in the wild to choose their own mates the offspring is strong and is able to evolve naturally. When they are forced to choose among a limited group like say an isolated grouping of animals in a zoo. The offspring is small and sickly and the mortality rate goes up. That's why it's hard to get a pairing of animals in a zoo situation to mate. They have the instinct that there are better mates out there and will refuse to mate with their cell mate. It would be kind of like putting you in a hotel room with Bill Gates, Howard Stern and Elton John and forcing you to choose one of them to have babies with."

"Gotcha, Bill Gates, would probably be my choice, because he's rich, a computer genius and age appropriate but I wouldn't choose him in the wild with other choices, he just the best of that bunch, Elton John being gay and Howard Stern being, well, yuck!"

"Ok, so you get my picture."

"So if it's true what Kit says and I have a wolf that thinks I'm his mate, how would that happen? I mean I'm not into furries, you know?"

Rick glanced down at his daughter wondering if she knew what that meant. But he answered her question anyway, "Well, I think Woofy sees you as his pack leader, not his mate. It's Kit who thinks Woofy is your mate. She must have heard me talking about imprinting before and used it in her game today. Obviously you couldn't be the one he would have chosen as a mate because your genes are incompatible. He might be able to mate with a dog and have unique offspring. But if he mated with a human, as if such a thing were possible, the DNA is too different. There would be no offspring at all. So by that definition alone, he could not possibly have imprinted with you."

"But what if he had? Is there any scenario you could come up with of a wild animal imprinting on a human?" Tess asked. "You know, in your wildest imagination?"

"Yeah," he said after a moments thought. "The Greek god Zeus came down to Earth in the form of a swan to trick a woman into mating with him. Clearly that falls into this category."

"A girl and a swan did it?" the older boy asked his father.

"No, it was a man disguised as a swan." Dawn told her precocious son. "Can we please change the subject?" she asked her husband.

"So what you're saying is that Woofy could only imprint on me if I was a wolf in disguise or if he was a human in disguise."

"Basically," Rick admitted. Tess looked down at her pet wolf who was looking up at her in adoration.

"You a werewolf?" she asked him, hoping that someone would laugh at the joke. Dawn and Rick both obliged but they were cut short by Woofy. He barked once and then after a pause barked twice more.

"Yes and No," Kit said. "He is but he isn't? Dad, what's he talking about?"

"Kit, I've told you this before. He's an animal he does not bark to answer yes or no questions. He was barking because Tess addressed him with her own vocalizations so he followed suit."

"But dad, I saw him."

"What did you see him do?" Tess asked.

"I saw him change, in his mind. He told me that he could change and he showed me how he does it."

"He's a Wolf, sweetie, he doesn't change into a human being," Dawn explained. She was being very patient with her daughter.

"It's good to have an imagination," Tess said. She patted the girl on the head. "But I think we have to go back to the tent now, it's been a long day and we have to find a way to get across the bridge tomorrow.

"We'd be happy to drive you," Rick said, "if this one is willing to sit in the back with all those children."

Woofy shook his tail in approval.

Tess gratefully accepted Rick's offer. They walked back to their own campsite and crawled into the tent. Woofy sniffed around a little but found nothing objectionable tonight. Tessa's clothing, pack and sleeping bag were all just as she had left them. She did some pre-packing for the morning then went down to the bathhouse for a quick shower before bed. When they crawled into the tent for the final time Tessa unloaded the mini-pack and gave Woofy his Wolf box. He gulped down the delicacies with gusto and then pushed the empty box to one side.

"I got you a present." She said. She pulled out the doggie backpack and showed it to him. It's your own backpack. She took it out of the wrapper and showed him that there were pockets for his snacks and his water. She showed him the water bottle that fit in the one side pocket. He looked at all of this with a tilted head and that tongue lolling smile of his. Then he licked the gifts and then her face and settled down to sleep.

I'm going to have to get you your own doggie brush," she told him. He opened his eyes one last time and then closed them. This time he slept. So did she, solidly and all night.

Part Two: Threats

Chapter 1

Tessa's Travels

Where am I heading? At the moment I'm exploring the wooded area known as Chippewa County in the Eastern Tip of the U.P. I plan to hit:

Drummond Island
Detour Village
Raber
Pickford
Kinross
Sault Ste. Marie
Bay Mills Reservation in Brimley
Paradise
Newberry
McMillan
Seney
Grand Marais
Picture Rocks Lakeshore
Munising
Marquette

June 25, 2011

Dead Dad, publishers and constant readers,

Woofy and I are traveling through the U.P. finally. We made several stops in St. Ignace and reviewed the Casino Restaurant. Casinos are famous for having great chefs so it was a real treat to taste the cuisine of this one. I highly recommend this restaurant even if you're not a gambler!

I was told about two interesting places on the far Eastern Tip of the U.P. but walking out there was a daunting idea. A Waiter from the Casino said he would get me as far as a little town called Cedarville where we spent the night in a stand of woods just on the west side of town. A deer came into our site that night and poked around. It was just before we went to bed. I muzzled Woofy long enough to get a good look at it, but as soon as Woofy got loose he let go with a long howl which effectively scared the thing into next week!

I walked all day today after having breakfast in a little restaurant called Angio's. Tonight we are sleeping on the beach about ten miles outside of a little town called Detour Village. I plan to visit a little place called Raber Bar which is purported to be a favorite establishment of the locals up here. Also there is a good place to eat on Drummond Island that caters to tourists that go up on hunting and fishing trips. I will try that out. Drummond, I have heard is not as big a tourist destination as Mackinac Island so I'm hoping the ferry will allow me to take Woofy with me. I really don't enjoy being away from him now that we are used to each other. I'm thinking seriously about getting him one of those vests and pretend he's a service dog. I think less people would be scared of him.

Dad I got him a doggie back pack so he can carry his own water supply and snacks. He loves it! He waits very patiently when I put it on him. The only thing is he doesn't like to have it on when he goes into the woods to do his business. He begs for me to take it off. I do so obligingly if only to keep it cleaner. After all he does carry food in it.

After Drummond and Raber Bar I plan to head up to a smallish town called Pickford and then up the Soo (which is what the locals call Sault Ste. Marie.) The famous Soo locks are there, I hope there are some Ore ships going through while I'm there.

In the Soo there are several Casinos and a few restaurants I wish to try. I anticipate being there in about five days time and I plan to spend two nights there in a motel, preferably one that doesn't mind dogs.

Did I tell you, Dad? Woofy is not really a dog. He's a full blooded wolf. I ran into a zoologist at the campgrounds in Mackinaw City who confirmed it. He theorizes that Woofy must be a trained wolf that they use in movies, because he shows abnormal intelligence for a wild animal. There are several theories however as to my place in his life. The expert says Woofy thinks of me as his pack leader, but his daughter has a more romantic notion. She thinks Woofy sees me as his mate. If only he were a man!

Again readers, if you are interested in any of the restaurant reviews I have proposed please contact my Dad at the E-mail in the box at the right. Hiking the trails at Picture rocks lake shore will be a departure for me. There are probably no restaurants through there from Grand Marais to Munising, a good 40 mile hike, but I think I will take this opportunity to try my hand at travel writing. It's supposed to be a beautiful hiker's destination. I'll report on the trails and the sights. I understand there are more than a dozen waterfalls in that area.

Thanks for your interest,
Tess and Woofy!

It took Tess two days to get to Drummond Island from Cedarville. It was farther than she thought. She stopped at a little grocery store with a strange name, Sune's, in Detour Village after walking the ten miles into town that morning and got into a conversation with a woman in the meat department by the name of Annie Warner. The woman had seen her Wolf and was a pronounced dog lover, she insisted on going out to pet the animal and give him some raw meat scraps. She also offered Tess a ride to Raber, her next stop, after she came back from Drummond Island. The ferry did indeed allow her to take Woofy with her and she didn't even have to pay for him. They did however insist that she keep him on a leash while he was on board. She didn't like this idea, but saw that it was probably best. Tess decided that if she needed a leash for Woofy she would purchase one for these types of situations. She talked it over with Woofy while they were on board the ferry and he seemed to agree with her.

After reviewing the restaurant on Drummond and making the return trip, she tried a cafe in Detour village. Tess spent about an hour in the café writing the reviews to those two places and uploading them to her father. Then she went back to the Sune's a few minutes before Annie Warner was supposed to get off work.

"Oh, you made it," Annie said to her as she exited the back door of the grocery store.

"Yep," Tess said to her. "I really appreciate the ride."

"Oh, that's OK," Annie said. "I go right by there."

Tess detected a hint of the U.P. dialect in this woman's voice. "Have you lived here all your life?" she asked.

"No, I grew up here and then married a career military man who took me off to Germany, Florida, and then upstate New York. Then after ten years I divorced him and got half his pension money in the settlement and moved back up here to home with my kids."

"Oh, I see," Tess said. She was a little uncomfortable with all this personal information after having only known the woman less than a day but people up here were very friendly.

"Yep, and I've been happy ever since!" A cackle of laughter emerged from the good-natured woman, and Tess couldn't help but laugh with her. "But I'd rather hear about your exciting life," the woman said. The sentence came out "I druther hear boat your exciten life."

"Oh," Tess said. "The exciting life of a restaurant reviewer that walks off all the food she eats between gigs?"

This statement elicited another stream of laughter. Tess felt like the wittiest person on the planet being around this woman. As they talked for a while longer Tess realized that she didn't want to leave this woman's company, so she asked if the woman was hungry and would Annie be her guest for dinner.

Not to be outdone, Annie asked if Tess would like to stay the night in her guest room. Tess said she would not like to put her out, but that maybe she wouldn't mind letting Tess and Woofy camped in her yard.

"I wouldn't mind at all," Annie said. It sounded like she said, "I wont mind tall."

Annie drove Tess back to her house in Goetzville where Tess spent a half hour putting her tent up. Annie had two grown children, Christopher and Nadine. Christopher was on his way out to work in the Soo, a late shift at a factory, but Nadine said she would be happy to accompany them to dinner when Tess extended the invitation. Woofy ran back into the field behind the house and was not seen again.

"He's just checking the campsite," Tess explained. "He always does this. We had a surprise visit from a raccoon one time so he thinks it's his duty to mark the territory where we sleep."

"I get it," Nadine said. "He's your protector!"

"Yeah, I suppose he is now," Tess said.

They had a good meal at Raber Bar. Tess ordered five meals and tasted them all, then the two women kept her talking non-stop about where all she had traveled and what unusual things she had eaten. At the end of the enjoyable evening she paid the check, there was a discussion about who should leave the tip, but Tess won that argument and left a 25% tip on her charge card.

When they got back to Annie's house Woofy was stationed in front of the pitched tent awaiting her. He was praised up and down for being a good Woofy, and was given his wolf-box with all the leftovers of their meal, including two t-bones from steaks they had consumed and half a bar burger. There was also plenty left of a pasty that Tess had gotten because of the contest. It would not make the finals, the bottom of the pastry was too greasy and the filling was just too ordinary. It was a passable pasty but not up to the standards of the contest.

The night was completely uneventful and in the morning, Nadine came outside to offer Tess a morning cup of coffee which she gratefully accepted. Nadine also offered her a ride to the Soo. Nadine had a morning class at the college and said she would be happy to drive Tess and Woofy up there. Tess accepted this too, but said there was a café in Pickford she wished to try out. So this cut 20 miles and a whole day off of Tessa's trip.

Tess took breakfast at the café in Pickford, which boasted the worlds best sticky buns. Tess actually agreed with this assessment having never had any better. They hiked the rest of the 25 miles up to the Soo, where she found a motel on the outskirts that was pet-friendly. When she turned to leave the office, key in hand, Woofy was no where to be seen. She called for him several times but he was just gone.

By this time she had walked off the sticky bun from the morning and the dry sandwich she had gotten from a gas station near Kinross, so she decided to walk toward the Casino up on the hill and see if she could spot her Wolf. This was a pretty busy road with lots of fast food and destination businesses on it. She began to fear that Woofy might be in danger. She sat for a prolonged time inside the Casino restaurant doing her review and finally admitted that it had to be done. She would walk back to the motel. She passed a PetSmart on the road and decided that she would step inside and buy a collar and leash. If she had had one today she would not have lost Woofy when she stepped into the motel office. She only hoped it wasn't too late. He had found her again at Annie's house in Goetzville. Woofy was smart and if indeed he wanted to stay with her, he would come back.

They next day Tess decided that since she planned on staying two nights here, she would find out where she could do laundry. So after reviewing a breakfast buffet restaurant on the hill she explored the area around the motel. There was a St. Vincent De Paul thrift store behind them on a side street and next to it a coin laundry. One more street of houses beyond that emptied into a stand of trees. She walked back there while her clothes were in the washer and called several times for Woofy, but the only thing she could hear in response was someone in the distance chopping wood.

On her way back to her room she noticed a man coming around the corner of the building. There was something strangely familiar about him. She looked at him as he walked by and then stopped him.

"Excuse me, but I think we know each other."

He turned and looked at her. "You know, I was thinking that same thing but I was afraid you might think I was hitting on you if I said something."

Tess smiled. "Yeah, that's a sure way to turn most women off, I guess." Her non-committal statement made him smile as well. "I've never been up here before though," she continued. "So I don't know where I may have seen you. You just look very familiar."

"I travel a lot. We maybe have run into each other before. It's a small world."

"So they tell me."

He smiled at her. She was sure she had seen that smile before. She just couldn't place where. The man had dark hair and eyes, his face was tan as if he spent a good deal of time outdoors. He looked like he might be as old as thirty, but the way he smiled and tilted his head, made him look younger, maybe her age. She shifted the bag of clean laundry to her other hand and he insisted he take it from her.

"Do you live around here?" he asked.

"No, I'm traveling. I'm a hiker. I walk from place to place and write restaurant reviews."

"You walk? Everywhere?" he asked.

"If I can't find a ride."

"Wow," he said, then qualified it, "I mean, walking is healthy. You must be in great shape." He then grew embarrassed by how stupid that sounded. Tess knew he had not meant it to sound like a line.

"I know, but I like to eat, and it's good for me to walk off all the food I eat."

She had begun to walk back toward the motel and he had followed still carrying her laundry bag. "I like to eat too," he smiled. "I'd ask you out to dinner but I find myself suffering some hard times just now."

"Really?" she asked. There was something about him that she instinctively liked. She didn't know what it was, couldn't put her finger on it. But she all at once knew she would be having dinner with him tonight.

"Maybe you would like to have dinner with me tonight and we can discuss it further. My treat."

"I don't . . . I mean I wasn't trying . . ." he stammered.

"It's nothing, I often ask people to dine with me. I'm a restaurant reviewer and I have to order several entrées when I go to a new restaurant. You would actually be doing me a favor."

"So this would be a business expense for you?"

"Yes, but you aren't one of those people who doesn't like to share his food, are you?"

"No," he said. "But I do enjoy eating. I might polish off all the rest of your food."

"Well, if you don't my Woofy will."

"What is a Woofy?" he asked, his lips going up in an amused smile.

"Woofy is my wolf." She said. Usually she told total strangers that he was her dog so as not to scare them but this man was different. She wanted to be totally honest with him.

"Wolf? Wow, not a lot of people have a pet wolf."

"He's not exactly a pet, I mean, not in the sense that I decided to go find myself an unusual pet and bought a wolf cub to raise. I just found him in the woods as I was hiking. He started to follow me and well now he's my constant companion."

"Really! I'd love to meet him. Where is he now?"

"Um, out back there somewhere. When I stop at a hotel he doesn't always like to stay indoors with me. He likes to go out and explore the woods."

"I see, but he'll be back?"

"I assume he'll be back tonight before I go to bed. He likes to sleep next to me."

The man looked away. He had a self-deprecating blush that she could see embarrassed him. He tried to cover it with a highly charismatic smile.

"What?" she asked.

"I just got jealous of a wolf," he said. Then he did something that made her think of the young man she had met in Northport. He looked up at her with a crooked smile and a tilted head.

She shook it off. This man could not possibly be Kicky. Maybe he was related to him somehow. Kicky was only 18 this man was at least eight years older than that, about her age she thought.

He was very attractive though. Down girl, she told herself.

"I hope this isn't a very fancy restaurant we're going to tonight. I don't bring good clothes with me on the road." She looked down at his clothes. He was wearing jeans that were a bit too tight, a shirt that was loose around the waist but was too tight around his muscular shoulders and chest, and on his feet he wore a pair of flip flops.

"You look OK for a tourist town."

"Maybe I can find something nicer in the St. Vinnie's store over there." He said nodding toward it with his head.

"You're fine," she told him. He smiled again. "I don't have many nice clothes either. Just my hiking stuff."

"I see, well, OK then. I'll, um, come by tonight to pick you up?"

"Sure, about 6:00 P.M?" she asked.

"Sounds good."

"My name is Tess," she said holding out her hand. He took it in both of his holding it. "I'm David." He said. He let go of her hand and leaned against her door jamb.

She keyed into her room. Closing the door on him was one of the hardest things she'd done in a while, but a girl can't be too eager. She didn't even know the guy.

She unpacked the laundry bag and laid out her best slacks for the evening. She had several hours to kill before lunch so now would be a good time to get some work done. She grabbed her laptop and took it out to the picnic table which was situated behind the motel just outside the back door of the office. By the evidence of cigarette butts littering the ground this was where the staff took their breaks. She opened the laptop and caught up on her reviews sending them off in an e-mail with attachments to her father. After uploading more photos that she had taken along the way she checked her financials and found that she was still in the black. She decided to make a double payment on her student loan this month and so arranged that. Next time it came due a double amount would go out automatically. She'd have to remember to change it back before the August payment though or she might find herself short. She also put some of the extra into her savings account. It felt good to have a few extra hundred dollars in there. Normally she only put about $200 a month in there, this month she had added nearly $2000. Nice feeling!

She started thinking about Drummond Island and how different it was from Mackinac Island. One was so entirely touristy, and the other was just like a backwoods retreat. These thoughts prompted an article juxtaposing the two places. She decided not to send it off just now to her dad hoping to expand it a little and polish it a bit more.

Thoughts of Woofy brought her back to the present. She whistled again and again got no response. Where the heck was that creature?

He'd be back, she was certain. Maybe he was off hunting. That was fine, he did that sometimes when they were between cities and game was more prevalent than stores or restaurants. She had no way of knowing how they were going to handle being back in Chicago. Maybe she shouldn't hit big cities at all. Maybe she should avoid them and just hit more rural areas of the country. She thought about hiking all the way to Arizona to see Harry. All plans are loose though. And they can afford to be because when one has to walk every where, one is not getting there fast! It will probably be months before they made it to Chicago, if at all. Anything could happen.

Tess sighed. As much as she missed her dad she had to admit that this trip had been wonderful so far. She'd met up with some really nice people, Kicky, and his family, the Krafts, Annie Warner from Goetzville and her son, and now David. Not to mention her wonderful Woofy. She really couldn't complain even if she never saw any of them again. There were so many nice people in the world. This trip was so different from traveling with Harry in the beat up Volvo. Harry kept her from meeting anyone. Of course, he thought he was protecting her.

She opened her laptop again and called up a new e-mail to Harry.

Harry,

What the heck dude, are you mad at me or something? I want to hear your voice. You got my digits, call me or write me or something. I miss you. Hey, we're still friends right?

I got something to tell you. I have a traveling companion. He's got grey white hair and when he stands up straight he's about six two. He has been hiking along with me since Charlevoix. If you are reading my Blog you know that I'm talking about Woofy, my wolf. It's been an adventure and it's not half over. I wish you would tell me what's wrong. If I've done something please, let's have it out.

Love you, my dear friend,
Tess

Tess shut off her laptop and took it back to the room. With nothing to do in the room she worried about Woofy again, so she wandered over to the St. Vincent De Paul's store and looked around. She didn't see anything in the line of clothing she wanted so she browsed around the books and house wares area. Nothing caught her eye until she got to the craft department. There was a set of size one double-pointed knitting needles and some other larger ones. Her boyfriend from college had said that a woman wasn't a woman unless she couldn't knit, cook and make love with abandon. She had wanted to please him so she took 14 weeks worth of knitting classes and actually got pretty good at it. It's one of the things that she didn't regret on coming out of that relationship. She loved knitting socks above all. She had bought some yarn and needles in that little town downstate just outside of Petoskey and had made a pair of socks for her father. But now, with two sets of needles she could make both socks as once. Plus she also now had a larger set of single point needles to make scarves and hats with as well. So she shelled out the two dollars on the price tags and left the store. She'd have to find a yarn shop somewhere next.

As she walked back to the room she kept her eyes open for Woofy. She hoped nothing happened to him. It just wasn't like him to be gone this long.

She got lunch at an unusual little sandwich shop half way down the hill toward town. They had a very good sandwich with Liverwurst and sweet onion slathered with cream cheese on a toasted ciabata roll. She ordered it and a steak sandwich taking the steak sandwich back up the hill with her. Maybe she would give it to Woofy and maybe to David if he returned early.

She decided to check her e-mail and then take a nap.

"Finally," she commented in the quiet of her room upon seeing a return post from Harry.

"Tess,

"Sorry, I sometimes forget that you aren't hearing my comments when I speak them aloud into the computer screen. I guess I've been Skyping too much with my mom. You should download Skype, I would have an easier time talking with you that way.

"Anyway, yeah, I've been following your Blog. But I'm concerned about those animal attacks up there. Are you sure it's not your Wolf?

"Nothing is going on here. I'm just busy with schoolwork. Nothing you would be interested in. I do have a girlfriend. She's almost as unusual as I am. Download Skype and I'll let you meet her.

"Don't be so quick to judge me, Tessy, I'm not mad or anything. Just trying not to be homesick. Arizona is SOOO not Chicago!

"As always, Harry."

Tess remembered how Harry used to make single syllable words into four or five syllables so she heard him say "SOOOOO!" quite clearly in her mind. She smiled, satisfied that she had done her part to keep that relationship going.

She set the alarm on her phone for 4:00 P.M. so she could be dressed and ready by six. That would give her about an hour and half to sleep. Surely Woofy would be begging to come in by then.

But when the alarm went off she went to the door. No Woofy. She walked out back again and whistled. Nothing.

She went back inside and got dressed for her date. She carried mascara with her, but that was the only make-up she felt she could not do without. She applied some of it just before 6:00 P.M. Shortly before six came a knock on the door. She invited him in. She had the mini-pack ready to go.

He had changed his clothes. He was now wearing a black shirt that fit him better and a pair of black loafers with no socks. Very chic, she thought. She greeted him with a kiss on his cheek which surprised him. But he recovered quickly and returned the kiss with one of his own.

"I hope you don't mind if we walk," he said.

"Hey, I don't mind walking. I do it all the time. The restaurant is downtown right down the hill here. We'll get to know each other."

And they did. David was indeed a Native American from a tribe down state. Part of the Ottawa nation, he said. His family still lived down there on the reservation. He liked traveling though. He enjoyed meeting new people.

Tess told him about her father in Chicago, about Harry and about her student loans. The topic of their personal lives had nearly been exhausted by the time they reached the restaurant.

They sat down at a table by a window that overlooked the Soo Locks. Tess looked out the window for a time trying to figure out how to describe the nuances of the atmosphere. The restaurant was situated in the Chippewa Hotel and had both Native American themes and shipping themes in the décor. But the view of the locks and the rapids beyond were the real draw.

She picked up the menu and began perusing it.

"Just in case I forget to mention it later," David said. "I really had fun tonight."

"Do you write movies in your spare time?" Tess joked.

He smiled his crooked smile again and shook his head. "Can't pull anything over on you," he said.

"Sorry, I'm just a little worried about Woofy." She told him.

"Your wolf?"

"Yeah, he didn't come back tonight. I haven't seen him all day."

"Maybe he didn't like the city. I know I would spend as little time here as possible if I were a wolf."

"Hey, jury is still out on that one. Just because you are showing some self-deprecation doesn't mean you're not a wolf," Tess said with half a smile.

"You mean, you're not fooled by my sheep suit?" he smiled again, as he stroked the front of his shirt. Oh boy, she thought, I could get used to that crooked grin.

The waitress came with their drinks and took their order. After a short conversation with her about the chef specialties, Tess settled on four dishes she would like to try.

"Would you like something else?" she asked her date.

"Yeah, I'd like to try that 16 oz prime rib." He looked at Tess, "OK with you?"

"Sure, get what you want. Leftovers belong to Woofy though."

"He's getting his own dinner tonight," David said. The Waitress left the table and they sat looking into each other's eyes for a second, and sipping their drinks.

"Hasn't Woofy ever let you go someplace by yourself, like into a town, and then met you again on the other side?" David asked.

"Oh, you want to talk about Woofy!"

"Sure, I know you're worried about him."

"I am. But we can talk about something else."

"No, actually I'm somewhat of a wolf expert."

"Really?"

"Well, yeah, I studies wolves for a while in school."

"Well, to answer your question, he has left me a couple of times. He wouldn't go into Petoskey with me. He just ran off and caught up with me on the other side. He hadn't been with me very long and I just thought he had gone back to his master. I thought he was a dog back then. But there he was, on the other side of the town waiting for me. He's pretty much been with me ever since."

"I think he will be again. When you head out of town I think he'll catch up to you again."

"You have more faith in the dumb animal than I do."

"Is he really that dumb?" David asked. In the split moment after saying this, Tessa thought that he almost looked hurt, but his expression changed to curiosity so quickly that she figured she imagined it.

"No, actually he's the smartest dog I've ever known. He's not a dog I know, but he's the smartest animal I've ever known. I have a feeling that he understands what I'm saying."

"Well, he probably does," David said. "Animals don't think the way we do. I studied animal behavior for a while and animals can sense pictures in people's minds."

"How do you know this?" Tess asked.

"There have been experiments with dogs, dolphins, and mice and the results were the same across the board."

"Tell me," Tess said.

David thought for a moment. "OK, it's like this. We had heard of a scientist that did this experiment with dolphins. He taught the dolphins to fetch things from the water, different shaped hoops. He would then look at a picture of the shaped hoop he wanted the dolphin to get. The dolphin got the shape he was looking at sixteen times out of twenty. He noted when the dolphin missed and it had been at times when he himself had been distracted, first by his cell phone going off, then by a student who had drawn his attention, then by a rumbling stomach. The last time he had just not been concentrating because he knew this would be the last time. So he did the experiment again only this time he eliminated all the distractions and the dolphin got the right hoop 20 out of 20 times. The dolphin actually even knew when the twentieth time was and afterward went back and fetched the rest of the hoops and handed them over without being asked."

"Really! Wow!"

"Yeah, so I tried the same experiment with a dog. I had a Rubik's cube, a tennis ball and a Frisbee lined up on three chairs and I looked a picture of the one I wanted the dog to get. At first I had to tell the dog to go fetch. But after a while he caught on and just went and got the thing that I was looking at. I did not show him the picture. I just mixed them up and drew one at random. The first time we did this experiment he got 12 out of 20. The second time about two days later, he got 18 out of 20. You see he was learning, from me what was expected of him. After that he always got 20 out of 20 and after the third time he even went to a box where we kept a lot of toys and objects and he picked out the three things I needed for the test."

"That's amazing." Tess said.

"Yeah, but that's not all. I tried to make the test even harder by adding first one and then about six other objects to the pile and then I tried to picture each one in my head. As soon as he got the picture from me he would go and try to find the object. As long as I was concentrating and not distracted he could find the right object. As soon as I got distracted though it confused him and he brought his favorite toy which was the tennis ball. He would always opt for the tennis ball when he couldn't focus on the thing I wanted. Or rather, if I couldn't focus on the thing I wanted."

The waitress brought the salads. Both of them dug in before continuing the conversation.

"I have a question." Tess said. "If you were in college studying to be scientist, how did you end up here with no money?"

"Um, poor choices?" he said doubtfully.

"OK, none of my business." She quickly acquiesced. She didn't want to spoil this evening.

"It's OK, Tess. I will tell you everything in the course of time. We will eventually get to know each other well enough for all our secrets to be revealed." He looked into her eyes so earnestly that she believed him. "This is not a one-timer, Tess," he stated. "I'm not letting you go so easily."

She didn't know what to say to this. It was far too intense a statement for their first date. It should be upsetting to hear such a thing, or at least off-putting. But she was somehow reassured by this statement.

She shook off all this and decided to lighten it up a bit. "So what conclusions did you come up with about the dog?"

"Oh, yeah, OK, well I figured that this dog and I had gained some sort of affinity so I had one of the other students try it and sure enough the dog preformed just as well with the other student. He had more right than wrong even on the first try. I thought that maybe I should try the experiment with something with a smaller brain. So I got three mice and built a room with two doors, one black and one white. Behind the white door I put food and behind the black door I put a picture of a cat. The mouse chose the white door each time. Then I took the picture of the cat away and put food in the black door thinking the mouse would be programmed not to go into the black door because of the cat. Guess what happened."

"The mouse went in the white door despite knowledge that there was food behind the other door."

"No, the mouse trusted me. He went in the black door because I had told him there was food there."

"Trust?" Tess asked. "Trust is the issue?"

"For animals it is. I had continually told the mouse there was cat behind the black door and the one and only time he had gone through it there was indeed a cat there. Not a real cat just a picture of a cat but he remembered it. So when I told him there was food behind the door, he hesitated a few seconds but then he went into the door. I even tested this. I got another student to do the experiment and tell a different mouse that there was food in the white door and a cat in the black door. The mouse went to the white door. Then the student told the mouse the cat was in the white door and the food in the black door. He went to the black door and there was the cat. After that it was a crap shoot. The mouse would sometimes go to the door with the food and sometimes to the door with the cat because there was no consistency. The mouse would sometimes choose the door with the cat thinking that the human was lying to him and he would really find food there. He stopped trusting the human for information. But worse yet. He stopped trusting his own sense of smell and his own instincts, all because the human was lying to him on an inconsistent basis."

"So the conclusion you drew from all this is that trust is the key ingredient."

"Yeah. If Woofy trusts you, then he won't desert you."

Tess thought for a moment. “Listen to this, and tell me what you think,” she said. “I get the feeling that not only does Woofy understand me, but that he answers yes or no questions. I haven’t tested this yet because I’m afraid to. I’m afraid to discover that I’m just anthropomorphizing him. You know?”

“Yeah, I thought that too.”

“But I swear to you, when he agrees with me he barks once and when he disagrees or wants to give me a negative, he will bark twice.”

“Once for yes and twice for no?” David said.

“Yeah,”

“You should test it. Obviously he’s getting clear thoughts from you, and making his own preferences clear. I bet if you had asked him if he wanted to come into town with you he would have barked twice.”

A friend of mine who met Woofy a while ago told me that he thought Woofy must be one of those specially raised and highly trained movie wolves.”

“Maybe, but a movie wolf might not be so at home in the wild as this one seems to be.”

“Really? Would a wild animal just come up to a human and start following her around?”

“It depends. He obviously has some sort of affinity for you.”

“There are two schools of thought on that topic too. Am I his pack leader or does he see me more as a mate?”

“Well, I could tell you this, if I was him, I would see you as a mate.”

“Ok, quit flirting for a second, this is a serious discussion.”

Tess was about to say more when the waitress came with their five plates of food. Conversation was put on hold while Tess got out her camera and laptop and did her job. After tasting everything on all five plates and allowing David to do the same she made some notes.

"Which is your favorite?" she asked him.

"I'm a carnivore. I want the prime rib." She sliced off a small portion of it and put it on the plate with the grilled Salmon plank and pulled that one over in front of her. They shared all the side dishes including the baked potato that came with his prime rib, and they shared the Chicken from the plate of spaghetti laden cacciatore. After cleaning up what was left on all five plates and asking the waitress for more wine, David brought the conversation back to Woofy.

"You were about to tell me why you thought Woofy thinks of you as his mate."

"Oh, well, it's not that exactly, but I think he has imprinted on me."

"Imprinted? Yeah, I can see that. That's not a big deal. I mean, in the wild when there is a shortage of female wolves, the males sometimes imprint on each other. It's just a sex thing. They, in effect, become gay and satisfy each other since there are no females to mate with. The same could be true for you. He might have seen as you as female before human, and imprinted on you as someone who could satisfy him."

"Sexually?"

"I don't know, has he ever tried humping your leg?"

"Well, I was rubbing his tummy one night and he got aroused."

"Really? Did you give him a hand job?"

"Of course not!"

"Why not?"

"Oh come on. I'm not a pervert."

"But you do get gratification from touching his fur and stroking him. How is that different than giving him some satisfaction sexually."

"I just couldn't do that, I'm a good Catholic girl."

"Oh, OK, that explains everything."

"OK, I know you're an animal lover," Tess said, "but I'm going to have to keep Woofy on the level of friend."

"OK, fair enough. Don't let me foist my beliefs on you and you don't have to burden me with yours either, OK?"

Tess smiled. "Fair enough." Tess made a few more notes and then closed her lap top and asked for the check. After a bit more small talk while the check was being paid, she packed up the mini-pack.

"So tell me about your hard times. Or don't you want to talk about that?" Tess asked him as they walked slowly up the hill.

"I just ran into some difficulties. I was stopped here between jobs and discovered that my wallet was gone. Without my I.D. I couldn't get paid for the run and without my driver's license they wouldn't allow me to take the truck out again, of course. So I had to stay here, and wait for a replacement license. I had no money so I had to have my mom send me some cash through the mail. When the envelope got here it was open and the cash gone. So I had to call her collect again and ask for more. It's just been a big mess. Finally I got some money, ordered my license and now I'm waiting for that to arrive. I have to go back to the

Post Office every day to check for general delivery. I found a couple of people who needed wood chopped, they've been paying me under the table to do that. I worked as a bus boy two nights under the table as well. I've been sleeping in the park, but the police are catching on and moving me along. I spent last night out in a shack in the woods."

"Poor guy, what about tonight?"

"Yeah, I'll probably go back out to the shack tonight. It was actually pretty nice in there. Warm enough and not a lot of mosquitoes."

Tess looked up into his eyes.

"Don't do that," he said. "Don't give me that pitiful look."

"Well, I'm too much of a Catholic to offer you a bed tonight."

"I know, and I would never ask. But I do appreciate the meal! That's the best meal I've had in a while."

When they reached the motel Tess leaned against the door jamb.

"Want to come in," Tess asked him.

"I was kind of hoping you would ask," he said.

Chapter 2

Tess woke dreamily the next morning about 7:00 A.M. David had left about Midnight. They talked for a good long time and even made out a little. Tess couldn't understand why his kisses even seemed familiar. The two of them had fallen into shorthand with each other. They had snuggled into each other's arms watching a movie on HBO. She could only remember parts of it though her mind had been elsewhere. They just kept talking about every topic they could think of. They never ran out of things to say to one another. At one point there was a lull in the conversation and he leaned in for kiss. When the kiss was finished he said, "Oh yeah, I remember what I wanted to tell you." And he went on to this new topic as if the kiss had been a comma in the sentence.

Tess switched it over to the 11:00 P.M. news to see how the weather would be tonight and tomorrow, since she was planning on leaving. She hadn't told him that yet, but they would have that discussion soon enough. When she turned it, to her surprise Annie Warner was being interviewed.

"I know her," Tess said. Their attention became riveted. They were showing the back of

Annie's house and there were claw marks along the back door jamb. It looked like whatever had made them had paws the size of dinner plates. The scratches were deep. The glass on the back screen door was broken and the aluminum doorframe hung off its hinges at an odd angle. Annie's voice speaking over this series of shots showing more damage to her house was saying, "Just after midnight last night. I wasn't home but my two adult kids were here in the house. They said they heard the howls like a really angry wolf howling. They looked out the windows but couldn't see anything. My son Christopher got out the shotgun and stood on the back porch and fired it hoping to scare the thing away, but instead it charged him. He said it had to have been a bear, because it was too big for a wolf. Christopher barely got inside the back door before the thing hit the door. They locked the wooden door and went around to the back bedroom to see if they could see it. But everything they did attracted its attention and the thing charged them at the window and broke the glass in the window too. So they got scared and went down to the basement and locked themselves in Christopher's room down there. There's just one little window in his room but the thing found it and kept scratching at it hoping to get through. So they ran again and locked themselves in the storage closet it the basement and barricaded themselves in there. About an hour later I came home and saw all this damage. I didn't see the animal that caused it though. I had to get the kids to open the closet door because they were still too scared to come out."

The scene changed to Christopher who said, "It looked like a huge dog, but it couldn't have been because there aren't dogs that big. It was bigger than a wolf too. It had to have been a bear, but it howled like a wolf. The way it came after me, it was mad. It wasn't scared of me at all. It looked like it wanted to kill me. I just ran and hid."

The newscaster came back on saying that the house sustained damage worth over $3000. And it is unsure whether this incident has any relation to the animal attacks that have been reported down state.

At the end of the report Tess looked up at David. "Oh, my gosh. I spent the night in her backyard two nights ago."

"Really?" David asked.

"Yeah, and you know what else is weird? Those attacks downstate that they've been reporting, I was in the vicinity of each of those as well. That's four attacks now. People were killed the first three times. I suppose it's good that the kids escaped this attack. I would have felt so bad if anyone had been hurt. Do you think it has anything to do with me and Woofy?"

"How could it?" David asked. "If it is an animal attack then the thing couldn't be following you, I mean, there is this kind of big obstruction between the Lower and Upper Peninsulas. I would think that anything that looked like they described would be noticed if it tried to cross the bridge."

"Unless it hitched a ride in the back of a semi," she said, trying to make it sound like a joke. He smiled.

"I can pretty much guarantee you that it just a coincidence."

"I better call her and make sure they are all right," Tess said. She looked up the number in the local phone book, it was there. As she dialed it, David kissed her hair and said he would be by in the morning for breakfast. She kissed him again on the lips and then heard an answer on her phone.

"Annie," she said. "This is Tess, I just saw you all on the news, are you all right?"

She spoke with Annie for a few minutes and then Annie got another call. Tess let her go. She was worried about Woofy out in the woods by himself. What if this thing were following them? Could it track Woofy's scent? She walked out to the corner of the motel one last time and called his name. He didn't come. There was nothing else she could do so she went back inside and tried to sleep.

Chapter 3

"Hi," David said, as he leaned against her door jamb the next morning.

"Hi, yourself."

He smiled and rolled toward her. He kissed her on the cheek and then bent in for a longer exploration of her mouth. Then he released her.

"You leaving today?" he asked.

"I was planning to. But . . ." she hesitated. "You?"

"No, I will stay another day if you do. I got no place better to be."

"There are a couple more restaurants we could try here," she said. "But tomorrow I have to be on my way for sure."

They kissed for a while longer and then decided it was time to get some food. They dressed and walked down to a restaurant on Portage Street that the motel manager said was the best kept secret in town, called Frank's Place. After looking over the menu and the buffet, Tess decided to just order two buffets for them. The waitress said they wouldn't be sorry. There were no huge surprises in the buffet items unless it was that they were all mouthwateringly good. Usually a chef's best efforts were not put on the buffet but this one was an exception. They both ate there fill and enjoyed it.

They took a back way back through town and ran across a Goodwill store.

"I love wandering around in thrift shops," Tess told David.

"Me too. If it weren't for thrift shops, I would have grown up naked!" Tess lifted her eyebrows and then laughed.

"Stop trying to make me imagine you naked!" she chided, but he laughed too.

"Why? It's working."

They walked around in the thrift shop for a while. Tess found a small ball of specialty yarn that she thought would make a good scarf. It was only 50 cents so she bought it. David found a pair of blue jeans that looked pretty good and he also found a man's tri-fold leather wallet that looked like it still had some wear in it. He bought both for a total of $2.50.

"Now you have a wallet all you need is something to put in it," Tess said. David smiled at this. He reached into his pocket and took out all of his money, $22.50. All that was left from the $25 that he had earned chopping wood. He put the bills into the wallet and shoved the change back into his pocket. Then slipped the wallet into his back pocket.

"I need to get some things at K-Mart," she told him. "Want to walk up there with me?"

"I live for it!" he said. But his smile took the sting out of his words.

At K-mart Tess picked up some shampoo and some new razors and some camping food in easy to carry packets. David bought a pair of black socks to wear with his loafers. He paid for it with cash out of his wallet.

"When do you get paid for the job you were talking about?"

"As soon as I get my driver's license," he said. "I wish I knew where my wallet was. The only thing I can think is that I must have left it at my last stop. I don't want to accuse anyone of pick pocketing me. But I'm beginning to suspect that might have been the case."

"So you lost everything?"

"Everything but the clothes on my back," he said.

"When did this happen?"

"Few days ago. It's been a tough couple of days. Yesterday when I ran into you, I was wondering where my next meal was coming from. That's how desperate I am. Sault Ste. Marie is not someplace you want to be broke and homeless."

"Is everything going to be OK? I mean, you'll get your license and then go get paid and take another run someplace?" She asked.

"That's the plan. I sure wish I had a computer so I could follow your whereabouts, maybe we could meet up again in one of these towns."

"I would like that. I could buy you dinner again." She smiled up at him.

He smiled back but he had a quizzical look on his face.

"Trust me, Tessa, the last thing I want you to think about me is that I'm using you for meals."

"It's OK," she said. "I am not thinking that." She paid for her few items and they began to walk back to the motel.

"So, I'm a little fuzzy. Do you own the truck that you drive?"

"No," he said. "The truck belongs to the carrier company. If it belonged to me I could have driven it without a license and gone home to get some money from my mom so I could apply for another one at home. But I'm not allowed to leave with the truck until I can prove I have my license."

"When will you have your license?"

"I put a rush on it. I'm expecting it today in general delivery. I should go down to the Post Office and check it again."

"I'll go with you."

"Maybe at lunch time."

"So what happens next then? Once you get your license and your money? Do you have to pay to get the truck back?"

"No, they have to pay me for the load."

"I see," Tess said. "Well I hope you have better luck from here on out."

"Yeah, I think my luck has change," he said looking down at her again.

They chit chatted as they made their way back to the motel. When they got to the room the bed just looked way to inviting and David fell into it. Tess sat at the table and wrote her reviews of Freighters Restaurant, where they had eaten the night before, and also Frank's Place. David slept for a couple of hours and woke refreshed.

"Do you mind if I use your shower?" he asked.

"My shower is your shower," she said and sent him on his way with a flourish. Tess continued to write expanding her article about the two Islands and also thinking about how she could jazz up the article on Freighters with a description of the Soo Locks which is the real draw of that Restaurant. Soon she heard the shower turn off. David came out dressed in nothing but a towel around his waist. Tess looked up from her laptop and smiled.

"You are very bad!" she said. "It's not enough that you were trying to make me imagine you naked, now you feel the need to just be naked right in front of me?"

"I didn't think you mind too much."

"That's the killer, I don't," she said smiling. But he had suddenly turned shy. He backed up into the bathroom again and she didn't see him again until he was dry and fully dressed in his new clothes.

Tess had done some research and told him that she wanted to check out a couple of tavern type restaurants, one for lunch and the other for dinner and did he have any plans this afternoon?

"I'm free as a bird," he smiled.

The afternoon went as planned. David went to the post office and when he came out he said he had the license and now just needed to check in with the dispatch office. But he was in no hurry to leave Tess. He made an excuse and said he would do it in the morning before he left.

After an unusual meal at Zim's Bar and some pleasant conversation they decided to go for a stroll along the park next to the locks. The setting sun was gleaming off the rushing rapids past the locks from where they were walking. Tess leaned into David who obligingly stood his ground putting his arms around her and holding her as they enjoyed the view.

"Let's head back to the room," Tess said with a gleam in her eyes.

"Absolutely," David agreed.

As they walked through town a car stopped just ahead of them and Rick Kraft got out. "Tess, I was hoping I'd run into you here," he said. "I knew you were coming here so I've been on the lookout. Something happened at the camp ground after you left."

"Oh no, what happened?" Tessa's mind ran ahead of his words.

"It was the night after you left. At least I know for sure it wasn't Woofy. He was with you on the St. Ignace side."

"Oh no, another animal attack?" she asked.

"Yeah," he nodded. He looked dead serious and in pain.

"Who?" Tess asked.

"Kit. She's in the hospital up here." Tess jumped.

"Let's go," she said and the three of them got into Rick's car. It only took a few short minutes to get to the hospital, but in that time he told her the gist. The younger boys had come up here with Rick but his parents had met them here the next day and taken them back to St. Clair Shores with them. So it was just Rick and Kit up here now.

"Where is Dawn?" Tess asked with tears in her eyes. Her worst fears were realized when he told her the story.

"Dawn, Kit and Colt were at the camp site. I had taken Jamie down to the bathhouse to wash him up. He had been playing in mud. It was a huge wolf, bigger than any I had ever seen. It attacked Kit and Dawn got between it and the kids. One of the campers nearby fired at it and it ran off. Dawn and Kit were airlifted to War Memorial Hospital for no other reason than they were the ones who could assemble a surgical team the fastest. I got the boys packed up. Colt was practically catatonic by the time we got in the car. He had seen the whole thing. We drove straight up here, but by the time we got here Dawn was . . ." he couldn't say the last word. His eyes just filled with tears and his voice hitched with sobs.

She reached over and put her hand on his shoulder. He had himself under control by the time he parked the car.

Kit's room was in the intensive care unit. She was sleeping fitfully. "She's fighting off an infection. She's got a high fever and I'm afraid she's delirious. She said you and Kicky were here in town and I should go find you."

Tess bent over the child. Her face was half covered with a bandage. It looked like she had been raked across the forehead and down the left side of her face. Miraculously the left eye was undamaged and not under the bandages that covered the rest of the left side of her face. She also had seeping bandages on her chest and torso.

Tess looked up at Rick. "Oh no, any permanent damage?" she asked him, her voice hitched with worried fear.

Rick shook his head. "Just scarring. They said that eventually they may be able to do plastic surgery and remove the scarring from her breasts and face."

"What a horrible thing to have to go through," Tess said, meaning the attack. She leaned over Kit again and pushed her hair back. Kit's eyes came wide open. "Tess," she said. Then the girl looked over at David. "Kicky!"

"No sweetie, this is David, my friend David."

"Kicky," she said, grabbing toward the tall man. "Tell her who you are. You're her mate. She has the right to know." The girl slumped then and fell back into a fitful sleep again."

"Sorry, David," Rick said. "She's been like this for three days. She was in a coma when they brought her in but then she woke three days ago and has been on about Tess and Kicky ever since. Kicky is what she calls Woofy. She claims that he told her his name was Kicky."

"Dr. Dolittle, huh?" David said, but realized this was no time for a joke. This family had been through enough. But Rick did smile a bit through the pain etched on his face. They stood as Rick sat down in the only chair in the room and took his daughter's hand. Tears came to Tessa's eyes and she circled around the bed to take Kit's other hand. David positioned himself at the end of her bed and took the two lumps of covers representing her feet and squeezed them gently.

Tess cleared her throat and said, "Rick is the Zoologist I was telling you about."

"Oh," David said. The room fell into silence again briefly.

"Rick, David was a science major and did some behavioral studies about dogs and ESP."

"Really," Rick said. Again silence.

"He said I should test Woofy, to see if Woofy has an affinity for reading my mind. He thinks that's what may be accountable for the barking once for yes and twice for no phenomenon."

"Does he?" Rick said. "It's worth a try I guess."

"Rick," Tess said. "Maybe Woofy could track whatever it was that did this."

"Don't, Tess." Rick said. "It's not worth another life. The Sheriff has been tracking it with dogs for more than a week now. The thing vanishes in thin air only to reappear miles away in another part of the county before it strikes again. No one knows how an animal could do that."

"But Rick, don't you get it? I think it's following me and Woofy. It's struck everywhere we've been. If it wasn't following us it might have gone off to some other place, not Mackinaw City. At Mackinaw City it might have gotten trapped between the dogs and the water. Why would it go there if it wasn't following us?"

"Don't blame yourself for this. I'm sure you have nothing to do with it." Rick said. "I'm more than sure that Woofy has nothing to do with it either."

"You don't understand," Tess said. "I know this thing is following me. It attacked a house where I had spent the night. The owner let me camp in her back yard. The next night I saw her on the news saying the animal that looked like bear but howled like a wolf had attacked their house and did a lot of damage."

"Tess," Rick said reasonably. "If it's really an animal, how did it get from Mackinaw City to the U.P.? Swim?"

"I don't know, but after what I told you about how it attacked people in all the places that I had spent the night downstate and again Annie's house in Goetzville? It can't just be a coincidence."

"Have you told anyone about this theory of yours?"

"No, but I will if you think it will help."

"No, you have a job to do. You have no obligation. I think it goes into hiding or something between attacks. The thing in Goetzville is just a coincidence. It's still down in the Lower Peninsula. It could not have come north with you."

"Rick, What if it's not just an animal attack. What if it's a person who has trained a wolf to attack people?"

"Why do you say that?"

Tess told him about the chipmunk carcass that had been put in her backpack and her stolen camera. Clearly a human had to have done those two things. Then she told him about the photo card that she found and that it was a picture taken of the t-shirt and the carcass before he had wrapped it up and put it in her pack."

"You didn't tell me about that," David said.

Tess looked at him, she was about to ask him what he meant, but Rick spoke instead, distracting her.

"How did you find the photo card?" he asked.

"I went to buy another camera at the local pawn shop before I went over to Mackinac Island that day. I asked for more storage cards and he found three extras that fit that camera and sold them to me. One of them was mine from the camera that had been stolen."

"That's a mighty interesting coincidence." Rick said.

"Yeah, I know," Tess agreed. "That's why I think it might have been done by a man with a trained Wolf. Maybe he trained Woofy too but Woofy didn't like him and escaped."

"That's assuming a lot of facts not in evidence," David said.

"Hey, it's just a theory." Tess countered.

"I got a better one." David said. "This creature, whatever it is, has absolutely nothing to do with you or Woofy and the guy, or rather psycho kid, who pulled the gross prank on you and stole your camera, also has nothing to do personally with you or Woofy."

"That sounds more plausible to me too," said Rick.

"I just feel like I got you into this mess by leaving Woofy with you and Kit that day. If I hadn't done that then maybe the creature would not have smelled another wolf at your campsite and gone there to investigate."

"You didn't know this was going to happen, Tess, I refuse to let you feel guilty over this," Rick said.

"I agree, even if Woofy being in that camp site was what drew the animal there, it still isn't your fault. You didn't know anything bad would happen and you sure couldn't have prevented it," David said.

"Then why do I feel so responsible."

"It's your Catholic guilt," David said. "You just feel bad that something happened to people you like. That's all it is."

"David is right, Tess." Rick said. "Listen to him. He's a wise man. Listen, I've burdened you enough for one day. The only reason I've been looking for you is because Kit wanted me to find you. She seemed to sense that you and Woofy were around. Look she's sleeping easier now."

Kit indeed was asleep and quiet once more. "She'll sleep all night now," Rick said. "Should I drive you back to your tent?"

"I'm staying in a motel tonight, up the road here. It won't take us long to walk back. I have to stop and the 7-11 anyway and pick up some jerky for Woofy incase he comes back tonight."

"What do you mean? He's not with you?" Rick asked.

"No, he vamoosed when I came into town and I haven't seen him for a couple of days. He did this once before when I went through Petoskey. I bought a collar and leash so next time I will be able to keep him with me when we go into a bigger town."

"Oh, he might just hate that," David said.

"I can't help it. I worry too much when he's not with me."

"I thought I was distracting you from all that worry," David said.

"Yeah, and it was working, but now . . ."

Tessa asked if she could keep in touch with Rick, he said he would be grateful for that and they exchanged phone numbers on their cell phones. Tess and David both kissed Kit on the forehead and said goodnight to Rick. They walked out of the hospital at about quarter to ten.

"Poor guy," David said. "He lost his mate and nearly his daughter. His son saw the whole thing and who knows what kind of mental problems that will cause. I just feel so bad for them."

"I know," Tess said. They walked back to the motel in silence. She stopped at the 7-11 and bought a bottle of wine and several pieces of beef jerky. Tess cracked the bottle of wine back at the motel room.

Despite the workings of the wine, the thought of Kit laying in the hospital struggling for her life kept Tess from succumbing to David's charms. But since he had no place else to go, they fell asleep in each other's arms.

The next morning Tess was in the shower when she heard David stirring in the next room. She left the water running and poked her head out to ask if he wanted to shower next. He ogled her towel clad body and then passed her to get to the shower.

"Are we ever going to see each other again?" she asked as he shook water out of his shaggy hair.

"I have a haul to Winnipeg. But I'm going to get another load back down here to the Soo with a stop in Marquette. I was kind of hoping I could find you on the road somewhere on my way back through."

"You want my cell phone number?"

"I don't have a cell phone, remember? Can I call you from the road and reverse the charges?"

"What is this? The 80's?" she said teasingly. "Yes, I don't mind." She smiled.

"Or, we could just pick a target date and say meet at a certain hotel on a certain date. Say the Holiday Inn in Munising on July 14th?"

"But what if I can't get there by that date or I decide to take a detour that gets me there sooner. Should I just wait or is there a way I can get a hold of you if the plans change?"

"Yeah, there is a way," he said. "Can I use your cell?"

"Sure," she said.

"Yeah, I'll check in at the headquarters. I check in there once in a while and they can get a message to me when I do."

"OK, sounds like a plan." She got out and put on her oversized t-shirt, the one that she normally slept in. She went over to her mini-pack. "Here," she said throwing the phone to him. He was trying to tuck a towel around his waste but made a catch for the phone instead and the towel fell to the ground. She smiled at the sight of his beautiful naked body.

David dialed the phone, and closed the bathroom door. "Hi, it's me. . . . Yeah, I'm in the Soo. . . . Yeah, she is. . . . I don't know, about 25 or so I guess. . . . I don't want to talk about it. Yeah listen, she's going to call you to tell you where she can meet me. . . . I'll figure it out. . . . No, I probably won't. . . . It's complicated. . . . I know, I think it might be a rogue or a Windigo. . . . Yeah, it's definitely after me! . . . Protect her I guess. What else can I do? . . . Thanks, sis, I'll talk with you later." He hung up and came out of the bathroom. She had stepped out of the room after she had dressed. She was probably calling for Woofy again. Her pack was sitting on the bed. He folded the good clothes he had worn last night as small as he could and stuck them down the bottom of her pack, loafers and socks too. And inside one of the socks was the wallet with the $20.00 bill. He didn't think she would find it there. Then he dressed in the jeans and the t-shirt that he had stolen out of the donation dumpster beside the St. Vincent's store. He would put them back this morning after saying good-bye to Tess.

She came back into the room as he was tugging on the shirt.

"OK, I guess I can make it to Munising by July 10th," Tess told him after consulting mapquest on line. "Can you meet me there, that day?"

"Yeah, I think so. I'll make my plans so that I can. That's ten days from now, how am I going to do without you for that long?" he said once again taking her in his arms.

"I don't know. How did you manage to go without me for 28 years?" she said. "I can't believe we just met on Wednesday."

"I've known you for decades," he said. "I have to have known you before Wednesday. I couldn't possibly be this in love with someone I only met two days ago."

"Yeah, right," she said, not wanting to admit it herself. "Hey, do you think you could give me and Woofy a ride to Bay Mills reservation?"

He shook his head, "Two problems with that. Company Truck, they won't allow me to carry passengers, and two Woofy, I'm beginning to think he's your imaginary wolf. I'd love to meet him someday."

"Yeah, I wonder how he would take it. If he really thinks I'm his mate he might challenge you."

"He'd probably kick my ass, too." David said with another of his crooked smiles.

"Are you really going to meet me in Munising," Tess asked, "or are you going to break my heart? I mean you could be just using me for dinner and a motel room."

"You bet I am. I haven't been paid yet. But I'll meet you." His face got very serious then. "Tessa, I don't know what I can do for you. I'm in no position to help you in any way. I just really want to be with you. I've never met anyone like you."

"I'm just maybe a little naïve and trusting. But I really want to believe you. Here." She said and called up the numbers he just dialed on her cell. She punched in the words "David's HQ" as the name on that number. She moved it to first in line on her call list. “There,” she said. “Now you can’t get away from me.”

“I don’t want to get away from you. I wish I was Woofy so I could just go with you everywhere.”

“Really?”

“Tess, I never want to lie to you. Someday we both will know everything there is to know about each other.”

Tess tilted her head. “You’ve said that to me before.”

“Yeah, last night when you asked about my turning from scholar to truck driver.”

“No, before that.” She thought. “No that was Kicky,” she commented under her breath.

“Who is Kicky?” he asked, “And why is that name all mixed up with Woofy and Kit?”

“Oh yeah, I was going to explain that to you. Let’s have breakfast together and I’ll tell you all about it. You do remind me of him and not just because you are both Native American.”

“Sorry, I can’t. I’m already late. If I get on the road any later than 9 am I’ll have to speed. I should have been gone already it takes an hour to start that truck in the morning.”

The time on her phone said 7:47 A.M. “Yikes, you better get moving then.”

“Yeah, you’ll have to tell me about Kicky next time.” He slid into the flip flops. “I hope you don’t mind, but I put my good date clothes into your pack. I didn’t want to lose them by leaving them in the truck. I can wear them when you and I are together.”

“No problem, they can’t weigh that much. I’ll keep them for you.”

He bent to kiss her again and made a pained look that she noticed. "Ten days," he said wistfully and then left the room.

For some reason, she felt in a big hurry to be off herself. She packed the doggie pack with the jerky, the two bowls, and the extra water container, and threw it into the top her pack. She dropped the key off at the lobby and walked up the hill toward the south end of town. She stopped at the same restaurant she reviewed two mornings ago with the breakfast buffet and ate her fill while managing to squirrel away about a dozen sausages and several slices of bacon for Woofy once she met up with him again. Now that David was out of her sight she wanted Woofy back.

She walked over toward the highway. She had used mapquest to find a route that would take her to Brimley without using I75. She got to the road she had to turn on and there he was. He was running toward her at break-neck speed. She quickly moved away from the road so he wouldn't accidentally over shoot and go into traffic. She got down on her knees. He ran straight into her arms knocking her over onto her back. To passers-by, she thought it might look like an animal attack. She hoped no one who saw them was packing a gun. To be on the safe side she stood up at once and bent over to pet her beloved wolf. OK, this must be clear now that he's a friend not foe, she thought. She calmed him down a bit and opened her backpack. She took out his pack and he stood patiently as she strapped it on him. She took out the container with the breakfast meats she had just gotten from the buffet restaurant and hand fed them to him. This job accomplished she stuffed the bowl back into his pack and they walked on toward Brimley.

They hadn't gone more than five miles toward the reservation and the casino situated there when a Sheriff's car came by. It ran up ahead of them about 50 yards and stopped. As Tess and Woofy walked up behind it the Deputy got out of the car and met them.

"Ma'am," he said by way of hello.

"Hello Deputy," she answered.

"Can you account for the whereabouts of this animal over the last two weeks?"

"Yes I can officer. This isn't the one that had been attacking those people downstate. He's been traveling with me. We've been in the U.P. for almost a week now."

"There was another attack two nights ago up here in the U.P."

"I know," Tess said, "In Goetzville, I saw it on the news."

"Have you ever been there in the last two weeks?"

"Yes sir. Woofy and I spent the night there in a friend's backyard. Let's see that was on Monday, June, 27th. When was the attack?"

"The attack was the 28th. A young man was out with friends and got home about midnight. He said he saw what looked like a big dog in the backyard. He didn't think anything of it until it howled. He went out and tried to frighten it away by shooting a round from a shotgun, But it angered the animal it tried to get into the house. He knocked himself into a picture window and nearly broke it. The young man's sister was also in the house and they locked themselves in the basement until the thing went away. It came around to the back door and battered it so bad that they were afraid it would knock the door down. The boy's bedroom was in the basement and so they ran down to his room and barricaded themselves in. It then came to the window and growled and scraped at the window. It scared them to death."

"But no one got hurt." Tess said.

"No, it finally gave up and went away. Then I get a call from someone on their cell phone a few minutes ago saying that a girl was being attacked by a wolf next to the Brimley road here in town. I don't find a body or blood but another five miles up I find you walking with what looks like a wolf."

"He was just playing. I was afraid it might have looked like an attack. I'm sorry deputy. I hope it didn't scare anyone too badly."

"This is your pet?"

"Yes sir. I'm very sorry for any inconvenience. If it's any consolation I hope you find whatever it is that's hurting people. Some very good friends of mine were hurt by this creature. Kit and Dawn Kraft. They were new friends, but we enjoyed their company and now they have to suffer through what this creature did to their family.

"Wait, you knew Kit and Dawn Kraft and you spent the night in a friend's backyard in Goetzville? Excuse me for saying so, but that's two coincidences. Is this thing following you?"

Tess asked if he could give them a ride to Bay Mills and in the car she would tell him the whole story. He agreed. Tess and Woofy got in the back seat of the squad car and Tess told him in a nutshell what she did for a living, how she met up with Woofy and where she had spent the nights which later became targets for these attacks.

"I think whatever is doing this is following me. My friend's all tell me I'm nuts and it's just a coincidence but I don't think so." She told the deputy about the prank with the chipmunk and the camera card and even pulled up the photo on her hard drive to show him.

"Hell, Ma'am, I think we have a serial killer here using a trained attack dog to do some of the damage and he sure has you picked out as a person of interest."

"I think so too," Tess agreed.

"Why didn't you come forward with this information?"

"My friends talked me out of it. I believe the words "facts not found in evidence" were used. But I must say that, a coincidence isn't always just a coincidence."

"No, Ma'am, you're right."

"Please my name is Tess, Tessa Gates. This is Woofy."

"Can you tell me where you plan on being in the near future?" he asked her.

"Well Deputy," she began.

"Morrison."

"Deputy Morrison, my entire itinerary is on my blog, Tessa's Travels. I anticipate that it will take me ten days to make it to Munising. I'm meeting a friend in Munising on July 10th."

"Ok, then, do you mind if I or another deputy checks in on you from time to time?"

"Not at all, sir, I would feel so much safer if you did."

They arrived at the casino at Bay Mills, hours sooner than Tess had hoped. Deputy Morrison came into the casino with her and introduced her to one of the managers, a Native

American named Clyde Morrow took Tessa's hand briefly. He was tall and barrel-chested. He looked about fifty years old with long hair fixed into a thin braid that went most of the way down his broad back. His face was completely over sized with huge jowls and a bulbous nose. His skin was pock marked and very tan.

"Clyde is one of the elders at the Bay Mills Rez." Deputy Morrison told her. "He'll make sure you have a place to stay tonight that's secure. And if you don't mind, tomorrow would you see to it she gets to her next destination?"

"Sure Guy," Clyde told him.

"We don't want her sleeping in the woods with this maniac loose, do we?"

Clyde was watching the wolf that was trying to be unobtrusive while standing next to Tess carrying a doggie backpack. "That your wolf?" Clyde asked her.

"Yep, this is Woofy."

"I bet he is." Clyde said. "He looks like a pussy with that saddlebag on him."

Tess knelt to unbuckle the pack and took it off.

"There that's better, now he looks more natural. Follow me," Clyde said.

Clyde took them to the elevator and pushed 16. When the elevator stopped Clyde took them down the hall and pulled a card from his pocket. He keyed in and led them into a suite. "We reserve this one for white bitches with their doggie mates." He said. "Not that you fit that description," he said with a wry smile.

Tess smiled as she looked the suite over and said, "I don't think I can afford this."

"You and your companion are here at the request of the law and as a guest of the Bay Mills Ojibwa tribe. Is he house-trained?" Clyde asked pointing his chin toward the wolf.

"Yes, I'll take him outside to do his business. Are you sure? It looks very expensive."

"You the one that monster Windigo is chasing after right?"

"What is a Windigo?"

"Demon. He dresses up like a wolf to make his kills. He's after that one, ain't he?" Again he pointed his chin toward Woofy. "What is he, skin walker?"

"What? I'm sorry I don't know what you're talking about."

"Yes you do. He's your wolf. Is he always around or does he leave when someone else comes around. You been spending time with any Indian humans lately? Does the wolf make himself scarce when the Indian is around?"

"How did you know all that?"

"I got a better question for you. How do you know, he's not the Windigo?"

"He's been with me every time there was an attack," Tess said.

"Including two nights ago?" Clyde asked.

Tess looked down. Woofy had not been with her two nights ago, but he was also not in Goetzville. He had been in the woods south of town waiting for her.

"Yeah, we'll see," Clyde said as he left the room.

"Am I trapped in here?" Tess asked Woofy. He tilted his head and whimpered.

Tess got out her laptop and decided to do some work. She finished three more reviews and e-mailed them to her father along with the photos. She walked around the suite and realized the bathroom had a spa tub. Boy! Luxury! She was intending to be here for dinnertime but it was nearly lunch time and she was getting hungry.

"Well," she said aloud to Woofy. "How would it be to review the room service at a luxury hotel associated with a Casino?"

Woofy agreed with one bark.

"Great, lets order!" She got room service on the line and ordered three of her favorite sandwiches and asked for a suggestion for a chef's favorite as well. Then she called the front desk and asked if someone could get key card for her room. Somehow she had misplaced the first one. A boy was sent up with a duplicate key card.

She paid for the lunch on her credit card when it arrived and wrote a review as she ate the lunch, tasting everything and then feeding what she didn't want to Woofy. Then she decided it was time to let Woofy go outside for a bit.

The hotel was situated near a bay just North of Brimley. She walked back into the forest toward the water. It was a mild day. It was cool out and a slight breeze blew off the lake. She walked along the shore and looked down at the all the pretty stones and pebbles. She spotted an Agate with swirls of color polished shiny in the surf. She picked it up and showed it to Woofy. He barked once at her statement of how beautiful it was.

"Glad you agree," she said, and put it in her pocket. They kept walking west along the shore. Soon they came to a group of buildings with people sitting in a circle in front of one of them. They were sitting around an open fire in a fire pit. They spoke in a language that she didn't recognize and every so often one of them would say something and the others would laugh jovially.

"Hello," she said to them.

"Oh, Hey," one of the women said. "You must be the one that Guy Morrison brought in, the Sheriff?"

"Yes, that's me."

"So this is the Windigo then," a man said looking at the wolf. He said something else in another language and they all laughed. Woofy put his ears back and whimpered looking away.

"What's the joke?" she asked, trying to be polite.

"Oh, he said, it looks like a wolf, not a pack mule." They didn't laugh this time. Tess smiled at the joke. She guessed it had only been funny once.

"Mr. um, Morrow, over at the Casino, said that a Windigo was a Demon. I think Woofy is really just a wolf. I don't think he's evil or anything."

The woman looked at the wolf solemnly and said, "I don't know. Wild Water, what do you think?"

"He's a skin walker." The one who spoke was an ancient looking man. His white hair framed his deeply creased face.

"You should listen to him, his Great Grandfather was Kineekuhowa."

"I'm sorry but who is Kineekuhowa and what is a skin walker?"

The woman looked at Tess and then back at the man across from her. She said a word in her language and they all laughed. Tess tried not to take it personally.

"A skin walker is a shape shifter. There is a clan of them down state. Is that where he came from?"

"Yes, I mean. He started to follow me around Charlevoix, so yes I assume he came from downstate. But what do you mean by shape shifter, you mean he can change his form?"

"He's a man disguising himself as a wolf." The old man named Wild Water said this.

"Interesting," Tess said, "But if he were a man really then why won't he change into a man and show me himself."

"He probably has." Wild Water said.

Tess was silent for a moment. The woman spoke again and the others laughed.

"I'm really happy that I amuse you," Tess said. She had gotten tired of being the butt of their jokes.

"OK, OK, sorry," the woman told her. "You obviously have a problem," she said to Tess. "We are just enjoying the fact that it's you're problem and not ours."

"What is my problem?" Tess asked.

"You are an attractor," she told Tess.

"I'm in a tractor?" Tess asked. She couldn't figure out what the woman was getting at. Everyone laughed at Tessa's statement though.

"No, you are attracting them." The woman said being as clear as she could.

"Who?"

"Well, first this shifter, and then the Windigo." She said. "There is something about you that is attracting these beings."

"About me?" Tess asked.

"Yeah," she said. "You feel it Tony?" She asked the man across from her.

"I don't. But then, I'm not a shape shifter," he said. They laughed again. This time Tess laughed too.

"You laugh," said Wild Water, "But here's something else you should know."

"What?"

"A shifter such as the likes of him wouldn't have chosen to walk with you unless he imprinted on you."

"Yes, I know, but a friend of mine said that when a wolf doesn't have any female wolves to mate with sometimes they imprint on male wolves. He didn't think it was a big deal that Woofy thought of me as a mate."

"Who told you that?"

"A friend of mine."

"Was this friend an Indian?"

"Yes, he was Native American."

"Oh, he was Native American, huh? From what tribe?"

"He said he was Ottawa."

"He's the shifter. Why'd you tell her that?" the old Indian asked the wolf and then broke into his own language. The others around the fire chuckled.

"What did you tell him?" she asked with half a smile.

"I told him he was a . . ."

"Never mind," the woman interrupted.

"Why do you think my friend David is the shifter?"

"Did you ever meet him before you met this animal?"

"David? No, I just met him a few days ago."

"Did you ever meet any Indians before you met him?"

"Yes, I met a family of Ottawa Indians down in Northport."

"Did any of them look like this David guy?"

Tess remembered that certain things David had said reminded her of things Kicky had said. "Maybe," she admitted. "But Kicky was very young, maybe 18 and David is like 28 or 30."

"How long since you've seen Kicky?" the woman asked.

"A month, maybe a little more."

"That's it," she said then she went into a long diatribe in her own language. But the others didn't laugh, they just nodded.

"What?" Tess asked.

The old Indian turned to face Tess. "Sit down," he said to her. She sat down on a log a few feet away.

"Your friend Kicky is the skin walker." He said to her. "He sits here next to you." The wolf looked at her his head was tilted and his tongue was lolling out the side of his mouth. "Tell me, were you physically intimate with Kicky?"

Tess sighed in exasperation but decided to answer the question. "No, he was too young for me."

"You didn't make love with him," the woman asked.

"No, I'm a Catholic, I don't do one night stands." Tess cringed at the lie. She had only spent the night once with David but it was not the first night they were together.

"You didn't even kiss him?" the woman asked.

"Who Kicky? Yeah I kissed him."

"I don't mean like a friendly kiss on the cheek, I mean like a lover's kiss."

"OK, yes, we made out a little before I sent him home."

"And were you physically intimate with this David fellow as well?"

"Yes, about the same amount, but what does that have to do with it?"

"Did you feel, when you met David that you wanted him right away after only being in his presence for a short while?"

"Yes, I felt that. There was just something about him. He was my age and very attractive. I felt like I'd known him before."

"Did you feel like you wanted to be around Kicky that same way?" she asked.

Tess thought back. "Yeah, I was attracted to him but he was too young for me. He was only 18."

"Is it important to you that your lovers are your age?"

"I don't have lovers. I have only had one boyfriend ever and yes, he was my same age. I'm not really that interested in being with someone who is not compatible with me and age has something to do with that."

"That's why," the woman said cryptically to the others.

"That's why what?"

"That's why he appeared older to you the second time. He used the name David, but he and Kicky are the same person."

Tess was stunned. "And you're saying that not only are David and Kicky the same person but that when they are not, I mean when he is not he is Woofy here?"

She looked down at Woofy. Woofy closed his mouth and looked up at her. "Are you David?" she asked Woofy. He stood up and barked at her three times.

"Are you Kicky?" she asked, he barked twice this time. "Do you have any idea what I'm talking about," she asked and got a single bark.

"So what about this Windigo?" Tess asked. She was fairly convinced it was a game they were playing, "Let's make a fool out of the pale face." But she was willing to go along with it as far as they were. It was pretty entertaining.

"The Demon," said the woman. "He's something else."

"In you're society you call them Psychopaths or Sociopaths or Serial Killers," the man named Tony said. "But in our culture we call them Windigos."

"A Windigo is an evil spirit that is possessing the body of a man and making him do terrible things to other people." The woman told her. "Wild Water can see the Windigo spirit inside a person. The spirit hungers for the souls of other beings. As he eats he gets bigger and bigger. He devours the soul of the person he eats but he cannot digest it and use it for fuel in his body, which is why he always feels empty inside. He can only go so long before he needs another soul to devour."

Wild Water looked at the girl, "You don't believe this, do you?"

"Well, I'm a Catholic," she said again, but this fact has started to sound like an excuse even to her own ears. "I don't believe the soul of a human being can be eaten, consumed by an evil spirit. No I'm sorry, I can't believe that."

"You know one of his victims personally, don't you?" Wild Water said. It was not a question.

"Yes, I met a man and woman and their three children in Mackinaw City. The night after I left, the campground was attacked. The woman died and the oldest girl was severely hurt by the creature. They said it looked like a wolf only bigger and it could stand on its hind legs."

"So you think that if you don't believe he could eat her soul then she is safe in heaven with your God and your Jesus?" Wild Water asked her point blank.

"Yes, I have to believe that. To believe that she is now a part of that creature is unthinkable."

"She isn't yet. But if the creature isn't killed soon, she may be lost forever."

"What do you mean?"

The woman took over. "Spirits can't survive long without food or a way to express themselves. The Windigo is preventing her from eating or speaking with others. She will die if she isn't released soon."

"She's already dead." Tess said with tears in her eyes.

"Her body is already dead," Wild Water said, "but her spirit will die too. The creature has to be stopped and killed and the Windigo must be sent away into the spirit world from whence he came."

"You think he's after me? I mean, because of the attraction?"

"Maybe he's after this one," one of the men from across the fire said. The man stood and came around the fire. He squatted in from of Tess and Woofy. He patted Woofy on the side and held out his right hand. "I'm Kent Robin," he said. Tess shook his hand.

"Tessa Gates," she said.

"We know. Clyde came down here for lunch and told us about you."

"Oh, I was wondering. Word sure travels fast on the Reservation!"

"Yeah, we're all terrible gossips." Kent smiled up at her. He seemed very friendly, but she was not attracted to him. She silently relaxed. For a while she thought she might just be attracted to all Native American men. She was glad that she was not, and if it turned out that Kicky and David are the same person, then maybe it's only him she was attracted to. This made sense but she wasn't swallowing it whole. Skin walker?

He stood and then poked the fire for a bit. He took a seat on the ground near her. He went around the fire and introduced everyone. The woman was Roseanne Baker, and Kent introduced Wild Water as the Chief Medicine man.

"I have a story to tell you." Kent said.

Tess looked around the circle of elders and realized that they were all settling themselves into comfortable positions and giving their attention to Kent. Beside her Woofy too lay down with his right paw on Tessa's left foot. Tess Moved down so that she was seated on the ground with her back against the log and crossed her legs. Woofy put his head on her knee. When she again looked over at Kent, he nodded his head and began his story.

Chapter 4

This story took placed in the time of my grandfather's grandfather. The Algonquin people were far separated back then. Not like today when Ottawa and Ojibwa live together as the same tribe. Back then the Ottawa were a separate people from the Ojibwa. There was a clan in the Ottawa nation called the Eagle Clan. Rumor has it that they still exist, but I cannot prove that.

The Eagle Clan had an ancestor that they believed came from the bird people. The bird people where known among the people as being people of powerful medicine. It is said that they could change their shape with the will of their minds. The Eagle Clan also could change. But they did not have all the powers of their bird people ancestor. Each member of the Eagle Clan could only change into one animal, the animal that his totem most resembled.

It is said that among the Eagle Clan there was a curse. Like with all curses, this came with a blessing.

The Curse was this: no member of the Eagle Clan could choose his own mate. Instead he had a powerful draw toward that one person who would be the best mate for that one Eagle Clan member. Sometimes that meant the best mate to further the goals of that shifter, other times it meant that she was the best mate to give strong Eagle Clan children to the shifter. No one knew who they would be mated to until they found this one person to whom they felt this powerful draw. And it could not be argued with. An Eagle Clan member might feel drawn toward his own sister or his aunt, or a small baby. And it didn't matter. The Eagle Clan shifter knew this was his mate and all other ties fell away.

The Blessing was that most members of the Eagle Clan lived much longer than regular people. They kept the look of their youth and their young bodies long after others in the tribe had grown old and passed to the spirit world. It is said they inherited this trait from their bird people ancestors. The bird people all lived for thousands of years.

During the time of my Grandfather's Grandfather there was a member of the Eagle Clan who had lived nearly 50 winters without finding his mate. His name was Wind Runner. He was still very young by the standards of the Eagle Clan and so he took it into his head that he would travel north to the Ojibwa people who were also of the Algonquin people, and he would try to find his mate.

Wind Runner traveled for days along the wilderness, and then came to Gitchee Gumee, the Great Lake, the one we sit near today. He fashioned a canoe out of a tree and a paddle from one of its branches and he set sail out onto the lake.

Many days Wind Runner paddled and every time he saw people near the shore he would stop and spend the days with them. But there was no one that attracted his interest. So he started out again.

It was nearing winter and Wind Runner had to find shelter. He could not stay on the waters of Gitchee Gumee in the winter, or he would surely die. So finally he came to shore and found a cave to dwell in until the winter had passed. He didn't know it but this Cave was the dwelling place of a pack of wolves, for there were still wolves in these parts back in the time of my Grandfather's Grandfather. Wind Runner changed into his wolf form and joined their pack.

Because of his human intelligence and his bigger stronger body Wind Runner soon was the pack leader and mated to the lead female of the pack who in the language of the wolves was called Dappled Sun.. Over the course of the winter he hunted with the pack and lived with them in their den. By springtime his mate had given birth to three young strong wolves. He could tell they were Eagle Clan cubs at once. By early summer the three cubs had grown and were learning to fight and to hunt from their pack members. And by fall they were well grown. One fall day Wind Runner took them all out to the field outside the pack's hunting grounds where he would not be seen and shifted into his human form. The three cubs were amazed, they had never seen a creature like the one their father turned into. He shifted back to the familiar form of their father, the wolf, and then he explained to them that he was of the Eagle Clan and so were they. He then showed them again how to shift into human form. One by one they all learned how to shift. The three children, now almost in puberty, were beautiful sweet humans. The oldest, a girl had raven black hair that hung past her shoulders. The two younger ones, boys, were strong and lively and rambunctious.

Everyday Wind Runner would bring them out away from the den and teach them how to be human beings. The girl caught on very well but the two boys would rather run and play and paid no heed to their father's warnings and teachings.

One day the following summer when the girl and her father were out walking in their human skin, they ran across a party of Ojibwa hunters. The girl felt the bond, the drawing for one of the hunters and from that day forward they were never apart. The hunter took her as wife and the tribe never discovered that she could shift, because from that day on she never did. She stayed in the form that her husband wished to see.

Wind Runner joined this tribe too, but he did not stay long. He longed for his wife, Dappled Sun, the wolf woman that he had been drawn to as mate. So his was a two spirited life. He would come to visit his daughter with the Ojibwa and then he would go back to his den and his wolf family.

The reason we know about all of this is because of what happened next. Years passed and the girl became a mother to many children. Some of the children were Eagle Clan and others were not. Those who were Eagle Clan were revered as great medicine men and women. Others were not Eagle Clan and they did not change when they reached adulthood. As Eagle Clan members married other Ojibwa mates fewer and fewer Eagle Clan offspring were born until only one in each generation was said to be Eagle Clan. Soon no one knew these people existed at all, except for the stories. The ones who were Eagle Clan were alone. They were still honored by the tribe when one appeared but they were more often feared because when they changed they looked like wild animals and sometimes were very fearsome.

The last one born to the Ojibwa was born in the time of my Grandfather. He discovered his nature one day when he changed into a wolf. He was very surprised that he could do this for he was among those being raised by the pale faces in the Christian schools. The pale faces were frightened of him and tried to train him to not change. But when he turned 18 he left them never to return.

His Christian name was Talbot, his Ojibwa name was River Shade. From time to time he came back to the tribe as an adult. Always he was angry and made trouble for the elders. Finally he left for a very long time. They say that he went to war. They say also that he spent many years in Europe where he took on the look and speech of many European countries. We don't know if he died or if he is still alive. All we know is that he lived long past others who were born at the same time. Some say that he became a Windigo, but there is no proof of that. Most people are glad he never came home. There are some of us who remember him and hope he never comes home.

Chapter 5

Tess had sat quietly and listened to the legend. But now the spell seemed to drift away. Kent had a gift. He had captured Tess completely and held her captive with his words. But then, the tale was finished and he allowed her to escape. She came back to herself slowly, and realized she had questions.

"May I?" she asked.

The story teller nodded once.

"This Rivershade," she began. "You think he's still alive?"

"It's possible. We haven't heard from him in a long time. Last time we saw him was in the early 60's. He killed one of our elders. That in itself is one of the worst things an Ojibwa can do, we are taught to respect our elders. But not only that, the elder he killed was over 140 years old. His name was Kineekuhowa. Legend says he was born the year the Fort at Michilimackinac was overtaken by the red coats."

"Michi . . .?" Tess asked.

"Michilimackinac," he said, "That's the fort on what's now called Mackinac Island."

"I'm sorry but I don't know anything about local history. Red coats? You mean the British?"

"Yeah," the woman said. "That war that started in 1812."

"The war of 1812? That was mostly a sea battle against invading British." Tess said, but even as she said it she wasn't sure if she was right.

The storyteller looked at her. "You may not know much about your own American history, but I know everything about mine. The war of 1812 was fought all up and down the frontier between Canada and the United States. We Ojibwa helped in the fight against the red coats. But in the end Michilimackinac fell, and was not returned until the war was over and the peace pipe smoked between the two leaders in the East."

"So what you're saying is that this elder, Kinee . . ."

"Kineekuhowa," someone supplied.

"Kineekuhowa was born in 1812."

The woman, Roseanne, spoke again, "Some say it was sooner than that. Some say he had been a boy when the fort fell. Others claim they had heard the story that his mother was having birthing pains when the attack began. But all agree that was about the time."

"And he was killed by this Rivershade in the early sixties?" Tess was incredulous.

"Yes," Kent said.

"That would make him nearly 150 years old."

"Yes," he agreed. "It is assumed that he was Eagle Clan, although no one ever saw him change. It is possible that he had only the attribute of longevity from his heritage, but none of the shape shifting abilities."

"So if Kineekuhowa was a member of this Eagle Clan, descended from the Bird People, why would Rivershade want to kill his own family member?"

"Jealousy," he said. He would say no more on the matter.

"Why do you call them the Bird People?"

"Because they came from the sky."

"You mean they were Aliens?" Tess asked with a laugh.

"Today, you might call them that. They may even have been what you call a UFO."

Tess stood. She turned and took a few steps away from the group.

"This is all just legend, right?" She said smiling nervously as she turned back to address them. "This is a game right, a game called 'Let's see how bad we can spook the white girl?' You can't be seriously telling me that the Bird People are aliens."

No one spoke.

"You are joking with me again, right?" No one was laughing.

She felt her knees start to buckle.

"Whoa, whoa whoa," the storyteller said. He was by her side and holding her up. He guided her back to the log and helped her sit down.

The woman spoke to her finally. "There is no translation in our language for the word "lies."

"Yes, I suppose I've heard that somewhere." Tess said. "So if all this is true then where is this guy now?"

"We don't know. We hear rumors," Kent said.

"Clyde said he saw him when he went to Washington that one time," Roseanne said.

"Someone pointed him out to Clyde and said that the man he pointed to was the most brilliant man alive, and that he had 14 degrees in every possible imaginable thing. The guy told Clyde that he was a philosopher."

"Someone else said they saw someone who looked like him in a newscast from England," Kent said.

"My daughter went to Egypt that one time to see the pyramids," Tony put in. "She said she thought he was one of the lecturers at this symposium on Anthropology."

"These couldn't all be sightings of him," Tess reasoned.

"Well, how would we know for sure? He's been alive for almost a hundred years and last time we saw him he still looked like he was in his 30's."

Tess considered for a moment. "Could he be this Windigo that all of you are talking about?"

The woman looked at the storyteller. "Finally," she said.

"He's after you for some reason though," Kent said. "You were chosen by one member of the Eagle Clan as being a highly acceptable mate. Maybe this Windigo wants you as well."

Tess shook with a sudden chill. She looked down at Woofy who had been listening intensely from his vantage point at her knee and had not moved, even when she got up. All at once the campfire site was all too public. She glanced over toward the thick forest. It could be watching right now, but no, she thought. If it was, certainly Woofy would have sensed it and would be tense. No, she felt certain that while she was here at the reservation she would be safe. Still, she had a job to do and maybe she should be getting back to it. Good excuse, she thought.

"I guess I better be going," Tess said. "Thanks for the stories, and I'll definitely be on my guard."

She turned and walked quickly away so she couldn't see the looks that passed between all of the elders that sat around the fire. Maybe they would stop her and try to bring her back. She walked through the clearing and back to the edge of the woods before looking for Woofy. He was still back at the campfire. He was looking at her, but hadn't moved.

"Come on, Woofy," she called. "Here boy." Reluctantly, the wolf began to follow her, then he sped up to a trot and soon he was across the field and walking by her side.

She keyed into the room a few minutes later. Just as she was thinking about getting dressed for the restaurant a knock came on her door.

"Tessa Gates, this is Special Agent Edward Marcus of the FBI," Morrison said to her when she opened the door. Morrison was a cop in his thirties with short hair, clean shaven and in a rumpled uniform. Agent Marcus was lean, forty-ish and had on a crisp grey suit that looked like it was steam cleaned daily.

"We are interested in hearing your part of the story," Marcus said. "I've gotten a bit of it from the Deputy here, but I'd rather hear it in your own words."

"I would like to tell you everything, but can we do it over dinner?" She asked. "My treat!"

The two men looked at each other. "I'm a restaurant reviewer," Tess said, "so it's not a bribe. I have to review the restaurant downstairs." She got the collar and leash and put them on Woofy. The whole time she was telling him how sorry she was. But with the FBI now involved she didn't want him out of her sight. She told him that he had to be on his best behavior and to make her proud! He yipped once in agreement.

All four were soon were seated in the restaurant, Woofy on the floor next to Tessa's chair. Having ordered twice the normal amount of dishes because of her added guests, she settled in to tell her story. As the food arrived she had gotten to the part where she had found the photo on her memory card. She showed it to the agent, allowing him to page through the photos on her laptop as she took more photos of the food that was now on their table.

"What are all these photos of people on the boat?" Marcus asked.

"I was getting paranoid. I felt like someone was watching me so I casually went around and took some candid shots of people on the ferry to Mackinac Island. I didn't recognize anyone so I chalked it up to neurosis."

He smiled at her joke, but jotted down an e-mail address on a card. "When you get a chance this afternoon, attach them for me and mail them to this address."

She glanced at the card. Special Agent Edward Marcus. The card contained all of his information, office phone, cell phone, e-mail with .gov at the end, and then the hand printed e-mail that she assumed was his personal e-mail account.

"Gee whiz, Special Agent Marcus," she said affecting an innocent air for the sake of humor, "You weren't ready to share your mother's maiden name with me?"

She was rewarded by another smile. No matter how funny her jokes were the FBI agent would not laugh outright. So she contented herself with the odd smile that she could elicit from this man. But even so she felt herself warming up to him. If a movie were to be made with Special Agent Marcus as a character, he would undoubtedly be played by Harrison Ford or Clive Owen, two men that emoted caring father-like figures in her mind.

After photographing each dish and then taking the perfect bite she invited each of the men to do the same tasting each dish. She made no notes at this point since Marcus was still perusing the laptop. Then she asked the men which dishes they wanted for themselves. When each had claimed a plate she settled back into her story and recounted the rest of the trip and the fact that it had to be more than coincidence that a house was attacked down in Goetzville within days after she had spent the night in a backyard in that tiny village.

"I must tell you," Marcus said. "Those Warner kids were frightened out of their wits. They said that when the animal rose onto its hind legs and tried to get inside the door, his front legs had been perched on the eves of the house. It was over nine feet off the ground. I measured it myself. The footprints of the thing were huge as well. Almost as big as bear. The young man said it made sounds like a wolf even though it was too big. He said it had a snout and eyes that glowed in the dark. He said it seemed like a giant wolf."

"Annie Warner is the one who told me I could spend the night in her yard. I called her after I saw her on the news to make sure they were all right," Tess said. "Her son, Christopher, was the one who drove Woofy and I up to Pickford the next day."

"Yes, that's what they said." The agent looked over at Morrison. "They remembered your wolf and told me that it was nothing like that one. This one was bigger and nastier. They both agreed on that. I had to see your wolf for myself."

"Woofy didn't do this," Tess assured them.

"I know," said Agent Marcus, "Your pet," he put emphasis on this word, "is too small to have made those footprints, even though he is a bigger wolf than I've seen."

"Am I under suspicion at all?" Tess asked. She was worried.

"Not for a crime, but I think you may be connected in some other way," the agent admitted cryptically.

"How?" Tess asked.

"Well, obviously whoever is perpetrating this is interested in you. Do you know any breeders of wild animals?"

"Breeders?" Tess was confused, "How could there be breeders of wild animals?"

"Yes, I mean, where did your wolf come from, for example? Maybe someone is breeding these animals on a farm in the area where you found your pet, and they want your wolf back."

"I did think of that. But I haven't exactly been keeping him on a leash," Tess said looking down at Woofy, she winced. "Well, until now. Before today, he's been free to leave all the time we've been together. So if he did belong somewhere else at one time, he was always free to go back there. I don't know any breeders personally and I'm from Chicago originally. I'm just traveling up here because of my job."

"I see," Marcus said. "It's obvious to me that he wants to stay with you. These are just theories." Marcus looked significantly over at Morrison and then back at Tess. Tess realized that they both had their own theory.

"What is your theory, Tess?" Morrison asked.

"Well, Rick Kraft said that he thought Woofy might be a specially trained wolf that they use in movies who somehow escaped. He's obviously used to being around people and is very fond of children. He's well trained."

"Yes, but what is YOUR theory?"

Tess thought for a moment. She thought about the information the Native Americans had given her around the campfire, the Eagle Clan and the shape shifters, the man who had lived over 140 years. What did she believe? That this creature and Woofy were somehow related even if it was generations back? Did she really believe that skin walkers existed outside of the realm of Ojibwa legends? She was almost grateful for the two law men sitting at the table because they were giving her a much needed reality check.

"It sounds more logical than anything else I could come up with," Tess said.

"Has this guy tried to reach you at all?" Morrison asked.

"Reach me? Other than following me you mean?"

"You have a cell phone and an on-line presence. Has he ever e-mailed you or called and left a message for you on your cell phone?"

"I don't think so," Tess said. Then on a whim she pulled her computer over in front of her. She booted up an internet browser and clicked on her Blog. She scrolled down to the place where messages were displayed from her Blog followers and found one that she had not seen yet. It was from someone who had no picture and signed his identity as T. It said simply, "There you are!"

"That's weird," Tess said.

"What?" Both men said at the same time.

Tess turned her computer and showed them.

The agent spoke the words out loud. "There you are. There you are. What does that mean?"

"Maybe he knows she's here at the Casino?" Morrison asked.

"Maybe," Marcus agreed. "But why reveal himself like this? I mean, he hasn't got her."

"Do you think he's stalking me so he can abduct me?" Tess asked. Real fear shook her voice.

"That's my theory," Morrison said honestly.

Agent Marcus pulled the computer over in front of him and began reading through it. He was very interested in the section on where Tess would be going next.

"He's tracking her through this Blog," he said. "Look." He moved the computer over so that the Deputy could see too. He paged up to the box where she put her itinerary.

"That's not quite true," Morrison said. "Look, she says she is going to check out a place called Raber Bar. But she doesn't say she's going to Goetzville. The attack took place in Goetzville. He must have known she had been at that house some other way."

"He's watching her," Marcus said, "tracking her maybe. Maybe he has the animal trained to track her."

"He knows every place she's been and exactly where she is going," Morrison said. "So why taunt her?"

"Is he just trying to shake me up? I spent last night in a hotel and now tonight too. It would be easier for him to abduct me if I was out in the tent like I normally am."

"I don't think it's a good idea for you to stay in the woods at night until we catch this guy," Morrison told her.

"I don't have a car, and I have to keep traveling. I don't know how I'm going to do my job if I can't at least get to the next town."

"That is a dilemma," Agent Marcus said. He offered no other comment.

"Well," Morrison said. "I understand that Clyde has taken a liking to you. I think I could have him allow you to stay here for the time being until we can catch the guy or guys responsible."

"Clyde likes me? He said that?" She remembered disapproval and disdain in his attitude when he showed her to her room, but no actual affection. "What did he say?"

"He said that you were like part of the tribe now," Morrison said. "I've never known him to say something like that about someone he just met. Usually Indians like to get to know people before they invite them into the tribe."

"I didn't get that at all. They don't treat me like a family member, more like a disagreeable in-law." As Tess spoke these words she realized how true they sounded.

"Well, they seem to have your safety in mind at this point. I'd take them up on it," Morrison suggested.

Talk turned to more pleasant subjects as they finished the meals. But Tessa's mind was on other topics.

Tess and the two law men exchanged cell phone numbers and she promised to keep closely in touch. As they left the restaurant, Clyde pulled Tess aside. He looked back over his shoulder at the G-men to make sure he couldn't be overheard. Then he hunched himself over her, the bulk of him obscuring her whole slender body from their view. Tess realized that as he did this she felt entirely physically protected. It was a very strange sensation!

"I want you to plan to stay here for the next few weeks," he told her. "We'll be sure the Windigo doesn't get you."

"I have a job to do." She said looking up into his huge face, "If I don't keep moving I don't get paid."

"Ok, I'll see what I can do," Clyde said. He stepped back, effectively releasing her from his hovering protection.

Tess decided it was time to take Woofy for a walk. She didn't want to have to explain to Clyde if there was an accident in the room.

As they walked through the lobby, a woman cowered frozen as she glimpsed the wolf even though he was on the leash.

"It's OK, he won't hurt you," Tess reassured the woman. But all she got in return was a dirty look.

Tess patted Woofy's head and led him out of the woman's sight. As she passed through the glass double doors to the front of the casino, a complete stranger stopped her at the door.

“Tess,” he said. She was surprised to hear her name. She looked up to see a young very handsome Native American man addressing her. “You shouldn’t go out there.”

“What do you mean? I have to take Woofy outside so he can . . you know.”

“Come with me,” he said. “It’s not safe.”

She was about to protest that everyone seemed instantaneously to know her business even though she was still getting used to the idea that she was in danger. But the young man had turned and was leading her back through the casino to a service hall. She had to follow or lose him in a crowd of tourists.

He led her around to a back door used by the casino and hotel staff. He took her and Woofy out toward a row of dumpsters. “Use this back way, if you need to. This area is fenced in, only the laundry service and the garbage trucks come back here and always with an escort. The Rez is back that way,” he said pointing to the Northwest.

“Can you answer a question?” Tess asked as she allowed Woofy to go out and explore the yard.

“I’ll try.” He said.

“Why are all of you being so nice to me?”

“A woman who speaks to Wolves? Powerful medicine! You were brought to us and you need protection, that’s all you need to know. But let me caution you. Not all Indians are on your side. You have a powerful enemy.”

“How do I know which ones are on my side? I mean, if this Windigo that’s after me is an Indian, how will I know?”

“Maybe you won’t know,” the man said, “But he will.” He nodded his chin toward Woofy. “It’s all been kind of much for you, hasn’t it?”

"Kind of," Tess agreed.

"Well, I'm Ondag Stark," he held out his hand.

"Tessa Gates," she said.

"I know."

"How do you know? I mean, how do all of you know so much about me already, I've only been here less than a day."

"We're big gossips around here. Not much happens up here, so when something big comes along, like you, we all talk about it. I heard about you this afternoon when I came on duty. They were talking about you because you came in with a police escort."

Tess smiled. "Yes, but Deputy Morrison said that you consider me part of the tribe already? Why is that?"

"Cuz of him," he said pointing to the wolf.

"Woofy?"

"Yeah," Ondag said, and then was about to say more but stopped.

"What?"

"Nothing," he said smiling, "It's not my secret to tell."

Woofy had heard his name and having done his business, was ready to go back inside.

That night Tess lay down on the bed and e-mailed her father about all that had happened. She attached the reviews and photos from the casino restaurant. She had sent the e-mail out and then set her computer aside still open when she heard the familiar sound of her father's ring tone. She answered the phone.

"Hi Dad!"

"Hello, Tessy, I'm a little worried."

Tess chuckled, "Get right to the point Dad!"

"Tess," her father said, a warning note in his voice.

"It's OK, I'm being held hostage here on the Bay Mills Reservation."

There was dead silence on the other end of the line.

"I'm serious, Dad, they don't want me going out of the hotel without someone along to protect me. They said I was part of the tribe, if you can believe that."

"Tess, please, just listen to me."

"What is it Dad?"

"I got this e-mail about a day or two ago. It was from some fellow in Sault Ste. Marie telling me that you were being very reckless and that I should not let you travel around like you do. He said that you spent the night with some stranger in a hotel."

"Did he sign a name?"

"No there wasn't a name on the e-mail and I dismissed it, I deleted it. I sure wish I hadn't done that, because I got another one today. This one says that the animal you are traveling with is a wild beast and that your life is in danger. How much of this is true, Tess. Your pet dog, is he wild?"

"He's a wolf, and yes, I think he may have been trained to act in movies or something like that. I'm not sure where he came from Dad, but I trust him and he's not the animal that has been attacking people."

"You're sure of that?"

"Yes, I'm sure, he's been with me the whole time."

"But Tessy, listen," Her father's voice normally very mild, became firm. "I don't want you fooling around with strange men on the road, you understand?"

"Dad, he wasn't a strange man. He was a very nice man, a Native American, a truck driver. He didn't want to leave me, but we made plans to meet up again in Munising in a week or so. I was planning to hike up through Picture Rocks and try my hand at a travel article."

"I know, I read your Blog," Her dad said.

"I know you do, but after that I was going to spend a night in the Holiday Inn at Munising and rest up before hiking to Marquette."

"I really don't think you should be out there by yourself."

"I have to keep moving, you know. If I don't keep moving then how will I keep making money?"

"Why don't you let the Wolf off the leash and get on a bus and come home? We can figure out how to get you a car, and while you're home you can use mine."

"I can't Dad," she said. "I want to make that appointment in Munising. I think I may be in love."

She heard her father take a deep breath through the phone. "That's great Tessa. I'm very happy for you, but if he loves you then maybe he will follow you to Chicago."

"Dad, it's still such a new relationship. I wouldn't ask that of him. I'm sure he would though, that's how sure I am that we made a connection. I just don't want to put him to the test before we even get started, you know?"

"I'm just scared for you, sweetie. I don't want anything to happen to you."

"I'm not going to take any chances. Besides, the Native American's here at the reservation seem to know more than they are telling me right now, and they are keeping a close eye on me. I don't think they will let anything happen to me. I have an FBI agent on speed dial too. For the next week I will be within a two hour drive of several people who are looking out for me."

"And you've got a wolf protecting you too," her father stated blandly.

"Yeah, Woofy does watch out for me." She sat back in the bed and began to tell her father the story about the raccoon carrying off her garbage at the camp site in Mackinaw City. She left out the part about the dead Chipmunk and the camera card so they were laughing together again before long and she put an end to the call just before 10:00 P.M.

Woofy slept with her in the bed. He was 6 feet long when he stretched out beside her. She spooned with him. He laid facing away from her and she snuggled in behind him putting her arm around him. They slept like that the whole night and neither of them woke.

Part Three: Rivershade

Chapter 1

Draft of an e-mail written on July 5, 2011.

My name is Talbot Rivershade. It is time that I introduce myself to you since our worlds are colliding. You may have heard about me. How I've spent time in Washington DC, my voice in the ear of President Nixon. How I gave lectures in Egypt on Archeology, how I have fifteen degrees, or has the story risen to 20 yet? Maybe you heard that I studied philosophy with Sartre, or maybe you heard that I was in the war: all of them since the First World War. Actually I hadn't been born yet. I was born in 1920. And right now, as I admire myself striking a pose in the mirror, I look to be only about 35. I have aged very well, but then I owe that to my recessive Eagle Clan gene. But you know more about that than I do, don't you? Or hasn't your lover told you about himself yet?

Tisk tisk, that little Woofy of yours is deceiving you. We "Native Americans" (as you like to call us) like to say that we cannot lie. But here's the real truth: we were taught how to lie by the best liars in the world, Europeans! Now it's second nature to us all. We tell you exactly what you want to hear and then we laugh about it behind your backs. Oh, I suppose I shouldn't talk as if I represent all Indians. Maybe it's just me that does that. Wouldn't want to upset the Elders now, would we? Your new family! Have they adopted you officially yet, or are they merely treating you like you belong to them? They do take an upper hand when they want to own something now don't they? Oh I had better not go on or I will upset the elders.

But despite all that, I am here to tell you the truth. That animal you travel with, your wonderful wolf you so lovingly call Woofy, has another identity. Believe me, I know, for he is a kinsman of mine, except for one thing. He is Ottawa. He comes from an entire clan of beings such as himself. He grew up, no doubt, knowing of his nature and that he would someday change his shape. They may not have known what shape he would take, but certainly they knew he would change. I've been reading your blog, my dear one, and I think you met him in the area now known as Leelanau. That word meant something different when I was a lad learning my native tongue, but I digress.

No doubt those Bay Mills kinsmen of mine told you of the legends, and they may even have told you that I'm a murderer. They claim I killed the old one, Kineekuhowa. But alas, I did not. I only wanted him dead. As near as I know, I am not as yet capable of wishing someone dead and have it come to pass. Kineekuhowa was an old man. The fact that he died in my presence is only coincidental. Don't get me wrong however my dear little evolved woman. I have killed! Oh yes, I have, and will again.

You may wonder why I call you an evolved woman. You are, you know, evolved to a very high level. You are almost one of the bird people. I'm surprised the bird people have not sought you out. You are so nearly one of them. Did you ever feel that you had been abducted by Aliens? Never mind.

I am well aware that you have been chosen by your little friend to be his mate, but you are a highly suitable mate for anyone of our species. I personally have never met the bird people. But I am assured by people who have that they are highly evolved and that they are in need of good breeding stock. I am thinking they just haven't found you yet. I wonder why? And I wonder if they would be interested in you. I wonder if there is a reward for someone such as you. And if so, I wonder how I could possibly contact the right "people" in order to collect. I'm very interested.

Well, all that aside, I just have to inform you that I can't allow your "friend" to survive. He is just too good, at what he does. I suppose I'm jealous. And rightly so. He's had every advantage. I wonder what his parents turned into, wolves? Coyotes? Mountain Lions? Human's usually turn into predators. Very rarely do they shift into bunnies or squirrels, or mice. Never actually, I would imagine. We human beings are too used to being at the TOP of the food chain. And me above all! But you see the gene in me has degraded. I do not turn into the pure form of the animal. I turn into a grotesque caricature of a wolf. Through the ages, they have called me dogman, wolfman, and werewolf. I used to terrorize Michigan. One time someone saw me turn and I twisted her head off. I horrified a van load of hippies one time on the beach. I clawed out the window of a woman who had done nothing to me except taken my parking space. I think she suffered a massive coronary as I tried to get at her through the glass of the window. I smile just to think on it.

One year I wanted to see if I could horrify a small town between Kalkaska and Grayling so badly that I could make it into a ghost town. Ah, that was a good year.

So you see, I don't have any qualms about taking your wolf-friend away from you.

You are destined to be MY mate. You, my dear one, will be the mother of a new breed of Bird People. And I will be their father!

(Found on July 8, 2011. Computer abandoned in a motel room in Newberry Michigan.)

Chapter 2

Tessa's Travels
July 7, 2011
Hello Dad and other readers,

I've had a busy week. Things are really happening in the forests of Northern Michigan. Woofy and I have eaten more pasties in the last three weeks than most people do in their lifetime. But we are getting a taste for them. There are subtle differences. Woofy tends to like the ones with lots of meat, go figure, and I usually like the ones with more vegetables and the pretty crusts. The crust, I think, is what makes all the difference. A good pasty crust is thick, yet flaky, and the meat juices give it a rich flavor that is absorbed. But I don't want to give too much away. I will expound on that later in my articles on the best and the worst of the pasties in the Upper Peninsula.

Traveling has been a breeze lately though. Who can complain with all this wonderful nature? I've seen more wild animals in this one trip than I had ever seen before. Possums, raccoons, chipmunks, deer, coyotes, a moose, sand hill cranes, ravens, an eagle, all sorts. I started carrying my camera around my neck so I could get pictures of them all. That of course is when they all vanished. I think wild animals are camera shy.

I managed to hit a number of restaurants in the northern areas along the Lake Superior coast, Gitchee Gumee, as the Ojibwa say. It means literally, "Big Lake."

I made it to restaurants in Paradise, Newberry, McMillan, Seney and Grand Marais. Then I caught a ride down to Manistique and am heading toward Escanaba as we speak. I've reviewed so many Casino restaurants up here that the Ojibwa now consider me a tribal member! Just kidding!

And always by my side is my faithful Woofy. He makes the perfect traveling companion. He's not picky about what he eats sometimes providing his own food in the wilderness, so I can eat the jerky myself. He protects me from intruders in the night, the animal kind, Dad, not the human kind. He is my friend and companion on those lonely nights by the fire. He listens to all my troubles with a sympathetic ear. Yeah girls, when did you ever find a man that just listens? Woofy is the perfect man! If only he really was a human man instead of a wolf-man. (Excuse the pun.)

Dad tells me that I have some followers for the great debate on the pasties so I will try to deliver on that score. I have heard that several places in Marquette have worthy pasties and I'll try to head up there next after Escanaba, or maybe I'll skip it and go west to Iron Mountain and the Wisconsin Border. I haven't decided yet. I'm told I have only a three month window of opportunity to explore the northern clime of Michigan, since there are 9 months of winter and (as one old timer put it) 3 months of damned poor sledding. Dad, as you know, I don't even own a sled, so I have to be out of here by September 1st!

As always, readers, if you are interested in purchasing any of my restaurant reviews for your publication my father handles the business end of this venture and his contact information is in the box at the right. I am open to suggestions as to where I should head next. Dad has put up a poll to cover this. Should I next explore Minnesota restaurants or head back down to Wisconsin in an effort to get home to the Windy city by Christmas? Or points west? When I get the results I will check mapquest and post on this Blog my next set of destinations.

Till then,

Tessa Gates and Woofy

Chapter 3

The last week for Tess and Woofy had been safe and uneventful. The creature doing the killing appeared to have dropped off the planet, but the elders were not convinced that he wouldn't strike again.

Members of the tribe had taken turns getting Tess to her destinations. Her most dedicated driver had been the front door security guard, Ondag Stark. He volunteered to drive and the only times he missed was when he had to take a shift at the casino. Tess was able to cover all the towns she had intended but always came back to Bay Mills at night.

Since she didn't have to walk 25 to 30 miles every day, Tess had a lot of spare time on her hands. Her day would usually start with a short breakfast either from room service or down in the hotel restaurant. She would then spend several hours with Roseanne Baker, who, Tess discovered, was Ondag Stark's mother. Roseanne made all the fry bread for the restaurant. It was her specialty. Tess learned how to make it for herself. It was pretty easy and could be made as a camp food with very few ingredients.

Roseanne treated her like an errant daughter, correcting her more notable mis-conclusions. Tess was a quick study. She soon realized that Roseanne was teaching her about the Native mindset. She listened carefully to all Roseanne said and took it to heart.

One day while baking, Tess began to wonder why Roseanne, Ondag and Clyde all had different last names. This prompted a discussion on names in general.

Roseanne's tribal name was Long Elk. Her son's name, Awn-dayg, translated to Crow, short for Blue Crow which was his tribal name, but everyone called him Awn-dayg. The first few times Tess wrote it in her correspondences to her father she spelled it phonetically as Ondag. Since Ondag usually only signed his name as Robert Stark, he didn't mind the new spelling so he told her he liked it and started correcting it when she spelled it any other way.

"When Ondag was born," Roseanne said, "I saw crows fly by outside the hospital window. One came and landed on the window sill and stood there and watched me as I labored. I asked the spirit of the crow to deliver my son whole and unharmed and I would name him after the blue crow at the window. For indeed the crow at the window had light shining on him in such a way that his feathers shone blue. You know how that happens when something is so black that it seems blue?"

"Yes, I know what you mean," Tess said. "I saw a cat once that was like that. He was so deeply black that he was blue."

Roseanne smiled her approval of Tess. In the short time since she'd been here, she found that she had begun to crave those moments when the woman's face would turn to her with that smile. It always made her feel worthy.

That night Tess had a dream. She dreamed that she was married to Woofy and that she had become a wolf herself like the Eagle Clan wolf and his wolf wife in the story Kent had told. But instead of Woofy turning to a human, it was she. When she was human and walking among other humans they would comment to her about how terrible it must be to be a wolf, always living in an underground den with bugs walking on them and always in the company of other filthy wolves. The prejudices of old came into sharp focus and her wolf mate was called killer and cattle hunter, and all forms of prejudicial pronouncements based on fear and loathing. She would cringe each time she heard them, and felt as though they were talking about her personally and right to her face because no one knew she was a wolf in her other form. But when she was a wolf she would mock the humans. If someone in the pack killed a cow in the field she would laughingly call him "Killer." If someone was infested with fleas, she would tease him calling him "Flea-bitten." Her fellow wolves would laugh with her because they knew she was one of them. When she woke she understood the difference. Furthermore she knew now that white people are never able to get away with saying anything racist because they invented racism.

When Blacks or Indians, or Wolf people, or anyone for that matter, co-opt the racial epithets, it is not only to take the sting out of the words, but also to mock white people for using them in the first place.

Tess told Roseanne about her dream and her conclusions the next day.

"You know of course," Roseanne said, "that that dream came from our ancestors?"

"It did?" Tess asked.

"Yep. It's good that you had that dream. It means the ancestors accept you as one of the tribe."

When Roseanne told her this, it felt to Tess like a warm woolen blanket had been wrapped around her soul.

Aside from getting to know Roseanne, she also got to know Clyde, Kent, Tony and Wild Water who told her stories around the camp fire at night.

One night she sat with Woofy's head in her lap and listened as Wild Water told the story of Skull Cave.

"It was in the times of the grandfather's grandfather that this story comes to our memory." Wild Water began. "It had been a time of great trouble among the people and many of the tribe hunters had been slain in war with the Huron. We lived in that place that you know as Mackinac the Island of the Great Turtle. On the Island was a cave in which the dead of the Ojibwa were lain. It comes down to us now as "skull cave." The women of the tribe were very restless because there weren't enough men to go around. Many of the women had been widowed, lost their husbands and sons in the fighting and were without hunters. They complained to the elders that there were not enough men and asked the chief to do something about it or they would have to leave the tribe and seek others with whom to mate.

"So the Chief, known as Kenu, the fire bird, made a spirit journey up to the top of the Island and looked out at the water. When he came down he knew what he had to do.

"He went to Skull Cave and dug clay from the ground inside the cave. With this clay he fashioned a dozen pipes and filled them all with his finest tobacco. He placed each pipe in the mouth of a skull of one of his ancestors and lit them. Then he fell into a deep sleep as the smoke from the pipes engulfed him.

"When he woke, the dozen pipes were being smoked not by skulls but by twelve young strong hunters. He told the hunters to come with him to the village and choose mates from among the women of the tribe. Which they did and from then on the women were satisfied, and they no longer complained or squabbled among each other."

"Is this a story about sex being the way to keep a woman quiet?" Tess asked.

This struck up guffaws among the men.

"No," Wild Walker said. "It's a story from our tribe, part of our *oral* history." Which made Tess and the other women, chuckle.

By the end of the week, Tess felt like a full member of the tribe. But she had had enough. She had to get back to work.

"I have to try to walk through the Picture Rocks Lake shore region," she told Clyde and the elders one night as they enjoyed each other's company around the campfire.

"Tessa you know it's not safe to be out the woods, even with your fur person next to you," Roseanne said.

"I know but there has to be some way to keep myself solvent and stop relying on all of you for rides everywhere."

"I can give you a job here at the Casino." Clyde offered.

"Oh, Clyde, that's very kind of you, but I can't do that," Tess said. "I really want to make a name for myself in journalism. I'm a travel writer and a food critic. If I quit now I'll never get back to it. One of my writing professors in college warned us that each time we get a job to make ends meet it will set our writing career back ten years."

Ondag said, "Too bad you can't tell him you're going someplace else and then go where you want to go."

"Who?" Tess asked, but then caught up. "The killer?"

"Yeah, I mean. I know you can't cuz he'll sniff you out, but . . ."

"Wait a second," Tess said. "He is using my blog to figure out where I am. Maybe if I put on my blog that I'm down on the shore of Lake Michigan heading toward Wisconsin, he'll go down there looking for me and I'll be free to travel up here."

She stood, "This is a great idea. I can still get to Munising by the 10th."

She started to leave. Kent stopped her. "Tess, you know, he's part animal and he's very smart. How long would you really have before he figured it out?"

"All I need is two days to get through the Picture Rocks area, and meet up with David at Munising. I mean, we're only talking two days. Do you work tomorrow morning, Ondag?" she asked her chauffeur.

"Not until 2 pm." He answered.

"You could drive me to Grand Marais tomorrow morning early so I can start walking."

"It's a forty mile hike," Kent said. Tess could tell by his tone of voice he was trying to discourage her.

"I know, I often walk 20-25 miles a day. I will just spend one night in the woods along the trail, take some great nature pictures of the waterfalls and the wildlife, and I'll be back in a hotel room by Saturday night."

Roseanne looked at Tess, "You can really cover that much ground in two days just walking?"

"I'm pretty good," Tess said smiling. In the week that had passed, staying here at the hotel with the tribe, they had gotten to know her. They spoke to her with the familiarity of parents and grandparents speaking to the younger generation.

"Well, What if you were to change right now," Clyde said to Woofy. "Then she wouldn't have to go to all the trouble of meeting up with you in Munising." Woofy yipped twice at the suggestion.

"We're still on that?" Tess asked.

"We can't actually stop you from doing this fool thing," Clyde said, looking down his bulbous nose at her, "But I want you to take some precautions. I want you to check in hourly with me. Ondag is going to go up to Seney and track you, so he will never be more than 20 minutes away from you. I also want you to put that FBI guy on speed dial. If something happens to you call Ondag first and him second. Ondag can get to you faster than The FBI way down in the Soo."

"What about my shifts?" Ondag asked.

"This is your job. I'll pay you for looking after Tess."

"You can't do that," Tess argued.

"Who's talking to you?" Clyde said giving her a stern look that clearly indicated she needed to mind her own business. This is how it was with Clyde. He saw a need and he filled it, no matter what others thought of it.

"I get it," Ondag said.

"Who is this guy that you are meeting in Munising?" Roseanne asked.

"David," Tess said. He's a truck driver. I told you about him. He's the one I was staying with in the Soo last week."

"What's his last name?" Ondag asked.

Tess grimaced. He must have told her his last name. I mean, they spent two days together.

Roseanne smiled, "He didn't tell you?"

"I . . . he must have told me, I'm just drawing a blank. He did say he would meet me in Munising though. And I believe him."

"No doubt," she quipped. She gave Woofy a hard meaningful look, but Woofy just turned his head, his tongue lolling out of the side of his mouth.

"So that's the plan," Ondag said. "In the morning I take you to Grand Marias and drop you off. You and Woofy start hiking and I go down to Seney to await a phone call saying that you're in trouble. Try to call me at least 20 minutes before the trouble happens, OK?"

"Yeah, right!" Tess said and shared a laugh with the others. "I have to write a misleading Blog tonight and call Agent Marcus. I should call Dad tonight as well and let him know what's going on. I should also get some travel rations."

"Let me get you some fresh jerky and stuff," Roseanne said.

"Yeah, make her some of that great fry bread of yours too, Mom," Ondag suggested.

So it was settled. Tess and Woofy went up to the room to sleep in the comfortable bed one last night. In the morning Ondag knocked on the door just as she was finishing the last of her packing.

"Here, pack these," he said handing her several gallon sized zip-lock bags full of jerky, fry bread and a combination of trail mix made with nuts, cereal and dried fruits. She packed them in her sack and told him to thank his mother when he saw her again.

They went down to the back entrance near the dumpsters. Standing there waiting for them was Kent Robin in front of a huge RV.

"What's this?" Tess asked.

"I don't use it any more. I bought it thinking I would take it to all the Powwow's around the country, but with gas prices the way they are, I can't afford to take it anywhere. You might as well use it."

"I'm not sure I can afford the gas either," Tess said.

"Just don't crash it the first time out, OK?" he said handing Ondag the keys.

"Are you sure about this?" Ondag asked.

"Yeah! Oh, and there's a charge card in the kitchen drawer from Clyde, you can use it for gas or parts or anything you want. He'll pay the bill on it."

"I can't do that," Tess argued. "That's too generous."

"Take it up with Clyde, it wasn't me," Kent told her.

"Come on, Tess, burning daylight here!" Ondag called from the RV. Woofy had already boarded as well. Ondag had started the thing and was in the process of rolling away. Tess gave a quick hug to Kent and told him to pass it on to the other elders including Clyde. Then she ran and jumped on board.

In a little over an hour they were at Grand Marais. Tess looked over the map momentarily and found a camp site about half way through the trail.

"We'll camp there tonight," Tess said.

Ondag looked the map over. "I'll go down to this parking lot here and wait for you. You can walk the extra four miles if you'd rather stay in the RV tonight."

"Did you bring a book to read?" Tess asked him.

"No, but I'll pick one up before I leave town. I think I'll get some groceries too." Tess thanked Ondag once again for the ride and all the help and then she and Woofy hit the trail.

The first part of the trail snaked around inside a line of dunes along the southern shore of Lake Superior. They were not on the trail more than 20 minutes before Tess saw a sign reading "Sable Falls" with an arrow pointing the way.

She heard them first. They were not loud, but there was a definite sound of moving water. Then she came around the bend and saw a beautiful water fall etched out of the outcropping walls and cascading down a three tiered slope. The top tier was horseshoe shaped with the water flowing in evenly around an outwardly curved flat boulder. It fell about seven feet down into a creek bed that was strewn with fallen trees and branches making a dammed pool about fifteen feet wide. White water was created as the rushing liquid overflowed this dam and cascaded down its second tier which was about five feet high. The second tier was split, most of the water falling through a four foot wide section of rock while a secondary fall about two feet wide off to the right handled the rest of the flow. A smaller pool concentrated the flow of water into a funnel shaped cascade that over decades had carved a weird shape out of the side of the canyon rock that looked vaguely like the three-toed webbed foot of some strange pre-historic reptile. From there the water went down through the canyon out of sight. A staircase made of wooden planks led down through the thick forest. Tess and Woofy took them down toward the Lake. In a few short minutes they reached the edge of Lake Superior.

After descending Tess looked up and took several more pictures of the lovely falls.

"How do you describe something like this?" she asked Woofy aloud. "I guess a picture is really worth a thousand words in this case."

At the base of the stairs she found another sign urging her to go back toward Grand Marais. The beach hike would only be about 2 miles to town, but the next waterfall in this area was west about 20 miles.

"Well, Woofy. Let's get started," she said, and turned west. She found it easier to walk in the scrub grass above the high water line rather than on the beach. The sand on the beach would have made hiking way more strenuous. A few miles up she ran into a sign telling her that she was on the Lakeshore/North Country trail and that is was about 42 miles to Munising.

She looked down at Woofy, "Piece of Cake," she said and Woofy agreed with one yelp.

But the rest of the tour that day could be described with very few sentences. She saw some pretty woods and a few meandering streams that she presumed ended in waterfalls, but she didn't see them. Mostly she was treading in scrub with mosquito laden marshes on the side of the trail or she was climbing hills covered in dense forest. Every so often she would glimpse the water off to her right and realized how high she was climbing. Then all at once she was walking along a cliff overlooking the lake. Huge rock formations under her made her start and hang back away from the edge. Some Park committee had erected a railing along there but a very determined hiker could crawl under it to get a closer look at the rocky edge and the plummet. Woofy walked right under it without even stooping and sniffed out over the edge.

"Get back here Woofy," Tess said with a nervous edge in her voice. Woofy looked back and came to Tess in an instant. He stayed by her side, between her right leg and the drop. Before the twenty miles was finished there were several more places like this, each higher than the last. Soon she estimated they were about 60 or 70 feet up from the level of the lake.

She saw a sign that read, "Spray Falls scenic overlook." She took the small side trail off to the right. It led out to a cliff which made her a bit nervous but she didn't get too close to the edge. The lake was its normal cold blue and the sky to the north seemed to match. But off to the West she could clearly see the curved cliff face jutting out over the lake and the water literally spraying out over the cliff. The cliff was made from layers of what looked like flat sedimentary rock with vertical dark striations of dark color. The cliff face was pock marked with cave shallow cave openings especially one along the water line. The beach was dotted with huge rocky boulders that had broken off the cliff face. It was magnificent. She took several pictures of it, each time edging closer to the edge of the cliff. She didn't notice the rock beneath her foot shifting until it was too late. Losing her balance, she began to swing her arms wildly trying to regain footing.

Just as she was certain she was going to fall she felt Woofy behind her. He latched onto her backpack with his teeth and yanked her quickly backward. She landed on her backside on the rock. Breathless with adrenalin coursing through her veins she looked up at Woofy and grabbed him around the neck. He dug in and moved backward dragging her along with him. When they were both safely away from the edge she said what was in her mind. "You saved my life," she told the Wolf. "You saved my life."

Woofy barked twice. "No?" she asked. "Well, then, you saved me from taking up cliff diving. All the same, by my estimation!"

Woofy gave her that Wolf version of a panting smile. He backed up a few steps so she could get her feet under her again. "This is beautiful and all," she told her friend, "but I think we need to find a camp."

They walked back toward the path and a few feet beyond they saw a sign directing them to the campground about two miles walk from where they now stood.

"Perfect," she told Woofy. As they walked up the trail on top of the bluff, over a foot bridge of running water that was the source of Spray Falls, and on into the campground, Tess grew more and more nervous. What made her go that close to the edge? She was berating herself for her close call. It wasn't like her to take a chance like that. She had the clear thought in her mind that it was so lucky that Woofy had been there. She kneeled down on the trail and called him to her. She hugged him fiercely.

"Woofy, I can't get over it. I almost died. You saved my life." Woofy did not bark or move, he just sat there next to her and endured the hug.

Another ten minutes of hiking brought them to the campground. It was not what she expected. It was certainly not like the KOA down in Mackinaw City. Regulated, organized, fenced in, secure. This was more or less an open space with sites where people could pitch tents and build fires in a stone fire pit over which to cook. "OK," she said to Woofy. "Let's get some firewood."

After dinner several other hikers arrived at the camp ground and began setting up. Tess greeted them in a friendly manner as they set up. The camps were within shouting distance of each other but Tess heard very little of the conversations the others were having so she felt free to talk with Woofy while she prepared their meal.

"Maybe we should see how far away Ondag is from us." Tess said.

Woofy got down on his front haunches and began to growl.

"Oh, you don't like that idea?" she asked. Woofy barked twice. "You think you can protect me yourself?" One bark.

"Sure you can. OK, but I'm going to call him and let him know we arrived."

Woofy whimpered. She unpacked the tent and had it pitched in no time. Then she sat down and began to call people. First she called Ondag and told him she was at the campgrounds about two miles from Spray falls. He looked it up on his map and found it. He was in the parking lot about 4 miles from there at a trail head for Spray Falls.

"Do you want me to come up the trail and stay with you two?" he asked.

"No, Woofy said he wants to protect me."

"He did huh?"

"Don't worry about me, I'll be fine and if something happens I can run four miles in half an hour, while calling you on the cell phone!"

"OK," Ondag said. "Have it your way."

Tess told him goodnight and called Clyde who actually put two other people off to talk with her. And when she hung up he said, "OK, but you're alright, dear?"

She almost laughed. He had never seemed the type for endearments. Maybe she had him wrong.

Then she called Agent Marcus and let him know where she was. She had a feeling she was going to be totally surrounded by morning.

"Why are we doing this?" she asked Woofy. "This is fool-hardy, putting ourselves at risk like this. We should just go on ahead and walk the four miles back to where Ondag is."

Woofy whimpered again. Tess thought about doing some work but looked at her pack. She had gotten out of shape in the week that she spent in the hotel. She was totally blitzed, way too tired to try to work. She left the majority of her pack intact for morning. All she did was rummage through to get out her oversized sleeping shirt.

After gathering wood and building a Tee Pee style fire, Tess was far too tired to start it, so as the sun was setting she got out the jerky and trail mix and that was their dinner. They got settled into the tent and cuddled up for warmth. Even though it was early July, the nights were still pretty chilly up near Gitchee Gumee.

Chapter 4

Tessa started awake when she heard noises outside the tent. Woofy was not there. He had left the tent somehow despite the fact that she had zipped the bottom zipper on the flap.

"Woofy," she said quietly. If he was out there scrounging around she didn't want to wake any of the other campers. There had only been a few other tents at the camp ground that night. They had kept pretty much to themselves all at separate camp fires, respecting each other's privacy.

"Woofy!" she said a little louder.

"Tess?" someone outside said. She sat up as this someone began to fumble with the zipper of the tent.

"Ondag?" Tess asked.

"No it's me, David," came the answer. Then he managed to get the flap open and crawled into the tent. He was naked.

"David," she was stunned even though her heart was flip flopping with joy at seeing him.

"We gotta get out of here," he said. Quick, pack up your valuables. We gotta strike camp and go, NOW!"

She got moving at once. Mostly she was packed but she tried to roll her sleeping bag.

"The tent," she said.

"We need to leave it, no time to strike it."

"What about the others?" The other campers!

"Yeah, we better warn them."

"David, how did you find me?"

"Tess, not now. We have to go."

"Do you want your clothes?"

"No! just . . ." He pulled her pack out of her hands and found the cell phone. He thrust it at her. "Call Ondag."

"How do you know Ondag?"

"Just do it, Tess!"

She fumbled with the phone as she pulled herself out of the tent. Ondag answered on the second ring. "Something's happened," she said to him. We're going to make a run for it. David is here, he thinks we're being stalked or something. We're going to wake the other campers. . . ."

"Don't worry. I'll be there in ten minutes." Ondag didn't bother to say goodbye, he just shut down the phone.

"Everybody, get up, your lives are in danger." David was rousing the other campers. Leave your belongings, only take the most valuable things that you can't do without. Everybody has to leave right now."

"Why, what's going on?" Someone asked from inside a tent a few yards off.

"You know that animal that's been attacking people down state?"

"Yeah," came the answer from inside the tent.

"Well, it's stalking this camp as we speak. If we all stay together and leave now, we might make it back to the road before he knows we're gone."

There was some shuffling in and around the campsite and soon about five people emerged. One of them was in the process of striking his tent.

"There's no time for that," David said. He was getting some strange looks from people. He still hadn't bothered to dress. Tess tried calling for Woofy. But she got a strange look from David. "Come on, he can take care of himself."

He ran out ahead of her in the darkness. He called back, "Follow me."

Four of the other five campers were hot on her trail. The one who was trying to strike his tent had mumbled something about the tent costing him $150 and he wasn't going to leave it.

There was a commotion up in front of her and some grunting noises. Then she saw Woofy come running back for her. When he saw her he turned and started toward the road again. Tess thought David must still be further up the trail. They were bound to catch up with him before they got up to the parking area. One of the campers who had left all his belongings behind started to sprint past her but shied up when he saw the wolf ahead.

"It's OK, that's my Wolf," Tess told him, but after that he stayed with the pack.

Ahead Tess could see headlights coming along up the trail. The RV was bouncing along the paved footpath. It was barely big enough to accommodate the huge vehicle but there it was. Woofy circled back around the way they came and watched the woods with a low growl in his throat.

They all ran toward the headlights and Tess turned to be sure that Woofy was following them. He was right behind the group. Ondag opened the door and the four campers jumped inside the RV, Tess and Woofy hot behind them.

"David is still out there," she yelled at Ondag.

"David who?" Ondag asked. "You mean the guy you were going to meet in Munising?"

"Yes, he's out there, we have to find him."

Ondag looked at Woofy and then started turning the RV around in the open scrub. "No we don't."

"Yes, we do, he's out there and I'm not leaving without him."

Ondag thought for a moment as he kept trying to find a place to turn the RV around. Low hanging pine branches were scraping along one side of the vehicle. "Tess, if he was out there then he must have gone out there with a vehicle right?" He probably went back to his vehicle.

"Why didn't he take me with him then? Why did he have me call you?"

He glanced back at the people in the back seat. "I don't know, Tess, you're going to have to ask him that when you see him."

"How did he know the Windigo was there?" she asked.

"Tess," Ondag said. "I have no idea. Please just shut up so I can think."

He kept driving.

A woman from the back seat began to cry. "Ted!" she said. "Where is Ted?"

"Was he the guy with the tent?" a young guy asked.

"Yes, he didn't want to leave it. It was brand new. He's still back there. He'll be wondering where we all are."

"There was someone else back there?" Ondag asked.

"Ted!" she repeated.

"Cripes," Ondag said after a moment's hesitation then he slammed on the breaks and turned the RV back toward the campsite. He drove as far as he could before the trees were too close to the path for him to be able to clear them any more. He honked the horn several times. One of the campers, the young man who had spoken before opened the door and began to call out. He called Ted's name toward the forest and waited to see if he could hear anything. After several seconds Ondag honked again and pushing his head out the side window, called again.

Woofy wanted to get out too. But Tess grabbed him around the neck and wouldn't let him go. He struggled only a little before he sat back down on the seat and waited. Ondag called one more time. Some branches near the opening to the trail shook a little and then all at once Ted burst forth from the opening. He was not carrying his pack or his tent but he was running for all he was worth.

"Common, Hurry," the young man called to him. "Don't look back!"

Tess thought the young man should not have said that because the man then glanced behind him and nearly lost his footing on the path. There was nothing behind the man. At least nothing that Tess could see. Then she saw it. It was huge, black and had a muzzle the size of a bear trap. Its arms ended in paws but it was running upright on two legs. It must have been 7 feet tall if not more. It was following in great leaps. Ondag and the young man were calling to Ted to hurry and cross the distance faster, but Tess could see that the huge wolf-like animal was gaining ground. She did the only thing she could think of. She leaned over and blared the horn. Everyone was startled but the adrenalin going through Ted's body helped him recover faster and he only tripped up a little getting back to his full tilt run within a nanosecond.

While blaring the horn Tess leaned into the gear shift and bumped the headlights up to bright by accident, but it worked. The beast was momentarily blinded and faltered just long enough for Ted to reach the RV and jump head first inside. Ondag pulled his head back inside and raised the window. The young camper slammed the door and fumbled with the lock. Ondag looked out the side mirror and started backing the RV up as fast as he could staying on the footpath. As he backed away, Tess could clearly see the beast advancing before them. The beast ran into the front of the RV, grabbing the top of the hood with his claws and clinging to it. Ondag looked forward again and screamed. He turned the RV off the path, throwing the creature off the hood and into the scrub. It was pure luck that Ondag hadn't slammed into a tree. The RV rocked off to one side, Tess prayed that it would not go over. But Ondag managed to shove the gearshift down into drive and pull back onto the footpath going forward.

"Where is it," Ondag shouted. But no one saw what happened to it and once Ondag turned the RV toward the parking lot no one saw it again.

About 30 minutes later Ondag pulled up in the town of Munising. The town was dead quiet.

The only thing open was the all-night Holiday gas station.

"Where do you want to go?" Ondag asked. "Holiday Inn?"

"How about the police station?" Someone suggested.

"How about the Holiday Inn and then we'll call the police from there," Ondag insisted.

"OK, sounds good," Tess said. She didn't feel good though. She couldn't get it out of her mind that Ondag was willing to go back for Ted but not for David. A thousand questions about this whole matter with David and Ondag bothered her. Maybe Ondag was jealous of David. Maybe Ondag wanted Tess for himself. She would have to speak with him about this. But not right now. She was going to have to talk with the police soon so she had better get her mind on that.

"Tess, I need to talk with you," Ondag said.

"What?"

"Come in here," he said and led her into a stair well. Woofy followed them. "OK, it's like this. What are you going to tell them?"

"I'll tell them that David woke me up and told me that we needed to go now, I don't know how he knew, or even how he found me, but he saved us all."

"You can't tell them that David woke you up. David was not there. Tell them Woofy woke you up."

"Everyone out there heard David, he woke everyone up."

Ondag looked down at Woofy exasperated. "I suppose everyone is going to say they heard David wake them up, right?"

"Because he did," Tess said. "And you wouldn't even go back for him."

"Stop." Ondag said. He looked down at Woofy. "There's nothing to do, we have to have David. We'll say you had your own car and you made it back here to the hotel where you were supposed to meet Tess. We'll say you got here just before we did."

Woofy barked once. "Do you have clothes for him?" Ondag asked.

"For David? He wanted me to keep his date clothes."

"In your pack?"

"Yes," she opened her pack and pulled out the slacks and the shirt. Ondag took them and then opened the door for her. She went back to the others in the lobby. What was he planning to do? Pretend he was David? Maybe no one saw David, just heard his voice. But everyone knows that Ondag was the one that drove them back to town. How was he going to pull this off?

A few seconds later Ondag came out of the stairwell with David following behind tucking in his shirt. He was barefoot.

"Where did . . ." then she realized that Woofy had not come out of the stair well. She whispered, "Where's Woofy?"

Ondag whispered back, "We've been trying to tell you for a week," he said and then said no more.

Tess went to David and leaned against him. "Good to see you again, my friend." She was still whispering. She wished she could scream and rant. But she had to keep it cool. The police were on their way.

Ondag called Clyde to tell him what was going on and Clyde said he would call the friends at the FBI who no doubt would want to talk with them all as well.

"You up for answering questions?" Tess asked into David's ear.

"I can handle the FBI," he said.

"I meant MY questions," Tess said.

"I can handle you too," he said giving her that crooked smile of his.

The police came and questioned each of the campers separately. This took the rest of the night. Then at dawn Agent Marcus arrived and questioned Tess and the others all over again. Meanwhile the local Sheriff called out a K-9 unit and starting at the campsite they tracked the animal. It took most of the day, but they managed to track it back to the road about ten miles to the east of the campsite and then the trail simply vanished. One local Sheriff said it was like the creature had a car waiting for him and he just got in and drove off. Agent Marcus looked at Tess and David significantly and then smiled. "Wolves can't drive." He said simply.

Around noon several of the campers decided they wanted to go back and get the rest of their belongings at the campsite.

"There isn't much left," the sheriff told them. F.B.I. Crime Scene Investigators had been there all morning and had not yet given the OK to allow others into the area. The sheriff said he would ask if it was alright. Another hour passed before Agent Marcus appeared.

"I understand you want to go back and collect your belongings?" he asked the campers as a group. This included Tess, David and Ondag.

"Some of us do," Ted said. He had been emerging as the spokesperson for the group. Ted had that type-A personality that so often takes over in a crisis situation. Marcus recognized this so addressed most of his comments to him.

"Let me understand," Marcus said. "Some of you don't want to go back?"

"No," Ted said. "Some of us," and here he looked sharply at one young man who was cuddling his girlfriend and had been doing so endlessly. Said girlfriend had been quietly sobbing the entire morning into his shirt. "Some of us don't want to ever see the forest again."

Marcus thought about this. "OK, here's the thing. I would like to go back there myself with some of you and question you as to what happened and when. There are some discrepancies in my mind, and there is one point of your stories that is totally out of whack. I'm hoping that if you all go back there you can help me put together the pieces."

"Is it an all or nothing thing?" the young man with the girlfriend asked.

"I don't want to cause any hysteria here, but yes, it's daylight, it's a nice day out there, sun is shining. The CSI is still on scene, there will be about ten other sheriffs out there and me. The animal or whatever it was that attacked you has been tracked by a K-9 unit and is long gone, so there is really nothing out there to fear other than the usual wildlife, bears, cougars, poachers. You'll be safe enough."

"Way to instill confidence, Special Agent Marcus," Tess said to him. He turned toward her to hide his smile from the others."

"It would be helpful to have you all out there," he continued.

"What do you say, Angie?" said the young man to the girl he has been holding all morning. The girl looked around at everyone watching her.

"Do you think it will be alright?" she asked her boyfriend.

"I think it'll be OK. You heard him, at least ten sheriffs, all with guns. I think it'll be OK."

She reluctantly agreed. The other five campers struggled in silence but in the end they all agreed to go with the Agent.

They made the trip in three squad cars. Ondag sat up front in the lead car with Marcus, Tess and David in the backseat. Ondag instructed Marcus on where to go. They parked in the parking lot and walked back along the paved footpath the four miles to the campsite. As they walked, Tess noticed all the signs of their movements through the woods the night before and pointed them out to Marcus.

"This is where Ondag turned the RV around to go back for Ted," she told Agent Marcus.

Then further up Tess showed him where he turned around the first time after finding them on the path. Even further along she showed where Ondag had made the final turn and there the confrontation with the creature had occurred. Ondag carefully recounted the whole incident, pointed to where the branches that scraped the side of the RV had broken off and where the creature had been flung after he made the turn. In fact there was an orange tag with a handwritten number on it on the ground and another tacked to a tree about seven feet above the ground.

"The dog tracked the thing back here. Then it went off that way," Marcus said pointing east.

"Was it injured?" Tessa asked. "Did you find its blood?"

"No, just some hair samples, definitely wolf. Which reminds me, I'm going to need a sample of your pet's hair to eliminate him."

"I'll get it for you when we get back. He's locked in the RV right now."

Marcus lowered his voice and guided Tess away from hearing range of the others, "Do you mind if I ask you a personal question?"

"No," she said, curious, "go ahead."

"If you have this RV now, why are you checking into a hotel?"

"I made the plans to meet David at the hotel before Ondag began driving me and before Kent gave us the RV. David doesn't have a cell phone so I couldn't contact him with the info on the change of plans."

"He drives a truck? A semi?" Marcus asked.

"Yes," Tess said, but realized there was a big hole in their story. Where was the truck now? In fact, she now realized that she had also not seen the truck while they were together in the Soo. Tess realized that David's story had holes in it even back then. She looked at David and saw that he was watching her closely.

"Did you find any hair or droppings back at the campsite?" she asked.

"Plenty," he said. "That's why I need samples from Woofy."

"Oh, yeah, you said that," she said. She was getting confused as to who was supposed to know what.

The campsite was a mess. Literally everything that had been left had been shredded by claws that cut deeply into tent canvas, sleeping bags and packs alike. Clothing was strewn around the ground and food stuffs were spread out over everything, ants and other insects feeding on the camp food. There was nothing left. Ted's knees buckled under him when he saw the shreds of his tent. He began to cry. His female friend went to try to comfort him. "It's only a tent, Ted," she said.

"It might have been me," he said, cries hitching at his voice. "I was more concerned over that stupid tent than my own life, or yours."

He put a hand to his head, "Stupid," he said into his fist and then slammed it against his head, "Stupid," he reiterated.

David came to Tess and took her into his arms as they looked down at what was left of Tessa's tent. Tess realized that if David had not awakened her, she may have been killed too, or worse: taken. Maybe Deputy Morrison had been right. Maybe this creature wanted Tess. The thought of being abducted by the creature they had seen last night made Tess want to empty the contents of her stomach.

She looked up again into David's eyes. Oh yes, they would talk. As soon as they were alone in the hotel room, there would be talking, there would be words.

"David," Agent Marcus said, "Can you tell me where you were?"

"I was here in this tent with Tess."

"Was the Wolf there with you too?"

"Have you ever known Woofy to be away from Tess?"

The Agent gave David a look.

"Yes," David said. "He was there too."

"Did he give you the warning?"

"Woofy woke me up and indicated that he needed to go outside, so I let him out. He started growling outside the tent and I got up to see what was going on. I went outside and realized that something was out in the woods."

"Did you hear or see anything?"

"Yes, I heard it. It was stalking the campsite. I went back inside and told Tess to wake up that we had to get out of there. She told me to wake everyone else up in the campsite so I went outside and started shouting for everyone to get up, that we had to leave. I told them I thought it was that animal that had been attacking people. Everyone got up and grabbed whatever they could. Then this guy, Ted wanted to strike his tent. I told him he didn't have time and better leave it but he wouldn't. Everyone was out of the tents now so I told them to follow me. I was running back to the parking lot and I think Tess was calling Ondag while she ran. She knew Ondag was in the parking lot and he said he would come and find her. So I ran around behind them, and tried to see the creature but I couldn't. I thought about trying to lead the thing away from Tess and the rest of them to give Ondag time to find them. But I got a little lost. So instead I ran back to where my truck was parked. I figured they were going to end up at the hotel where Tess and I said we would meet tomorrow. So that's where I went. I got there just before they did."

"No one else said they saw your truck. Everyone said they heard your voice and someone responded. Someone else said they saw you come out of the tent naked. Did you put on clothes or were you running along in the woods naked and barefoot? And why didn't they see you after you started running down the foot path? They said they saw Woofy, but no one saw you."

"I don't know," David said. "I guess because I was ahead of them. Then I circled around to the back and got lost like I said."

"If you were lost then how did you find your truck? You were four miles out in the woods lost in a place where you might have wandered for a few days before coming to a road or a stream. How did you find your truck and manage to get back to the hotel before the rest of them in the RV?"

"Luck?" David said. "Look, I already told you. I don't know how to explain the discrepancies in my story. I don't know why some people saw me at the campsite but others didn't see me on the footpath. We were running for our lives."

Agent Marcus nodded. "Good story," he said. "Now will you tell me the truth?"

"You don't believe me?"

"No one saw your truck. It's a semi, right?"

"Yeah," he said.

"Where is it now?"

"Outside the hotel."

"No it's not. I checked. There is no semi parked outside the Holiday Inn."

"I parked it behind the building where they told me to park it. I had to walk all the way around the building to get in this morning."

"But you were there within minutes of Ondag and the other's arrival. The night clerk told us that."

"She's wrong. I showed up about couple minutes before they got there."

"Everyone pretty much agreed that you were there already when they arrived, they said you must already have had a room there because you came downstairs from the stair well. You came in with Ondag. Are you and he good friends?"

"I've known him for a while."

"Did he know you were staying at the hotel?"

"He, I, I don't know. I imagine Tess probably told him about meeting me there."

"Did he know you had a room already and where that room was?"

"I don't know. I told you. I went up to my room when I got here and . . ."

"You said you didn't have a room, you said you were staying out in the woods with Tess. Which is it?"

"Tess and I were planning to meet here today," David said. "I got here yesterday, a day early, and got a room. I was worried about her, having heard the news stories, so I went down to the campground and found her campsite. I surprised her. I asked if she would rather I take her back to the room. She said no, she would stay at the campsite and then finish the walk into town tomorrow. There were still a few sights she wanted to see. I had really missed her so I stayed with her."

"Oh, I see. OK, well you've managed to explain your whole story except for one thing."

"What's that?"

"How did you turn your truck around on that road out there? It's not much more than a two track, gravel, pitted with bumps, and pot holes. Swamp land on both sides for miles. If you had gone off the road with a semi you would have been mired in swamp until late fall. So how did you turn the truck around?"

"I didn't go off the road," he said.

"What?"

"Have you ever driven a big rig?" David asked the Agent.

"No," he answered "But I know that thing needs more than a tiny dirt road to turn around in."

"No it doesn't. All it needs is for the cab to not leave the road. The trailer can be put anywhere at all and as long as the cab can get traction it can haul the trailer out of anything, even foot deep mire. And that's about how deep it was."

Tess had been listening to all of this. She realized that she wanted to believe all this was true, just as he had said it. She wanted him to have a room in the hotel, and to have come out to her last night with the truck, and turned it around in the swamp like he had said. She wanted it to be true that he returned to his truck and met them back at the hotel minutes before they got there. She wanted Woofy to be her pet and David to be her boyfriend and to not mix up the matter. And how did Ondag know all of this?

The Agent looked at David. "You are hiding something my friend," he said. "What is it?"

David sighed deeply. "I'm afraid of getting in trouble with my bosses. I'm supposed to be on the road going to the Soo. I'm not supposed to make any stops. I've already been here longer than I should."

Agent Marcus looked severely at David. "It's more than that. There is something hinky about your story, but I can't figure it out." He paused watching David for a long time. David took several deep breaths and stayed silent.

"Where is your truck now?" Marcus asked.

"Behind the hotel. I parked in back away from the road."

"And that is no doubt why I didn't see it the whole time we were there today?" Marcus asked.

David said nothing.

"Go find your belongings. Maybe you will be able to find your shoes in the rubble."

Tess was in the habit of staying packed as much as possible. So she could get on the road fast in the morning. Usually all she had to do was roll up her sleeping bag, strike the tent and she would be off. She understood why this was a good practice now. She had nearly all of her belongings with her. The only things she had not been able to save were the tent, sleeping bag and some socks she had hung to dry on the tent line. She had grabbed her pack and Woofy's pack. She didn't know where Woofy's pack had gone. She might have dropped it on the footpath or it might have made it to the RV where it was dropped and forgotten. She was wearing her backpack while running through the woods and had not taken it off until Ondag asked if she had any of David's clothes. At that point she had put the pack down. She had put it back in the RV before the ride out here to the woods. So her laptop and camera were safe. She hoped Ondag had had the foresight to lock the RV before they left.

David took Tess by the shoulder and led her away, out of earshot of the others.

"I'm sorry about all of this Tess," he said.

"Do you really have a hotel room?" she asked.

"Tess," he said raising his eyebrows. "I was with you the whole time, remember?"

"I'm confused. I can't get used to this."

"You will," he said and kissed her solidly on the forehead.

"OK," she said. "You had me convinced you know?"

He looked slightly puzzled, "Of what?"

"All that stuff was true. I wish it was true and not this other thing."

"We'll talk about it later, OK?" he said. He took her in his arms and held her close for a good long time. He took a deep breath through her hair and said, "I love you Tess."

He let her go and went to talk with Ondag.

"Tess," Marcus called to her.

"Yes sir?" she answered. The distraction made her turn away from the two men.

"Is this yours?" he said. He had found a camera lying on the ground. She picked it up and looked at it. If this was not the camera that had been stolen, then it was one just like it. The camera had only been a few months old when it was stolen and had no distinguishing marks or bumps. But after inquiries with the other campers it was determined that no one who was camping that night had a camera like it. He was holding it with a pencil by the short strap.

"It looks like the one that was stolen in Mackinaw City. But it would be an extreme coincidence if it were," she told him. "Have you checked the data card?" she asked.

"We need to test it for prints," he said.

"What if it is mine?" she asked. "My prints would be on it."

"Possibly, but more to the point, it would mean that our theories are correct, he is following you."

"I thought that had been established," she said.

"Well, this is evidence, proof, that can be presented in court." He bagged the camera and put it in a carrying case on the ground. Then he looked back up at her, "Which was your tent?"

She led him over to her tent. It was in shreds. The tarpaulin that made up most of it was in four or five pieces lying around. The only way she could identify it was by the color and part of the screening was still attached in places. One of the socks was found still attached to a line with a notebook clip. Marcus had the Deputies bag up the main pieces that could be identified.

"That's about all we can do here. Maybe you should head back to the hotel and get some rest," Marcus suggested.

"Yeah, I think so," Tess agreed.

They caught a ride with one of the Deputies and also two of the other campers who were totally stunned and could not stop talking about how much they owed to Tessa's boyfriend for waking them up and getting them out of there.

Once back at the hotel she tried to check in and found that she already had a room in her name. She asked for the key and went up, but before she could key in the door opened. David grabbed her in his arms and closed the door behind her.

Once their initial joy was over Tess backed away from him and looked at him from head to toe.

"Woofy?" she asked.

"Yeah, and Kicky," he confirmed.

"Kicky?" she asked. "You can't be. Kicky was only a teenager, you're in your thirties."

"Thirty? Really?" he said going to the mirror. He sounded like he was expecting to see grey hair. He regarded himself in the mirror for a few seconds. "I have to stay human for a while."

Tess began to laugh, and even to her own ears it began to sound hysterical.

"What?" he asked.

"You have to stay human for a while?" She asked incredulously. "Whatever for?"

"I'm aging too fast. I need to stabilize." She was laughing again and he said, "Wolves age faster than humans, I've been spending too much time as a wolf."

She stopped laughing then and was dead serious. "What kind of game is this? You knew you would age faster if you stayed a wolf so you purposely stayed a wolf so we would be more the same age?"

"It seemed important to you," he said.

"So you purposely shortened your lifespan because you thought it was important to me?"

Now it was Kicky's turn to smile. "I don't really have to worry about that. My life span is going to be longer by at least half than even the oldest human beings. I'm Eagle Clan. My Great Grandfather is still alive."

"So how old are you really?" she asked, her chin up in the air, daring him to tell her the truth.

"How old do you want me to be?"

"Answer the question," she demanded.

"Old enough to know that I love you and that I can't be without you. I've imprinted on you," he said.

"You told me that wasn't a big thing."

"Well, I lied. I didn't want to lie but I did. Here's the thing. I will tell you about every single lie and from this night forward I will not lie to you again, how would that be?"

"You said you would never lie to me," she said. She hated the fact that she was pouting.

"I won't, from this moment forward. Ask me anything."

She thought for a long moment. There were so many questions in her mind. She couldn't settle which was the most important. So she decided to ask the one that was first. Others would come later.

"Why did you tell me that imprinting was nothing big?" She asked, "When clearly it is the biggest thing in your life. I mean you changed your entire direction in life because of me."

"I just told you that so that you wouldn't be afraid of it. You still have a choice even though I've imprinted on you. You are not Eagle Clan. You don't have to be stuck with me."

"Stuck with you?" she said. "Believe me, I missed you every day. When I was in Charlevoix I couldn't stop thinking about you. In Alden I almost turned around and went back for you. And I must say that I'm relieved you are Kicky and David both, because for a while there after the Soo I thought I was going to be attracted to every young handsome Native American man I met. But I'm not, it turns out, it's just you."

Kicky smiled at this and bent his head. "Thank you," he said.

"For what?" she was still perturbed, but was beginning to recover.

"For telling me that. The only time you ever said you cared about me was when I was Woofy. It's easy to love an animal, not so easy to love a man."

"And harder yet to love a skin walker!" She exclaimed. She was still angry. Kicky couldn't help himself though. Her use of the term "skin walker" made him laugh. He laughed so long and hard that she found she had to laugh too. It cut right through the anger.

She walked into his arms and hugged him fiercely around the waist. He embraced her too, bending to kiss the top of her head. Then he became aware of the fact that she was crying. She had literally laughed so hard that she began to cry.

"What's wrong?" he asked.

"I nearly lost you," she said. What was I thinking leaving us both open like that? We knew this thing was after us and I purposely and stubbornly went out there hiking anyway, spending the night in a camp ground with no security after knowing that he could get to us even in a campground that had security like the KOA. I should have realized, but you just kept being the faithful hound following after your mistress and going where she told you to go," Tess sobbed as she said all this. Kicky stopped her.

"OK, that's enough. You have to quit this now. I could have stopped you at any time. But I know how important it is to you to keep working. That's all part of the imprinting thing. What's important to you becomes important to me. You don't get it yet, I know, but I'm the dream supportive boyfriend. Anything you do I will be for. Any idea you have I become its advocate. Anything you wish to accomplish, I will be behind it, no matter what."

"So, in other words, you're my yes man?" Tess said. The joke almost made her smile.

"No, if you purposely put yourself in danger I will stop you."

"Good to know," Tess said. This time she did smile.

That night they talked for hours. She asked him where he had gone that first night in the Soo. He had been out in the neighborhood trying to earn enough money for some decent clothes. The ones he had stolen out of the St. Vincent's dumpster were not adequate for dinners in nice restaurants. Not even in a tourist town. He had found a local who needed some wood chopped and spent several hours chopping wood for minimum wage. The guy paid him in cash.

"So, when you change, do you think like a human still? Is that why you can answer yes or no questions with a bark or two?"

"I still have all the cognitive functions of a human when I am in wolf form yes. Not all shifters can, I can because I'm Eagle Clan. We are the purest descendents of the Bird People in the country. There are other skin walkers that turn into animals when they change and only change back because they fall sleep. It's kind of a stop gap function. I had to make sure that I woke before you everyday so I could change back into a wolf before you saw me. Last night in the tent I woke up as a human and heard the footsteps outside. More to the point, I smelled the other wolf. I knew that getting up and shouting would make him pause and wait so that's what I did. I started to shout and get everybody going. I figured that if we all stayed together maybe he wouldn't attack the whole lot of us. But then that other guy stayed behind. I had warned him but if he wasn't willing to listen to me it was his neck, not yours, and not mine."

"I would have felt so guilty if he hadn't survived."

"Me too," Kicky buried his face into Tessa's shoulder, a move reminiscent of something he did as Woofy. "I'm so glad that girl was able to talk Ondag into going back."

Tess absently stroked the back of Kicky's head much the way she did with Woofy. Then she pulled free from his embrace and sat up. "I want to see it," she said.

"See what?" he asked.

"I want to see you change."

"Really?"

"Yes, I guess I need to see it to prove it's real, you know. I mean yes you are what you are and there is no other explanation for it. And the Bay Mills Elders had been trying to tell me for a whole week, and Ondag already knew in the stairwell when he was trying to get the story straight. But I just really feel like I need to see it to believe it once and for all."

"Ok, I guess I can understand that." He stood up and took off his shirt. He was already barefoot having been in bed with her for hours and now he opened the fly of his pants and let them drop. He stood there naked before her and she allowed her eyes to travel the length of his beautiful tan and muscular body. All at once he began to morph into the form of the wolf. Hair grew, his nose turned into a muzzle, his jaw began jutting out, his fingers shortened and became paws, his legs changed shape and his feet lengthened into the dog leg haunch. His waist shrank and his arms shortened. He fell to the floor on all fours and when he shook himself one last time to settle the fur of his ruff, the transformation had become complete. The familiar form of Woofy stood in front of Tess. He then jumped back up on the bed and came to her, licking her face.

"Stop that," she scolded him. He did and sat down on the bed looking at her. He lay down next to her and tucked his head down into her breast. She stroked him for a while. Then he rolled over back facing her so she could spoon with him. She put her arm around him and stroked his tummy, as she knew he liked. But when she discovered he was aroused she stopped.

"Sorry, I just can't," she said to him. "It's just too big a taboo, there is something sick about it." He barked once and then closed his eyes to sleep.

"I'm glad you agree," she said. And she settled in for some rest as well.

Chapter 5

Tessa's Travels:

Sunday July 10, 2011

Dear readers and Dad,

Woofy and I have traveled down to stop for a while in Manistique, Michigan. There is a very clear spring here that is very cool to see, and I'm going to be writing an article about it for sale in the next couple of days. What's nice about it is it has not become a major tourist trap. You can literally go there and see it for next to no money. It's only slightly off the beaten path, and it's very cool, literally. The water temperature coming up from the ground below is a constant 35 degrees, which is also why it's so clear. But more about this later.

We are staying in a motel near the edge of town and will be here for the next two days at least. The rain has us holed up. I had a mishap with my tent and I have to find another one, but in the mean time Woofy and I will be staying here. I will review three restaurants from this town before we go on, so if you're interested in where to eat in this neighborhood, check back in a day and I'll have those reviews for you.

From here we will be heading south toward Gladwin, Escanaba, Iron Mountain and Menominee and then on into Wisconsin where I already have Chicago buyers interested in the Wisconsin restaurants. I'll be there soon Uncle John! (John Galbreath of the Sun Times.)

As always, if you wish to buy any of the articles I have mentioned, please feel free to contact my father whose contact information is in the box at the right.

Thank you to all the readers who voted for me to come to Sweet Home Chicago! I am looking forward to seeing my father again!

Thank you,
Tessa Gates and Woofy

E-mail: Sunday July 10, 2011

Dear Dad,

When you read the Blog please note that the whole thing is a fabrication. We did not go down to Manistique from Munising. We are still here in Munising. I did have a mishap with the tent. It was destroyed when the creature that has been attacking people attacked me and Woofy at the Spray Falls Campground. We got away but only because my friend Ondag had been sleeping in his RV about four miles away from the campground. I called him the night before letting him know where I was. He was supposed to keep an eye on me under orders from the Bay Mills Elders who have sort of adopted me into the tribe. They think it's good medicine that I talk with wolves. I don't know. You'll have to ask them what the reasoning is. Anyway, if it weren't for Ondag there would have been major casualties that night. Not to mention Woofy, who woke up and warned everyone that someone was near by.

The FBI is involved now and they tell me that I need to stay put for a time. Rain is in the forecast for the next two days anyway, so I guess it's a good time to be holed up in a hotel. This one is pretty nice too, because it has an indoor pool and a Jacuzzi. I plan to use both a lot. Plus I'm meeting Kicky here. Dad, you are going to love Kicky. I do. You'll get to meet him soon enough. I think we will be heading toward Marquette next. Clyde, the elder at Bay Mills, has arranged for me to use an RV owned by one of the other Elders. They also sent Ondag along as my driver. No more walking from town to town. I'm afraid I might be gaining some weight in the near future. Kicky will be traveling with me from now on. He didn't have much of a job and I think the protection he affords me is well worth the extra money he will cost. I'm not sure how long Woofy will stay around once we get into more populace areas. He may decide to stay in the wild. I wouldn't blame him.

Anyway, I just wanted to write and tell you that the blog is a fabrication, and I am planning to keep with the original plan. At least until the FBI manage to catch this murderer. We are helping all we can. The blog is a false lead for the killer, so there may be another false blog if this one doesn't work.

Dad I don't want you to worry about me. The FBI is not using me as bait. They just wanted me to lay down a false trail in my blog so they can lead the killer away from me and maybe catch him in the act of stalking me. It's really as simple as that. Meanwhile I have Kicky, Ondag, and Woofy to protect me.

I just got a phone call from Clyde down at Bay Mills. Ondag is going to drive us up to Marquette tomorrow and he's also been authorized to stay with us as long as we need him. So I'll be very safe! Don't worry about us, OK? Meanwhile, you can call some of the regulars and let them know I have reviews from Munising and Marquette. And I will have reviews for the towns named in the blog, hopefully next week after this guy gets caught and we can get back on our regular tack. I'll let you know if anything changes.

I Love you Dad!

Tessa.

Chapter 6

The number of interesting looking places to eat between Munising and Marquette gave Tessa pause. She treated Kicky and Ondag to breakfast at a place in Christmas. They stopped in Autrain for a swim and lunch. Then they saw a neat looking Inn a few more miles down the road so Tess suggested they park the RV and have dinner at the Inn. It turned out to be a very nice place with a chef that was very creative with his Northern Michigan ingredients, especially blueberries. Tess even talked him into cleaning the grill so he could make them an order of his blueberry pancakes which he normally only made in the morning before he began cooking meat stuffs on it. It was worth it too because Tess assured him a good review for two meals, breakfast and dinner.

That night in the RV, the three of them made up a list of all the things they needed to make the RV into their home. The back bedroom had three very cozy single beds lining the room. There was storage underneath them and curtained windows around the perimeter of the room. One closet was tucked up next to the area which was the bathroom on the driver's side. There was a bank of cupboards on the passenger side that stretched from the bedroom door to the side door entrance. In one of them was extra bedding, sheets and blankets. Another one housed slatted metal security shades to fit all of the windows. Kent had had these made to fit either the inside of the window or the outside. Ondag explained that Kent planned to do a lot of traveling in this RV including to places where there was often golf ball sized hail. He wanted something that would protect the windows.

"Windows?" Tess exclaimed. "I think he was planning for the zombie apocalypse."

Ondag smiled at that joke but didn't deny it.

The bathroom was customarily tiny. There was a tank that ran above the bathroom and kitchenette that held wash-up water. Many signs recommended them to not drink it. But it was perfectly safe for them to shower in, and wash their dishes. Except they had no dishes. Kent must have removed his dishware from the RV. They would have to get some. Kicky was all for just buying paper plates and red solo cups having worked as a bus boy at his sister's restaurant. But Tess insisted she needed a coffee mug in the morning.

The one really good thing about the RV was the full sized refrigerator. Ondag thought it would be great to keep a stockpile of beer in there. But Tess wanted to make sure there was room for good fruits and veggies and plenty of bottled water.

"Let's make a habit of stopping at every farmer's market we see," she suggested. "With all the restaurant food I eat, I hardly ever get my fill of fresh fruits and vegetables."

"Just keep the steaks coming for me," Kicky said. "I'll be happy."

Past the kitchenette was a living area. There was a fold down table behind the passenger seat with enough seating for four and there was another built in couch behind the driver's seat. That night Ondag made it clear that the built in couch was going to be his bed. The other two could sleep wherever they wished.

"Me and Woofy get the back bedroom," Tess said.

"What about me?" Kicky asked her. Tess laughed.

"I'm used to sleeping with Woofy. I'm not sure I should be sleeping with you." She nudged him playfully. Ondag just looked at them.

"There's always the pull down," Kicky said. Above the front window there was indeed a pull down bed on a hinge. It could be pushed up in the daytime for a better view out the front window, but it could sleep at least one adult or maybe as many as three small children. Kicky said he would sleep there if Tess didn't want him in her room. She laughed but said nothing more.

The next day they made it to Marquette about 10:00 A.M. Some internet research had indicated that there was coffee shop on Third Street, called, oddly enough, Third Street Café, that had great sandwiches. They had brunch there and she wrote the review while Kicky and Ondag walked around a department store called Shopko

Tess finished her review and did some research to choose their dinner restaurant, a place out on the lake called Coco's.

The men had not come back by the time she was finished so she slipped on her shoes and went inside to find them. They were having an argument in sporting goods. Kicky had wanted to get a big gas grill that they could haul on the back deck of the RV. But Ondag argued that they weren't going to be cooking much. What he wanted was a portable fire pit. They could build a fire in the evenings in the wilderness and they wouldn't have to clear a place for it everywhere they went. Tess looked at the price tags on both items. "We don't need either," she said and walked away. She went to the house wares department and picked out a set of picnic table wear, plastic plates in ocean blue, with matching bowls and cold drink cups. She also found huge coffee mugs with saucers. She bought a set of four of them that sort of matched the picnic plates. There was also a set of six place settings of silverware with the same ocean blue handles that came in a container that would also hold napkins and a salt and pepper shaker.

"This will do us quite nicely," she said. She also loaded up the cart with bottled water and juice drinks which were on sale. Two large bags of Hershey's minis also accidentally fell into her cart, but they were on sale two for one so it was all good!

She placed a frying pan into the cart on a whim but then put it back when she went down the isle with the small appliances and discovered how inexpensively she could buy a microwave oven. She had picked out a coffee maker already but was still looking at the various microwaves when the men found her.

"We decided on the portable fire pit," Kicky told her. "Ondag's right, we're never going to cook in the RV, but we might have a campfire at night."

"No, we won't be cooking, but we might be warming food from take out boxes. I think we need a microwave."

This prompted a discussion amongst the men that ended with them buying a tape measure and measuring the space under the kitchen counter to see which one would fit the best. After Shopko they hit the SuperOne grocery store. By the time they were finished they had everything they needed to call the RV home.

At each place she asked the checkout girl where she could get the best pasties in town. She got a variety of answers but the two most mentioned were Jean Kay and Lawry's. She chose one at random.

"Let's go get some pasties for lunch," she said to the guys. She gave Ondag the address and then sat back down at the table while he drove them there. Ondag had used Clyde's credit card to buy the fire pit along with a Satellite GPS system. While Kicky and Tess were shopping at SuperOne, he was reading the manual for the GPS and installing it in the RV.

Before they got to the Jean Kay's though, Tessa's phone rang. It was Agent Marcus.

"Stay put, I'm taking you into protective custody," he told her.

"What?" she asked, "Why?"

"I'll explain when I get there. Suffice it to say that he figured out the ruse. There was only one motel on the edge of town here. He went there and tortured the proprietor into confessing that you had not been there. He went crazy did a rampage down here and killed about half a dozen citizens whose only crime was to be staying at this motel last night. I have no idea where he is now but I'm on M94 heading up to Munising. I should be there in two hours. Where are you?"

"We're on our way to Jean Kay Pasty shop on Presque Isle Dr. We were talking about just parking the RV in the parking lot at Shopko while we're here. I'm not sure if there is room in the tourist park, it's the middle of summer after all."

"OK, we'll find someplace to park it. I'll be in touch with Marquette Police. I'm taking you to a safe house in Marquette. When we catch this guy you can go back and retrieve your RV."

"What about Kicky and Ondag?" Tess asked him.

"Kicky and Ondag? Who are they? I thought David was your boyfriend."

"He is. I mean, his nickname is Kicky, that's what he likes to be called. Ondag is part of my entourage, my driver."

"You do seem to collect champions."

She agreed to meet him at the local Sheriff department.

After they disconnected, Tess did a search for the address of the Marquette Sheriff department. Ondag punched it into the GPS. After getting three pasties at Jean Kay, they went straight there.

"Where are we supposed to go?" Kicky asked when they parked at the back of the lot.

"We have to stick around here until Agent Marcus gets here," Tess told them before taking a big bite out of her pasty. "He wants to take us to a safe house. I think I'll go back and get a nap after lunch."

"Does he think Rivershade is on his way up here?"

"I don't know, he said he would give us the details when he got here."

They finished their lunch and Tess made some notes about the tasty crust on this pasty.

“This was good,” she told them. “We might have a winner!”

“It’s the best one I’ve had so far,” Kicky agreed. Tess went to the back bedroom and crawled into one of the bunks. Kicky tucked her in and said he may join her in a bit.

But if he did, Tess was unaware. She was out almost at once.

Chapter 7

My dearest most darling Contessa,

How I long for you. I have acquired another computer, having lost the last one when I had to flee from the motel room in which I was staying as I searched for you. No doubt the FBI has that one now. I suppose they are trying to figure out who I am from all the clues I left them on that little e-mail draft that I couldn't finish. Did they share that with you my dear? No? I doubted that they would. Everyone seems to wish to protect you above all else. Even to the point where they will not give you information you need to survive! How Un-gallant that is!

I would not be like that with you. If you and I were together I would not treat you like a fragile flower that could wilt with a breath. I think you are made of sterner stuff than that. When we are wed, (and yes I do mean to wed you, bed you and procreate with you) you will be a part of my master plan. I do not coddle my wives. Because you are an evolved woman I think your children might be truer in the nature of the bird people, possibly, than anyone I've ever met before. I would be very happy to add you to my harem of happy brides. I have a collection of evolved women who have all bore me sons. I have only one daughter so far, but there may be more on the horizon. I will collect a menagerie to rival the bird people themselves. You will become part of it.

Ah, me! As I was saying, I had lost the last computer, so I acquired a new one. This one used to belong to a motel desk clerk in Manistique Michigan. As you know, I have been reading of your travels. I jumped ahead of you this time, instead of following behind. I got to Manistique and killed the desk clerk so that I could look up on his computer your blog to see where you were. Imagine my surprise when you said you were staying in the same motel. Well, I searched for you. There wasn't anyone there that even resembled you. There were some honeymooners from Manistique who had just been married last weekend and from the smell of them they had not left the room in three days. There was another young couple who were traveling through Michigan on a wildlife tour. There was an older businessman with a brief case. There was a young woman who was fleeing from an abusive husband and the motel owner. I killed them all trying to get at you. The motel owner I killed longest because he kept insisting that no one by your name had checked into the motel in the past week.

So imagine my chagrin when I realized YOU had LIED to me. The effrontery! How could you? Honestly. Where are you? Munising still? Escanaba? Marquette? I woke this morning in my human form and waited. I waited in my car for the Federal Buffalo Interpreter to get here so I could find out where you were. He and that idiot deputy from the Soo arrived together and spoke with the locals I was watching from the diner. They came in and sat talking for a while. They were very careful not to mention any details of your whereabouts. But at one point your brave hero stood and his phone slipped off the newspaper. I happened to see it and grabbed it. You see I was sitting just behind them in a booth. I quickly programmed the phone to ring in to my cell when he used it for any reason. Then I kindly offered it back to him, "Excuse me sir, I think you dropped this." The whole of the operation took nearly four seconds. Isn't technology wonderful these days!

Well, it wasn't more than fifteen minutes later that I got a call. It was him calling you, and telling you to stay put in Marquette, you had an RV and he was taking you into protective custody. Not only that but you had picked up another hanger-on. You're entourage, you called him. You can surround yourself with fifteen Ojibwa Warriors, and I will still get through them all in order to get to a specimen such as yourself. You are my destiny, my dear Contessa Gates. You are going to be my bride, and you will bear me sons. Maybe more than one! Would you like that, my princess?

I will not make the mistake again of thinking I have time to refine my letters to you. This one I will send as soon as it is finished. Oh and in case you are worried about the Federal Bureau of Fuck-ups, I intend that before you see him, he will be dead and I will be at your doorstep. You see, I'm ahead of him. I left toward Marquette a full twenty minutes before him. He will be coming through Escanaba right about now and I will be waiting for him in Gladwin. Do not fret about me killing law officers. It's a little hobby of mine. I take their canine teeth as trophies. It's especially good if they are vampires, oh how they screech when their teeth are pulled. Or did you not know that there are vampires in the world as well. But then again, how could you not? If there are werewolves, how could there not be vampires? It just makes sense, silly girl. The Bird people, as my home tribe calls them, are very wide reaching. They have procreated many times with humans. Most notably was the seduction of Queen Leda by Zeus in the guise of a swan. Ancient myth, you say? How does that differ from me and you mating? I suppose that if I had been born in the times of ancient Greece I too would be considered a god! That is very apropos and fitting to my character. In fact, maybe I'll have my wives start worshiping me! Beginning with you my dear one!

I hope you get this message before I arrive. It would broaden the excitement of our first mating immensely if you were anticipating it.

Are you eager now my love? My mate to be? As you read this I could be outside your room right now. I could be walking past your door, waiting for you to make your move. I could be just behind you having already dispatched your pet and your adopted brother.

Oh I am getting all shivery with excitement. I will send this too you, so you can be shivery too!

All my sweet sticky love to you my darling,
TR

Chapter 8

Agent Marcus stopped for Gas in Gladwin, Michigan and went inside to buy himself a coke. When he came out he found that he had a low tire. The gas station where he stopped had no air pump, so he inquired inside where he could find one. He was directed to a tire shop about two miles away and he started for it. Knowing he would be delayed, he called Deputy Morrison on his cell phone. Morrison was going through Christmas, Michigan when the call came. Marcus let him know that he was delayed and to go to the Sheriff Department in Marquette, where they would all meet up in an hour or so.

Talbot Rivershade was speeding in his jeep toward Marquette, as near as he could figure ahead of everyone descending on Tess, especially since the reception of that last phone call from the Federal Balls of Intoxication. Rivershade was certain he could get there ahead of everyone. He could easily dispatch her pet and that new brother of hers.

The fact that Clyde had adopted the girl pissed him off more than he was willing to admit. Last time he had seen his Nephew Clyde was in the Sixties. Clyde had exacted a promise from Talbot at that time. Talbot had been allowed to leave the reservation under two circumstances; one was that he never comes back to Bay Mills. The second was that he never harms one of his own family members. For the last 50 years he had abided by these two promises. This past summer he had broken the first. He had crossed onto the rez once to assure himself that she was being protected there. And now he would break the second by taking as wife his own grand niece. But then Clyde had no business adopting the girl. If he had not she would still be fair game and no promise would have to be broken. So in his mind he decided that the adoption was null and void, it did not matter. She was not a blood relation.

The other thing that was making him angry at the moment was that it had been so easy for them all to spot the pet. If it had not been for the fact that they had dealt so severely with him all those years ago, not a one of them would have thought her little Woofy, as she so quaintly called him, was a shifter. In fact had it not been for the fact that he had been exiled from the tribe in the first place none of them would have known that shifters really existed.

Indeed this young shifter may be closer related to the Eagle Clan than Talbot himself. He had the advantage of knowing that he would grow into adolescence and change into a predator. He would have the advantage of being able to shift at will. For Eagle clan members it is painless to shift and they keep their human cognition when they shift. That would be a grand advantage.

Talbot Rivershade had none of these advantages. Talbot Rivershade did not know he would shift when he entered puberty. He did not know how to shift at will. He could only shift when he grew angry enough to shift or when in the throws of other strong emotion, fear and lust most notably. It was always very painful to shift which embittered him to it. But the driving lusts of the predatory animal's life was something that he had become addicted too, and thus would be willing to go through any amount of pain to partake of it.

But the advantage of keeping his human mind inside his wolf form the way the young Eagle Clan Ottawa seemed to be able to do, now that was an enviable state. Talbot remembered nothing while he was in his animal form, acting on instinct only, driven by passions. It was only afterward, after a good long sleep to recover himself that he could adequately recall anything at all that had happened when he was animal.

It had been a long time before he even knew what form his animal nature took. He had the face and features of a wolf and yet could stand on his hind legs. The first time he had heard a radio station in Traverse City play the song about the Dogman of Michigan, he realized that someone had seen him. The song was about him.

He had been the one who terrorized the hippies in the van out by Lake Michigan. He had been the one who attacked the woman's house. He had been the one who had shown up at the woodman's campfire. He had been the one outside of Reed City who had chased down the car full of teenagers. They had come too close to his property and angered him. This was back in the 90's when he was trying to lay low for a while. He had been studying for his doctorate in Anthropology and wanted someplace quiet to write his thesis. So he had taken the house at the end of the long lane about ten miles outside of Reed City. The area was very quiet, rural and densely wooded. When he felt the urge to change he would simply allow it to happen instead of fighting to deny the urge. This is something he had always tried to do as a young man, and when he lived in Paris, Madrid, Egypt and later at Eton and Princeton as he explored his education.

The woods North of Reed City were secluded enough to allow him the full range of his animal tendencies. This is when he became hooked on the feelings that emerged when he changed. But living in the same place for almost a decade and changing there at least once a month whether he wanted to or not, eventually the place got a reputation and soon people began to come out to the house and explore the surrounding forest. After turning away about the tenth such visitor in two weeks, Talbot grew angry and decided that it was time for an encounter. That time, the lads in the car had gotten away with their lives, but only because Talbot had been cautious about approaching a car full of young men. He did give chase though and later laughed as he read about the encounter in the paper.

Of course that incident spurred on other young men to try their luck and soon Talbot realized it was time to abandon the place. He quickly finished his thesis and went back to Princeton to submit it, but not before staging a very dramatic fire in the forest north of Reed City. He was please to read that the fire had destroyed about 3000 acres of forest. That would serve those people right who would deign disturb his solitude.

Talbot had been lying in wait for The Fucking Bureau of Ingenuousness to come by so he could drive him off the road, but that was not to be.

Who ever heard of a flat tire on a rental vehicle? So instead he decided to break some speed laws on the back roads and try to get to Marquette ahead of Deputy Idiot. He was a little out his jurisdiction, but things like that didn't seem to matter much in the U.P. With the wide open spaces and tourism running rampant most of the law enforcement agencies up here tended to back each other up when needed. But usually it was Marquette backing up all the other one horse towns not the other way around. But, Deputy Idiot was familiar with the case and because Talbot was involved it was considered a capital case. After all Talbot was what they called a Serial Killer. It was strange how in one hundred years the term went from Tribal Warrior to Serial Killer. My my, the times, they are a changing!

Twenty minutes passed at the speed of 95 MPH, and Talbot was breezing by K.I. Sawyer Air force Base when he saw the lights flashing behind him. Damned M.P.'s were as bad as the tribal police in their overblown sense of importance. Well, he would stop. Oh yes. He would stop for sure. After all he hadn't killed anyone in the last 14 hours.

Chapter 9

While Tess slept, Ondag took the metal shades out one by one and locked them down on all the windows on the outside. Once locked in place the RV was like a vault. And Ondag had the key!

Tess woke from her nap in near total darkness. She was getting hungry. Checking her watch, only three hours had passed. Tess thought that the reason she had been so tired today was because she hadn't had any exercise. She would have to remedy this. Just because she had this wonderful new RV didn't mean she could become a couch potato. They would have to work something out.

She expected to see Kicky in one of the other beds when she turned on the light, but he had not appeared. It was nearly four hours since Agent Marcus had called her. Where was he? He said he would be here in an hour.

Tess left the back room. The entire RV had been swaddled in the darkening metal shades. She sat down at her laptop powering it up to use as a light source. She opened her pack to find her cell phone. It wasn't there. Kicky must have it.

She opened the door and peered outside. That's when she noticed they had moved. They were no longer parked in the back parking lot of the Sheriff's Department. They were parked in an alley behind a row of two story houses. She couldn't see Kicky or Ondag and wondered if she dared step outside to look for them. With the metal slats locked on the outside of all the windows, the door was the only exit or entrance to the vehicle. Very little could be seen. The men had chosen this alley because it was well hidden from any main thoroughfare. What were they hiding from? Where were they?

There was nothing to do but wait. She turned on the little TV set that was placed strategically so that anyone sitting in the dining area and the passenger seat could see it but the driver could not. She found the 5:00 P.M. news on one station but they had already passed into news that was not news, but filler content. She thought about ordering a pizza but didn't know where to tell them to deliver it. She looked into the fridge. It had been stocked with wine, beer, water, juice, and soft drinks. But they had not bought actual food. Chocolate. She had those mini Hershey bars. She wondered now if she should have bought those. Kicky might not be able to eat chocolate being that it was poisonous for dogs, even though he was not really a dog but a wolf, and not even really a wolf but a human shape shifter. Oh, my god, this was confusing. Tess was still getting used to the idea that her loving David was really Kicky and Kicky was really Woofy and Woofy was not her Woofy either. And what did Ondag mean when he said that Clyde adopted her? She felt like going back to sleep. Instead she sat down at her laptop and plugged it into the outlet wondering if this would run down the RV's battery. At this point she didn't care. She needed to get her mind off stuff. She began to write a review of the pasties they'd had for lunch but she was too hungry to think about food. Soon she abandoned all work and wrote an e-mail to her dad. But this too didn't help because what could she tell him? She didn't know what was going on. And where are those two men? Her protectors! Is this how they protect her by leaving her with no method of contacting them in an alley in a strange city god knows where?

She made up her mind to leave the motor home and go look for them when she heard her cell phone ringing. It was definitely her ring tone, but she couldn't find it. She followed the ring note to the back of the motor home when it abruptly stopped.

"Yeah?" said a voice. It was Kicky. He had been stationed at the back of the motor home this whole time. She couldn't see him through the metal slats. He was probably sitting on the aft storage shelf.

"No, still sleeping." Kicky said. "OK, we'll be here." Kicky hung up the phone with a snap. Tess tapped on the window to get his attention. He came around the motor home and she unlocked the door for him.

"What's going on?" Tess asked.

"Ondag thought he saw a jeep circling the parking lot about an hour ago. He thought it looked suspicious, so we decided to get the hell out of there"

"Agent Marcus told us to stay put. I mean how much danger could there be in the parking lot of the Sheriff's department."

"We just got nervous," he said. "So we found this alley which seemed secluded and I went over there to the house and asked if we could park here for a couple of hours. So I stayed here with your cell phone and Ondag went back to the Sheriff's Department to wait for Agent Marcus. Are you hungry? Would you like me to order a pizza? There's a good Italian Restaurant just down the street here on the corner."

"Oh, well, hasn't Agent Marcus called to tell you why he's late? I mean he was supposed to be here about an hour ago at least."

"Nope haven't heard." Kicky opened the lid on the phone and experimentally pushed a button. "I'm not sure how to work this. Maybe you have a message."

Tess took her phone from Kicky and looked at it. The message light was not flashing.

"Ok, I'm going to lock the door behind you. Here's my card. Get enough pizza for us and Ondag and whatever other stuff looks good on the menu. Get it to go and while you're down there take some pictures of the inside of the restaurant. Maybe tonight will not be wasted after all."

"OK Tess." Kicky said, taking her camera and credit card. "If they have a problem with you using that have them call me and I'll OK it. I guess maybe I should apply for one for you too, huh?"

"This is the only instance I can think of why I would need it."

"But it would have come in handy this afternoon, Huh?"

He smiled at her, kissed her on the lips and then stepped down out of the motor home. "Lock the door," he said as she watched him go.

She did so at once. OK, so she had the cell phone now. She could call her father. So why was she thinking about calling Clyde instead? The burning question in her mind was the adoption. What did it really mean to him? Did he really consider her his daughter? And what obligations did that put on her? Did she really need to be part of the tribe? How many fathers did one grown woman need after all? She was very touched with the loan of Ondag and the RV. But she knew this was only because of this Windigo character whoever he was. She sat down at her computer again and thought briefly about trying to write another Blog entry. She hadn't checked her e-mail lately. There was still ten minutes before 6:00 P.M. when another news program would begin. So she logged on to her account and found the e-mail from TR. He had sent her other correspondences? That was news to her. She checked her spam folder, nothing was there. She remembered the one line message on her Blog, "There you are," it had said. Signed "R". Did "R" stand for Rivershade? That's what Ondag and the others from Bay Mills called this Windigo, Rivershade.

She was plenty spooked now. She wished she could see outside to make sure no one was watching her. Oh god, she had the willies but bad. She remembered the e-mail's her father had told her about at his web address. He had been frightened by them. She had no idea what they said, but if they were anything at all like this one she understood why he had been so concerned. Where was Kicky? What was the name of that restaurant? She began to do a search of Italian restaurants in Marquette but she had no idea which they were near. She didn't know enough about their whereabouts to know which one was the one Kicky had gone to get their dinner. Maybe she should call Ondag. She needed to be in touch with someone she trusted, and right now too.

She called Ondag's cell. "Yeah?" he answered.

"It's me, Tess."

"Yeah?"

"I got an e-mail from someone who signs TR."

"Talbot Rivershade?"

"It is scaring the life out of me. He is seriously twisted. Do you think he can find me?"

"Don't say anything else. I'm coming over there. OK?"

"Do you think he knows where you are? Maybe he's waiting for you to give away my position."

"Damn, Tess, I hadn't thought of that."

"Have you heard from Agent Marcus or Deputy Morrison?" she asked.

"Not in more than an hour. Morrison called to say that they had to check out a call down in Sawyer at the base."

"What base?"

"The air force base."

"A call? Is it related to us?" Tess asked worry tingeing her voice.

"He implied that it was."

"He's on his way here," she said with the surety of something more than intuition. "If you come to meet us, how will you know you aren't being followed?"

"If he is driving that Jeep Wrangler I saw earlier I'll recognize it. I won't lead him back to you, Tess, trust me."

"Ondag," Tess said trying to keep the tears that were leaking down her cheeks out of her voice. "He says he wants me to be his wife."

"Gawd," was all he replied to that.

"You be careful," she said. "He doesn't care who he kills, and I don't want to lose you."

"You won't lose me. I'm your brother now you know?"

"What?" Tess asked.

"Yeah, I'm Clyde and Mary's son. They adopted you and that means you're my sister."

"Really? How many other siblings do we have?"

"A few."

"OK Bro, you be careful. I want you back!"

She snapped her phone closed. She noticed that it was 6:00 P.M. and turned on the TV. Top story of the evening on the local news was that the FBI had been called to the scene of a grisly murder which took place this afternoon near the former K.I. Sawyer Air force base. An M.P. had been killed after making a stop for a traffic violation. The offender, witnesses say, was a Native American man about age 25-30 wearing a black leather jacket and driving a white jeep wrangler. He had been clocked doing speeds in excess of 110 MPH. The perpetrator left the scene heading at top speeds toward Marquette. If you see him or the white jeep wrangler call local police at (it gave a number which Tess began dialing at once.). Do not try to approach this man, he is considered armed and dangerous.

"No fake," Tess said aloud as she waited for her call to connect. "My friend saw a jeep wrangler fitting that description in the parking lot of the Sheriff's Department about an hour and half ago."

She reported to the policeman who answered the phone. He asked for her to identify herself and she did so. "My friend is afraid he might be following him." She explained that the guy was actually after her. But she would tell her friend to call the police if he saw him again. The officer acted as though she was an hysterical paranoid and gave her the bums rush off the phone. She hung up swearing. Maybe she did sound crazy. But she called Ondag again right away.

"They just gave the profile of Rivershade on TV. Does he look like he's in his late twenties to thirty?"

"Yeah, he does, and so did the guy in the jeep." Ondag confirmed.

"Was it a white Jeep wrangler?" Tess asked.

"Yeah it was."

"That was him. He's here. I'm going to call Agent Marcus," Tess said.

"No, don't. Don't make any more calls. Rivershade might be able to triangulate and trace you. I'll call Marcus."

"OK, but listen, tell Agent Marcus that Rivershade has rigged his phone to call into his own whenever it gets used. I didn't even know people could do that, but in his e-mail, he said that he was intercepting all of Agent Marcus' phone calls. That's how he knew where to find us. I'm going to turn off the phone as soon as Kicky gets back."

"Where is Kicky?"

"He went down the road to get us some dinner."

"When did he leave?"

"About fifteen minutes ago."

"What's he getting?"

"Italian, Pizza, whatever else is on the menu that looks good."

"OK, I'll eat the leftovers later."

"Where are the keys to . . .?" Tess started to ask but Ondag interrupted her.

"Kicky knows." Ondag stopped her from saying anything more. "I'll see you soon, bye." He abruptly ended the call.

Oh this was infuriating, Tess thought. Anything could be happening out there. How would she know? It was certainly a bad idea to have sent Kicky out to a restaurant. Who knows how long it would take for what he ordered. She absently fingered the cell phone while watching the rest of the news broadcast. She was glad to see that it would not rain here in the next few days. If Agent Marcus catches Rivershade tonight, she and Kicky could still walk to the Copper Country over the next week. Yes, that was the right thing to do. Get your mind off of current difficulties by planning the future. Perfect.

She managed to ignore everything for a total of five minutes while she did a web search of restaurants in the Copper Country. She marked a few of them as possibilities and then looked at mapquest to plan how long it might take to hike up that way and back out again.

She was interrupted by a knock on the door and Kicky's voice. He was heavy laden with three pizza boxes a paper bag of food on top and a larger plastic bag with three different take out boxes hanging from his left wrist. She relieved him of the pizza boxes as he climbed into the motor home.

She quickly got him caught up with the news, as he set out the boxes on the counter and the take out containers on the table pushing her laptop to one side to make room. She took down a plate and began to choose the bits of the three meals and the three pizzas she wished to eat. She barely noticed the taste of the first bite because of telling him about the e-mail from Rivershade.

Kicky got an intense look on his face and then pulled the computer over in front of him to read it for himself. She told him that the white jeep wrangler that Ondag had seen had been heavily emphasized on the newscast. She hoped Rivershade had been arrested by now so they could contact Agent Marcus, and get their lives underway again.

All at once she realized that she was eating something that tasted fantastic. It had Italian sausage in it that was rife with flavorful seeds and herbs and it was encased in a pasta shell that was also stuffed with a variety of cheese and then baked. She decided maybe she had better start paying attention to her job.

This focus change happened for the best. Soon she was making notes of all the food before it was totally gone. She tugged the computer away from Kicky who had finally finished reading the e-mail and was sitting there with a dark look on his face. He stood abruptly and paced across the short distance between the table and the driver's seat.

"We gotta get this mutha!" he said. "This guy is way too sick to stay alive."

"I know, right?" she agreed then went back to making her notes.

"How can you just sit there doing your job when this guy is out there after you?" he shouted at her. He pounded his fist on the back of the driver's seat after looking around to find something that might withstand the attack. He didn't want to punch holes in the only thing that had the possibility of keeping them safe.

"What do you mean? What can I do about it? I have no control in this situation. In the mean time, I still have bills to pay and a job to do. So why not just do my job and not think about irrelevant things like getting raped by an insane werewolf."

She began to laugh, a note of hysteria tingeing the sound. "Hellfire, Did you hear what I just said. This whole thing is crazy, so don't get mad at me!"

"Hellfire?" he asked, amusement tipping his word. "You even swear like a Catholic girl."

They both broke into laughter. But it stopped abruptly when they heard a sound behind the RV. Kicky stood and went to the door. He opened it quickly and went outside closing it again behind him. Tess moved to the door and locked it. She wished again that she could see what was going on outside. Soon came a knock on the door. She unlocked the door and let them in.

Ondag went to the cupboard. Inside an upside down coffee mug he found the keys. He went outside and quickly removed the metal slats from the whole front of the RV and the two side windows so he could see the rearview mirrors. Then he came back inside and locked the door behind him. He drove onto a deserted side street and then kept to similar streets, turning every couple of blocks.

"Let's go over to the tourist park," Ondag said. "We scoped it out earlier. No one will think to look for us there."

"Hide in plain sight, good plan," Kicky agreed.

Ondag turned to look at the food, "I'm teaching you to drive Kicky. So I can eat once in a while."

"Sure, I know how to drive. I just don't have my license."

Tess looked at him sideways. "You don't?"

"Never actually got around to it."

They made it to the tourist park and when they turned in they pulled behind the office building. Kicky got out and watched the road closely while Ondag went into the office.

No one came by the road or pulled in. Kicky acted like he was rearranging the items on the storage shelf. When Ondag came out they got back into the motor home.

"I got a space in the woods by the back fence. No one will be able to see us from the road. It'll be fairly secluded back there." He told them.

"You'll be able to work back here. Kicky and I are going to go buy some second hand bikes. There's a St. Vincent DePaul a few blocks from here. We can go get some bikes to get around on. Or do you think we should buy an old car?" Ondag asked.

"I thought this RV was going to be our transportation," she said.

"We need something to get us around while we're parked."

"You're talking to someone who is used to walking everywhere."

"That's not safe right now," Ondag argued. "Maybe we should rent a car."

"Maybe we should all just chill for the night until we can get in touch with Agent Marcus and tell him where we landed."

There was a power hook up and a bath house at this park, something to be happy about, and they would all be able to sleep well tonight. All they needed was to set up a night watch.

Kicky sat next to Tess at the table. Ondag came and sat across from them. He opened a take out box and began eating. As they sat and ate together like a family the conversation took a decidedly more positive form. They made small talk about things they still needed for the motor home, ways they could trick it out to make it more useful and how Tess and Woofy could still hike through wilderness areas if they wished while Ondag drove on ahead to a camp site and parked to wait for them. In the end Tess agreed that the RV would work out just find for them all. Still, it seemed wrong to not have a tent or a sleeping bag just in case. But she agreed not to go out and buy them right away.

After they had their fill, Tess started writing up her review. The two men had a discussion about whether they should call Agent Marcus. The consensus was that they should if only to arrange a different meeting place.

Ondag dialed up Agent Marcus' number and handed the phone to Tess.

"Marcus," he answered.

"This is Tess, are you up in town yet?" she asked him. She had the instinct that she should keep this conversation to the point.

"Not yet, on my way. He's ahead of me so maybe you better move your location."

"We have, we're safe."

"Where are you?" he asked.

"I can't tell you that right now. Rivershade has your phone tagged somehow. He is hearing everything we are saying."

Abruptly the line went dead. Tess hung up on her end.

He called her back in minutes.

"I'm at a land line," he explained. "I am here in town at the police station. I've been waiting for you to call since you weren't at the rendezvous. Where are you?"

Tess gave him their location and he said he would be there with a car for them in a matter of ten to fifteen minutes.

"Pack up boys," Tess said. "We're going into protective custody."

They busied themselves gathering up the last of the food containers and their few belongings. As they waited Tess did the dishes and added a dish drainer and some kitchen towels to the list of things they needed for the RV. Ondag and Kicky put the metal slats back on the front windows again. Then Ondag walked down to the office to tell someone that they were staying longer. He had put the fee on Clyde's credit card so he told the woman in the office to charge that same card any additional expenses.

Ondag met Agent Marcus near the building and brought him back to their campsite. After making sure everything was stowed and locked they got in Marcus' car and left.

"What smells so good?" Marcus asked, looking at their luggage.

"It's some leftover Italian food," Tess told him, "from a local restaurant, Casa Calibria. It just got a great review from me. Are you hungry?"

"You bet," he said. "I'll eat something when we get to the safe house." They traveled a few miles on the back road and then he turned onto the highway going west. After another few miles they got on a road going southwest and then onto another heading west again. This road was entirely deserted and it wound through dense forest. He looked back through the rearview mirror often but there was nothing there. It was still light out but the sun in front of them was beginning to set. They turned off this road onto a two track in the woods. About a mile in they came upon what looked from the outside to be a hut.

"You kidding me," Ondag said. "Who offered up their deer camp as a safe house?"

"Hey it's got a working toilet, and a deck of cards, and sometimes the fridge works too. When there is no power outage."

"Are you sure about that?" Ondag said. Marcus opened the hut with a key. "I'm thinking I could have torn some boards off the siding and gotten in that way."

"I think that would be considered breaking and entering." Marcus said dryly.

"Not if I put the boards back up when I was finished!"

"It's summer so heat shouldn't be a problem. But if it gets too cold at night go ahead and make a fire. There's a wood pile back that way." He told them indicating a direction away from the road.

"Here's the key, I have to go back." Marcus told Ondag.

"We don't get a protective detail?" Tess asked.

"I'll send one of the guys out with some breakfast in the morning." He told them. "You aren't under arrest and I seriously doubt you will be found out here. You are free to come and go as you wish."

"We were traveling for about half an hour," Ondag said. "So we're what about twenty miles from town? With no vehicle? Yeah, I'm sure you want us coming and going as we wish."

"She just hiked across half of Alger County, I'm sure she could make it, I'm just saying you shouldn't try."

"We know this is for our protection, sir," Tess said to him. "But there should be someone here with a gun protecting us. After all there is a serial killer out there targeting us."

Agent Marcus took Tess by the shoulders, "No, Tess. He is targeting YOU!" he looked down into her eyes. "He will not find you, not out here. He's looking in the wrong place. As long as he keeps looking in that wrong place he will be caught. The best part about this plan is that we know what he looks like, where he is and what he's driving. He can't get away from us."

"OK, well what about food?" she asked.

"I told you, I'd send someone out with some tomorrow morning."

"No I mean you, right now, want some cold pizza?"

He bent his head and smiled. "Yeah, sure," he said and went inside the deer hut with them.

Twenty miles away in the back of a newly acquired van that he had traded a perfectly good Jeep Wrangler for, Rivershade watched the stolen computer screen as it tracked the GPS chip on

Agent Marcus' phone. It showed that he had stopped, but if he had started again in a few minutes Rivershade may have thought he was stopping to gas up. The fact that he stayed longer than a five minute rest stop, led Rivershade into thinking that he finally had them. The location of the safe house was locked into his tracking software now. He could bide his time and wait for all of them to go to sleep before he nabbed the girl.

Chapter 10

There was plenty of food left for Agent Marcus to eat. He finished off the supreme pizza saying that the sauce was one of the best he'd tasted ever. The manicotti also had its supporters. Everyone wished Kicky had bought two of those dinners.

It was an hour later when Marcus made his excuses and left their company. Tess followed Agent Marcus to his car to say goodbye. As Marcus drove off, to the East back toward town Kicky put his arm around Tess.

"Alone at last," he said in her ear.

"What did you do with Ondag?" she asked, 'Kill him?"

"Don't even joke like that," he said. "Much as I'd like to be alone with you right now, we are stuck with Ondag."

"Hey, what do you want," said Ondag from behind them. "I'll take a long walk in the woods so you can do the deed, but I'll be back in half an hour."

"Half an hour? Give me a break," Kicky said.

"What? Shouldn't take you longer than that," he said, pushing Kicky's shoulder.

"Stop you two," Tess interjected. "Enough of this. Who knows how long we'll have to be cooped up here together. We might as well make the best of this."

They went back into the cabin. Tess took out her computer and hooked up to the internet.

"Maybe that's not such a good idea," Ondag said.

"Why not? Do you think he might be able to trace me using my computer?"

"Is it worth the risk?"

Tess shook her head, in essence agreeing. She turned it off. She put the computer back in its slot in her pack with finality. The world would have to do without for a time.

"So what do we do?" Tess asked.

"Do you want to play cards?" Ondag asked. They all agreed this was probably the best thing to do until bedtime. But a search of the cupboards in the cabin came up with a Monopoly game that lacked the houses and hotels and the money. They also found a dice cup with four dice in it, not enough to play Yatzee and a picture puzzle in a plastic bag with no picture.

"What are the chances all the pieces are in here?" Tess asked hopefully. But both men just laughed.

Finally in a drawer in the kitchen area they found a deck of cards held together with a rubber band. It seemed short of a full deck though and when they examined it closer found that it was only the 9s through the aces and with the added fives.

"Wanna play Euchre?" Kicky asked.

"What's Euchre?" Tess asked.

"We need a fourth player for Euchre." Ondag said.

"Yeah, but how bored do you have to get before you start making up another person to play the fourth," Kicky quipped.

"He would be a really lousy player. He probably wouldn't even do the following suit rule."

"What's Euchre?" Tess asked again.

"We could teach Tessa to play, and then when the cop gets here in the morning with our breakfast we could corral him into a game."

"Are you thinking that this is the only game in this building that has all the parts to it?" Tess asked.

"It's a full Euchre deck, yes," Ondag told her.

"Well then, let's do it!" Tess agreed. They sat down, dealt the cards and gave her an overview of the rules playing a few rounds open and giving her some strategy hints. She had played Hearts before which is a similar game, but it took her some time to get used the jacks being the highest cards in the deck and the off jack being the left bower and counting as the trump suit.

"With only five tricks to take you would think that it would be a much simpler game, but it's not," Tess said. "It's actually harder because you can't make any mistakes or you end up losing the hand."

"True," Kicky said. He smiled at Tess. He was very proud of her, that she was able to catch on that fast.

They tried to play a few hands with Kicky and Ondag as partners and Tess playing both her own hand and that of her partner. Then they tried playing with Ondag as Tessa's partner and Kicky playing two hands at once. But in the end they gave it up. Tess suggested they try to play Monopoly and keep track of their money on paper or on a calculator. But the cabin had no paper and the idea of Tess using her computer was nixed at once.

"What is that smell?" Tess asked. Neither man could smell anything unusual so Tess tracked it down by herself. It was a pile of rags under the sink that had gone musty. She pushed them onto a snow shovel she found outside the shed and took them outside. Then she tried very hard to clean the spot where they had lain for several months with a paper towel and a bar of soap from the bathroom. But when she went into the bathroom to look for the soap and some towels she came out shuddering.

"This place has not seen a woman's touch ever!" She exclaimed. She then sent the men to find buckets and anything that could be used to clean with. They found a half a bottle of bleach and brought the rags back into the house. This was it. Tess filled the sink with water and poured in a cup of bleach. She swished the rags around in it for a while and then emptied the filthy water from the sink and repeated the process. In between she sent Ondag and Kicky into the bathroom with wet rags to wipe down the shower and sink. She told them not to touch the toilet until the shower and sink were clean. When the two men pronounced them clean she went in to check them herself and she herself re-cleaned both to her own satisfaction. She went back to her laundry, wringing out the rags she had used and washing them in the sink. She told the men to start on the toilet.

The two men were determined to do a better job on the toilet so that she wouldn't have to reclean it. And they were gratified with their efforts. When she came in to inspect it she was satisfied.

"If I get bored tomorrow, I'll come in here and see what I can do about this floor." She said.

She washed the rags one more time in the last of the bleach and hung them in the closet on wire hangers to dry.

"The wire is going to leave rust stains on all the rags, but it's the best I can do," she said.

The exertion had made them all a little tired. Kicky sat on the couch and Tess came to sit next to him. Ondag got comfortable in the chair across from them. Soon Tess scooted over and put Kicky's arm around her.

"We should make a list of things we need so we can give it to the guy when he comes with our breakfast." Ondag suggested.

"How about if he just brings the motor home? That would be good. That would be nearly everything we need." Kicky said.

"Hardly," Ondag disagreed. "We still need a lot of stuff to make that thing livable."

"Still, it's better than this place," Tess said.

"When your right, your right," Ondag agreed.

They fell silent for a time, each in their own thoughts. Then Tess blurted out what was foremost on her mind.

"Why did Clyde decide to adopt me?" she asked Ondag. "It couldn't have been just because of Kicky. I don't get it. What did I do that was so special that made him want to adopt me?"

Ondag chuckled. "It's not such a big thing, really. I'm not saying it happens a lot, but it does happen. Clyde sees someone in trouble and he wants to help. All of us do it. It's a feeling we get.

I can't explain it very well. Kicky must know about it."

"I've heard of it happening. But I come from a pretty exclusive clan. We don't often adopt members into our clan. If someone is Eagle Clan they usually show signs of it by the time they are in the 8th or 9th grade, and then we know that they are family, even if we didn't know before that. Up here though you only get one Eagle Clan person every third generation or something so it's harder for us to find those who are Eagle clan up here and adopt them into our clan down state."

"I didn't know you would do stuff like that," Ondag said. "We could have sent Rivershade to you all those years ago when we discovered he was Eagle Clan."

"Yeah, and the younger the better."

"But why did I get adopted?" Tess persisted.

"That wasn't an Indian thing. That was a Clyde thing." Ondag explained. "You gotta know my dad."

"Wait," Tess interrupted, "Clyde is your father?"

"Yeah, I thought you knew that."

"But his last name is Morrow and yours is Stark."

"Yeah, my birth father was Four Elk Stark. He was just passing through on a journey from a Canadian Huron tribe. My mom spent the night with him and got pregnant with me. They never got married, but she named me after him. Then she married Kevin Baker who was my dad for about six months until she caught him gambling and kicked him out. But then she married Clyde and decided not to change her name again because she said it was too much of a hassle. So we all have different last names. She had two more babies with Clyde, our sisters Kathryn May, and Whispering Girl. They are both away at college or you would have met them. But then there are the others who were adopted as well. Most of them have gone their own way but they all come back for the powwow in the summer."

"So again, you still haven't told me why Clyde adopted me, and why he is so willing to spend all this money on me."

"Clyde is a philanthropist. He has the means and the inclination. My mom kicked one guy out for gambling, but Clyde owns a casino. How do you figure that?"

"Yeah, I was wondering about that too." Tess said.

"Clyde doesn't gamble. He never risked anything in his life. He earned a bunch of money by opening a Bingo parlor in the late 70's and then turned it into a casino by selling shares to the other Indians up here. He keeps fifty-five families solvent with the earnings of the casino."

"Really?" Tess was amazed.

"Yeah, of course he has controlling interest, but he uses his share of the money to help people. He's got a scholarship fund and pays the tuition of sixteen different students. If he can't get them a scholarship then he adopts them and sends them to school with his own money."

"Wow, really?"

"He'd hate that I was telling you all of this, but you kept asking."

"So he saw that I needed help? I don't think I needed any help."

"You kidding me? The police brought you to the rez. Of course you needed help. The only thing he hates is to see people he admires mixed up with the police."

"I wasn't mixed up with the police. Deputy Morrison was just giving me a ride."

"Yeah but then he brought back the worst police, the FBI. Clyde hates the FBI more than he hates the police. The one thing he wanted more that anything else these past few weeks was to see that you got away from the FBI in one piece. That's why he sent me with you."

"Why?"

"To make sure you were safe, not just from Rivershade but from the FBI as well."

"And here I am in protective custody," she said, irony tingeing her voice.

"Yeah, well, this is better than dead at the hands of a lunatic."

Tess backed up a bit, "Yeah, but, why does Clyde admire me?"

"Well, aside from the fact that you are the chosen mate of an Eagle Clan man?"

"Yeah, aside from that," Tess said.

Ondag's face lost its mocking joviality that it usually displayed. He sat back in his chair and considered his words carefully before answering.

"Tess, think about who you are. You refused his offer of a job at the casino, and believe me, he would have made up a position for you that would have satisfied every need you had both financially and artistically. But you would rather be self-sufficient even if it puts your life in danger. You are paying your own student loans. You created a job for yourself in the field you wanted to be in. No one is beholden to you and you are beholden to no one. The only connections you have in your life are those that bring you joy and comfort. I think Clyde recognized all this in you and was touched by it."

"Is that why he called me "dear" last time I talked with him?" she asked trying to get the jovial nature of their relationship back.

Ondag gave her his half-smile and the joviality was back. "He said that to you?"

"Yeah, shocked the living hell out of me."

"Yeah," Ondag agreed. "It's not like him to use endearments."

"But, he gave you a credit card. Why would he do that?" Tess asked.

"It's a prepaid credit card," Ondag told her. "It has $20,000 on it."

"What? I can spend all that on my trip? Why would he do that? Why would he give me $20,000 to spend?"

Without missing a beat Ondag countered, "Because he didn't have 30 grand to spend on you."

Tess laughed. "No, I mean really. Why so much?"

"Think about it. What kind of a yearly salary do you think he could have? He owns a freaking casino. He probably makes millions of dollars every year. He pays dividends to his share holders, he puts probably 90% of his own income into charity work for the scholarships, and other charities to benefit Native Americans around the country, but he's still in the highest tax bracket the U.S. government has. So what does he do? He sets up trust funds for everyone he knows and he hires people, he gives them jobs and pays them to make up their own positions. I had no idea what I wanted to do with my life. I wasn't very good in school and didn't really want to go to college, so he gave me a job at the casino. I just enjoyed being a watchman and a bouncer, so that's what he paid me to do. Then when you came along, he had me drive you around and he asked me if I wanted to be your permanent chauffer. I jumped at the chance. I'm still on his payroll. He's paying me to be your chauffer and bodyguard."

"OK, so I get it now. In order for you to be paid to protect me, he had to adopt me."

"No, he adopted you because he wanted to adopt you, and then because you were adopted, he felt the need to have me protect you."

"Which came first?" She asked, "The chicken or the egg?"

"You came first," Ondag was clear on this issue. "You were adopted into the tribe practically the moment you checked into the hotel. When Clyde used his pass key to get you into the largest suite in the hotel we all knew that he was going to adopt you. You saw how fast word traveled on the rez."

"If all the elders knew I was going to be adopted then why did they treat me so badly that first day? They were making jokes about me and Kicky at their campfire in their own language and laughing at us in front of our face."

"I know. That was to see how long you would take it. Mom said you didn't take it very long. You stood up for yourself within about ten minutes, wanted to be let in on the joke."

"So I passed the test?"

"Yeah, with flying colors. You were always respectful of the elders, never giving insult or belittling anyone. You always listened to what they had to say and considered it before making your own decisions. That's exactly what they respect.

You did everything right. They approved of you by the second day, and agreed to the adoption."

"Why was there no ceremony, I mean why wasn't I told I was being adopted?"

"What would you have done?"

"I would have declined. I don't need another father. I have a father in Chicago. I don't want another mother, my mother died of Breast Cancer when I was fourteen. I am a grown woman, on my own and doing my own thing. I don't need extra family ties."

"Yeah, Clyde figured all that out. So that's why he didn't invite you to the ceremony."

"But, he's not legally required to do any of this. He's not my legal guardian. I don't even need a legal guardian. I'm 28 years old."

"It's not that kind of adoption. It's more like the kind of adoption that they used to do in Ancient Rome. Remember how the Roman Emperors would adopt someone as their heir, even if the person wasn't related to them at all."

"OK, so I'm heir to his Empire?" Tess asked, sarcasm tingeing her voice.

"Um, no. You are however protected. Clyde exacted a promise from Rivershade that he would never hurt someone who was related to him.

"So by adopting me, Clyde was making me part of the promise."

"Yeah, that's just a side benefit though. I don't believe that was the initial reason for the adoption."

"Alright, so I had no say in the matter at all."

"Not really." Ondag said.

"I should take this, not as a circumvention of my will but as a charitable act on Clyde's part."

"No, you should take it as an expression of his affection for you."

"Just that simple?"

"Yeah, just that simple," Ondag said, "Everything else is just a side benefit."

"The promise to not hurt his relatives, me being a relative. The $20,000 to outfit me in any way you see fit," Tess said, marking the list off with her fingers.

"Yeah but that was just the top figure," Ondag tried to interject but Tess spoke over him.

"You as my bodyguard/chauffer, not to mention the truck you were using before you got the motor home," she slowed then.

"It's my total pleasure," he said. "I do love you like a sister, you know."

She paused and smiled briefly, "Thank you," then she went back to counting on her fingers, "Next thing you know he's going to try to pay off my student loans."

"He probably already has," Ondag said.

"Has what? Tried or actually paid them off?"

"I know he's probably tried already. I don't know if he succeeded."

Tess stood and went to her computer.

"You shouldn't do that," Ondag warned her.

"You aren't stopping me," she said. She opened her computer and turned it on. Within minutes she was at the bank site requesting the balance on her student loans. It showed that the balance had been paid four days ago. There was a notification pending when the interest due was cleared. She would have been notified within about five more days that the balance had been paid.

"I did not ask for this," she said.

"You didn't ask for me either," Kicky interjected. "I supposed you could have done without me too?"

"You hardly fit in the same category."

"I kind of do," he said. "Am I not a protector of sorts, am I not someone in your life that you didn't expect or ask for?"

"But you're not a gift, your not charity. Unless you think that you are making a big sacrifice to be with me?"

"I am!" he admitted. "I'm making a big sacrifice to be with you. I sacrificed my senior year of high school so I could travel with you. I sacrificed my youth, I'm a thirty year old man now. Old before my time so I could be with you."

"High school?" she asked, "How old are you?"

"I told you, I'm a thirty year old man. And I will be for the next 90 years."

"Kicky," she said, but then she faltered. She didn't know how to respond to this. She just stammered, almost thinking she should apologize to him.

"It's OK, Tess. I would do anything for you. You're my mate. But what I said to you in the Soo is true. I have nothing to give you but myself. I'm not in the position to help you at all. I don't have Clyde's money, or Ondag's skill with vehicle maintenance, or your education. I have nothing to give you but my love."

Tess was dumbfounded. She had no idea what to say to her beloved Kicky. She would not have wanted to go on with out him. Not even after finding out what he was. After all was said and done she knew that she would want him around for life. It didn't matter why or how or if he ever amounted anything more than what he was now. He was hers, nothing else mattered.

"Listen," Ondag said. "I got something to say about all this."

Tess, still at a loss for words, looked at her brother. So did Kicky.

It took him a few seconds to gather his thoughts but then he began to speak. And they listened.

"Tess, you are the focal point of your life. You do realize that, correct?"

"Yes but everyone is the focal point of their own life."

"No, that's not true. Some of us have others as their focal point. It just so happens that you found Kicky and I nearly at the same time. You needed us and we were floundering. Kicky had a direction in which he was going but when he came across you, you became his new direction. I was just sitting there in my life waiting for a direction, and when I ran across you, you gave me that new direction. You are the focal point of both of our lives. There is nothing you can do about it. We're just here. I'm your brother, and Kicky is your mate. Age doesn't matter, or what we do for a living, or how we get out next meal. Nothing matters now except the three of us being together and doing what you need done."

"But Clyde's money," Tess began.

"Really doesn't matter!" Kicky said. "Clyde is not focused on you the way we are. He's just helping out however he can. Don't you think your own father would have paid off your student loan and bought you a motor home if he could have?"

"Yes, he would have," she said. "He offered to take out a second mortgage on the house in

Chicago to get me a van that I could sleep in. I refused because I knew he couldn't afford it."

"Well, Clyde can not only afford it, but you are helping him out with his tax problems by accepting his gifts," Ondag said.

Tess sat back and thought about this. "But," Ondag held up his hand to stop her from saying anything more.

"No, do not start your next sentence with that word," he told her.

"But," she said.

"Nope, think some other thought," he said.

"But Ondag," she began again.

"Nope, not going to let you speak until you accept this much."

"Accept? How can I . . ."

"Nope, stop right there." He said. He kept stopping her from speaking every time he heard a negative thought begin to come out of her mouth.

Finally she said, "All right." She waited and he did not stop her.

"All right," she said again and then wondered what could come next. "I will accept that you and Kicky are my entourage, and lord knows I need you both. But . . ."

"Nope," he said. "No buts, you are not allowed to continue this conversation while using that word."

"But," she said again.

"Nope!" he said.

Tess took a deep breath. "Are you saying I'm stubborn?"

"Very, and this is the only way I'm going to show you reason, by refusing to allow you to express your negativity."

"OK, so," she began.

"Nope." He said.

"You don't even know what I'm going to say," she said, exasperation tingeing her voice.

"OK, I'll listen but no negative statements, I mean it."

"I was just going to say that I accept that I have you and Kicky with me, and I accept that you will be my brother and my protector and my driver. I also accept that Kicky will be protecting me and staying with me and sometimes he'll be a wolf. And I accept that I will be financially responsible for both of you even though I can't pay you a salary yet."

"Nope," he said.

"Nope what?" she asked.

"Nope, that's a negative thought. You don't have to pay me, or even be financially responsible for me. I work for your father. And I'm your brother, I would do all of this for free because I love you."

"You love me?" she asked.

"Sure, in a brotherly way, why not?" he said, then realized this would require a negative statement on her part so he added, "Don't answer that."

"Do you have anything to say about this?" she asked Kicky.

"I don't care who loves you, as long as I'm the only one that gets to sleep with you." Kicky said.

"You are," she acknowledged, "You're the only one."

"Good." Kicky said and put his hand on her shoulder. "In fact, I don't see really how everyone who meets you doesn't automatically fall in love with you. I'm kind of blind that way. I see so much in you to love, that I can't understand why everyone doesn't love you like we do."

"You're so sweet," she told him.

Kicky just smiled and in that smile she saw the Kicky that she had met at the Great Moose restaurant, the young 18 year old that had given her a ride. She once again secretly hoped he was at least 18.

"As far as Clyde is concerned, you don't really even have to worry about his involvement. Now that we have the motor home, and as soon as we get back to it and can trick it out to meet all our needs, Clyde will more than likely be out of the picture. He's done his duty by you. I'm sure he feels that. He paid off your student loans, and he bought you some transportation. He's set me up with a trust fund that I can draw from for my own upkeep and he's paying me a salary on top of it to do this job, so I think he's finished. All you have to do is accept in your heart that he's done this much for you. You should probably not expect anything more until you and Kicky get married. Then he'll want to throw you a big wedding."

"I think my father will have something to say about that." Tess said.

"And no doubt you'll try to circumvent any entanglements by insisting on getting married in Vegas or something similarly ridiculous." Ondag said.

"Ondag, what about you? Don't you want to get married someday?" Tess asked.

"Someday, when I find someone else to revolve my life around."

Tess chuckled at this statement.

"How old are you?" she asked him.

"Old enough to know better," he said, then to Kicky, "What is it about her and age?"

"I've been thinking about it," he said to Ondag. "I think it's her way to place herself in the natural scheme of life. She needs to know how old everyone is so she knows if that person is wiser than she, or more experienced, or if she can teach them anything. I know that she treated me differently when she thought was 18 than when she thought I was thirty. I liked being thirty better. She was more respectful of me at that age."

"OK, so I'm thirty," Ondag said.

"Come on, really. I really want to know,"

"OK, I'm 24," Ondag said. "I've been working as a night watchman at the Casino for 6 years since I graduated from High school. How old are you?" he asked.

"I'm 28. I graduated from college 2 years ago. I have my master's degree in journalism, but couldn't find a job so I started out with the job that I wanted all along. I love food and I love to travel, and I love to write about both. So it's my dream job!"

"Good for you," Ondag said. "It's nice to have that clear of a focus as to what you want to do with your life."

"Yes it is," she said. "What about you, what did you dream about becoming when you were in High school?"

Ondag smiled sardonically, "I dreamed about being a high school graduate."

"Really, nothing past that?"

"Not really. Well, there was one thing that I thought about doing." He dropped off, reluctant to mention it.

"What?"

"When I was a kid," he said and hesitated again.

"Yeah?"

"I wanted to be a cowboy," he said grinning.

"Come on, tell me the truth," she said.

"Really, that's it. I wanted to be a cowboy. I wanted to ride horses and rope cattle and go on the rodeo circuit. I love horses."

"Are you kidding me?"

"Well, yes and no." he admitted.

"I do love to ride horses. Our tribe didn't really have many horses historically we only had a few, but I really liked them. I'm good with animals. I thought about opening up a ranch and teaching young people how to ride. I have a piece of land in mind. I was kind of thinking that I should buy it and go for it. I was on the verge of doing it but this came along."

"So you did have a direction that I took you from."

"Not really. It was a back-up plan actually. I didn't have enough money for the horses yet, and those type of businesses need a lot of start up capital or they end up failing. It's just a dream, I'll do it someday when I accumulate enough wealth, like Clyde says."

"What about you Kicky? Do you have dreams?"

"You fulfilled them all," he said.

"No come on, really. I want to know."

"OK, I had a dream. It's like this. Every person in my family has the same dream. My mother was in her late fifties when she found her mate. My father was in his early twenties when he imprinted on her. My oldest sister is now in her fifties and she still hasn't imprinted. My youngest sister, is now 25 and she imprinted on her mate when she was 4 years old. Very rarely does someone in my family imprint on their mate when they are in their early to mid twenties and their mate is too. My sister's husband is ten years older than she is. They were playmates at first then he was her babysitter, then he was off at college and when he came back she was in high school and they started dating. She got pregnant when she was 17 and quit school. Now she's 25 she has three kids of her own, one of which is five and has already imprinted on the neighbor girl who is also five years old."

"Every year of my life as I blew out the candles on my birthday cake, I've asked the same wish. I want to meet my mate this year. That's my dream. It's always been my dream. Before I knew you Tess, my life was a question mark. I don't care what kinds of sacrifices I have to make for you. It's worth it. I found you now rather than later. I didn't have to wait until I was half way finished with my life before finding you. I didn't have to wait for you to come of age. I didn't have to search you out. You just walked through my door one day and there you were, in my life. And you felt it too. I know you did."

"Oh please tell me your 18," Tess said.

"I've already told you, I'm thirty," he said in his deep rich voice that was wise past his years. "For the next thirty years no one is going to know any differently."

"Will you go grey when I do?"

"I will arrange that, yes."

"Will you live longer than me?"

"Probably. I'm probably going to live to be about 90 or 100."

"Will I live that long by association?"

"No, but our children will."

"How many children do you want to have?"

"That matters not at all, as many as we want, as many as God gives us."

"You believe in God?"

"Of course, you do. You still don't get it, what it means to be imprinted on me. You and I we are totally alike. We have the same thoughts and the same opinions. We are in love with each other and it will settle into a deep abiding love and appreciation for each other and the persons we are. Everything you have a strong opinion about will become my opinion also. Everything I feel strongly about, you will too. We are a united front for our children and all other outsiders, and everyone is an outsider, everyone but you and me. That's why I've been staying out of this conversation because I needed you to come around to accepting Clyde on your own, so that I could too."

"You have already accepted his gifts. You were the one telling me that I needed to pick out dishes for the motor home."

"I knew that you needed the motor home so I accepted it and knew that you would soon accept it too." He smiled at her. "Besides, it's not yet perfect. When I was Woofy I so wanted you to treat me like your mate but you refused. You wouldn't even touch my private parts when I was a wolf."

"I'm not a pervert," she said. She looked at Ondag when she said this. Ondag looked down at his hands

"I'm a human being, not a wolf. You are not a pervert who is in love with an animal. You are a healthy young woman in love with a man who happens to be able to shift into the form of an animal."

"Yes, and you'll have to shift back into a man if you want to be sexually intimate with me. Those are my strongly held opinions."

"I know that, but while I was stuck in that form, a little hand job might have been nice."

"Ok, I'm going out for a walk," Ondag said. Before anyone could object he was out the door and they were alone.

Tess looked up into Kicky's eyes. "What else is there about the bond we share that I need to know?"

"I can usually tell how you are feeling." he said. He waited for her to say something.

"You mean, ESP?"

He smiled. "That's kind of an antiquated term for it. It's actually closer to an acute sense of empathy."

"Can you read my mind?" she asked.

"No, not yet. I think people have to be together for a lot of years before they can tell what the other is thinking, and even then it might be that they just know each other really well. My Grandma and Grandpa say they sometimes have full conversations without saying a word aloud."

She sat there thinking about this for a long moment.

Then came a clear thought through her mind, I want you to kiss me, it said. He leaned over and kissed her. Then he sat back waiting for his next instruction. It came. Again.

He again leaned over and kissed her. He kept kissing her then. He lifted her at her command and took her into the only bedroom with a good bed. He laid her down on the bed and continued to kiss her. He closed the door when he stood to remove his clothes.

Ondag stayed outside for as long as he could but the mosquitoes were beginning to get thick in the woods, and he was driven back into the cabin just after the sunset. He lay down on the couch and put his head between two pillows so that he could not hear the sounds coming from the next room, and in this way he managed to get to sleep without dwelling too much on the fact that he was alone in this world.

Chapter 11

Rivershade slept. He woke shortly before the alarm went off at midnight and hurried to dress in his customary loose fitting jeans and t-shirt. Most of his clothing was purchased at thrift stores because he lost it every time he shifted. He always made sure there was an extra set of clothing in his car though so that he would not have to drive back to a peopled location naked. Only once had he lost his car in all these times shifting. He presumed that it was because he had begun to shift while he was still in the car and didn't know how to find it once he shifted back. But that was a fluke. He made sure to never do that again.

He checked the stolen computer for the GPS chip tracking. It was still in the same place. The safe house had to be in that vicinity. He folded up the laptop and stowed it in the front seat of the car. It was about 1 am when he finally arrived at the location. It was back in the woods behind some trees. He grew impatient and pulled over to the side of the road. He parked the car just off the road and got out. He could detect a smell through the trees but it was not strong. It smelled like someone had left rotting garbage in the garbage can too long.

This was undoubtedly someone's deer camp or cottage. They would have a bad surprise when they came back here in November. He started to make his way through the trees.

He still could see no structures but he thought that he might as well turn now as later. He would have a better shot at killing the two men if he were in his wolf form. He would have to try very hard to remember that he was going to use the woman for a mate and to not kill her right away. It didn't matter if he crippled her, she would survive. He reminded himself firmly that he was to bite her legs only and not too high up on her legs. He should only hamstring her so she couldn't run away from him while he slept off his change.

He was ready. His plan was set in his mind. He walked further into the forest. The smell was a little stronger. The house must be just ahead. He began to think about the injustices the world had dealt him. This always was a handy trigger for the change. He felt himself slipping into the vague state of mind that he had become addicted to. He broke through the trees just as he was about to phase into his wolf form and saw the terrible truth of his situation. There was no house before him, only a vast hillside full of garbage. He was in a dump. The cell phone that he had been tracking must have been thrown into a garbage truck and taken here. All at once he was so angry he could not keep himself from changing. His clothing tore off his body and he went mad with wild anger. After this his instinctive mind took over and his rational thought was lost to blind rage.

He woke the next day naked in a pile of garbage with insects crawling all over his body. He vomited at once upon awakening and barely withstood the pain of the experience. He purposely did not examine too closely what it was that he had eaten in the dump that night. He hoped it would pass soon.

But it did not. Whatever it was stayed in his system for two more days after that and by the time it was gone he was left weak and dehydrated. After several hot baths in an out of town motel room, forcing swigs of pink stomach medicine down with water to wash it down and then vomiting it back up almost at once, he finally was able to keep water in his stomach for more than an hour. It was then that he decided he had been out of it for too long already and went out for the first time to hunt his prey.

He began to look for camp sites as he had done before. The obvious choice was Marquette's tourist park. There he found no tents that smelled like Tess, but he did manage to catch a whiff of her on a motor home that was there. He decided to move out of the motel room and into a nearby camper that was occupied by an older couple. They were up from their winter home in Florida for the summer. A few quick questions let Rivershade know that they had no relatives nearby and that they had been planning to move on in about a week. He dispatched them in three minutes time and stashed their bodies in the back bedroom of their camper. He planned to be gone long before they would start to ripen.

While he stayed in their camper, situated right across from the motor home that smelled like Tessa and that animal she was fucking, he kept on e-mailing Tess, taunting her.

"Come out, come out, wherever you are. Ollie Ollie oxen free! Safe harbor, come on in! I am waiting patiently for you! Have you gone to

Chicago to see your father? I do hope so, because if you have we will soon meet, I have been here for days waiting for you. Your father I'm afraid, could not wait however."

He could come up with all sorts of interesting and insidious lies for her. After all, he had been taught to lie by the best liars in the world, white men.

She did not answer him, ever. He supposed that if the rolls had been reversed he would not answer either. So he didn't really mind. But it did bother him that no one seemed to care that there was a vehicle in that space across from him that didn't have anyone coming or going from it. No doubt that it belonged to them. Although where they got the money for such a thing he would like to know. Possibly that wretch Clyde Morrow was helping the girl. He did adopt her after all. It made Rivershade angry, so angry that he could feel himself slipping again. He had better get out of the tourist camp if he was going to change. He walked out behind the campgrounds and jumped the fence. Soon he was wandering aimlessly looking for food, walking sometimes on all fours and other times rising up on two legs and looking around the countryside for whole minutes stretched out to his full height of over seven feet. Soon he saw a herd of deer silently walking along bending their graceful necks to pluck up grasses from the ground, now and then eating vegetation right from the tree branches at eye level. Rivershade stalked and killed one of them. He howled when he did so. The howls were heard by neighboring houses in the forest and reported. When Rivershade woke again around 2:00 A.M., it was at the sound of barking dogs. He stood and tried to run. He was covered with the deer's blood and naked again. But he ran. He ran through the woods and finally found a house on a small tree farm. He broke into the garage and found in there a pair of work overalls and a ford ranger. He slid quickly into the overalls and hotwired the ranger in record time. As he drove out of the driveway a gun shot exploded the back window of the ranger but did not hit Rivershade. He was out of range in a minute's time and heading toward the back entrance of the tourist park.

Part Four: Abduction

Chapter 1

Tess, Kicky and Ondag stayed in the deer camp for three days.

On the first day, Tess handed over her computer to Special Agent Marcus so he could track any communications that came in from Rivershade. He asked to see her cell phone, called up the SIM card and added a tracking package onto it. This was a precaution. Marcus told Tess that she should wear her hoody with the big pocket everywhere she went and keep the cell phone with her at all times, even possibly sleeping with it in her pocket. He also downloaded the SIM card from Ondag's cell phone in case that would be useful to have as well. They were only to use the cells in extreme emergency.

Rivershade continued to elude the police. They couldn't track his location from his e-mails. He was using stolen computers with various ISD signatures. He was hiding his tracks well by going through upwards of 15 different servers all over the country. More than a few were in Chicago though. Marcus got an e-mail saying that Rivershade was in Chicago, a quick call to the Chicago office of the FBI proved that to be false.

Tess was spared the knowledge that her father had been questioned and taken into protective custody in Chicago. He had been released about ten hours later and told that it might be good for him to visit out of town friends for a while. He made arrangements to go to his sister's house in Benld, Illinois, and left without so much as packing a bag.

Kicky and Tess shared the bed in the back bedroom of the cabin. It was a thirty or forty year old mattress set up on an old fashioned spring bed and because of that it sagged so badly toward the center that the two of them found themselves cuddling together in the center of the mattress whether they wanted to or not.

"It's a one person bed for sure," Tess argued.

"I don't mind sleeping on the floor if I'm in my wolf form but I doubt you would like it," Kicky said.

"I'm not giving up the couch," Ondag informed them both. So they tried it that way one night, Kicky on the rug in front of the fire, Ondag on the couch and Tess in the bed. She woke the next morning with a back ache and complained even louder that it was too cold in there without her heater-dog of a boyfriend.

On the bright side, that first night was the only boring one that they had to spend. The deputy that brought them their breakfast in the form of groceries from a local market and camp store told them that the market was about a two mile walk from where they were. He also showed them an old camp trail that kept them out of sight of the main road. He drove them down to the market and back that first time and then stayed on for several hours on the temptation of a game of Euchre. Tess replaced the bottle of bleach with a fresh one and got some other cleaning supplies as well. She spent at least part of her days making the place barely livable. Kicky and Ondag ended up doing most of the cooking.

"Well, why do you think I wanted to be a restaurant critic," she quipped. "I can't cook!"

But she did the dishes almost entirely by herself. She claimed that the men couldn't get them clean enough for HER to eat off of.

By the third day she had broken out the puzzle in the plastic baggie again and started sorting the pieces for it. The pieces were smaller than any puzzle she had ever put together having given up the occupation when she was in her early teens. On the fourth day she realized that these were not the pieces of a puzzle but the pieces of two puzzles. So she swept one of them to one side of the table and began setting up the other one. Everyone who came into the cabin took up the challenge of sorting the pieces between the two puzzles. Luckily they both were not the sort of puzzles that would mesh in subject matter. One of them was a scene depicting what Tess thought was a covered bridge. The other was clearly an ice covered lake that looked like some sort of animal was walking on. Only the pine trees were similar but after a while Kicky said he could see the minute difference between the pine trees in the bridge scene and the ones in the snow-covered lake scene. He said that one was brighter than the other. So he was given the job of putting them together outside of the puzzles in order to fit them in later once they were connected.

They took a break on the fourth day to walk to the market. They met with no cars going there but they had to hide in the woods twice coming back. Ondag bought a Sudoku book. Tess opted for a new deck of cards and a variety puzzle book, along with their groceries. She also bought pens and a spiral bound notebook. She was used to writing every day and missed it. So she figured she would keep her hand in possibly by writing a short story or at least some journal entries.

This was also when they discovered the two lonely shelves of used books near the back of the store, and each picked out two for their own reading pleasure.

On the fifth day Tess woke with a pain in her lower back so bad that she complained ceaselessly.

"OK, that's it," Ondag said. "I'm sick of listening to you complain about that damn bed. You and Kicky can have the couch tonight and I'll sleep in the goddamn thing."

Kicky looked over at Tess and Tess looked back. It was the first time either of them had ever heard Ondag get angry about anything.

"Tell us how you really feel," Tess said. Ondag tried to keep a straight face after that but found that he couldn't and they all ended up laughing for a full ten minutes. It released a bunch of tension that they all realized had been building for a few days. They ended up sitting next to each other on the couch with Tessa's arms around both men. It felt so good to just be there. That they stayed in that position for some time.

But that night Ondag got angry again when the deputy arrived with yet another message from Agent Marcus that they would have to be there for another two days.

"Do you have any idea how uncomfortable this cabin is? There are only two places to sleep, the couch and the bed. That other room just has a bare mattress on the floor and it smelled so bad that no one wanted to sleep near it let alone on it. Tess has had the bed for four nights in a row and she has such a bad back ache that she wakes up complaining every day. Kicky sleeps on the rug in front of the fireplace and I have been sleeping on the couch. We want out motor home. I think if you go get it from the tourist park and bring it out here no one will be the wiser, then we can all get a good nights sleep."

The deputy said he would take it under advisement and see what Marcus thought about the idea.

"My brother," Tess said, patting him on the arm, "you are one heck of an arguer. I'm glad you're on my side!"

He smiled and gave her a big hug.

The next morning Agent Marcus and the Deputy both came out to the cabin. The deputy was driving the motor home and Agent Marcus followed behind in the sheriff's car. It was a bright Sunday morning and all three were happy to see the two law men and their RV.

"How about a game or two of Euchre?" Tess offered the two men.

The Deputy agreed but Marcus was more interested in how the two puzzles were faring. He sat down at the coffee table and added his two cents to the puzzles while Kicky and Tess trounced the other two in two games of Euchre.

"I'd almost say you were cheating," the deputy said to Kicky. "But I can't for the life of me figure out how. It's almost like you can read her mind."

Kicky just smiled. "Naw, no such thing," was all he would reply.

After the two law officers left Tess asked if Kicky wanted to go out for a walk in the woods. Ondag could see that she wanted to be alone with him so he said he was tired and wanted to take a nap.

They walked through the woods away from the road for a few yards. Then Kicky turned and swept Tess into his arms and kissed her soundly. She laughed.

"Put me down," she said.

"No," he said and kissed her again. "Isn't this why you wanted to come out here? So we could fool around a little?"

"No, it isn't," she said still laughing. "Quit tickling me or I'll pee my pants."

"Oh is that how it is?" he asked jokingly and kept his hands busy around her waist and backside.

"Stop it," she shouted. "I'll sic my brother on you." She could not stop laughing.

"Oh no, you won't. Besides I think he would be on my side."

"Oh no, he wouldn't. Our father sent him to protect me, possibly against you."

"OK really? You think so huh?" he finally set her down and walked away a few feet. "OK, I'll be good then. I really don't want to be on Ondag's bad side."

Tess calmed herself down and came after him jumping on his back. He grabbed her legs and held her on his back as he walked further into the woods. She kept giggling a little as they went and for a while he acted like he was her pony trotting and galloping with her on his back. But soon he just began to walk and they both became quiet. He still held her on his back and she draped her arms over his shoulders holding him around his chest. She found herself thinking about his arms and his legs and his broad muscular shoulders. How fortunate she was to have this fine man in her life. She laid her head against his neck and locked her legs around his waist, feet tangled together in front of him. He leaned his head back against her shoulder and turned it slightly so he could kiss her hair. She was overwhelmed with the feeling of joy. How could she love a man this much? She barely knew him but already she knew she loved him more than she would ever love another, or ever had. She thought about her father whom she loved dearly. Not even a contest. She loved Kicky more. She could barely stand how much she loved him. She thought for a brief moment that it was obscene how much she loved him.

"Methinks thou dost protest too much," said Kicky.

"What?"

"I love you too, you know," he said. "You don't have to prove it, we can just feel it and grow into it and act on it. We don't have to prove it, at least not to each other."

"What are you talking about?" Tess asked him.

"I just am saying. I know you love me, you don't have to make such a big issue about it."

"I didn't say a word," she said.

"I know, but you were feeling it."

"How do you know what I'm feeling?"

"I've always known what you were feeling," he said.

"Always?"

"Well, yeah," he said. "I mean I get the gist, I don't hear your thoughts like they are words spoken in my head, but I can usually tell the emotion and the pictures and the basic ideas you have in your mind. I can tell when your hungry, I can usually tell what foods you want to eat, and I can tell when you are dissatisfied with something, and usually I can make a good guess as to what is causing the problem."

"How long has this been going on?" she asked.

"Since the beginning," he answered.

"Ever since the day we met?"

"I imprinted on you the very instant I laid eyes on you. So, yeah," he said.

"Oh so it's an imprinting thing?"

"Well, maybe. I'm not entirely sure about that. Maybe it's just something I can do."

"But you have been listening in on my thoughts ever since you met me?"

"I think so. I mean, well, yeah I guess so." He still carried her on his back as he walked. She rather liked this position even though she was afraid he might be getting tired of carrying her.

"I'm not," he said.

"You're not what?" she asked.

"I'm not tired of carrying you."

"It's that clear? You literally can hear my exact thoughts?"

"Well, you were kind of broadcasting that one. You're a very clear broadcaster. Your thoughts are clean and well ordered."

"You were cheating at Euchre!" She accused.

"Well, yeah," he admitted. "I could very clearly hear what suit you wanted to name and I could also hear what good cards you thought you had so I played out to you so you could take as many tricks as could be. I didn't know how to tell you that. The thing is, I would still be able to hear your thoughts if you weren't my partner and I'd play purposefully against you in that case. So it would still be cheating."

"Can you hear anyone else's thoughts, Ondag's or your family members?"

"Since Ondag has been with us I've tried to figure out what he's thinking but I can't. He's very guarded. I could never do it with any of my family members. There were times when I thought I heard my mother's voice in my head but I'm not sure if it was mind reading or just her voice in my head, you know?"

"Oh yeah, I know what you mean. I sometimes hear my Dad warning me to be careful on the road, because he says that every time we talk. That's his voice in my head. But there has been no one else that you could communicate with telepathically?" she asked.

"Well, yeah, Kit."

"Kit?" Tess thought. "You mean Kit Kraft? Rick's daughter?"

"Yeah, she came up with all that stuff about Kicky being my real name instead of Woofy and she saw in my mind how I change. I asked her how she could understand me and she told me that she didn't know. She just could. We spent a good deal of time together that day and when I realized that she was hearing my human thoughts inside my wolf head I tested her out. She could hear and visualize everything I gave her. I found out most of this later when she started telling you about it."

"Wow," Tess said. Then realized what she said and reiterated, "WOW!"

"Yeah, I know, right?"

"But how come I can't hear your thoughts?"

"Well, let's test it. I was feeding love back to you when you were thinking about how much you loved me just now. Maybe you can hear me."

"OK, well let's stop talking now and just see where the conversation takes us."

Kicky did not say anything but Tess thought he agreed. He had stopped talking when she asked him too so it stood to reason that he was in agreement. This was hardly proof. Not a test at all, Tess thought.

Then what would be a good test? She thought. She waited for an answer but none seemed to come. So she allowed her mind to wander. Pretty soon she was once again thinking about his strong shoulders and wondering if he was getting tired yet. There was something about the way he shrugged his shoulders just then that let her know that he was not tired. She felt like she wouldn't mind if he carried her like this all day long. She wasn't sure how much exercise she was getting with him doing all the heavy work of carrying her, but she loved being in such close proximity of him and holding him like this in her arms while he had hold of her legs. It was romantic, it was fun. And Sexy.

Wait, this could not be her own thought. She never thought about things being sexy. It was her Catholic upbringing. All at once she was thinking about Kicky's naked body and about how as a wolf she would stroke his stomach and how that one time he had become aroused. She thought about how she had stopped stroking him and thought about the fact that Woofy was probably reacting toward her as if he were her mate. But clearly if Woofy was Kicky he was indeed her mate and what would be the harm if she were to move her hand down onto his Wolf member and stroke it. She was indeed picturing herself doing just that when she stopped.

"You are putting that thought into my head aren't you?"

"Of course I am. You already know that you would never touch an animal in a sexual way. You yourself said that it was too big a taboo."

"So why are you putting that thought into my head?" she accused.

"Because it was clearly not your own thought, but mine, it was a test, to see if you could hear my thoughts."

"Wait," she considered. "The thought about carrying me being sexy, that was your thought too wasn't it?"

"Yes, I'm finding this very sexy," he admitted.

"What other thoughts were yours?" she asked.

"I told you I could carry you all day, because I was really enjoying it, I told you that I loved you being so close to me and holding me with your arms and legs. I then told you that I'd love it even more if we were both naked and holding each other like this. That's when you started picturing me as a wolf with an erection and I told you that I'd love it if you would put your hand on it. You started to allow your mind to picture it. It was a total two sided conversation."

Tess considered all of this. "All of the thoughts seemed to be my own," she said. "Only the sexy thoughts were foreign ideas to me. I never think about things being sexy," she said.

"I know. I heard that part."

"Also the last part about the giving Woofy a hand job, I knew that wasn't my thought, at least not entirely."

"Actually, it was more yours than mine. I was thinking about us being together as totally human, you were the one who brought Woofy into the picture."

She shook her head. "I'm sure I only did that because I'm starting to accept that you and Woofy are one and the same."

"I'm not at all sure about that. I think you know it in your mind that we are the same, but I don't think you have accepted it in your heart. You still call me Kicky and him Woofy, like we are both two different entities. It's still that way inside your mind. I'm not sure if you will ever totally lose that, no matter how many times you see me shift."

"I agree that it's still pretty new," she admitted. "But I think I'll eventually start calling you Kicky even when you're a Wolf."

"We shall see." He said. "You want to try another silent conversation? It could be that the more we do it the more you will be able to distinguish between my inner voice and yours."

"Sure," she said. "But this time keep your mind out of the gutter."

"I will if you will," he smiled.

Chapter 2

The morning that Talbot Rivershade noticed that the motor home across from his camper was gone was also the morning he was going to try to do something about the stench emitting from the back bedroom. He was just as glad that he didn't have to. He grabbed the laptop belonging to the old couple and loaded it into a newly stolen car. He followed the GPS signal out into the city of Marquette and toward the southwest. He stayed a good five to six miles behind it at all times. Then it stopped in an area of state forest. He pulled off to the side of the road and waited.

In the time that he had spent in the camper with the two dead bodies of its former occupants he had changed his thinking about the shifter and about Morrow's son. They were kinsmen after all. He had promised Clyde that he would not hurt anyone related to him. He had no quarrel with Clyde Morrow's son. And the shifter, well, the shifter was Eagle Clan as was he himself. He would have to see the shifter as his kin. He had not harmed anyone that was his own kin not since the tragic accidental death of the old man Kineekuhowa. How much longer would that old man have lived though really? No one even knew how old he really was. There were rumors that he might have been as old as 140 years, but really, he didn't look much over a hundred. It was hard to tell.

But the girl, she was not really kin. Clyde may have adopted her but she was white, not at all a blood relation by any stretch. And yes, the shifter probably thought of her as his mate, but he would get over it. They were not legally wed. Rivershade could tell that she was highly evolved. He didn't know how he could tell this, but he could. He could always tell. Part of it was that the shifter had chosen her as mate. That was actually proof enough for him. He wouldn't know for sure until he tasted her.

Yes, that was it, wasn't it? The evolved females tasted different. He wasn't sure about evolved males. He was certain that he had eaten one or two of them as well but really it was the females that were his passion. That one at the KOA in Mackinaw City was not as evolved as the Contessa. But she was up there. He was certain that Contessa would be the most evolved human he would ever taste. He would try to keep her alive long enough to get two evolved babies on her. Meanwhile he could still nibble on her fingers and toes now and then. As long as he stemmed the blood flow and allowed her to heal in between. Then when she was in labor with her second child he would help her along by ripping out her guts and feeding on her entrails. He could hardly wait. His jaws began to leak saliva at the thought.

Discipline, Rivershade reminded himself. You cannot turn yet. You must wait until night fall at least. He calmed himself by thinking of the two men. He had not yet decided whether it would actually cause more anguish in her to let her think they were dead or to let her think they were alive and could not find her. The second one would give her hope, and a little bit of hope might go a long way to making her fight him. Sometimes the chase was good whether it was you chasing someone else or someone else chasing you. It was exciting. Will they catch me? Will I catch them? Will I get away? Will I have to turn and try to kill them if they get too close? Oh, the delightful dilemmas involved in this whole sticky business!

Rivershade clicked on the computer again and saw that the blip on the screen was still about five miles ahead of him. They were not moving. That was fine, maybe they would not move tonight. They thought they were safe enough.

He moved his car forward another mile and a half and found a two track off to the side of the road. He pulled into it and when he was satisfied that his car could not be seen from the road he shut it down, rolled down the windows and went to sleep. He awoke with the setting sun in his eyes and sweat trickling down his face. He got out of the car and went to the trunk. In the trunk was a cooler full of melting ice. He dipped his t-shirt into the ice water and sponged himself off. Then he moved the cooler to the back seat. After all, he would need more trunk space in a few hours.

He watched the sun set in front of him patiently waiting as it sunk into the ground before him. After dark he turned on the computer again and moved his car closer to the blip on the map. He was within a quarter mile of the Contessa. He would be so happy when she was finally his. He was very happy that he had gotten some sleep today. He was up for a long drive tonight. He would first get her out of the state. There was a small community up in Minnesota where he had a cottage on a lake. He could take her there. No one would find them there. He could keep her there for a few years, tasting her and giving his seed to her to make children. Maybe he wouldn't grow tired of her and use her up too fast as he had done with all the others. His offspring were scattered all around the world, being raised by grandparents and foster families, by strangers who know nothing about how special these children are. He prayed that someday he would find one that was Eagle Clan, that had his shifter gene, and together they would walk the earth. Mere humans would tremble at their passing.

Maybe the Contessa would be able to give him the Eagle Clan baby he craved. She was destined to be mother to a new generation of Eagle Clan. He just knew it!

He looked at the time in the corner of the computer screen. It was nearly midnight. He had been lost in his thoughts for more than five hours. Discipline, Talbot, he reminded himself. You must have discipline.

Another hour went by, and then another. He decided to chance it. He took his car to within a few thousand feet of the cottage. The motor home was there. Everything was dark. He turned off the motor and allowed the car to glide a little way further up the two track driveway. When it stopped he opened the car door as quietly as he could and then walked around to open the trunk. He left both open as he came closer to the motor home. He sniffed. Shifter and girl were in the motor home. Where was Morrow's boy?

He kept sniffing. He was not in the motor home. He went to the cabin. Sniffing he could tell, past the prevalent smell of bleach, that Morrow's kid was indeed in the back bedroom of this cabin, and further, he could tell the boy was asleep by the way he was snoring. He went back to the motor home. All was quiet inside. There was another prevalent smell in the motor home, but it was not bleach. It was semen. The wolf had ejaculated recently.

No, he thought. The bitch was in heat, was she? Well, good then. First I will clean out his seed from her womb and then I will insert my own. She will bear me sons but never him, he thought. He puffed out the air from his nostrils. Disgusting bitch! She would pay for this!

He quickly opened the door to the motor home and was surprised to see as he entered that the two people were not asleep. They had been wide awake, both of them and lying in each other's arms. They sprang up and the shifter was at the door of the bedroom before he could get there himself. The shifter barreled into him and knocked him backward sending him off balance and onto his back. That shifter was on him, his naked body splaying out over him. He could feel the disgusting bulk of his manhood against his own body and wanted to wretch. He pushed the cloth containing the chloroform into the shifters face and when the man had two swift breaths in him Rivershade pushed his unconscious body away from him. He kneeled on the shifters chest as he poured more chloroform into the cloth. He looked up at the bitch who was screaming her head off as she was getting dressed. She had pulled on shorts and a blue sweatshirt with a hood and big pocket. He smiled at her.

"That's all right," he said to her. "I'll take them off again when I want you."

He came toward her and she lifted a huge flashlight over her head and swung it down at him. He dodged it just in time and caught her arm. He so enjoyed the panicked look in her eyes as she realized she was well caught.

"No, no, no," he warned her. Then he pushed the cloth over her face. When she was down and out for the count he took her over his shoulder to the car and put her in the trunk. He was in the driver's seat in a moment. He had not thought about the other one, Morrow's boy, until he was already in the car and the car was running. Certainly the sound of the starting engine would wake him. Oh well, he had what he wanted. He left.

As he drove down the two-track to the road he saw the Morrow boy come out of the cabin. With his sharp eyes he could see a cell phone in the boy's hand and he could also see the boy getting up into the motor home. It was not long before he could see the lights of the motor home behind him. He just sped up a little. That motor home could not in any way keep up with the stolen car he was driving. He topped out at about 90 and soon he could no longer see the motor home's headlights in his rear view mirror. But he kept driving. Minnesota was still a three hour drive away. He would lose them once he crossed the border.

Chapter 3

Kicky became aware of a pounding headache and shortly after that he became aware of the movement of the RV under him. When he opened his eyes he could see that he was lying on the floor of the RV and Ondag was behind the wheel. A sharp pain on the back of his head made him groan and Ondag looked back at him.

"Get up bro," Ondag said to him. "You gotta strap in, I need to go faster."

"What's the matter?" Kicky asked. "Where's Tess?" With this question came the realization. Rivershade has her. He remembered everything now. Two simultaneous feelings in his head fought with each other, one the sharp pounding pain which made him long for about 12 more hours of sleep and the other, the sickening feeling that Tess was in danger and he couldn't find her. He couldn't give in to either of these feelings. He needed to focus on Tess. Where was she?

He gained his feet with the abiding grace of a buffalo calf and managed to make it back to the bedroom where he found his jeans. He sat on the bed to get them on his feet. Every movement seemed to be taking too long and was much harder and more strenuous than it should have been. But eventually he got them up over his hips and buttoned. He grabbed his t-shirt and headed back to the front of the RV. He took a bottle of water out of the fridge. That smell of chloroform still in his nostrils told him that he needed the water.

When Ondag saw him coming he said, "We gotta call Marcus, maybe he can track her. Does she have her cell phone?" Kicky quickly pulled his t-shirt over his head and grabbed Ondag's cell phone before he took the passenger seat next to Ondag. He pulled the seatbelt over him.

"Do you know where she is?" Kicky asked.

"No, not really. They were heading this way before I lost them. Damned RV," he said. "Thing might be a great place for us to live but it's not that good for a high speed chase."

"How long ago did you loose sight of them?" Kicky asked.

"Almost 20 minutes ago," Ondag said. "Man, I am so sorry. It was my idea to bring the RV out here, this is all my fault."

"What do you mean?"

"If we had left the RV in town, maybe Rivershade wouldn't have been able to find us."

"No. You were thinking of Tessa's comfort. So was I. None of this is your fault. Man, if it weren't for you we wouldn't be this close to her even now," Kicky said as he looked up Marcus' number and then connected. "Besides, Rivershade has been after us for a while. He would have found us no matter what."

"Maybe, but . . ." Ondag grimaced and pounded his fist on his thigh. Kicky knew the feeling. But he wouldn't let Ondag take the blame all onto himself.

Marcus answered the phone by saying his name.

"It's me Kicky. Can you tell me where Tessa's cell phone is right now? Rivershade has her."

"Aw, crap," he said. He could hear Marcus clicking a key board on the other end of the connection. "Yeah, I got her. She's coming up to 35 where it crosses the East branch of the Escanaba River. Are you calling from Ondag's phone?"

"Yes," Kicky confirmed. "Why?"

"Because you are only about three miles behind her. Stay on the line and I'll tell you when they turn."

"I have to plug in the charger so I don't lose power."

"Never mind. If they turn off I'll call you back, I'm on my way. If you see them stopped don't approach them on your own. Wait for me."

"The hell I will," Kicky said.

"The hell you will what?" Ondag asked.

"Wait for the cops to catch him. I'm not waiting for nothing. We're going to keep the pressure on him so he can't stop."

"Agreed," Ondag said. He smiled then, and Kicky understood what that smile was all about. He was happy to be doing something instead of beating himself up over losing her in the first place.

Kicky found the charger for Ondag's phone and plugged it into the lighter. As soon as that task was accomplished the phone rang.

"He's turned onto 41 heading west, past Ishpeming. How fast can you get on 41?"

Ondag made a turn without slowing down and they approached the highway.

“We’re almost there,” Kicky said.

In a matter of seconds they were on 41. Now that they were on the highway Ondag tried to crank up the speed to 80 MPH, but the RV would not get there. It seemed to be topping out at 74 MPH. Kicky saw that he was rocking in his seat trying to get it to move faster.

“Don’t sweat it, man,” Kicky said. “We’ll get there. Marcus is calling ahead to Baraga County Sheriff’s. They’ll stop him. Did you see what he was driving?”

“No, man, it’s too dark.”

“It’s OK, don’t sweat it. We’ll get her.”

“I know you have to believe that,” Ondag said.

“Nope, don’t even go there. I’m going to find her and she’ll be alive. You can count on that!” Ondag said no more. Kicky had to believe he was capable of keeping his mate alive, or what good would he be? Kicky is Eagle Clan. He was certain he had the powers to find his mate.

Kicky automatically focused on the one power that would give him the most information at this moment. He could read Tessa’s emotions, and sometimes her thoughts. Focusing on the road ahead of him, he pushed his mind forward, forward two miles, three miles, four miles. In his mind’s eye he raced ahead of the car like an eagle flying through the air. He passed car after car, swerving through curves on the road and soaring over trees. He finally caught up with a vehicle, a dark SUV with tinted windows. In the trunk, lying unconscious, was Tess. He tried to get into her mind to tell her they were following her, but he couldn’t so he stayed with her. His eyes were closed in his physical body but he was still aware of

Ondag. He thought Ondag might like to know what was going on.

"I'm with her," he told Ondag. "She's still unconscious."

"He probably gave her more chloroform," Ondag said. His voice was coming from miles away but Kicky could hear it like he was right next to him.

"I'm going to stay with her," Kicky told him. "They are in a Black SUV."

"Give me the cell phone," he told Kicky. Kicky felt around for it and found it in the cubby on the dash. He handed it in Ondag's direction. Ondag took it out of his hand.

Kicky focused entirely on Tess. He could see her face. Her eyes were closed. Kicky was right in front of her, not three inches from her nose. He would see when she opened her eyes. Would she see him there? Maybe if she started to come to before she opened her eyes he could get inside her mind and warn her to stay quiet and sham sleep. He pressed as close as he could to her face. He realized he was trying to get inside her head. He kept pressing, each time he was rebuffed. Nothing was more important than him getting in touch with an awake, alive Tess. His need was great.

He remembered when they first met. Tess was in her tent on the Grand Traverse Bay, on the beach. She had awakened in the middle of the night and he was keeping watch outside in his wolf form. She had awakened him and seen him. Later on that morning he had crawled back into the tent and lay next to her in his human form. He had been sleeping soundly when he was awakened by a feeling of mild anxiety. He woke to find that Tess was having a dream. He got dressed and left the tent before she knew he had been there.

He pushed again. This time there was less resistance. He kept pushing and pushing until finally he was in. She was no longer unconscious, she was sleeping. In fact she was dreaming. He addressed her directly in her dream. "Tess," he said. "When you wake up, keep your breathing steady and your eyes closed. Do you understand?" He looked straight at her.

"Who are you?" she asked. "You seem so familiar, like someone that I know intimately, but I've never seen you before."

"It's me, Kicky," he said.

"No, Kicky is a fantasy. You are too . . . ," she did not come up with a word.

"Did you hear what I told you?" he asked pointedly.

"Yes, but if you are Kicky, and I'm not saying that you aren't, then why would you care if I'm asleep or awake?"

"Just, do what I tell you," he said. "It's for your own safety."

"I'm safe enough, I have Woofy to protect me."

"Tess," he said. "I'm not there with you. You have to protect yourself."

"But who are you?" she said. "If I'm really asleep then I'm dreaming you and I must say you are so truly the man of my dreams. But if I'm dreaming then you are nothing more than a figment of my subconscious."

"I'm not going to argue with you, Tess, please just do as I ask?"

"I will, because if you are a figment of my subconscious than you have a vested interest in keeping me safe. And I will very definitely listen and do what you say. Now," she looked up at him sideways, "What is it that you want me to do?"

He repeated his instructions on what to do when she woke. No sooner did he finish that last of them that he felt the dream fall away. She was awake. She had not opened her eyes. He could feel that she too had a headache, or maybe it was his headache translating over to her. Her breathing was quiet. He decided to try to communicate with her again. He pushed a thought into her brain.

"Tess if you can hear me than answer silently," he waited.

"Kicky?" came the silent answer.

"Yes, Tess, it's me, now listen." He told her quickly what her entire situation was, how far behind her they were. They were in the RV and Marcus had called ahead to the Baraga County Sheriff's department and soon she would be free, but she had to stay quiet and asleep and not move. As long as she was unconscious Rivershade would keep moving and not bother her. At least this was Kicky's fervent hope.

"Where are you?" she asked inside her mind.

"I told you, I'm about 3 or 4 miles behind you. We're on 41 heading west. Ondag is driving the RV and we're closing in on you as fast as we can."

"Why can I hear your thoughts, you aren't here in this vehicle with me are you?" she asked.

"No, I'm sitting in the passenger seat of the RV. Ondag is driving. I've flown up here to be with you."

"Mentally, you mean?" she asked, puzzled. "I mean you can't change into a bird can you?"

"No, I can only change into a wolf." He

gave her a picture of his own face smiling and then he picked up her hand and kissed it.

"You are very good at this," she said. "I can see mental images that you're sending me?"

"Yes," he answered.

"We're slowing down," Tess said to him. "Can you feel that?"

"Yes, keep your eyes closed. Keep your body limp, don't brace yourself against the movement."

Kicky spoke aloud to Ondag without opening his eyes. "He's slowing down."

"Something is wrong. He is totally stopped now. Wait, something else."

Silently to Tess he said: "What's happening?"

"We made a left turn and now he's picking up speed again."

Kicky relayed this info to Ondag.

Ondag pushed the send button on his phone. Marcus answered on the first ring. Ondag told him that he thought Tess had turned off the road.

"According to the GPS they are still heading northwest on 41." Marcus said. "Do you think he found her cell phone?"

"Maybe," Ondag said. Kicky silently asked Tess, "Do you still have your cell phone? Can you check your pockets without stirring too much?"

He became aware of Tess moving her body slightly. The phone had been in her right hand pocket and when she slid her hand into it she found nothing. She left it there hoping her movement seemed like natural sleep adjustments.

Kicky felt himself get closer to her physical body. Ondag was traveling well in excess of 70 MPH and Tess seemed to be traveling at a comfortable 60. When they came to the turn off to 28 and Ondag kept going up to the north toward Baraga, Kicky realized that they were getting further away.

"You didn't take the turn," he told Ondag.

"What turn? I thought she was going north."

"No, you need to go west. She's going west. I can feel her getting farther away."

Ondag pounded on the brakes and pulled to the side of the road. He let several cars go past and made a K-turn. Soon he was back at the turn off for Highway 28 toward Duluth. "He's taking her to Minnesota," Ondag announced.

"I know," Kicky said, and then went back to Tess. "I'm with you," he said. "We just had to turn around. We are about 8 miles behind you."

"Good because if he stops then you'll be here," she told him.

"You bet I will," He said and again he sent her a mental picture of himself smiling at her.

Another hour passed in which nothing much happened. They stayed in contact with Tess who shammed sleep as long as she could. When they got to the Wisconsin Border the GPS in Rivershade's new car told him to take the exit toward U.S. 2 and continue on this road for a while. Tess relayed the information back through Kicky to Ondag who was about 4 miles back by this time. Rivershade was following all the speed limits, and Ondag was not. Ondag was only slowing when he neared a town where there might be police. At this rate, by the time they got to Duluth they would have caught up with him.

Meanwhile Ondag called Marcus every half hour with updates. They informed him that the tracking was no good, because Rivershade must have found Tessa's cell phone. Marcus's reply to that was, "Nuts!"

Ondag assured Marcus that they had another way to track her but he didn't elaborate. He told Marcus that they thought he was taking her to Minnesota. Marcus got on the horn and called the Duluth police, the Minnesota State police, and the Minneapolis office of the FBI, putting out an APB on the black or dark colored SUV, tinted windows, no info on the license plates, passengers included a man of about 30-40 years of age of Native American decent, and a Caucasian woman of about 25-30 wearing a hooded sweatshirt, possibly laying down unconscious in the backseat or trunk area. Approach with extreme caution. The man is a known serial killer.

The Amber alert went out even though Tess was not a child.

Chapter 4

In Ashland, Wisconsin, Rivershade stopped to get a bite to eat. He went into a diner and asked for two rare burgers to go and while there helped himself to a set of keys from the pocket of a jacket hanging by the door. The keys had an automatic door lock attached to it so when he left five minutes later with his take out box and the keys it was easy to find his new vehicle. He had cleverly left the keys to the SUV in the same jacket, as if someone would consider it an even trade. He then grabbed Tess and hoisted her into the front seat of the new car, a harvest gold Honda Matrix, and strapped her in with the take out box perched on her lap. He got in the drivers seat and they were off.

Rivershade thought it an equitable trade. He didn't even have to bother himself to kill anyone this time. He was truly anticipating the fun he would have with this tender young female of the evolved variety. She had been shamming sleep for the last hour and a half at least and even when he stopped for the burgers she had not let on. That take out box must be burning her bare legs badly but still she is shamming sleep. Maybe he should try to put an end to this sham.

Instead he took the box from her lap and setting on the dashboard, opened it to grab out a burger. They had been on the road for three and half hours, it was now nearly 6:00 A.M. He was just happy to have found an all night diner where he could get burgers for breakfast. He abhorred eggs. There was just something about his animal nature that could not eat an egg. He would not lower himself.

Once finished with both burgers (she would not get anything to eat unless she begged) he set about trying to figure out the best way to beat her sham. She was good. She had allowed her head to slag backward and her mouth to drop open. She might even allow drool to escape if he waited long enough. This thought amused him.

Now that he had a new car, he didn't think the authorities would find him as easily. Of course, the car was stolen but he had noticed that stolen cars got less notice than stolen people, and stolen people sometimes got little enough notice. That doggy of hers would stay on the trail right up to the copper country, but by the time he figured out his error they would be in Minnesota and at his backwoods camp by the lake. No one would find them. He would get rid of the car which no one would also find. They could then just live out their domestic fantasy life. She would bear him a son, maybe one like himself, and then she would bear him a daughter. At least he hoped she would be evolved enough to survive mating with him twice. Then they would live out their lives together up here like a true family. He could teach his children everything they would need to know as full members of the Eagle clan. Maybe they would be evolved enough to be like bird people. That would be sweet! He could give birth to bird people with all the powers that they possess. And he would be father to these bird people. They would be loyal to him. He could start his own clan and they would revere him as their leader, chief medicine man and grandfather. He could then gather all his children from across the globe and they would all flock to him like lambs. They would all become part of his grand scheme. He would take back the tribal lands, and he would set his children to cleansing the people of their white neighbors.

Oh but, these grand plans will have to wait. First I must convert the mother of my first bird people son. Her conversion would take months. Rivershade knew he would triumph though since he had the Stockholm syndrome to count on. He had abducted this young woman. And eventually she would begin to see things his way simply as a matter of survival.

But oh, this sham sleep was upsetting. He was sated now with those two rare burgers in his stomach. He wasn't in danger of eating her, as he had been not an hour earlier. It was time to stop this.

"Hm, my," he said aloud. "I wonder what she would do if she were awake." He waited a moment then added. "That spider is dropping down right into her mouth."

Her head was facing a bit away from him but he could tell from the tightening of the one eye on his side that the other eye had opened to make sure there was no spider. Too late she realized her mistake.

She closed her mouth and opened her eyes. "How did you know?"

"My dear girl," he said. "You snore. But you stopped snoring nearly two hours ago. I've only just gotten tired of your sham. We have a few more hours ahead of us and I want to start doing some planning with you."

"Where are you taking me?"

"Oh my darling, evolved girl," he said. "That is on a need to know basis and you don't ever need to know. Let us just suffice it to say that I am taking you home, for this will become your home and you will be mother to all my children. I intend to begin a new tribe with myself as the grandfather, and you as the grandmother."

"I don't understand you," Tess said. "How is that possible? Would you have our children marry one another?"

"Oh my dear, yes. My children are out there spread far wide. I will begin to gather them in. They will all live on my plantation with us as their parents and when they choose mates it will be among their siblings, at least until we have culled out all of the undesirable DNA from our tribe. You, my evolved one, will be their mother as well as mother to our own natural children. I will try to be gentle with you, not like my other wives. I want you to have many children, a dozen at least, and share my body many many times. I cannot wait to introduce you to my first son. He will be your servant. He is up at the compound right now. He is awaiting your arrival. He will make sure you have everything you desire."

"He's to be my jailer," Tess said.

"No, don't think of it like that. I don't wish you to be a prisoner there. I just want you to look upon it as your home."

Rivershade saw that Tess had closed her

eyes again. Maybe the light was too much for her. The rising sun was at their backs. He checked the mirrors. They were not reflecting sun into her eyes. Maybe it was a headache from the chloroform. He dismissed it from his mind. His true focus was not with her minor ailments. He had a bigger job to do. He had to begin her indoctrination.

"You really should consider yourself very lucky," he told her. "There are not many women who are as evolved as you. You must have some of the powers of your ancestors. Have you noticed any?"

"What do you mean? I don't have a clue what you're talking about. My ancestors came from Ireland."

"Yes, I've studied anthropology and sociology. You're descended from the Druids, a line of very powerful magic users, or as they used to call them, Witches. Oh, excuse me, the P.C. term is wiccans. Or did you not know?"

"I've heard of the Druids, but I didn't know I was descended from them. How do you know this?"

"Do you remember the chipmunk? The camera is not the only thing I stole from you that day. I took one single hair from your hair brush. It contained your DNA. I have also studied medicine and forensics. I was able to extract your DNA molecule from the hair. It told me a great deal about you. Of course I never would have found you if it hadn't been for that Eagle Clan dog that has been following you around. You like mating with dogs? You will love me then!"

"You disgust me," she spat.

"Oh that's neither here nor there. You my dear one, have not answered my question. Have you any of the powers of your ancestors?"

"I have no idea what you talking about. I'm just a regular person. I'm a reporter and I have debts to pay, and a job to do."

"No, no, certainly not, that's all behind you."

"No, I have a lot of people who won't rest until they find me."

"Not if they think you are dead," Rivershade said. He felt warm satisfaction come over him. "I have a daughter about your age and height. She just hasn't lived up to her potential, you know. It will be a very simple thing for me to make her look like a dead version of you. Dress her in your clothing, put your cell phone in her pocket and leave her beaten in face in a burning car. I would have to beat in her face and remove most of her teeth, because your dental records wouldn't match hers. With her fingerprints removed with fire the only things to identify her would be the personal effects found with her body. Your loved ones would mourn, oh it gives me shivers to think how that dog of yours will howl, but eventually they would go about their lives and forget all about you."

Tess had her hands over her eyes the entire time Rivershade was giving her this diatribe. But now she was looking up at the road. Stress? Perhaps? He thought. Good, keep going. I will have her yet.

"You see," he said after a pause, "I have studied for a good long time. After I found out what I was, I wished to find others like me. I didn't know about the Eagle Clan until about twenty years ago, so I was unable to go to them as some of my ancestors might have. By the time I found out about them it was already too late. My plans had been set." He lifted his shoulders in a shrug. This studied move was one that he had determined would put people at ease. But his evolved woman had not even noticed. Was she even listening to him?

"Am I boring you with all my plans?" he asked. "I don't wish to bore you."

She looked over at him. "I'm just, I'm thinking," she said.

"You don't have to think, you know. I'll do all the thinking for the clan from now on."

"Can we stop and get some food. Look there is Burger King in another two miles. A quick drive through and I'll be in a much better mood to talk."

Rivershade looked up at the sign they were passing. Burger King 2 miles ahead.

"Of course, my dear," he said and reached over to stroke her cheek with one finger. He was happy to see that she barely flinched at his touch.

Chapter 5

Two minutes after Tess mentioned the sign for Burger King, Ondag and Kicky came upon it. Kicky mentally told Tess that they were only about two miles behind her. If she was able to get Rivershade to stop even long enough to use the drive through, they would have caught up. Marcus was still about twenty miles behind. Soon Tess relayed the message that they had indeed stopped. She told him mentally to pull around to the back of the parking lot and she would make a run for the RV.

She knew that it would take a few minutes for Kicky to get there, so she waited in line with Rivershade and told him what she wanted to eat. Then she excused herself to use the toilet.

"You aren't planning to bolt on me, are you?" he asked quietly in her ear, he had his hand at the back of her neck and squeezed it. A young man in line behind them saw her tense under Rivershade's grasp so he backed off, "Ok, honey," he said. "I'll wait for you in the dining room." Tess realized he had tried to make it sound sweet and thoughtful. He hadn't pulled it off. The young man behind her in line looked like he wanted to follow her to see if she was OK. That's all she needed, another white knight getting in the way of her rescue. She smiled sweetly at Rivershade and gave him a kiss on the cheek.

"I'll be right back," she said. She glanced at the fellow behind her and smiled brightly at him.

The smile faded quickly as she made her way to the restroom. There was a back door next to the restrooms and she tested it to make sure it was open. Too late she looked back to be sure Rivershade hadn't noticed this. He could not be seen from his place in line. She went into the restroom and sat down. Once her overstuffed bladder had been voided she contacted Kicky again. They were pulling into the parking lot. Kicky reported that he saw where the gold Honda was parked and he could see no one inside it. They were pulling up behind the drive through lane where there were several parking places for vehicles pulling trailers. It would be a short run. Tess slowly washed her hands and dried them pushing the button on the air drier twice before all the moisture was gone. She didn't want hand slippage to ruin her chances. She took several deep breaths and then bolted out the bathroom door and out the back door of the restaurant.

Once outside she saw Rivershade ahead of her holding a long Bowie knife. He moved to intercept her. She darted away from him and barely missed the slash of the knife that might have hit her arm had she not lifted it at the last instant. She ran out and away from him and angled back in an all out sprint to get to the RV. As she ran she saw that Kicky had come out. He saw Rivershade close behind her. She shouted for him to get back inside. He ignored her. It was his intension to get between them and possibly get himself killed, she thought. She screamed again.

"Get back inside!" Her voice startled him and he did as she said. He turned to get back to the door. She came around the back of the RV and saw that Kicky was holding the door open for her. But just as she was about to ease up on her speed to make the jump into the open door she felt someone grab her hair. Her head was yanked back hard, her forward momentum halted. She fell on her backside next to the back tire of the RV. Kicky turned back to help her, but saw the knife. Rivershade had the point of the knife on her neck. One slow movement would sever her jugular. Kicky stopped and held up his hands.

"Let her go," he said.

Rivershade laughed. He took the knife away from her neck and put it across her throat. One swift movement would still be the end of her. But he didn't slit her throat. Instead he slashed the tire of the RV. He lifted Tess by her hair and put the knife back at her neck. He then began moving the two of them at once backward toward the back of the RV. The young man who had been behind them in line was standing next to a truck, one foot inside the truck and he had his cell phone out.

"Look at who's calling the police," he told Tess in her ear.

He went over to the man and asked very politely for his phone and truck keys. The truck had a logo on the side "Bob's heating and cooling."

"Are you Bob?" Rivershade asked the man.

"No," he said. He handed the keys and the cell phone over to Rivershade and stepped away from the truck.

"Explain this to your boss then," he said and pushed Tess into the truck ahead of him. He climbed in and started it up. As Tess watched Kicky race around the back of the RV, Rivershade pulled the truck out and sped into the lane of traffic causing at least two cars to swerve and brake hard. Kicky kept running after them after all hope was lost that he would catch up.

"There," Talbot said. "That should put some distance between us." He looked down at the phone. It was engaged. He put it up to his ear. "Hello?" he tested.

"Are you alright sir?" came the voice.

"Yes, we're fine, to whom am I speaking?"

"911 dispatch. Are you certain your fine?"

"The former owner of this phone just had his truck stolen. But I'm fine."

"Can you give me the details of the theft, is he alright? Does he need an ambulance besides police?"

"Possibly, um, how long will it take for the police to get here?"

"I've dispatched two cruisers which were in your area. They should arrive in about five minutes."

"Good, the man's truck was a delivery style panel van with the words something Caterers on it. It was white I don't know the make."

"Thank you sir, you've been very helpful, he said that someone was being abducted, did you see anything like that going on?"

"Why no, nothing like that. My girlfriend and I were simply having some breakfast and we saw the theft as we were getting into the car. It had something to do with an RV with a flat tire. I think maybe one of the owners of the RV needed a ride and stole the vehicle. The thief left two of them on the scene. They will probably know something about the whole mess."

"Thank you sir, I'll inform the police. How did you get a hold of the man's phone?"

"He dropped it in pursuit and I picked it up. I saw that he was trying to call the police so I decided to help out and finish the call."

"So you are still at the scene?"

"Yes, I am. It's not legal to leave the scene of a crime is it?"

"Is the man OK?"

"I think so. He is cursing up a storm. Not sure how he's going to explain this to his boss. There must have been several hundred dollars worth of equipment in his truck." As he said this he glanced out the rear view mirror to the back of the truck.

"The police are coming, I can hear the sirens," he said. "I'll hang up now."

"Yes sir, and thank you."

Rivershade pressed "end" and flung the phone out the window. It barely missed an on-coming car. He laughed as he put his hand back on the steering wheel.

He looked over at Tess. Tess had dreaded this moment. When he pulled her hair he had given her whiplash, her shoulders and neck ached horribly. She had bruises on her backside. She was afraid her tail bone might be broken because she was having a hard time moving her legs. On top of that, when Rivershade pushed her into the front seat of the truck he had accidentally slid the knife blade along her arm and there was a two inch long gash in her arm and sweatshirt that was bleeding enough to cause the entire arm of her sweatshirt to be saturated. When Rivershade looked over at Tess he smiled again.

"Blood! No wonder I'm so hungry," he said. "Don't make me angry, or I might just devour you."

He pulled over to the side of the road and bade her take off the sweatshirt.

"No," she said.

"No? It's soaked with blood."

"I'm not taking it off, it's all I'm wearing, that and my shorts."

"Oh," he said smiling again. "And you wish to keep me in suspense of your body a while longer. Don't worry about that, I'll see you naked soon enough."

Tess clasped her hand over the wound and tried to put enough pressure on it to stop the bleeding. All she got for her efforts was a wet sticky hand.

"I'm going to bleed out soon if this doesn't stop and then you won't have anyone to rape."

"Indeed," he said. He pulled over to the shoulder and undid his belt buckle.

"So you're going to rape me now?" she asked.

"I'm going to tie a tourniquet. It will hold until I can get somewhere that I can buy some bandages and a first aid kit. We'll be in Duluth soon. That's a big enough town to have a Riteaid. And what's the matter with your neck?" he asked.

Tess realized that he had noticed how she turned her upper torso instead of just her head. "I think you gave me whiplash when you pulled on my hair."

He made a clicking sound behind his teeth

and shook his head at her. "Poor Contessa, you are in bad shape, aren't you? But, I suppose that all explains why you didn't just jump back out of that side of the truck and run again. Are you even capable of running now?"

"I would enjoy the opportunity to try," she said.

"Well, first we need a new car." He told her. "I suppose any old thing would work." He got out and lifted the hood of the truck. He stood looking under for a time. Soon an elderly man pulled up, got out of his car and came up to Rivershade. "Got engine problems?" he asked.

"Nope, just needed a change," he told the man. Tess watched helplessly as Rivershade stabbed the man high under his ribs and then went through his pockets. He took keys, wallet and even the change in his front pocket. He pulled the dead man over to the side of the road and hid him in the ditch. Then he went to Tessa's side of the car and opened her door. She didn't move to get out fast enough for him so he pulled on her good arm.

"I'll do it, you beat me to hell and back and you want me to be as good as new? Forget it," she told him. She turned her body outward and lifted herself laboriously out of the passenger seat. She limped over to the new car, a Lexus. "Let me get in the back and lay down. I think you busted my coccyx," she said.

He opened the back door of the Lexus and she climbed in getting blood all over the white leather interior.

By noon, they had gotten to Duluth. No one seemed to be behind them and no one stopped them in their new vehicle either. There didn't seem to be much Tess could do about her situation so she just lay in the back seat and tried to stay in contact with Kicky, who was falling further and further behind her.

In Duluth, Rivershade stopped at Wal-Mart. He used some wet-ones that he found in the glove compartment to clean up the blood from his hands and then sat for a moment.

"Now," he said aloud. "How am I going to make sure you don't leave while I'm in the store?" he asked her.

"I can barely move," she said.

"Barely. But I think you might try if I don't devise some scheme to get you to stay. I supposed I could take you with me. But that wouldn't look good, now would it?" He put a finger on his cheek as if pondering. A woman walked by wheeling a cart with a toddler in it. He opened the door.

"Oh Ma'am," he called to her. She stopped for a moment. "Could you come here? I have a question for you."

"I'm sorry," she said. "I'm in kind of a hurry." She walked on a little faster pushing the cart away. He went after her. Tess covered her face. She didn't want to see him kill her. But nothing happened. He was just talking with her. When they came back to the car he was laughing and telling her, "No really, see. I'm not a bad guy. She's just really hurt bad. I have to get her some bandages and some new clean clothes."

"Well, OK." The woman opened the car door and sat on the back seat the whole time holding onto the cart with the boy in the child seat.

"I'll just take your cart in with me while I get the stuff I need." Rivershade told her.

"No, let me get my son out then."

"No, my dear lady," he said. "I'll be taking

your son with me. Let's call it insurance. You need to watch my girlfriend and make sure she doesn't leave. If you or her or you both are gone when I get back, your son will pay with his life. I promise not to hurt him, if you do as I say. Oh, one more thing. Have you a cell phone?" She reached into her bag. He didn't bother with that, he took the whole bag. The boy in the cart began to cry almost at once as they walked away. The mother had started after him but he flashed the knife as he put it back in its sheath at his back. She sat back down in the car.

"Will he do as he said," she asked Tess.

"I don't know. He kidnapped me. He murdered someone right in front of me. He's got me pretty badly beaten up. He wants to rape me, but he has to lose my friends first. They are following me. If he does let you go will you call the FBI and ask for Special Agent Marcus in Michigan. He's the one on my case. If you can tell which way we are heading when we leave tell him that and also tell him that we're in a tan colored Lexus, see if you can memorize the license plate number."

"Do you think he will let us go, knowing we have seen him and can identify him?"

"I don't know. I don't want to lie to you. I just don't know. If you act all docile and thank him then maybe he'll let you go. When he comes back just tell him thank you over and over and grab your kid and carry him away. I'll try to distract him so you can get away."

"Will it work?"

"I don't know. We have to try."

They sat silently for a time and finally she saw him come out. He was wheeling the cart and the baby seemed to be alright. His face was smeared with chocolate and he had a giant ice cream cone in his hands. It was dripping all over the cart. "There you go," he told the mother. "He should be wired for speed all afternoon now. You won't have time to report anything now, will you?"

"I won't report you, I promise. Thank you, thank you so much. I'll just go now." She grabbed her son so fast that the ice cream cone came down on her shoulder and got in her hair. She walked away as quickly as she could. She hadn't even noticed that he still had her bag. She walked back to her car and when she realized she had no keys she walked away from the car. Rivershade just watched her for a long time. Joy shone on his face.

"She's so happy to be alive that she doesn't even care about anything else." He said. "Once in a while I leave people alive just so I can see their idiocy. It gives my heart such a warm feeling!"

He took the bags out of the cart and threw them into the back seat. He got in the front and drove out of the parking lot.

Tess struggled to sit up and looked inside the bags. First of all there was a receipt. She thought this was odd then realized that he had bought all of these things with the woman's credit card which was also still in the bag. There were new clothes for her, two sizes too big but that was better than too small. There were bandages, a sewing kit, alcohol, matches, and antibacterial salve. She wondered if he was intending to sew her wound closed himself. In another bag there was a bottle of whiskey and some snacks. He had gone down the candy isle and filled a bag with chocolates, M&M's, truffles, chips, pretzels and all other forms of junk food. Some of the bags were opened, probably to shut up the youngster while shopping. There was also about three hundred dollars worth of 20's in the woman's purse. She looked at the receipt again. He had made a cash withdrawal on her MasterCard. How could he have done that without her PIN number? But upon closer inspection a four digit number was drawn onto the card itself with black fine line ink. How foolish to do something like that, she thought. But then, Tess thought, she would rather be this trusting and lose a few hundred dollars than be untrusting and lose her son. She hoped someone came along and helped the woman soon. There couldn't be two Rivershade's in the area today.

"Has the bleeding stopped yet?" he asked her.

"It's not seeping as much," she said.

"OK, I think we need to get out of town. I'm not going to spend the night here. Your friends all know that we were headed to Duluth. So I'm going to go somewhere else now." He had gotten on the highway again and was headed west, she thought. Sitting up in the back seat she was able to confirm this and send this thought to Kicky. But soon the highway turned to the North and she saw a sign that said, 53 North. But again, in another twenty miles he turned off the highway again heading west, she thought. He kept turning after this about once every 20 miles or so. He kept up this zigzag pattern of travel for the rest of the day and well into night. He stopped only at drive through restaurants and handed food back to her. On one particularly lonely stretch of road he told her to open the whiskey and get herself drunk. When she was feeling the alcohol he pulled over and stitches closed her wound. After he wrapped it up, he removed her torn sweatshirt and threw it along the side of the road in a ditch. He took his time putting the new one on her though. He was enjoying her naked breasts with both his eyes and his hands. She was drunk enough to not care though.

"Kicky is behind us. I can feel his presence," Tess said. If not for the booze she would not have tipped her hand like this. But it had the desired effect. Rivershade looked down the road.

"He can't possibly," Rivershade said. But he let her put on the new shirt and he circled around to the driver's seat again.

Whenever she could see a road sign she would mentally send it to Kicky. She could feel that he was still behind her. But with all this indirect route travel they couldn't tell how far behind they were.

At one point he told her that he was going to go to sleep for a little bit. He'd been driving while Ondag slept and now it was his turn to sleep. They had traced the pattern of turns, and although they felt it was to confuse them, they thought that maybe he was trying to eventually get to Fargo. So Ondag was planning to head straight for Fargo and then when Kicky woke up in a couple of hours they would check her position.

She agreed to this plan. But she decided that maybe it would be a good idea for her to sleep off the whiskey too. She lay back down on the back seat after trying to clean the blood off the major areas where her arm had been. She was asleep in moments.

Chapter 6

Kicky woke with a start about 5:00 P.M. that evening. He at once reached his psyche out toward Tess. She was not where he had left her, so to speak. She had been about 30 miles north of them heading west when he went to sleep. She was not there. He reached out to her again scanning ahead of them in a wide arc. He panicked, he couldn't find her.

He slipped out from under the covers, the covers still smelled like her even though she had only slept there twice, and the second time they hadn't actually slept. But he couldn't think about that now he had to find her.

He went up to the front of the RV and asked Ondag where they were.

"We're almost to Fargo, and guess who caught up?"

"Marcus?" Kicky asked, "He's here?"

"In the car right behind us. He and Morrison caught up about an hour ago."

"You got any idea where Tess is?" he asked.

"You're the one inside her head," Ondag

said, concern was showing on his face.

"I know, but I can't feel her. Maybe she's sleeping too."

"We're almost at Fargo. Do we just continue on to the west or do we stop here and wait?"

"Not stopping. We need to keep going no matter what. I should never have gone to sleep."

"You know why you slept. It's one advantage we have over him. We can take turns sleeping he can't. He has to stay ahead of us."

"Wait, he has to stay ahead of us. What if he didn't? What if he was going off the beaten path like that so that he could lose us and hole up somewhere to get some sleep?"

He stood up and sent his mind out to the east of the RV. He hoped that there wasn't a limit to how far away Tess could be from him before he could no longer detect her. He kept searching out back behind him.

"Pull over," he told Ondag. Ondag did so at once.

Kicky stood and exited the RV. Marcus had pulled up behind them and got out of the car.

"David, what's wrong?"

"I can't sense her any more. She could be sleeping, but I should still be able to sense her."

Kicky sent his mind outward from himself. He flew over the terrain they just crossed, circling ever higher. He sent out a message to the Great Spirit to help him find her. He then sent word to her God as well, "If you care about your daughter, help me find her so I can protect her." He spoke these words aloud.

"David?" Marcus said.

"I'm praying for help," Kicky told him.

Then he silently sent his mind outward again. There was nothing.

Finally in utter frustration he cried out, both mentally and out loud at the side of that highway, "Tessa!"

In the back of the Lexus 50 miles to the south of them, Tess woke from a dreamless sleep. She started awake and when she did she spoke his name, "Kicky?"

Kicky heard. He wheeled around facing south. "They are heading toward South Dakota," he said. He was so sure of this that he at once got into the RV and told Ondag to go. Marcus too got into the RV with them. Deputy Morrison took the wheel of his car and followed.

"You're south of us," Kicky told Tess. "Where are you?"

She groggily thought that she had been asleep, she didn't know where she was. But she would find out.

Kicky stayed with her, inside her head until she saw a road sign "I 29, Watertown 62 miles."

Behind him he heard Marcus on his cell phone, calling Watertown Sheriff's. He reported their current location and the latest description of the car, Tan Lexus '11 or '12 model. He also furnished them with a description of the two people in the vehicle. The woman age 28 was hostage. Cover all exits from highway between their location and Watertown, the suspect will travel back roads to escape police detection. "This is not a high speed chase," he said. "Suspect is obeying all traffic laws. If he thinks that we know what vehicle he is driving he will steal another vehicle. He has been known to kill the occupant of the stolen vehicle, so be very careful with this one. He is armed with a Bowie knife and should be considered very dangerous."

Kicky heard Marcus ask for confirmation on this information, they got it. He signed out then called Morrison on the shoulder short wave. "Morrison, you take the lead. We want to get on I 29 toward Watertown. Use the lights." Morrison pulled out ahead of them and used the lights and siren to clear traffic all the way through town to the junction. Once they were on I 29 south he killed the siren and only ran the lights. Ondag had topped out the RV speed at 74 MPH and Morrison was pulling away from them.

"Bet you wish you were still in the fast car," Ondag joked to Marcus.

"I'll stay here where the intel is," Marcus said looking at Kicky.

It was not long before Kicky saw a road sign. Wahpeton 60, Sisseton 98, Watertown 158.

"No," Kicky said. "How the hell did he get 100 miles in front of us?"

"He was zigzagging on back roads remember. We were going straight on highways." Ondag told him.

"We're never going to catch up. We just have to make sure he thinks we are hot on his trail." Kicky said.

"How are we going to do that?" Ondag asked.

"Yeah," Marcus agreed, "How are we going to do that without tipping our hand as to our secret informant?"

"I don't know," Kicky said. "I'll have to figure that one out."

He silently told Tess about the conversation and asked for her opinion. He was informed that they were on an exit ramp. They were leaving the interstate, still heading west.

"I wonder if he's going to the Rez?" Ondag asked. They both knew there were several Reservations in South Dakota including the Pine Ridge Reservation of the Lakota Sioux. It felt right. He would take her somewhere where he would be protected because of his Native American heritage. He could tell lies and they would help him. They would believe him since Native Americans pride themselves on being honest people.

Kicky plugged the location of the nearest Reservation into the GPS and for good measure also added the Pine Ridge Reservation. In both cases there were faster ways to get there than staying on the interstate. Kicky spent the next four hours telling Ondag where to turn. Morrison followed them in the agent's unmarked car. Marcus kept everyone, Morrison and other local authorities apprised of the situation.

Chapter 7

Tess sat up in the back seat. She had slept for nearly the entire afternoon, but Kicky had awakened her with his mental cry. He was so worried about her. She thought that maybe she would try to not sleep again, so that this wouldn't happen again.

"Were you dreaming about your pet?" Rivershade asked.

"Yes, dreaming," she said.

"Hm," he said dreamily. "Were they pleasant dreams? They didn't sound pleasant. Does he mistreat you my love?"

"Dispense with your endearments, they sound phony."

"I've been doing a lot of thinking, while you were asleep. How did your dog find you in Wisconsin? It's almost as if you still had your cell phone and had just called him to tell him where to meet you. But I know that can't be it, I put your cell phone in a truck going to International Falls while you were asleep. Yet they still seem to know exactly where you were."

"They have been following us. They probably just realized where we were and kept a lookout. When they saw the car you'd stolen parked at Burger King they pulled in."

"Yes, but you knew they were there. How did you know?"

"I saw them. How else could I have known?"

"Hm, yes. How else could you have known, witch?"

"I'm no witch. I have no idea what you're talking about."

"No, I suppose you don't." He drove silently for a while. "Do you just have a connection with him? Or are you reading my mind as well?"

"Reading minds now? Are you insane?"

"Of course not," Rivershade said. He quickly swerved off the interstate onto an exit ramp. "I bet you didn't see this coming." He grinned at her through the rear view mirror. They turned west and traveled the potholed road for a good long while, again never exceeding the speed limit. There were no road signs, even though Tess kept her eyes busily checking each intersection. They were on a paved country road with few enough intersections. The only signs she saw were small ones pounded into the ground in front of farms, "Eggs" one announced. "Quilts" another advertised. "Clean fill wanted" begged another.

"I was thinking," Rivershade said, "that we should call our new clan the Hawk Clan. Once we consolidate the DNA strand through selective breeding we will have as pure a line of shifters as if we were direct descendants of the bird people."

"Who are the bird people?" she asked.

"Who are . . ." He stopped. "Surely our

kinsman Clyde or one of his lackeys told you about the bird people."

"No, I've never heard of them," she lied. She wanted to keep him talking. Keep his mind off of her mental communications with Kicky.

"I can't tell if your lying to me or not. Very good. I'm going to have to keep my eyes on you. First a sham sleeper and then a cool liar. I'm going to have fun breaking you to my will."

"So, who are the bird people?" she asked. Rivershade paused briefly before answering. So she disarmed him by looking at him straight in the mirror with the most innocent look she could manage.

"All right then, I'll play your game. The Bird people are advanced life forms that have been on this planet for eons. I have yet to discover where they came from, but I do know that they have been here for the entire time that life has been on this planet. In fact, they are probably a main part of the primordial ooze that created life. Not only that, but they have influenced the life on this planet greatly at many times. Do you remember hearing that we were made in God's image? I believe that is from the book that you believe in."

She acknowledged him briefly.

"Well, if that is indeed true then the Bird people are the gods that we are made from."

"And they are shape shifters? Like you?" she asked.

"No, not like me. I am but a paltry shadow of what they were. I am a copy made from a copy made from a copy." He sighed with this analogy. "But you are a bit further up the ladder from me. You are only a copy."

She glanced over at him. "And your son?

The one you are taking me to meet?"

"Oh yes, he is a bit more pure than I, his mother had been very evolved. I didn't know it at the time, or I might have allowed her to live a little longer."

"So, these bird people. Are they still around?"

"They have always been around, I assume they still are, but I don't know where. I have never met one of them. They are well versed in inter-dimensional travel. They flit into another dimension at will, you see. And they can change shape to disguise themselves. So it could be that one is here in this car right now, sitting like a spider behind this rear view mirror and listening to our conversation."

"So then, how do they travel?"

"They travel in vehicles made from their own mind energy. Sometimes they are metallic looking objects in the sky, other times they partially shift into birds with huge wings and take aloft that way. Angels, demons, UFO's all can be traced to them."

"Truly," she said. And in this one word she was able to discount the entire race of people.

"Yes," he said. "I am, and well, we both are descended from them."

"But we both also have human blood as well."

"Yes, but with selective breeding we can rid the human DNA from our offspring and concentrate the Bird people DNA."

"And this is your plan?"

"It is," he said. "And I was hoping you would add your own enthusiasm to this endeavor."

"If you really plan to do human selective

breeding then you probably should include a true member of the Eagle Clan, my mate Kicky."

"Your mate?" he said. He didn't know why this term bothered him so much but it did. There was an extra meaning in it that he didn't understand. He dismissed it. It couldn't be that important, after all. "No, the Eagle Clan is too organized. I am not trying to recreate another Eagle Clan I want to try to rear a more unique strain of Bird people. The Eagle Clan has become polluted with the blood of other tribes, take me for example. I wish to refine the strains."

"Yes, but you admitted that the Eagle Clan is a lot closer to the original than you yourself are. You said something about a copy? How many times have they been copied down through the millennium?"

"You are arguing with me, my dear."

"Tess," she said.

"I know your name," he said.

"Then call me by it. Do not call me 'my dear' any more, those words when they come from your mouth sound like food, not endearments."

"Tess," he tried it on his tongue but it was not to his liking. "I think I would prefer to call you by your full name, Contessa. There is a name, regal, worthy. Contessa is a fit name for the mother of a new race of beings."

"So, as to specifics of your plan," Tess said. "Do you plan on breeding me with your evolved son? You said he had better DNA strands even than you yourself."

"Oh no no, Contessa," he said. "I plan to bed you myself and in my animal form too, but then you are used to mating with a wolf so you won't mind."

"What I mind is not your concern, because if I am to mate with anyone besides Kicky it will be against my will, so you can have anyone at all rape me if that is what you are after, it will make not the slightest difference to me who it is."

"Rape, is such an ugly word. That night I left you the gift of food in the form the chipmunk, I smelled no fewer than four men on your clothing. You are no virgin. What does it matter to you who fucks you? A woman who doesn't keep herself for her husband alone even before they are married is nothing more than a whore and any man can use her as he wishes."

"Is that what they taught you at the Rez? It's not true you know. If a man can have several women without it reflecting on his honor or status than why can't a woman?"

"Because a man is putting out, he is spraying the world with his seed. There is a bit about seeds falling on fertile soil in that book you profess to believe in, is there not? That's all a man is doing. A woman takes things in. A woman brings things inside of herself and they become a part of her. That is why it is frowned upon for a woman to have more than one man in her lifetime."

"And yet, you still want me, for what I can give to your seed. Do you see what a hypocrite you are?"

"I am not a hypocrite, I am simply going to father your first two children. Then my son will father the next two, and then one of your own highly evolved sons will father the next ones. How exciting will that be? The babe that suckled at your breast will then become your lover and father his own brothers. Yes, and you will take it, my dear, Contessa, because you only have two good things about you, your DNA and your womb. If I could chop off your head and keep you alive long enough to have one baby every year for the next 25 years I would gladly do it. You don't need a mind, Contessa. You only need a body."

She snorted a short laugh. "Then you might just as well let me go now, because I'm not going to be any good to you. I'm sterile."

He looked back at her with angry eyes. She took his stare with defiance. Then he began to laugh.

"You would say anything to me to get out of your fate. Would you not?" he asked. "Oh my dearest Contessa, a very cool liar, I see that now. But don't forget. I was taught how to lie by the best liars in the world, your own people. I can spot a lie like a crow in a wheat field. You forget. I saw your pack. I also saw the pills in your pack. If you were truly sterile you would not be so concerned about birth control. I also know that you are going on three days without your pills, so it's possible you are fertile even now."

"I've had nothing to eat all day but candy. Could we stop and get something with protein and maybe vegetables?" she asked.

"You want a real meal?" he asked. "Why yes, indeed. We can stop as soon as we find a place. I'm a bit on the hungry side too. I sucked on your bloody sweatshirt earlier, and that was my lunch, but it was not very filling."

Tess didn't know if he was lying about that but she couldn't help the shudder of revulsion that went through her. They came to a tiny cross road village with a diner in an old social club. The side of the building still boasted the words, Grange Hall. He stopped the car and helped her out. Her body had stiffened with the sleep and the lack of use sitting in the car for the whole day. Before they went inside he grabbed her arm and squeezed it hard enough to form a bruise.

"You will not embarrass me in there, now will you?"

"No one here is capable of protecting me against you," she said.

"My dear one, you are catching on."

They went inside. There were several other patrons sitting at the bar and in booths, but Tess chatted up the waitress anyway as they ordered. She smiled easily at the girl and said, "This is a mighty small town, what is it called?"

"You're in Roslyn, home of the National Vinegar Museum." The girl said proudly.

"Really, well, we'll have to check out the museum, I've always wondered about vinegar." Tess said brightly. "Is there a famous vinegar on my salad?"

"I can bring you a salad with a balsamic vinaigrette dressing."

"Please," Tess said. She was exuding joy and bounciness in her enthusiasm. "How about you, Honey?" she said to Rivershade and she hoped she put too much saccharine in the last word.

He smiled charmingly at her and said, "Yes my dear one, it sounds superb. Make it two."

They sat smiling at each other.

"OK," the waitress said doubtfully and walked off. Tess smiled a bit more genuinely then. The girl would remember them now. If she played her cards right she might be able to get the girl to call Marcus. She began drumming her fingers on the table. She was trying to remember Marcus's cell phone number. She had programmed his new number into her cell phone, but could she remember it from just that once. 906-565-something, something, 3, something. She drummed her fingers absently, staring Rivershade right in the face. Kicky supplied the rest of the phone number in her mind. 906-565-4239. She drummed her fingers, four times, pause, two times, pause, three times, pause, nine times. She kept doing it. The girl brought the salads. They both dug in and the Vinaigrette was the best she had ever tasted.

"I wish I had my laptop, I'd write a review of this restaurant and give it four stars." Tess said.

"You really do enjoy food and writing?"

"It's my life. Of course I enjoy it."

"What exactly would you have said about this place if you could?"

"That it's off the beaten path but well worth the extra miles to find it. That it takes its inspiration from the National Vinegar Museum and that it is the best balsamic vinaigrette I've ever tasted. I would embroider it up a bit more and describe some of their other food, making it as appealing as it could possibly be. It's close enough to Wisconsin that some of the Green Bay and Chicago clients would buy the review. And anyone traveling through South Dakota seeing the sights might be interested, so I could tap local markets as well. This place could have made me about $600 in sales. But alas, I have no computer now."

"This is truly how you make a living?" he asked.

"Yes, for the last two years."

Rivershade shook his head. "Contessa," he said. "There are so many better ways for a writer to make a living than wandering around the country with a big overgrown mutt and sleeping in tents just to make ends meet."

"This is the life I have chosen and I plan to be back at it as soon as I can."

"You are going to be busy procreating for the next 30 years, so get over it."

After they finished their meals Tess excused herself to use the restroom and asked to take the purse that they had gotten from the woman in Duluth.

"Up to something, Contessa?" he asked.

"You said it yourself. I've been without my pills for going on three days now. If they have a dispenser in the bathroom I am in need of some products."

"Fine, take it. There is nothing in there anyway. Pay the bill while you're at it." He intoned.

Tess took the bag and went to the restroom. Before she used it she wrote on the wall with a sharpie she found in the purse: For a good time call M. 906-565-4239. She bought three tampons from the machine using change from the woman's purse because, although she didn't need them now, she would in another day or two, she was sure. Then she used the toilet. As she stood washing her hands, Rivershade came in. He looked around. He saw nothing out of the ordinary. He took the purse from her and pulled out several twenties placing them in his own wallet then he left leaving the bag behind for her.

She came out too right behind him. Rivershade left the building. Tess asked the waitress for her check and winked at the girl several times as she paid the bill with the stolen credit card. She quietly said to the girl, "M. Is a friend of mine, he's looking for me. Could you give him a call?"

The girl looked confused. "In the bathroom," she said, winking again. "M."

Tess signed the receipt and walked away. He was waiting for her outside the door. She got in the front passenger seat and they drove away.

"So," Rivershade said, once they were back on the road. "Where are our pursuers? I take it you contacted them somehow from the bathroom."

"How could I have? I don't have a cell phone; there was no pay phone back there. And despite your own personal beliefs I do not have a psychic connection to any of them."

"Of course not," he said. "You are just a simple journalism major traveling the world looking for the perfect bite!"

"And you are just a simple werewolf doing the same thing."

"No, I'm much more than that. Oh, and by the by, I am not enamored of the term 'werewolf'. You need to stop calling me that if you wish to stay on my good side."

"That is my soul goal in life, at the moment," she admitted, "staying on your good side."

"You are very cheeky. When we get to where we are going, I'm going to have to beat some of that out of you."

"Where are we going?" she asked.

He broke into laughter again. Tess knew that sometimes there is laughter that can be shared between people. When one person laughs, others become infected and they too laugh. Rivershade did not have this type of laughter. When he laughed it felt like he was sinking teeth into flesh. If anything his laughter made her want to cry.

"My dearest Contessa, I can't have you

knowing at this stage where we are going so that your lovers can jump ahead of us and be waiting there before we get there. In fact, why don't you go to sleep? If I keep driving we will be there by morning. Then the fun will begin."

I'm not tired," she said. "I slept all day practically. I can keep you company. Maybe you need some sleep. I could drive while you rest. You just have to tell me which way to go."

He answered her with another of those flesh eating laughs.

She sat back and watched the countryside go by. It was still early. The sun would not set for at least 4 hours and it was coming around to the front of the car even now. Soon they would be driving right into it.

"Would you like to get in the back and lay down?" he asked. He almost made the statement sound kindly meant.

"No thank you," she said.

"Truly," he said. "You look worn out. You should rest."

"Nope," she said. "I'm fine." She looked at him though. "I would almost think that you were concerned about me."

"I am. I am most concerned about your well being. I want you to thrive and be happy with us. It would make things so much easier if I could have your cooperation."

"Yes, I suppose all rape would be easier if the woman were cooperative. It's still rape though."

"I do not ever intend to rape you."

"You so much as told me that you plan to rape me."

"No, no, of course not. That is not my

intention at all. I plan to make you the mother of a new species. I am planning a family here, not a brutality. I wish you could see that."

"You were just calling me whore and telling me the only good parts were between my legs and all that. Now you're trying to sweet-talk me?"

"I was angry before. But now that I've had a steak and a salad, I am just sweet as honey. You yourself called me Honey in the restaurant. It was said with very little sarcasm too, so I hope someday to hear you call me that with true love in your heart."

It was her turn to laugh. She kept it inside though and it only showed as a smile which she used to her benefit.

"Only when I am able to forget that you abducted me with chloroform."

"But Tess, that was a kindness. I could have done to you want I did to that poor little evolved girl's mother."

"Who are you talking about?"

"That little evolved girl, the one that babysat for your pet in Mackinaw City."

"Kit? Are you saying Kit is evolved? Like me?"

"Of course, not in the same way as you. But yes, she is very evolved."

"You killed her mother," Tess said. She no longer felt like laughing.

"Yes, she was in my way. I was after the girl, the mother got in the way like a lion defending her cub."

"You're sick," Tess said. "She's just a little girl."

"I know, but soon she would be putty in my hands. Have you never heard of the Stockholm syndrome? It's amazing what people will do to continue surviving, even if their new life is hardly worth living. Take you for example. You have already begun this transformation. You said yourself that no one in the restaurant could protect you from me. You went along with me because you knew that if you hadn't, I had the power to take all of their lives."

"It's not power," she said through gritted teeth.

"Not power? What ever could you mean?"

"You should not call it power, you should call it what it is, evil."

"Oh Contessa, there you go again. You are confusing nature with religion. In your religion there are definite ideas about good and evil. In nature there is not. In nature, as all Native American's believe there is only the power of nature, the sun and moon, the winds, the stars, the trees and the animals. None are good and none are evil, they just are."

"If you weren't trying to hurt her, then why did you?"

"She got in the way."

"No I don't mean Dawn, I mean Kit. You nearly killed Kit. You nearly tore her in half."

"I'm sorry about that. When I am fighting anger I sometimes forget myself. Like when I grabbed your hair and cut you. I had no intention of hurting you either. I simply needed to control the situation and the same thing happened there in Mackinaw. If the woman had just let me have the girl, I would have left them both alone and no one would have gotten hurt. If anything you could say it was her fault."

"No mother is going to allow you take her

child without a fight."

"No good mother," Rivershade agreed.

"Are you implying that Dawn was not a good mother?"

"She had already let the girl play with your pet wolf. What good mother would allow that?"

"You are sick," Tess exclaimed. "Woofy would never harm a little girl not in his wolf form and never in his human form."

"You are so swift to champion him. What is it about him? Are you that in love with the creature that you can't see his shortcomings? I can see them. I smelled his wolf seed on your clothing even back in Mackinaw."

"Stop, talking." She sat back in her seat again. She looked out the window and realized she had lost track of where they were. She sought contact with Kicky again inside her mind.

In the short exchange that followed Kicky admitted that Kit was aware of his psychic abilities and she had her own as well. He saw no harm in telling her about himself though since it would appear to others that she had a vivid imagination. Kit was indeed a highly evolved girl, he admitted. In many of the same ways that Tess herself was evolved. But he had not imprinted on her. He still belonged to Tess, body and soul.

With this reality check firmly in place she stared out the window in hopes of seeing some sign as to where they were or where they were going. The sun came around to the front of the car, bathing it with dazzling baking light. Rivershade rolled up the windows and turned the AC on full blast. Soon it was an even 70 degrees inside the car. Tess closed her eyes to rest them from the light and did not open them again until the sun had dipped below the horizon. They turned several more times always heading toward the southwest. Then they came to a road with a lot of signs. 212 going toward Seneca, Lebanon and Gettysburg. She relayed this info to Kicky.

Kicky told her they were getting closer. Ondag was resting for a while and Marcus was driving the RV, he reported. They were about 60 miles behind her, but they were catching up. If Tess could talk him into stopping at a diner for breakfast they would be able to catch up.

She said she would try.

Kicky told her to get some sleep, that he would need her in the morning.

Tess sent him mental misgivings about this. Last time, she reasoned partially to herself but knowing she was broadcasting to Kicky, there was a tense moment when they couldn't find each other.

He agreed that the moment had been tense, but he told her to remember that they had indeed found each other and that he would always find her no matter what. So she should try to sleep.

She bundled up the purse and put it under her head next to the window and closed her eyes. In a few minutes she began to sham snore. She heard Rivershade quietly say the word Contessa. She did not answer him. Then he said, "Tess?" His voice was so contemplative and quiet that her heart was almost touched. She would not acknowledge it though. Rivershade would never get any of her sympathy. He was evil. He would always be evil. But as long as she had Kicky's voice in her mind, she could withstand his mind games.

Chapter 8

Tess slept until well after sunrise. She didn't notice the sun coming up because they were parked under a thick canopy of trees. She had no idea where she was. There was underbrush all around the car, they seemed to be on a two track and she could not open the car door because Rivershade had pressed her side of the car up against a thicket. When she tried to open the door it would only open three inches before the wood blocked it from opening further.

Her movements woke Rivershade from his sound sleep.

"Oh, my dear, you're up," he said.

"I need to relieve myself do you think you could pull the car ahead so I can get out. There is a small clearing right up there."

"Of course, my dear one," he said. I just didn't want you getting up in the middle of the night and going over the side."

"The side of what?"

"The bluff," he said. He indicated the left side of the road. They were indeed perched at the edge of a bluff that dipped down through the trees about 60 feet. It would have been a bad fall.

He started the car and pulled ahead a few feet. She got out and went back into the woods making sure she was in his blind spot before she pulled down her pants. She came back to the car.

"There might be some wet ones in the glove compartment. I found a few there yesterday."

She checked and there was. She wiped her hands on one.

"Where are we?" she asked.

"Please," Rivershade said. "You still haven't learned. It is to my advantage if you do not know where you are."

"Yes, but I was just wondering if there was another diner around here somewhere. I'm hungry again."

"Hm, so am I," he said. "Alright, you win. I'll go find a diner."

He pulled the car backward a few yards and swung out into a turn-out drive. He snaked his way down the narrow dirt road and then back out onto a paved road. A few miles more and there was a diner.

She pulled no shenanigans like she had the last time. This time she simply ordered some bacon and eggs and an order of sausage gravy and biscuits and settled in to wait. When the food came she casually asked the waitress if there were any sights to see around here.

"You mean other than the mountain?"

"What mountain?" she asked.

"Mount Rushmore," the woman said.

"Oh yeah, we plan to see that, of course," Tess said. "Anything else?"

"Yeah, there's the Crazy horse monument,

and several Native American museums up here in town. Lots of stuff to see down on the Pine Ridge Reservation. You from there?" she asked Rivershade.

"Nope, I'm from Minnesota."

"Oh, well, you got kin down there then?"

"Not as far as I know, but then you never know about them Eagle Clan people, they get around."

The waitress left a ticket next to Rivershade's elbow and walked off.

"Very clever," he said.

"Yeah? Maybe you do need my mind after all."

"Not if that pet of yours shows up here in the next hour. Witch."

"Oh eat your steak before it gets cold. I like you much better when you're sated."

"I need more sleep. I think we'll go back to our hidey hole up there in the park and sleep this morning off. No one will find us there I'm sure. But to be sure, maybe I'll blindfold you."

"You can if you want. I have no one to tell. I'm beginning to despair that anyone other than you knows where I am."

"I don't believe you for a second!" he said. But he said nothing more until his steak had been devoured and he had refused more coffee.

The truth was that as soon as Tess has awakened, she had felt the close proximity of Kicky. He was so close that she could probably run to his side in a matter of minutes. Kicky had been anxiously waiting for her to wake for hours.

Their mental conversation was taken up at once. Kicky had tracked Tess in a dream but had lost her in an anxiety filled dream landscape about an hour ago. He had been unable to find her during that time and it made him very nervous. He admitted to her that he almost woke her to make sure she was alright. He asked her if she was scared.

Tess told him that she had gotten less and less scared of him the more they had talked. She now had nothing but contempt for him. Other than vague threats about rape and beatings, he had not mistreated her in any way except for the chloroform. He was a very sick contemptible person though and whatever punishment he got he would deserve.

Tess relayed the information about Mount Rushmore to Kicky and their whereabouts at the diner. Kicky informed her that they were only two miles away from her and she should keep an "open channel" so he could track her and they could take him.

When they got back in the car, Rivershade took the blood soaked sweatshirt and tied it around Tessa's head. She let it happen. The blood was dried and she could hear it crackle as he tied it tight around her head.

They drove for about half an hour before they stopped. He removed the blindfold. They were not in the same place they had been. But he was stopped right next to a large tree so that she couldn't get the door open again. She settled back into her seat and pretended that she was trying once again to fall sleep.

Rivershade looked over at her. He looked tired, beat in fact.

"Where is your pet?" he asked her.

"I don't know," she said. "And I would appreciate it if you would stop asking me about him. He's probably worried sick about me wherever he is."

"He's not going to climb into the back seat any minute now, is he?"

"I know he and my brother would have tried to find me, but I don't think they could after our plans changed so many times. They certainly didn't follow us all the way to South Dakota."

"I think you underestimate him. Or maybe you know that they did and are just lying to me again." He made a clicking sound with his tongue. "Naughty little Contessa. Listen to you trying to remind me that Clyde's little brat is your adopted brother. I've already told you that I will not harm you. There is no need to remind me of my promise to my nephew Clyde that I not harm any of my own relatives. Or did you not know that I had made that promise?"

"What promise?" Tess asked.

"Now you are truly trying to make me angry, my dear. I need no reminders that I have gone back on my word. I went on the reservation to make certain that you were there being protected by my kinsmen. And then I find that Clyde had adopted you so that you would also be my kinswoman. As such I am going against the promise I made to him about harming my own kin."

"Is that why Clyde adopted me? To protect me against you?"

"You knew that, you little witch!"

"I didn't. I asked Ondag why Clyde adopted me but he evaded the question."

"You ignorant little tease. You knew very well."

"Alright, Calm down," Tess said to him. "I don't want to argue with you. It's already too hot in this car. Why don't you open a window?"

Kicky had outlined the plan to Tess while she was maintaining her end of the argument and the plan hinged on the window next to his head being open.

"You condescending little bitch," he said absently turning the key to release the power windows. He kept her locked and up tight, but his own window went down all the way to the bottom.

"I just need some air," she said. "It's going to be 150 degrees in here before noon."

"Air, you don't deserve any air. I should take the air from you right now," he turned toward her. Tess could tell that he was getting angry.

"Don't get angry," she told him. "You'll turn and end up killing me, and then you won't have any breeding stock." She spat this last statement at him with all the venom she had been building up to over the last two days.

That's when he pounced. She could see his eyes turn from brown to yellow. His teeth went nearly at once from human to canine, his snout growing to a protrusion. His hands were around her neck, they were still hands. They sprouted course hair but did not turn into paws. She could feel her wind pipe blocked. Her head felt woozy, he was also blocking blood to her brain. All at once she passed out going limp in his hands.

Rivershade did not stop strangling her. His jaws snapped above her as his transformation continued. Soon he was standing full on top of her and biting down into her shoulder. He was trying to turn her around and put her in a position to further violate her when he felt something sting him on the backside.

He turned his huge head to see something

pink with feathers sticking out of his rump. He grabbed the dart with his teeth pulling it out. Then another one lodged itself in his great hairy neck. He swiped at it with a paw and then he tried to bite at it, but could not reach it. It was only then that he began to feel groggy. He fought it with all of his animal instincts. But a third and then a fourth dart lodged themselves in his body and he crashed down on top of Tessa's prone body.

Kicky was at the window at once pulling the door open and tugging the huge dogman off of Tess. As soon as the animal was out of the car two men with bar nooses slipped ropes around Rivershade's neck.

Kicky then saw Tess.

He made a strong howling cry as he lifted her body from the car. He placed her carefully on the ground and checked for a pulse, the whole time calling her name. She was bleeding from the shoulder wound and also from the cut in her arm where the stitches had torn in that last struggle.

"Tess, wake up, Oh Tess. Please," he howled.

Marcus came over to her side and checked again for a pulse. "Call for a bus," he told the deputy. He began chest compressions trying to keep her alive. With each compression blood spurted from her shoulder wound. Kicky bent down to her mouth and blew air into her lungs. He watched Marcus for a signal and each time blew in again. Marcus told another of the many law enforcement people who were there to put pressure on Tessa's shoulder, so she wouldn't bleed out. In less than ten minutes an EMS truck arrived on the scene and took over the life saving procedures. After shocking her chest four times they found that they had a heart beat and were then able to transport her to the hospital in Rapid City.

Chapter 9

Tess was clinically dead for a total of fourteen minutes. She woke briefly in the EMS truck and asked the paramedic where the old man was. Then she lapsed back into a coma.

In the ER, Kicky and Ondag took turns holding her hand and talking with her quietly encouraging her to return to them. They contacted her father in Chicago and also the tribe at Bay Mills. Kicky tried also to find Rick Kraft and let him know what was going on. He caught up with Rick at his in-laws house. He thanked Tessa's organizational skills for keeping Rick's cell phone number in her contacts even when she knew she might not ever call him again.

"They caught the maniac who killed Dawn," Kicky told Rick.

"They did? Oh, Thank God." For a few seconds Rick dropped the phone and then finally picked it up and quietly said into it, "Is he alive? Will he stand trial?"

"Yes, the trial will be in Marquette County I think. I'll let you know for sure when I find out."

"Yes, please do. Where are you now?"

"Tess is in a coma. She's in the hospital in Rapid City, South Dakota."

"South Dakota? How did . . . He took her all the way there?"

"Yeah, it's a long story but I'll tell you later, I have a few more calls to make."

"David," Rick said, "Kit and I will be there tomorrow. I'll fly out tonight."

"You don't have to. I just called because I knew she would want you to know that we have Dawn's killer."

"I'll be there. You and Tess need us."

"OK, you're right. Kit might be able to help get her back."

"Yeah, she might."

Rick severed the connection and Kicky sighed with relief. He was hoping that Rick would bring Kit. Kicky was in dire need of someone with Kit's abilities.

Kicky was with Tess when she woke from the coma. She woke not just with a fluttering of eye lids, but she woke with a strong inhale sitting straight upright in the hospital bed, eyes bulging.

She went straight from this to a coughing fit. There had been no need for a respirator since she was breathing on her own after her heart beat had been reestablished. And a four hour coma was the best any of her doctors could have hoped for. It meant that maybe there wasn't any brain damage.

"Kicky," she said. Her voice was raspy, barely audible.

He shushed her. "Don't talk, baby," he said. "Let your neck heal. I love you. Remember I can do all the talking for you."

She broadcast into his mind. "Where is the old man?"

What old man? He asked inside her mind.

The old one, Kineekuhowa. Tess showed Kicky a complete replay of what they would begin to refer to as her coma dream.

She had stood up, independent of her physical body. She had watched as Rivershade had begun to turn into his Dogman creature, half wolf and half man. He was strangling her. She waved goodbye to her body, and her body winked at her once. She felt the separation of the two souls after that wink, and she was free. She flew up and away from the scene in the car. She saw from a distance that the police were surrounding the Lexus. Then she turned and traveled south toward a vast desert. She was flying low over the terrain, traveling miles to the second. Ahead of her she could see her destination: a large area of sandy desert. Here she saw a lone man standing. She came nearer to him.

He was a very old Native American man. He stood alone in the center of the sandy waste. He wore deer hide from top to bottom, a long hide tunic decorated with many beads and shells. He wore leggings of black buffalo fur tied with sinew. And on his head was a hollowed out slice of a tree with deer antlers set into it. Strips of deer hide covered the wood and kept the antlers tied into place. It was a marvelous head piece.

A name came to her, whispered into her ear by the northwest wind. Kineekuhowa. She repeated the name; she did not wish to forget it. Kineekuhowa. The corners of his mouth turned downward but Tess could see that it was not a frown. She could see that he was pleased with her.

"Who are you?" she asked him.

"I am your children's ancestor," he said cryptically.

"I have no children," Tess told him.

The look in the eyes of the ancient Native said volumes. All at once Tess knew where she was. She was in the realm of the dead. She knew also that she did not belong there. She was too early. Her time on earth was not yet finished. She knew that when next she saw this place she would have grandchildren.

"I am not ready to be here yet," she told Kineekuhowa.

He put messages in her mind. No she was not ready. She had to go back. There was more she needed to do.

He told her to wait here for a few moments longer because he had a message for her to give to his grand nephew. She waited for him to speak the message. But he did not. Instead she felt the information enter her spirit and become a part of her.

"Touch his heart like thus," Kineekuhowa said to Tess. "Then he will know the message."

"You are the one who died in Rivershade's presence?" Tess felt a driving desire to know this since she too died because of him.

"I did," Kineekuhowa acknowledged. He placed his hand near her ear and she experienced the truth of Kineekuhowa's death.

"I see," she said. But she wasn't sure if she had, not in reality. She wasn't sure if she had completely understood all there was to know about this wise medicine man's death.

"It is time," he said. "You have no more time."

Then she felt herself pulled back by her solar plexus and slammed back into her body. She opened her eyes and she was in an ambulance.

"Where is the old man?" she asked and then fell into a coma.

The first thing that Kicky realized was that it had not been a coma dream, even though that's what they would call it. Tess had not yet been in the coma. She had been dead. Plain and simple. Dead. But he didn't point this out to her, at least not yet.

He put her hand to his chest, the way Kineekuhowa had told her to do to transfer the information, but he didn't seem to get anything. This meant that he was not the recipient of the information. Maybe Clyde or one of the other elders.

Over the course of the next few hours, Tess and Kicky told Ondag about the coma dream. He mostly sat quietly listening to Kicky's voice as he translated from Tess. Ondag realized that Tess had described a Native American afterlife and he asked Tess if she saw anything that might be described as heaven or angels or pearly gates.

She confirmed that she had not. Ondag and Kicky looked at each other significantly.

Tess spoke out loud, "Just a dream," she said.

"Don't talk," Kicky reminded her. "You're right, it was just a dream."

Not long after that Tess fell asleep and the next time she woke, Rick and Kit were sitting at her bedside. Kit was holding her hand and they were talking to her.

"Kicky, she's awake!" Kit said excitedly.

As Tessa looked over at Kit, she once again was sent into despair by seeing poor Kit's injuries. It had only been about three or four weeks since they had seen her in the hospital in Sault Ste. Marie.

The most terrible gashes had healed and the stitches were gone. Angry red scars marred her perfect child face though and would for a while longer before they faded.

And yet, Kit showed every sign of being the same vivacious girl Tess had first met. Over the course of the next few days before Tess was released from the hospital Kit kept them all entertained with her stories and her wit. Whenever Kit came up with another seemingly hair brained idea, Rick would simply shrug as if to say, "Don't ask me where she gets this stuff."

After extolling largely on canine physical attributes Ondag asked Kit if she was going to be veterinarian like her father.

"First of all, he's not a veterinarian," Kit told him.

"Oh you mean he never served in the military?" Ondag kidded with her.

"NO," she said all exasperation, "He not only is not a Veteran but he also doesn't take care of dogs and cats and horses and cows. He's a wildlife biologist. And no I'm not going to be a wildlife biologist. I'm going to be a Xeno-biologist."

"What's a Xeno-biologist?" Ondag asked innocently.

"I'm going to specialize in alien biology."

"Alien? You mean like little green men?"

"Well, first of all they aren't green, their grey. But second of all, no that's not what I mean. I mean Alien as in, hybrids that have occurred because of the interbreeding between aliens and humans or aliens and animals."

"Where do you come up with this stuff?" Rick asked his daughter.

"It's a totally new and open field. There aren't a lot of people in it so far but I think I can open up a niche for myself," she said in all seriousness.

"What are you talking about?" Rick asked.

"Kicky knows."

"David?" Rick asked.

"It's another coma dream," Kicky explained.

Chapter 10

When Tess was finally discharged from the hospital, she and Kicky checked into a motel on the outskirts of the Pine Ridge Reservation. Ondag and all the Bay Mills Elders were staying on the Reservation, honored guests of the Lakota Sioux tribal council.

The first thing Tess did was shower. Kicky wanted to climb into the shower with her but she mentally asked him not to. There would be time for love-making later. She had other things on her mind. So he sat on the toilet seat and waited patiently for his turn to shower.

"Thank you for not killing him," she said.

"Not killing him?"

"You know, it had to have been your idea to tranq him," Tess said.

"Yeah, well, I didn't think you'd want him killed. I figured you would probably want him to stand trial for his crimes, at least for killing Dawn and hurting Kit."

"Yes, you were right," she said. "He's a despotic lunatic, but he needs to be incarcerated and studied."

"We really don't need any publicity," Kicky said. Tess, through reading his mind, realized that he was talking about his own clan.

"I know, but maybe if he could be tranquilized with drugs, he wouldn't change while in prison and no one would find out what he is."

"That's pretty optimistic even for you." He sent her a mental dimpled smile, and she could feel the love emanating from the thought.

"He's a freak of nature," she said. "No one will want to speculate that there could be more than just him, just like people can't fathom a family of Loch Ness Monsters or a family of Jersey Devils."

"Or a family of Sasquatch?" he said. "Aliens? Vampires? Werewolves?"

"Fiction," she said. "Just fiction that's all. The definition of insanity is not being able to tell the difference between reality and your personal fictions. Most people won't believe he's really a shifter because they themselves don't want to be considered insane."

"But what about the people who will have to deal with him every day? The guards, the inmates. They will know what he is."

"Are you saying he should die?"

"No," Kicky said, but she could tell that he was conflicted about this. He wanted to share the same opinion with Tess, but he just couldn't.

"Kicky, you don't have to agree with me on everything."

"I'm really surprised that I don't. My sister, when she imprinted on her husband to be, she went from being totally non-political to being a republican like overnight. It was bizarre. I figured that I would be a carbon-copy of the person I imprinted. I have no idea why I still have my own thoughts."

"Maybe, because I want you to," she said.

"Do you?"

"I don't want you to be a slave to my thinking," she said. "I couldn't be with someone who didn't inspire me and surprise me once in a while. I love that you have your own mind and point of view and opinions. You have the ability to make me laugh, and that's so important. Because if you are in a relationship and you can laugh with that person, there will always be happiness."

"I think that too," Kicky said.

"See?" she said, "We agree on the basics."

"Not sure I came up with that one independently though."

She stepped out of the shower without turning it off and Kicky dropped his towel and stepped in.

As she was toweling off her hair she thought about her father.

"Oh my God," she said. "I have to call Dad. Oh my God, what am I going to tell him?"

"Tess, hang on, I'm almost finished."

"I don't need you. I need to call my Dad."

"You just had a strong emotion, I felt it way over here," he called from the next room.

"He's going to be so upset," she said. She sat down next to the phone and dialed her father's number beginning with a zero. She didn't even know if this trick still worked but it did, an operator came on the line and asked what she needed. She said she would like this call to be collect from Tess. When her father answered he accepted the charges at once.

"Dad, I first have to tell you that I'm OK, I

mean, I'm not hurt, or injured. I'm doing just fine."

"Are you still in the hospital?" he asked. "Someone named Ondag called me to tell me you had been abducted and were in the hospital. I couldn't get away just then because I was visiting your aunt in Benld. But you're out of the coma now and your OK?"

"I'm fine."

"How did it happen? I mean, you're always so careful. Does this have anything to do with that Indian guy you've been talking about? David?"

"His name is David Redwing, but he goes by Kicky. And no he had nothing to do with the abduction. I mean he was there, but he could stop it from happening. The guy used chloroform on us."

"Oh Tessy, are you traumatized? Did he rape you?"

"No, Daddy, I didn't get raped. But yeah, I suppose I'm a bit traumatized." She sniffed. Talking to her dad she was not able to hold it together. She had cried a little with Kicky when they were back in each others arms but now, talking with her dear old Dad she lost it entirely. Kicky emerged from the shower soaking wet. Bits of lather still clung to parts of his body. He came to her and put his arms around her. Her Dad was crying on the other end of the line.

"I'm going to come get you," he said.

"No, not yet. I still have to do a couple of things." Tess told him once she got control of her voice again.

"I'll help you. Are you still in Munising?"

"No, Daddy, I'm in South Dakota, this is where he brought me."

"I'll get on a plane and be there right away."

"No Dad. I won't be here that long. Oh, a

lot has happened. I'll tell you about it later. But just hold tight for a while. I'll call you once our plans get settled."

"Our plans? Who do you mean? Is that David guy still with you? Or Kicky or whatever."

"Yes, him my adopted brother, Ondag."

"Ondag, that's the man who called me? So you have two men traveling with you?"

"Yep, and Ondag has an RV. That's how we are traveling now-a-days."

"Do you trust these guys?"

"With my life, Daddy," she said.

"OK, then. I'm glad to hear you have a door you can lock when you sleep. It's always bothered me a little that you slept in a tent by the side of the road."

Tess laughed. She laughed harder than she thought she should at that joke. But it was such a relief to laugh out loud.

"I love you Dad," she said.

"I love you too Tessy. You call me later tonight after you figure out what you're doing. I miss you, and I want to come see you. So you figure out where and when we can meet. OK?"

She assured her father that she would call him the moment her plans were set and said goodbye to him.

No sooner had she hung up the phone and started towel drying Kicky's body then the phone rang. This time is was Agent Marcus.

"I've contacted the States Attorney in Michigan. His major crimes were committed there so we're taking him back to Marquette to stand trial. He's going to be tried for the murder of Dawn Kraft and we are also likely to be able to link him with the MP's from Sawyer, the rampage in Manistique and the murders in the Lower Peninsula as well. He's being called a rampage killer, and since most of his victims were in Michigan he has a better chance of being convicted there."

"Good, so you need us to go there?"

"Yes, the States Attorney will need your statements before the hearing since one of the counts will be abduction and crossing state lines."

"So that's what we'll do. We'll go back to Marquette to talk with him."

"Yeah, and if you could be there in about five days, that would be great."

"We will be there," she assured him. She put on her sleep shirt and climbed into bed where a still damp Kicky was waiting for her. They held each other in the cool morning light filtering through the shades for a long time, their thoughts intermingling. When every topic had been exhausted they fell asleep.

They woke about six hours later. The clock said 6:15 and for a short few seconds Tess wondered if it was A.M. or P.M. Someone was knocking on their motel room door. Tess got up, threw on some shorts and answered it. It was Ondag.

"Hey bro, what's doing?"

"I'm hungry, how about you guys?" He stepped into the room and revealed two big pizza boxes and a smaller one.

"Fabulous," she said. She took the boxes from him and set them on the dresser, opening the lid to discover the flavors, a meat-lovers and a supreme, with an order of those cheesy breadstick things that people are so fond of.

"I'm glad you guys aren't lactose intolerant," she said.

"I'll pretty much eat anything," Ondag said.

"I love pizza," Kicky agreed.

"Perfect!" Tess smiled as she bit into a piece and handed Kicky another. He was still lying in bed naked with a sheet covering him.

"What did the elders have to say?" Kicky asked Ondag.

"They said we would be welcome to stay on the Rez as special guests if we don't want to stay in the motel."

"We need to leave in the morning. We have to be back in Michigan in five days. Plus, I want to meet my dad back in Marquette as soon as possible." Tess couldn't read Ondag's mind but she could see he was a little disappointed about this decision.

"You're the boss," he said.

"But, what would you think of us coming back this way?"

"I think there are a lot of good restaurants through here." Ondag said, brightening a bit.

"Yeah? I was planning to head back down through Wisconsin to Chicago and then decide but maybe we should work our way out this way."

"Sounds good to me."

After dinner Tess grabbed her laptop from the RV and checked her finances. The travel magazines were taking off. They had bought another $3000 worth of her reviews for placement in their magazines and two travel magazines had shown interest in the article about hiking in Picture Rocks. There was an E-mail from one editor stating that the article would have to be rewritten to include ways to see these sights by car. Tess wrote back at once and said she would be happy to re-write with that slant and that they would have it in a day or two.

She looked at all her clothes, and Kicky's and decided that it would be good for them both to go get some new clothes. She could afford it with this new $3000, addition to her already inflated bank account. So they drove over to the Rushmore Crossings mall and they looked through T.J. Max. Tess bought them all two good outfits for fancier restaurants. Then they all bought new jeans, shorts, t-shirts and sweatshirts, clothes that looked like things tourists would wear. On their way back to the motel Tess saw a second hand consignment shop and asked Ondag to stop there as well. There she found some older comfortable clothing for them all and some dishes and glass wear for the RV. She also bought a whole set of flat wear and some cookware. Then they stopped at a grocery store and outfitted themselves with canned goods, condiments, snack foods and a few fresh veggies and meats for traveling. She kept reminding the men that they would be eating out a lot and would only need this stuff if they were hungry on off times when they couldn't get to a restaurant.

"Oh," said Ondag. "In that case, I need to go back to the snack isle."

He also walked down the baking isle and got a bag of flour, sugar and corn meal and some yeast, and baking powder.

"You going to take up baking?" Kicky asked him teasingly.

"I don't have to take it up, I already know how," he said, and didn't sound a single bit defensive about it.

They spent a nice long time that night setting up housekeeping in the RV and Ondag even threw together some biscuits just to see how the oven worked. Tess and Kicky were both astonished at the outcome.

"These are the best baking powder biscuits I've ever eaten," she exclaimed.

"Glad you like them. My grandmother taught me how to bake. Ma is too political, she never cared for it. So if I wanted something I just did it myself."

"So, you are a mechanic," Kicky said. "And a driver, and a baker. And you," he said turning to Tess, "are a writer and restaurant reviewer who is keeping us afloat financially. But I'm just a kid with no skills, no job and no reason to be here."

"Other than the obvious," Tess said. "Because I need you."

"For what?"

Tess walked up to Kicky and stroked his hair to one side. "You're my Woofy. I need you more than anyone."

"I just wish I was more use to you," he said shaking his head.

"You protect me," she said.

"How's that?" he asked looking doubtful. "I sure protected you from Rivershade. First I attracted him to you, then I made him think that you were worthy of his notice, then I practically helped him steal you."

"No," she said. "You did none of that. He was delusional, he thought he was creating a new master-race. He wanted me to mate with him and then his sons and then my own sons, so that the DNA would become more and more pure with each new generation. It was sick!"

"Yeah, I know, and I allowed him to just take you."

"You couldn't have known he was going to

do that."

"I should have smelled him half a mile away. But I was distracted. I'm so sorry."

"You are not to blame yourself. And by the way, neither are you," she pointed an accusing finger at Ondag too. "It just happened, and now it's over, so no more looking back at things that could have happened when they didn't. My time machine is on the fritz, it only goes one way, forward, and only at the pace of one minute per minute. So no going back, don't even talk about it any more, agreed?"

She put her hand out between them both. Kicky agreed and put his hand on Tessa's then Ondag did the same. When they broke from the huddle she grabbed them both into a group hug.

When the hug broke, some minutes later, Tess said one word, "Onward!"

"Onward," they both echoed.

Chapter 11

The next day just before they checked out of the motel Tess e-mailed her dad and asked him to buy her two new cell phones on their plan and to bring them to her in Marquette. She told him to check into the Ramada on Washington St. and wait for her. They were on their way back there and she would go straight to the hotel to find him.

They stayed on main highways this time and only stopped to change drivers and to eat once a day. All other meals were taken in the RV. It only took them 18 hours of constant driving to get back to Marquette. They had even beaten Tessa's dad. By a weird coincidence George walked into the lobby of the Ramada just as Tess and Kicky were heading back to the RV after inquiring after him.

"Kicky this is my father, George Gates. Daddy, this is him. This is David Kicky Redwing, my mate."

"Mate?" George said. "What do you mean? Like Gooday mate?" he said putting on an Australian accent.

"No Dad, I mean," she began.

"Stop, right there," he said. "I really don't want to know that much about your love life."

She smiled. "I was going to say that he's my husband, Daddy."

"Are you married?" he asked alarmed.

"No, we aren't," Kicky said. "But if you would give us your consent I hope we soon will be."

"Are you certain?" he said to Tess and Kicky both, "You two have known each other such a short time."

"Dad, there is more to this than meets the eye," Tess said. "Let's discuss it over supper, shall we?"

That night they had supper at a restaurant out by the lake called Coco's. The décor was unique and the food was fabulous especially the sweet potato fries which they served with a maple flavored sauce.

During dinner, Kicky and Ondag told George how they had managed to trace Tess across three states without letting on about Kicky's super power. It sounded almost plausible. Then George changed the subject.

"Tess, about your career, you need to branch out a bit," he told her. "I can sell your writing to national magazines and not just travel magazines. This thing about the pasties, that's an interesting take. Maybe you should try the best pizza in the country or the best barbeque, or the best salad, I don't know. The regional stuff is good but you need to be thinking more nationally."

"Do you think you could sell an article on the Dogman of Michigan?" Tess asked.

"The WHAT?" her father countered.

"I've been hearing a lot of legends lately, and they are pretty interesting. It would be a Halloween type pseudo fictional first person type article. *I was abducted by the Dogman of Michigan.*" She said putting her hand out to suggest a headline.

"I assume he was a maniac, but a Dogman?" George asked.

"I agree it's a little fanciful, but if you could find a buyer for such a thing, we could publish it under a pseudonym. Maybe Clarissa Moon."

"And does Ms. Moon have more such interesting ideas in her repertoire?"

"I'm a writer, Daddy. I'm sure there are many more!"

By the time they all said goodnight, Tess was back on track with her career and her father had met the two men who were very important to her. He seemed to approve of her travel companions too, which was a great relief to Tess.

"I have to go back to the park and write up this review."

"Why don't you come back to the hotel with me so we can talk for a while? There is an Irish pub across the street from the hotel, they can go over and get a drink there while we talk." This strategy was adopted at once and put into motion. Once back at the hotel George wanted to know about Tessa's plans.

"How long are you going to stay in Marquette?" he asked.

"I think a few more days yet. We still haven't heard from the States Attorney."

"I hope you don't mind if I stay with you for a while," he said.

"Not at all. I'd love to have you around while I work this town."

"I'm interested in the big pasty debate," he told her. "I've never eaten a pasty."

"I'll get you one. I think we've found the best one right here in this town. At least it's the best one I've had so far."

"I look forward to it."

"Dad, if you want to stop being my agent and start enjoying your retirement, I would understand."

"What?" he asked. "Is this your diplomatic way of telling me that you don't want me to handle your business affairs any more?"

"No, I want you to keep doing it. I just thought that maybe you feel stuck doing it, and if that's the case then I want you to know that I could find someone else to take over if you wanted out."

"I don't want out," he said emphatically. "You are my daughter and I love working with you like this. Your whole career is on the verge of taking off and I want to be involved when it does."

"Daddy, thanks."

"Besides, these new travel pieces you're doing are great and I'm having no trouble at all selling them. I think you need to do more of them. You could keep food as your focus but start adding local color as well as interesting destinations. You have a unique voice."

"Dad, really? I mean, we've never really

talked like this before about my career."

"Well, I've been having long lunches with my old friend, your 'uncle' John Galbreath. He has referred two more writers to me and I've taken them on. I'm a full-time agent now, honey." He winked and leaned in to tell her this next item. "I get 15% of the proceeds from every article they sell."

"Well, then you should be taking 15% from me as well. You shouldn't be working for free."

"With you it's different. You have bills to pay. You have student loans to pay off and now it looks like you have a travel staff to support."

"I don't have to pay Kicky, because he's my mate, I support him. And I don't have to pay Ondag because he works for Clyde."

"Who is Clyde?"

"My adopted father," she said. George gave her a look which she interpreted as confusion. She quickly added, "It's a long story and I will tell you all about it later. I'm not trying to replace you."

"I look forward to hearing all about it."

"I think he only adopted me because of Kicky," Tess said. But even to her own ears this seemed a lame excuse. "Oh, and Clyde paid off my student loans."

"He what?"

"Yeah, he's been very generous to us. I feel guilty, like I'm taking his charity when I don't need it."

"He must like you."

"Like I said, I think it has more to do with Kicky and it might have been a measure of protection against Rivershade, but that backfired."

"I don't understand," George said.

"Yeah, not sure if I do either, but . . ."

"Will I get to meet this man?"

"Yes, he'll be here in a day or two. If you stick around that long I'll introduce you to him and all of the elders."

"Elders, well!"

"But, Dad, from now on, I want you to transfer 15% of all my sales into your own account. I mean it Dad."

"You always were one for paying your own way," he said. "But you have just added a big expense. How did you afford the RV? And how are you going to afford running it?"

"Kent, one of the tribal elders, owns the RV and Ondag and his father are keeping it going. Ondag has a credit card that Clyde told him to use for gas and for outfitting the RV. Of course, all of this might change now that Rivershade is out of the picture."

"Rivershade?" George asked. "What does he have to do with all this?"

"It was because of him that Clyde felt I needed more protection. Now that Rivershade is incarcerated I might have to give the RV back."

"Really?" her dad looked at her. "Because I was thinking just the opposite. I thought that you should accept the gifts and try to keep going. You could still walk everywhere you go if you want and just plan out with Ondag where to meet up with you in the evening. Or if you need a break or want to get somewhere fast you could just ride. You could go everywhere in the Western Hemisphere this way. Just imagine it. There is literally no end to this lifestyle."

"Really Dad? Do you really think I could just freelance my entire life and support me, Kicky, Ondag and you?"

"I don't see why not. You're a good writer,

Tessy."

"Thank you, Dad." Tess had never before felt this much encouragement about her hair-brained scheme to travel and write restaurant reviews. She had adopted this whole business because of the simple fact that she couldn't get into an internship with the Sun Times in Chicago after she graduated. She had never been unemployed before, not since she was 12 and went out to get her own paper route. She had taken over payments of her own braces in Junior high and in high school she had paid for her own senior pictures, yearbooks, prom tickets, class ring, cap and gown and announcements, not to mention all the other little necessities that all high school kids need and want. When confronted with the new class ring her father said to her, "Boy I'm sure happy you don't spend all your money on drugs, Tessy."

She had laughed at that.

Her dad had never actually discovered his calling in life, and like so many others of his generation he had served a term in Viet Nam and came back scarred. His wife had held things together for him but when she died Tess felt the need to take over for her. George had nearly fallen apart then, but Tess was there for him. Together they made it through this tough time and emerged on the other side of it by working hard and keeping themselves focused on taking care of each other. Tess was convinced that alone neither of them would have been able to handle their loss, but together they thrived.

This was how they were even to this day. Tess had become as self-sufficient as she could possibly be and now it was difficult for her to take help from anyone, including her father. The help offered by Clyde and Ondag and the tribe rankled her but she swore that she would be able to pay it back someday. And she would!

The next day Tess called Agent Marcus to let him know that she had her cell phone back and it was the same number as the old one. He informed her that the States Attorney would be calling her later to schedule an appointment.

"Oh, by the way, some friends of yours are coming up here for the hearing. Rick Kraft and his family."

"All three kids?"

"No, just two. There were two kids who witnessed the attack on their mother."

"Yes, Kit, who was injured and the older boy, Colt, I think is his name."

"Yeah, that's right. Anyway, they are coming today and the State is putting them up in the Ramada until the hearing."

"Thanks for letting me know. I'll get to see them again."

"Tess," he said and he sounded serious.

"Yeah," she answered, he had her full attention.

"Are you all right?"

She thought for a long moment. "There is a thing that I have to work through, but I know how to do it. Kicky and everyone will help me."

"Wait, what about David?"

"Kicky is David, they're the same person."

"I thought . . ." He said. After a pause he finished the thought. "I thought Kicky was the name of your wolf."

"Oh no, Woofy was the name of my wolf."

"Where is he? I haven't seen him around recently. He never used to leave your side."

"Actually, last time I saw him was in Munising. I have a feeling he'll show up again soon."

"Are you going to try to find him?"

"If he wants to be with me, he will find me again. It's not that difficult. I'm going to start hiking again soon. I'm pretty sure he'll find me. He's a wild animal you know. He has his own ideas about companionship. The one thing I would never do is leash him."

"OK, I suppose that's a good attitude. Most people I think would claim ownership and make sure he stayed near by."

"I think he is nearby. I think I'll be seeing him before we leave Marquette for sure. I would never imagine that I owned him though. We have our affections for each other but we don't own each other."

"I disagree. I saw him with you. I think he does think he owns you. You're HIS human."

Tess laughed. "If that's the case then I think I will be seeing him again."

After Lunch Tess checked her accounts and sent $450 to her father's account for his share of the last payment made to her. If nothing else it would help him with his travel expenses. She did some research and found a few more places to eat around town. Just as she was about to make a decision Ondag came over and plopped a book on the counter next to her. It looked like one of those "for dummies" books that have been so popular. But the title of it was "Yooper Bars."

"Oh no, you didn't," she said picking up the book.

"Oh yes they did," Ondag said. I picked that up at the pub we went to last night. I thought it might come in handy for the rest of our tour.

She paged through it and stopped at several places. She had been to some of these places. The Raber bar, where she had met Annie Warner, the Pine Stump in Newberry. Andy's in Seney. The Log Jam in Munising. And that place here in Marquette that had the great Chicken Club Pizza, Stan's Dry Dock. Tess spent the whole next hour just paging through the book and thinking that maybe they should go to some more of these places.

"Man I wish I'd had this when I crossed the bridge," she said. "How accommodating it would be to have this sort of book for every place we go."

"I'll keep my eyes open."

"Look, the Gay bar, in Gay, Michigan. We have to go there." She said. Ondag just smiled and nodded.

"Well, now that we have someplace warm to stay we could just travel all winter," Kicky said.

"No, actually, I'm sending Ondag back after the hearing. We'll buy a tent and just continue on from here ourselves," she told him.

"Actually, no, you won't be doing that. I have my orders." Ondag said.

"No, you will do as I say," Tess insisted. "I have taken enough from Clyde, this RV belongs to Kent and I can't keep you from your job any longer."

"Yeah, well, Kent was the original owner of the RV, but Clyde bought it a while ago. He doesn't really need it, and he doesn't really need me either. You however, need both me and the RV, so I'm staying."

"I can't afford the RV or you," she said.

"Don't matter."

"It does to me," she said.

"Well, you and he will have to talk when he gets here."

"Yep, I have several bones to pick with him."

"Well good," Ondag said. "Because he and the elders will be here by this afternoon." He took the seat across from her at the table. "I'm worried about something."

"What?"

"I was opposed to Kicky's plan to tranquilize Rivershade. I thought they should just shoot him when he ran. In the end I got on board with the whole trial idea because I figured that if he was tried in South Dakota he could be executed there. Then they brought him back to Michigan and we don't have the death penalty here."

"Why are you so keen that he has to die?"

"He's a Windigo, Tess. He has to die so that the souls he has stolen can be released to go to their own versions of the afterlife."

"What are you talking about?"

"All those people he killed. Some of them were Christians. Your friend Dawn. Their souls are all trapped. They have to be freed."

"And they can only be freed if Rivershade dies?"

"Yes, he has to die," Ondag was convinced of this fact.

"I can't believe that Dawn's soul is not in heaven. She was a very good woman and kind, a good mother. I don't see how she possibly could have gone to purgatory let alone hell. She's in heaven with her maker."

"She's not in any of those places. She's trapped inside Rivershade's spirit stomach or some place like that. Windigos eat the souls of their victims and the souls struggle inside the Windigo until they finally die. We believe that a soul cannot live without food, air, light, love and creativity. When a soul is trapped inside a Windigo it has no access to these things and it dies. When a soul dies, it dies. There is nothing else. There is no afterlife, there is no salvation, it just ends."

"That's terrible," Tess agreed. "But I can't believe that."

"Rivershade believes it and he told his lawyer that no matter what he has to stay alive. He said he didn't care if he spends the rest of his life in prison, so long as he stays alive as long as possible."

"Who told you that?"

"Prison guard I met in the bar last night." Ondag stated.

Tess looked dubious.

"Yeah, I heard them talking and struck up a conversation with them."

"But what if he's not a Windigo?" Tess asked. "I mean, what if you all are wrong about him, about his nature. I got to know him a little. He's been living in the white world so long he started to think like a white man. He was definitely delusional, but I think he had a lot of emotional scars that led him toward those delusions. He is smart too. Did you know that he got a degree in Anthropology just so he could trace the bird people ancestry?"

"Really?"

"He is a very intelligent person, even though his conclusions all ended up being faulty and more along the lines of wish fulfillment than actual objective research. I mean, he was an expert geneticist but he thought he could breed a Bird

Person by concentrating the selective genes through a few generations of highly evolved humans."

"And you can't, I take it?"

"Not starting with the degraded material he was planning to start with. I told him that maybe if he started with Kicky it might work, but not his own, he was a mutation of the true Bird People gene. He admitted that himself."

"I think he just wanted to rape you," Ondag said.

"That too is true, undoubtedly. But you see my point. His theory was erroneous from the beginning. He was just trying to perpetrate as much evil as he could."

"And for that alone he should die."

"No he shouldn't," Tess said. "No one should ever be put to death by the state, but further, he should not be put to death because he could be studied by psychologists to determine why he became this evil man."

"Tess, he's not a man. He's a monster."

"He still deserves to live," she shouted.

"NO!" Ondag shouted back. "There are monsters in this world that do not deserve to live. And Rivershade is one of them."

Tess was stunned. She sat back in her seat. She had never seen this side of Ondag before. It frightened her a little.

Actually it frightened her a lot.

"Tess," he said. "I'm sorry. I didn't mean to yell like that. Look, I don't believe you're a cannibal just because you eat Jesus' body, or a vampire because you drink His blood. So don't discount my religion either, OK?"

"I'm sorry," Tess said to him. "I'm not saying there is nothing valid in your religion. All

I'm saying is that there is no proof that Dawn's soul is not already in heaven. There is also no proof that Rivershade is one of these soul eating Windigos."

"That's why I called in the Elders. Wild Water is the great-grandson of Kineekuhowa. It is well known that Kineekuhowa could speak with the spirits. I was hoping that Wild Water could speak with Rivershade and we could find out if he is a Windigo."

"Kineekuhowa? He was a real man?" Tess asked.

"Yeah, why?"

"I dreamt about him. Remember my coma dream?"

"That's the other thing. That was no dream. That was your spirit traveling to the land of the dead."

"No, it had to have been a dream. I'm sorry. It just couldn't have been real."

"Because if you were really dead, you would have seen the tunnel and the light, and Jesus? Heaven, angels, everything you've heard about?"

"Yes," she said.

"You didn't though. You saw the Big Sands. You traveled south to the land of the dead, the land that all the Algonquin people believe they will go to when they die."

"You're saying that the desert I saw is some sort of Happy Hunting ground?"

Ondag smiled. "No, you saw the true afterlife. The one that all Algonquin people see upon their death."

"How do you know this?"

"They same way you know it. People can go there and come back. It's hard to do, and the journey is never easy. The people who go there and come back are changed."

"But Kineekuhowa, he was a real person?"

"Yes, I don't remember him. I only remember my father talking about him. He died in the 60's. He was over 150 years old. People say he was born the year the British took Fort Michilimackinac."

"What year was that?" Tess asked.

"1812."

Tess had heard this story before. Kent had told her this back at Bay Mills. But that was before her coma dream. Tess was dumbfounded. She said nothing for a whole minute. When she regained her tongue she said, "Kineekuhowa told me that he was the ancestor of my children. Do you think he and Kicky are related somehow?"

"It's possible. Kineekuhowa would have been a young man back in 1830. He probably traveled all over the state. The Algonquin's ruled a land mass that was greater in pure acreage than the so called Louisiana Purchase."

"Really."

"He could have been Kicky's 3 or 4 times great grandfather."

"Wow."

"See what I mean? It don't matter if you *think* you're a member of this tribe or not. You still are. Clyde didn't adopt you so much as he acknowledged your connection."

"All right then," Tess said. "You did the right thing. I'm sorry I yelled at you."

"You didn't yell at me. You stayed utterly calm. I yell. I guess we need to know these things about each other, huh sis?"

Tess smiled at this. "Yeah, we'll figure it out."

They took a cue from the Yooper Bar guide and had lunch at a place called Stucko's Pub and Grill. It wasn't Friday so they couldn't try the fish fry, and they also didn't serve pasties, but they did have the best bar burgers in 100 miles, and they had Onion Rings that looked like donuts.

That afternoon things started to happen really fast. Tess got the phone call from the States Attorney, and was asked to go meet him at the Sheriff Department as soon as she could get there. Anson Weynecker was a middle aged man with male pattern baldness and a thick middle. He was nicely dressed in a black suit jacket and tie around his over-sized neck. He had the red-veined nose of an habitual drinker and a voice like Darth Vader with a yooper accent. As soon as he smiled though Tess liked him. She could tell he would always be counted on to do what was right.

"First of all," he said as he escorted her toward a chair in the interview room. "Are you OK? I mean, you look OK, but do you need any help. Maybe some counseling or something. Being abducted is not a nice thing to happen. Whatever you need to do for yourself I would like to encourage you to do it."

"Thank you, but I think I'll be fine, for now. I have a very supportive family."

"Oh good, that's good to hear," he said. "Now tell me what happened to you step by step."

Tess talked for about an hour first giving him a sketchy time line of events and than filling in some of the details. She told him about the threats, about the intended rape and the theory that was in his head for breeding her with himself, his son and then her own offspring in order to get a more pure breed. She did not let on that Rivershade was a shifter. If that became known later then she would admit to knowing that he believed himself to be a shifter. She had not seen him shift in the time that they had been together so she would not admit to anyone that she herself believed him to be a shifter.

"He believed some very crazy theories," Tess told Weynecker.

"Such as?"

"He believed in something he called 'Bird People'. I asked him what they were and he said that's what his people called what we think of as Aliens."

"Aliens," he stated flatly.

"That's what he told me. Crazy right?"

"Are you telling me that he thought he was one of them?" Weynecker asked.

"Yes, he did. He also thought I was part Alien and his whole breeding theory was to concentrate the Alien DNA so he could breed an actual Alien from us humans who had high levels of Alien DNA. I don't know how he figured out which people had it and which didn't. He thought I had a lot of Alien DNA. I think it was just an excuse to rape me cloaked in Science."

Weynecker nodded. He had a grim look on his face. "At least they caught him before you could be raped."

"Yeah, Thank God for small favors huh?"

"They did right?"

"Yes," she said soberly. "I did not get raped. He had a very hard cruel mouth though so I was privy to all of his thoughts on the subject. He admitted to raping and murdering other women."

"Hearing what a bad man is planning is part of the rape, in my considered opinion," Weynecker said. Tess nodded in agreement.

"OK, based on your testimony alone, we can convict him of kidnapping. But I also want to get him for as many counts of murder as I can get. Do you have anything to say about Dawn Kraft?"

"Only that I met her and her family in Mackinaw City the week before she was attacked. I had a pet wolf at the time that followed me around and I left the pet with her family when I went over to Mackinac Island one afternoon. Dawn's husband Rick is a wildlife biologist. He told me a lot of information about my wolf so I figured they would make good wolf sitters. They became good friends with us and they also drove me and Woofy over the bridge the next day. Then later, I went to visit the little girl Kit in the hospital in the Soo. I didn't know anything about the attack until I ran into Rick in the Soo several weeks later."

"Did you know any of the other victims in the Lower Peninsula?" he asked.

"No sir, but I had camped near a lot of the locations where murders occurred. Namely Alden, Charlevoix and I had also been through Pelston but I didn't camp there."

"And you witnessed him killing several people in Wisconsin and Minnesota?"

"Just the one in Wisconsin when he felt the need to switch cars."

"What about the one in Minnesota?"

"He didn't kill her or her baby. He just took the baby into the store as a hostage so that I wouldn't try to run away. I felt so sorry for her that I didn't even try. I hope she's OK. I hated what he did to her."

"Do you know her name? I could get her as witness and that would be two abductions."

"Do you have the stuff that was in his car

when he was caught?"

"Um, yeah, I think I do."

"Her purse was in the car. He used her credit cards and her money for a while on the trip. I'm sure that her I.D. Must be in there."

"Thank you, I'll look into that."

"Anything else you can think of?"

"Annie Warner," she said. "Her two adult children were attacked after I spent the night camping in her back yard, in Goetzville, Michigan."

"Yes, I've spoken with them. They were attacked by an animal. An oversized Wolf it sounds like. Do you think he had such a pet?"

"It would explain a few things," Tess said.

"OK, not sure what, but. Anything else?"

"No, not off the top of my head. I'll go over it again tonight to make sure."

"OK, but don't drive yourself crazy."

Tess smiled and started to leave.

"Oh, by the by," he said. Tess looked back at him, "Why would I want a Native-American Shaman looking in on our guy?"

"You let other prisoners see their clergymen, right?"

"You think Talbot Rivershade is looking for spiritual guidance?"

"Maybe," Tess said. She knew why Wild Water wanted to see him, but this statement would insure that he wasn't turned away. Everyone had a right to pray for their own soul.

When Tess walked out of the interview room Kit, Rick and Colt were sitting in the chairs. Kit jumped up and ran to Tess. Tess got down on her knees and hugged Kit for all she was worth.

"You are looking fine, girlfriend," Tess said.

"You look good too. Better than in that old

hospital."

"I know, I hate hospitals."

"I know, me too." Kit said sadly. "Where is Kicky?"

"Kicky is back at the tourist camp."

"Can I see him and play with him?"

"Yes, you may." She looked up at Rick. "Are you staying at the camp too?"

"No, the kids want to be inside at night. No more camping for us."

Tess nodded. "Come out to the camp tonight. We'll have a bonfire and you'll get to meet all the Ojibwa Elders. Would you like to meet a lot of Native Americans?" she asked Colt and Kit.

"Yeah," came their answers.

"I'm going to cater in a pizza party I think. BYO snacks and Beverage," she told Rick. "And don't forget the marshmallows," she said patting Kit on the head.

Weynecker came out and ushered the family into the interview room. Before the door closed though, Tessa's phone was ringing. It was Clyde. The elders just arrived at the Ramada.

"This is a nice hotel, our room is overlooking the pool," he told her.

Within minutes they were all gathered in Clyde's hotel room, even George. Clyde greeted George like a brother, giving him a big hug. "Good to meet Tessa's real father," he said. "I'm Tessa's adopted father."

"Does this mean she's part of the tribe now?" he asked.

"Well, she's not a full member of the tribe yet because she wasn't at the adoption ritual. There were only two people there, me and her mother, Roseanne."

"I was there too," Ondag said. "I witnessed."

"There was a ritual involved?" Tess asked.

"Yeah, and you can't be a full member of the tribe unless you participate. We can have another one anytime you want though."

"What if I don't want to be part of the tribe at all?"

"Don't matter, you already are, at least partly. If you never do the ritual then you will always just partly be part of the tribe."

"Right," said Tess. "But, why did all of you come?"

"I need to talk with Rivershade," Wild Water stated. "Then we have to decide what to do."

"He's going to be tried and convicted and spend the rest of his life in prison, if I have anything to say about it." Tess was adamant.

"Yeah, we want that too, Tess." Clyde patted her shoulder. Her spidey sense was tingling. She could tell when she was being shined on. But she supposed the tribe had their way of doing things, and she would just have to wait and accept. He was in prison now awaiting the hearing.

"After talking with him in the car all that time, I know that he's just delusional. I really hope he gets sent to someplace where he's just not going to rot in a cell. He needs help," she said.

"Stockholm Syndrome?" Roseanne asked. Wild Water nodded.

"Well, listen," Clyde said. "You got the appointment this afternoon. We'll know what we need to do by tonight."

"Oh, speaking of tonight. You are all invited out to the tourist camp tonight for dinner and a bonfire. I'm buying pizza and pop. One other family is bringing stuff to make s'mores and it's BYO snacks and beverages."

"OK, sounds good. Where are you ordering from?"

She almost answered that question and then knew that would be a mistake. Clyde would end up footing the bill for her entire party.

Ondag handed Tess the car keys as she walked toward the door. "I'm going to stay here with my family," he told her. She shrugged. She couldn't blame him for that. George, Kicky and Tess left and went to arrange for the party that night.

Sure enough, when she went into Casa Calibria to order the Pizzas for the party, she was told that it was already paid for on the credit card of one Clyde Morrow. There were half a dozen places to order Pizza in this town. He must have called them all with those instructions. So Tess stopped at KFC and got a couple of buckets of Chicken with all the sides as well. They went back to the tourist park to wait for their guests to show up. Kicky went out to gather wood for their bonfire and ended up having to buy some from the office.

They had a quiet time for a while before Rick showed up with his kids. George spent this time getting to know Kicky. He jokingly began the conversation with the question of whether or not his intentions were honorable.

"Yes sir," Kicky answered, and to his credit, Tess thought he didn't sound a bit defensive. "Tess is my mate and always will be."

"Always?" George asked.

"Yep, I'm not going anywhere. Except where she goes, of course," he amended.

"I thought your name was David?"

"David Kickingstone Red Wing. My family calls me Kicky."

"Kickingstone? How did you get a name like that?" George asked.

"My sister was babysitting for me when I was about three I think. I tried to kick a stone out of my way with bare feet and ended up stubbing my toe. They called me Kickingstone after that."

"Like Stands with a fist," he said.

"Dances with Wolves," he smiled at his mate. Tess was setting up a folding table that they had found hidden under the bed.

She had a pile of paper plates on it and the napkins and utensils from KFC. She dumped the pop into the cooler and the ice on top of it. Then she was done for the time being. The chicken was staying warm in the oven. The little fridge was full to overloaded and the za hadn't arrived yet. She came over to sit down on the lawn chair in front of Kicky. He pulled her into his arms and there they sat chatting with George.

"It's good to see you happy," George said.

Tess smiled. "I gave you 15% of the last deposit," she told him.

"I knew you were going to do that," he said. "I don't need it you know."

"Like my adopted father says, don't matter."

"Tess?" Kicky asked. "Do you mind if I use your cell phone to go call my mom?"

Tess had totally forgotten that she had not given him the second cell phone that George had brought for him. "Sure," she said. "Here. Keep it."

"Mine?" he asked.

"Yep," she said.

"Wow, Thank you! This will come in handy next time you get abducted."

"Shush on that," she said smiling. "It's about time you had one."

"Why didn't he have one before this?"

"Because when I first met him he didn't have a pocket to put it in."

"What? Does that mean something?"

Tess smiled. She wanted to discuss the topic with Kicky before she reveal his secrets. It wasn't her secret to tell. She wondered what he was telling his mother. She thought about listening in on his conversation mentally, but decided it would not be good form. Then a clear thought came to her. "You can if you want. I have no secrets from you."

"Oh yeah?" She asked mentally. "Then how old are you really?"

She got back the flash of a wrinkled old Kicky with white hair that hung down in long braids on both sides of his head. Right!

"What are you thinking about?" George asked.

"Dad, I don't want to keep secrets from you, but it's not my secret to tell."

"Does it have anything to do with your wolf being missing? You do still see him right?"

"Not in a while, but I have a feeling he'll be around. Maybe tonight."

Kicky came back in the room and sat. He was pushing the touch pad of his phone and discovering all the features.

"Where does your mother live?"

"My family lives in Sutton's Bay and Northport, and some of them live in Peshawbestown. All in that area north of Traverse City."

"How many of you are there?"

He cleared his throat. "There are five kids in my immediate family and my parents. But our clan is over 150 people. They are all our relatives, you know extended."

"Wow," George said. "When you all get together I bet it's a big occasion."

"We all get together every week. And yeah, it's big. Our clan leader has a club house that we all fit in. It's kind of like a hall that you have a wedding reception in."

"Is that where you plan to get married?" he asked. Then he added, "You are planning to get married right?"

"As soon as ever possible," he said. He pulled Tess closer into his body. She turned her head so she could rest it on his shoulder.

"Is there a ring and a date?" George asked.

"Not yet, Dad, we haven't got the money for all that."

"I do to," Kicky said. "I just called my mom so she could send me my last few paychecks and my I.D. She had to get it reissued and she did that but didn't know where to send it until I called her just now."

"I'm sorry," Tess said. "I should have thought of that sooner. Besides you need to get in touch with your family more often than this."

"No, I don't. It's OK, Tess. You are my family now."

"I'll pay you back for the phones Dad." Tess said.

"You don't have to do that you know."

"Yes, I always pay my own way."

"It's true. Ever since I've known Tess, I know that she has a highly developed sense of pride in her self-sufficiency and her work ethic." Kicky said. “I think it makes her sick to take money from people. It’s not a matter of whether she deserves it. I think she does, but that’s not the issue. She just believes it’s wrong to take money except for services rendered. The only services she wants to be paid for is her writing. I don’t think there is anything wrong with that.”

“To be sure,” George said. “You seem to know my daughter very well for only having met her recently.”

“I know her very well. I’ve imprinted on her. I know exactly what she wants from me and I’m hers no matter what.”

“Imprinted? What does that mean?” George asked.

“Tess wants to tell you this. I think you have the right to know.”

“Tell me what?”

“Actually I’ll show you.” He climbed once again out of the chair and went inside the RV. A few minutes later Woofy emerged from the RV.

“Was he in there that whole time?” George asked his daughter.

“No, he was out here with us.”

“No, I mean the wolf. Was he in that motor home taking a nap or something?”

“No, this is Kicky.”

“No,” George said. “Kicky come out here,” he shouted toward the motor home.

“Go see for yourself,” she said. He went to the door of the motor home and went inside. He was there for a few minutes and then came out. “The clothes he was wearing are on the kitchen floor, but he’s not there.”

“No, Dad, because he’s right here.” She petted the gray ruff around Woofy’s neck.

"Are you telling me that he is a werewolf?"

"No, he's a shape shifter," she confirmed. "He can only shift into a wolf but when he does he keeps his human mind. Want to see proof?"

"Yeah, will he turn in front of me?"

She looked into the wolf's mind. "Yes, he said he would but only inside. He doesn't want anyone else to see him change. He doesn't even really like me watching his transformation."

"Oh, OK." He got up and went into the RV with Woofy. They both emerged a little while later. George was as white as a Halloween ghost. Woofy was still Woofy. Kicky had decided to play out the party tonight as the wolf. Tess mentally asked him if that would age him. He said it would not. He just didn't want to disappoint Kit and he thought it would be good for Colt to see a good wolf after having seen the bad wolf.

"Daddy, are you alright?" Tess asked.

"I'm stunned. I never thought there were such things. Who would think there were? Crazy people."

"I know, right?"

They had to put the topic aside because Rick showed up just then with his two kids. They had a box of graham crackers, chocolate bars and a bag of marshmallows along with a bag of pretzels, he explained, for those who would rather have salty than sweet. He had half a dozen juice boxes with him and a six pack of Molson's. He offered one to George after Tess introduced them and he asked where David was as he popped one for himself.

"Kicky is here," Kit howled and then ran straight for him. The wolf jumped up and down several times as Kit tried to hug him and they both ended up lying on the ground, Woofy licking her face as she giggled. Colt was a little more shy about Woofy, at first hiding behind his father's legs, but soon he was approaching as he saw what a good time his sister was having with the wolf. Kicky approached the boy calmly and straight forward allowing his tongue to loll out the side in a friendly manner. Pretty soon he was laughing and roughhousing with his sister. It wasn't long after that when the Ojibwa Elders began to arrive. They rode in four cars. They each made two trips to the cars and back, first to get chairs to sit in, and then to bring food and several coolers full of beverages. When Clyde saw Woofy playing with the kids, he shook his head.

"Tess," he said. "I think your G-man is coming, maybe Kicky would like to make an appearance."

"He had to go out of town, but Woofy came back."

"Yeah, good for him." Clyde said. Tess went inside to bring out the food from the fridge and the oven. George came in to help her.

"Does Clyde know about Kicky?" he asked.

"Yeah, Dad, Um, lets just say that Native Americans have their own belief system, and leave it at that. They knew even before I did."

"Really?"

They got the food out and just as they were starting to line up to get chicken and fixings the pizza arrived.

The party was going good by 8 pm. The chicken was gone, the pizza leftovers had been reduced to one box, and everything with mayo had been taken back into the fridge by Roseanne, who was very careful about such things. Kicky had not shown up at all and Kit and Colt had been told that when the law enforcement officers were present they should only refer to the wolf as Woofy. Agent Marcus arrived just as the marshmallows had begun to hit the campfire.

"Hey, G-man," Clyde called to him. "Come meet Tessa's father."

Clyde remembered his name having met him weeks earlier when they had brought Tess to the reservation. He introduced Marcus to George.

"You eat yet G-man?" Clyde asked him.

"Not yet," he admitted. "I've been meeting with witness all afternoon, making phone calls. I just now only came over here to let you know that the hearing is tomorrow morning at 9:00 A.M. They will set the trial date at that time."

"Is that all?" Clyde asked. Roseanne had just come out of the RV with a plate full of food and handed it to Marcus. He at once took the fork she offered and began munching potato salad. "OK then, you've done your duty. Time to party. Want a beer?"

"No, I'm driving. But, Kit?" he said raising his voice. "Can I have one of your juice boxes?" He had noticed she had been sipping on one and when he looked inside the cooler had noticed several more there.

"Sure," she said. She bounded over and knelt in front of the cooler lifting the lid. "Do you want apple, grape, cherry, or strawberry/banana?"

"I don't know, which is the best?" he said looking at her.

"I think," she said turning her head sideways and putting one finger on her cheek, "that you are a cherry guy."

"I was hoping you would say that," he said.

She handed him the red box and then helped

him by pulling off the straw and poking it into the top for him. “There, that’s how it’s done.” She turned and said, “Commere, Kicky.”

“Kicky?” he said. He turned to Tess. “I thought you said David was Kicky.”

Tess pretended to be busy corralling a marshmallow between two graham crackers and a chocolate bar for Colt. She didn’t acknowledge the question.

The wolf was prancing all around the campfire jumping up to lick Kit’s face and then running after her when she hopped off. He would outdistance her and then stop to wait for her to catch up. When she did she fell to her knees before him and he edged in to knock her down. She got up and put her arms around his neck and pronounced in a loud voice, “I love you too, Kicky!”

Tess noticed that the kisses he was giving her were mostly on her scars. The bandages were off and the scar tissue was a red ugly streak going down the middle of that side of her face. There was a very fine ridge though and Tess thought that in time the ridge might fade to white and not look quite so bad.

“Rick,” Tess said. “Did the doctors say that maybe Kit could get plastic surgery in the future to get rid of the scar tissue?”

“Yeah, they seem hopeful.”

“How is Kit feeling about the way she looks?” Roseanne asked.

“She doesn’t even seem to notice it. She doesn’t look in mirrors any more, not even in the bathroom to comb her hair. So I know it’s having an affect on her. But she’s more worried about her mother.”

“Her mother?” Roseanne asked.

"Yeah, she's been having nightmares lately. She says that her mother isn't in heaven. She claims that her mother is in some dark pit of a place and can't breathe or eat or speak. This just scares her to death."

Ondag looked over at Tess.

"Does she know where her mother is?" Clyde asked.

"What?" Rick was stunned by the question. "I think it has to do with the fact that we buried her in the ground. I think she's afraid that her mother is still alive in the coffin. I tell her that only her body is in the coffin, and that her spirit is with Jesus. But she doesn't understand."

"Do you mind if I ask her?" Clyde asked.

"If you want," Rick said. "Kit come over here for a second will you?"

Kit came running Woofy at her heels.

Clyde called her over to him and she stood out in front of him facing him. Tess thought she looked very courageous.

"You've been having dreams?" he asked her.

"Yes sir," she said very formally. She didn't know what this was about but she lifted her chin determined to answer his questions the best she could.

"Did you know that we Indians put a great stock in dreams?" he asked her. "We believe the dream world is another world that we live in, like this one. And we can go back and forth there all the time. Did you know that?"

"No," she admitted. "How do you do it?"

"Just like you do, we go to sleep and go over to that other world. Things are different in that other world. We can sometimes see people over there that died in this world."

"I do to, all the time. I see my brother there, the one that died."

"You have two brothers," Rick said. "They are still alive."

"No, I mean the one that died in Mommy's belly. She had me, but the other one that was with me died."

"What?" he said.

"Rick?" Tess asked. She grabbed his arm because he looked like he might fall over.

He whispered to Tess, "There was two heart beats at first," Rick said. But then she started to bleed and we thought she had miscarried. But when it stopped she was still pregnant with Kit. But how did Kit . . .?" he stopped to listen more because Clyde had kept asking her questions.

"Do you ever see your Mommy in that world?" he asked.

"Sort of," Kit said.

"What do you mean?"

"I know it's her because she's sort of crying for me, but not with her mouth, with her wanting."

"With her wanting?" he asked.

"Yeah, she wants to reach us so bad. She's in a lot of pain. She can't breathe in there, she's in a sack, like a stomach sort of. She can't see or feel or hear or anything. All I know is she wants to get out of there."

"Is it like hell?" Clyde asked.

"No, not exactly," Kit told him. "It's more like a big wet plastic bag that she's in."

"Is she struggling to get out and you can see her arms push it outward like this," he asked, and then pushed his arms out away from him.

"Yeah, sort of."

"How do you know it's her?"

"I can feel her. She's my mother, I can feel her." Kit knew this statement was inadequate but didn't know how else to say it.

"How do you know that she can't breathe in there?" he asked.

"Because she is doing this," Kit closed her throat and made a gasping noise as if something were constricting her airway.

"Are there other people in there with her?"

"Yes, but they are all separate. They can't talk to each other."

"Kit," Clyde said to her, "This is really important. Do you know where she is?"

Kit closed her eyes and thought. Tess realized that she had already said that she didn't know where her mother was, but that she wasn't in heaven. But when Kit opened her eyes she said, "I think it's kind of like a jail."

"A jail," Clyde repeated. He looked up at Wild Water. "Do you mean the sack IS the jail, or is the sack IN jail?" Tess didn't know what he was getting at. The two sounded the same to her.

"The sack is inside the jail." Kit said. "Is my mommy going to die in there?"

"Sweetie, Your mother is already dead," Tess said to her.

"No, I know she's dead from this world, but she's not dead in that one." She looked desperately back at Clyde, "Will she die in that one?"

"I hope not, sweetie," Clyde said. "Not if I have anything to say about it."

Kit stood in front of Clyde for a moment, her lips were turned down. Tess thought she looked like she was trying not to cry. The two regarded each other somberly for a few seconds and then Kit collapsed into Clyde's arms. She held back her sobs even though several tears fell from the corners of her eyes. The big man gathered her up into his arms and held her for a long time telling her, "It's OK, I'll see that she gets out of there. It's OK, don't worry," he kept repeating this for several minutes while everyone looked on.

Chapter 12

The party broke up about an hour later. Kit had stayed safe and warm in Clyde's lap that whole time, falling asleep in the big man's arms. Woofy stayed in his wolf form getting up onto the bed in the back of the RV. Before they went to bed though, Ondag had to explain something to Tess.

"He's going to have to die you know," he told her.

"I don't know what you're talking about. That was all just a little girl's anxiety over losing her mother."

"Didn't you hear her though. There were other people in there with her, they were all separate, they couldn't talk to each other, they can't breathe, they are all suffering and the sack they are in is inside a jail, that's because Rivershade is in jail and they are inside Rivershade. It's exactly as Wild Water confirmed earlier when he went to see Rivershade in the prison today."

"I refuse to believe that Dawn isn't in heaven where she belongs."

"It's your refusal to believe in anything except what your religion teaches that's going to be your downfall Tess." Ondag shouted. "You didn't believe Woofy could be a shape shifter until you saw it for yourself with your own eyes. You don't believe in the Bird People, but they are as real as you and me. You probably don't believe in Sasquatch or in The Lock Ness Monster, or in dinosaurs.

"I believe in dinosaurs, they've found bones. But they have never found fossilized remains of big foot or the Loch Ness monster. There is no evidence."

"OK, no evidence that you will take. That's different. You need to see for yourself. You won't take eye witness accounts of my people that have been handed down from generation to generation in our oral histories."

"No, I don't, because have you ever played the game telephone?"

"I'm really sick of that argument. But our historians hear the old stories again and again when we are young until we know them by heart. Then we say them to our own young again and again so they can remember then correctly. We only speak the truth, especially where our history is concerned. You can rely on that."

"So you're saying that all those stories are true, even the one with the guy in the cave who made a pipe out of clay and put it in the skulls mouths. They came to life then." This had been a story that was told to her in the campfire at Bay Mills while she was staying there. She thought it was a very scary story but there was no way she would believe it.

"Yes, the old warriors came back to life to repopulate the tribe. Don't you get it. They were dead and they came back to life long enough to mate with the women. It's a spiritual story. You don't understand it, do you?"

"No, because it's impossible. Once you are a bones in a grave you cannot come back to life and father children."

"I know many people who believe that once you are bones in a grave you can come back. Like the Hindu's, they believe you can come back to life after you die."

"Yes, in a different body, that's reincarnation."

"OK, what about Jesus. He came back to life in his own same body, and so did that other guy that Jesus saved, Lazarus."

"Those were miracles and they both still had flesh, they were not just skull bones, smoking on clay pipes."

"But they were dead. They came back. Who's to say what is possible and impossible in the spiritual world. Or are you going to argue that you're God can do miracles but ours can't?"

Tess stopped herself from saying what had come into her mind next. She realized that she was such a Catholic that she couldn't lend credence to any other religion but her own and ones that were similar to hers.

"So where is Kicky? He should be in on this

conversation. He is my mate, if he feels the same as you, I should know about it."

"He went to bed on purpose. He doesn't want to fight with you."

"I'm sorry, but we might have to agree to disagree on this topic. I'm just not going to ever agree with capital punishment."

"We can't afford to disagree. Rivershade needs to die. As the person who was abducted by him, you need to step up and tell us that it has to happen. Whether you do or not, we all know that he must die. He cannot be allowed to go on living indefinitely."

"We are in a state that has no death penalty. If he is convicted he will spend the rest of his life in prison, no matter what. Who is going to kill him? Clyde, you? Then you will spend the rest of your life in prison. Don't do it. Do not sacrifice yourself over this. It's just not worth it."

"Tell Dawn, it's not worth it." Ondag said. "Tell all his other victims their eternal spirit being snuffed out is not worth it."

"If their eternal spirit could be snuffed out it would not be worth it. But it can't be. It's eternal. By definition it cannot be snuffed out."

"You're own bible says it can be," he countered.

"What do you mean?"

" 'If thy hand offends thee, cut it off. If thy eye offends thee, pluck it out.'" Ondag quoted.

"That's from the Old Testament." She said.

"No it's not," he countered, "It's from the New Testament. It can be interpreted that God is the source of all spirit, of all life. He puts a spark of Himself into each one of us. If one of us offends God, then he has no choice but to cut us off from his divine spark and snuff out our existence. He doesn't like to do that of course because it's like plucking out one of his own eyes or cutting off his own hand. He will only do it in extreme cases."

"So how is it that this Windigo can cut off the spark as well? If God is all powerful than why would He allow such a thing to exist?"

"How many times has that question been asked?" Ondag said. "People ask it all the time. If God is all powerful why does He allow evil to exist? It's a question without a good answer. Have you ever heard a good answer?"

"Yeah, I have. It's so that people can choose the good over the evil. Good could not exist without evil."

"OK, that's a good answer, but it might be too easy of an answer. What if it's not clear which is the good choice and which the evil?"

"It's always clear."

"Destroying a life is always evil?"

"Yes," Tess said.

"What about a lame horse? Is it evil to kill a lame horse or is it kinder to put it out of its misery?"

"I see what you mean, but that's just an animal, not a human."

"What about a human with cancer who can't eat any more, has a colostomy bag and can't shit any more, and has so much pain that they are on massive doses of morphine just to get through the day. They are praying for death, they ask someone to help them die to put them out of this miserable state of existence. Which is more evil, letting them suffer or helping them die with dignity?"

"My religion says that human life is sacred and helping someone die is tantamount to murder." Tess said, but she was now weeping openly.

"Now, what about this situation. Kit's mother is trapped in a place where she will not be able to survive. She has an immortal soul, but she will lose hope and eventually she will die. When the soul dies, it is snuffed out of existence. Her soul will be released when Rivershade dies. But Kit's mom might be dead already by the time he dies. Which is more evil. To allow him to live and let all those people that he has trapped die from their immortal existence or kill him and let all of them go on to their own versions of heaven?"

Tess wept. She mentally called for Kicky but got a stone wall of silence back. She knew what that meant. Kicky believed as Ondag did. So much for imprinting.

Ondag silently stood and went back into the bathroom. As he passed her he said, "Go to bed, Tess. You need some rest."

The next morning Tess was lying in bed with a naked human Kicky. She slowly came awake enjoying the view of his beautiful body. Then she heard his clear thought, "No time for that this morning. We have to go to the hearing."

She glanced at the clock on her telephone and got up to dress.

Ondag had scrambled eggs and warmed over pizza on the breakfast table. They grabbed some food on the fly and soon were off to the court house.

Everyone was searched on the way into the court house. No one had a weapon of any kind. Tess was happy for that. She didn't know what Clyde had planned, if anything. But it wouldn't involve shoot or knifing the defendant. Court came into session exactly at nine. Several other defendants were called before Rivershade, registered a plea and were told what their court date would be. Clyde had seen which door the criminals were entering through and managed to get into the seats just behind it. Tess sat watching him from across the room. Kit was sitting on Kicky's lap to her right with Rick on the other side of them. Ondag sat to her left with George and Roseanne to his left. The rest of the elders sat in the row behind her.

Tess remembered this room from the movie. James Stewart had played the part of the lawyer in Anatomy of a Murder which was filmed in this very courtroom. Tess remembered watching it once or twice as a girl. It was interesting being in a place that she remembered from a movie. She was about to comment on it when the court clerk announced in a loud voice, people v. Talbot Rivershade. Rivershade was ushered out into the courtroom. He was shackled both on his hands and ankles and he was wearing gray horizontally striped coveralls. The moment he came through the door he looked straight at Clyde. Clyde smiled at him.

He was being escorted by two police offers, neither of them were wearing guns. The only reason Tess noticed this was because she was at once afraid that Clyde might try to steal a weapon and kill Rivershade. But he couldn't.

The two officers held Rivershade's arms and forced him to face the judge. The clerk read the charges, two counts of abducting a person against their will, one count of terrorism, five counts of murder.

"How do you plead?" asked the judge.

"Not guilty," he answered.

Weynecker stood, "Your honor, we request remand. The defendant is facing multiple charges, and he has unknown resources of wealth that he can pull from. I believe him to be a flight risk."

"Your honor," Rivershade's attorney stated. "My client is an upstanding member of the tribe of Ojibwa Indians and is not at all a flight risk. He had strong ties to this community and is not overburdened with casino money. Like some of his neighbors that are here in this courtroom." He looked significantly over at Clyde who smiled again.

"He abducted a young woman and fled the state, your honor. He does have the means to flee."

"Yes, yes, we want him to stick around," said the judge. "Remand. Court date will be set for three weeks from today in courtroom 12, Judge Halkonen presiding."

"Thank you, your honor," Weynecker said. The other attorney murmured something similar.

The two police officers turned Rivershade and began to escort him out the door. But Clyde leaned in and said something to Rivershade. Tess couldn't hear it. One of the officers put a hand on Clyde's chest to push him away from the prisoner. But Clyde leaned in again and grabbed Rivershade by the collar. He brought Rivershade's face very close to his and spoke. Then he let Rivershade go, throwing the collar away from him in a gesture that Tess thought meant that he was through with Rivershade.

The officers tried to get Rivershade under control again, but he was getting angry and pulling away from them. Clyde had turned and was walking swiftly out of the courtroom. Tess stood. She could not believe what was happening. Rivershade had evaded one of the officers and was climbing over the railing trying to get at the quickly retreating Clyde. Tess watched helplessly as he elbowed the nose of the officer that still held his arm. This officer fell backward over a chair and went sprawling on the floor behind the defendant's desk. The other officer made a grab for Rivershade from the back and managed to catch hold of the back of his collar. The coverall slipped backward and tightened around Rivershade's neck drawing him backward. He snarled at the man and pulled at the tightened collar. It came out of the man's hand tearing like paper. Rivershade vaulted over the railing and bounded over the seats falling on his hands and then taking off again like a wolf. He snarled again and the next time he bounded upward his hands had turned into paws. He easily slipped the shackles with only a couple of short movements. He kicked his legs several times and the shackles were gone from those limbs as well. He was full on Dogman skin for certain now and bounding after Clyde. Clyde was running. He made it out to the lobby and kept running. Rivershade ran on all fours and heading straight toward the door, knocking people down as he went. Several people were injured by his claws.

He got outside the court room. Tess moved toward a window but too many people were in her way. Ondag had climbed on the bench and managed to walk its length jumping over several people who still sat down. He made it to the window. Tess came after him and got to the window too in time to see Clyde run from the building, yelling help. He made it across the lawn before Rivershade emerged from the building. Then Tess heard the pop of several guns and Rivershade stopped upright. He fell to the ground and as many people watched he changed back into a man. Not the man he had been in the courtroom however. He changed into a man that looked to be over a hundred years old. Tess watched this all in stunned silence. Clyde had not killed him, but whatever it was that Clyde had said to him, it made him angry enough to turn. In that way Clyde had assured that the law enforcement officers outside would kill him. Tess was angry. She would speak to Clyde about this. She looked back toward Rick. Kit was holding onto her father's leg like her life depended on it. Colt was in his father's arms, face buried into his father's neck as if not wanting to see the bad wolf again. Kicky bent down to take Kit into his arms but she wouldn't let go of her father.

He stayed down on one knee and held Kit as he looked up at Tess. She heard the clear question in her head. "Is he dead?"

She nodded. He was most assuredly dead.

Chapter 13

In the aftermath of the attack, somehow, most of the Elders were able to avoid police scrutiny. Clyde was not among those happy few. Since he had been the focus of the "animal attack" he was questioned for hours. In the end the police outside the building clearly saw what they called a large wolf that ran upright on its hind legs, three of them open fired on the thing and killed it in the front yard of the Courthouse. Inside the eye witness accounts were a little more sketchy. One young woman said the Native American man had whispered something in the defendant's ear and then the defendant had turned into a wolf, jumped into the crowd and escaped still wearing his human clothing. She also happened to mention that his clothes didn't tear off like they normally did in the movies. She was the only one in the court room that stuck with the story that Rivershade had turned into a wolf. All others said that there was a lot of confusion but the escapee had not turned, even though four people said they thought they had seen him turn, later they recanted. Still others in the courtroom claimed the man had just transformed in anger. They describe his face getting angry and then he attacked. When pressed about the facial transformation one woman elaborated saying that he was so mad that his features twisted into a wolf like mask of anger. But she did not admit that she had seen him change. He had remained the same, a man, a very angry man.

One man told police that the attacker must have had a knife of some sort because he saw the man "slash and claw" a woman who got in his way. The woman who had been attacked called the weapon a hook. And still another who had seen it described the "knife" in perfect detail. When police asked these people how he could possibly have gotten a knife they all agreed that he had not drawn it from a belt sheath, and that it must have been up his sleeve because at one point he did not have it in his hand and then the very next second he did.

Tess and Kicky sat in the police station across from each other at two adjacent desks while they filled out the reports. One of the cops had told Tess that this was pretty crazy. He had a theory which he related to Tess before she gave her statement. He said that he thought Rivershade had gone crazy attacked several people inside the courtroom and then ran outside where he was shot. The "dog" that everyone was claiming to have seen was simply someone's trained service dog that went a little crazy in the commotion and had nothing to do really with anything. This is all proved by the fact that the dog disappeared. He probably ran off and went home to his master. Having heard this version of things, Tess gave her testimony with very little embellishments on this same theme. Kicky insisted that he was watching Tess the whole time and didn't really see what was going on. He said he looked up to see his friend Clyde being chased by a dog. It must have been the seeing-eye dog the guy had told him about.

By two that afternoon the police had completed their investigation and the body of Talbot Rivershade was in the morgue undergoing an autopsy which showed that he was a normal healthy man of about 110 years of age who had died of three gunshot wounds to the upper torso and head. On closer inspection the autopsy revealed that he had been in very good shape and had probably exercised frequently. He had the lungs and musculature of a much younger man, that of a man in his 30's. The Coroner reported that Rivershade must have run marathons and kept in very good shape by running daily. There were no signs of any of the usual aging diseases such as optic degeneration, muscle or joint degeneration or indeed any signs of colon or digestive tract problems. In fact the only indications that this was not a man in his 30's were his teeth. Even the skin still had elasticity and there were no wrinkles or age spots. His hair was thin and gray but only his teeth gave away his true age. Tess knew that he had worn dentures because she saw him put them in one morning. But beneath them there had been nothing but empty holes and nubs of rotted teeth.

Tess was hungry. She and Kicky walked up the hill to the Ramada and knocked on her father's door and then Clyde's. Clyde, Roseanne, and Ondag were all sitting around the room talking, when they arrived.

Tess went to the bed where Roseanne was sitting propped up on pillows against the headboard. She climbed into the bed and put her head on Roseanne's lap.

"Tough day, sweetie?" Roseanne asked.

"You said it," Tess agreed.

Clyde sat forward in his chair. "You know why I had to do it?" he asked Tess. It was not really a question, more like a cry for understanding.

"I know why you thought you had to do it," she said. Even in her own ears this sounded bad, disrespectful.

"I know that in your religion there are very few things that are worse than murder. But in our religion it is not a sin to release someone's spirit into the next realm."

"Enough," Tess shouted, sitting bolt upright in the bed. Everyone was stunned into an uncomfortable silence. She sighed. "What's done is done," she said calmly. "You didn't kill him, and I don't know what you said to him to make him so angry, but it was clear to me that you wanted him to change in the courtroom so that he would have to be put down like an old dog."

Kicky and Ondag smiled sardonically at each other. This look was not lost on Tess.

"I told him that I forgive him."

"Forgive him?" Tess asked, "For what?"

"For hurting someone in his own family. He is my great uncle. I asked him as a favor to his family and his tribe that he not harm anyone to whom he was related. He promised he would not and he had kept that promise right up until the day he took you captive. Did you never wonder why he killed so many people so frequently but he left Ondag and Kicky alive to pursue you when he took you?"

"I admit that crossed my mind, but I didn't want to question it because I was so happy my mate and brother were still alive," Tess said.

"Ondag is his direct kinsmen, and Kicky is Eagle Clan, therefore kin to him as well. You were adopted by me and therefore kin to him by adoption. So he should have left you alone. But he didn't. He hurt you. He committed acts of terror on you and on everyone he met while you were with him. So I gave him absolution, I told him he was forgiven for having lied and gone against his promise to not harm his own family members."

"Don't for a moment try to convince me though that you didn't manipulate him into changing."

"I would not, being that I am an honest man. I would have you know that I knew exactly what would happen and wanted it to happen too. He could not live, Tessa, he had to die, so that the souls he had eaten could live."

"I don't believe that," Tess said to him.

"I told you," Ondag said to Clyde. "She is totally intolerant of our religion."

"I'm not, I just believe that spirit is in the realm of God and no man has domination over other men's spirits."

"That is simply not true," Clyde said. He spoke calmly to her but logically. "All human beings are in charge of their own soul. If they have strong beliefs then they hold fast to their own souls, if they do not have strong faith in God, or in the Universe, or in some religion, then they will never be able to hold on to their souls and may end up losing their souls to others who would capture them and manipulate them. If people knew what could happen to their souls they would not be so careless with them."

"Clyde I can't believe that someone with goodness in them like Dawn, could lose their soul so easily."

"To be sure, she couldn't. Someone who uses their soul for good is more likely to hang onto it than someone who is careless of it and only uses it for self-gratification or to hang onto others or, worse yet, doesn't think they have one at all and thus ignores it."

"Self-gratification?" Tess asked. "You mean like masturbation?"

"Tessa," George said. But he was watching Clyde at the time so didn't notice her look toward him.

"No, I mean the more evil kind of self-gratification where a person has to belittle someone else in order to make themselves feel better. Bullies, and people who have low self-esteem who have developed the mechanism of making others feel inferior so they can have the illusion of superiority."

"You consider that evil."

"That is the face of evil personified. There is nothing more evil in this world. It is literally the cause of every evil, where one man or woman or group of men and women think themselves superior to another individual or group and therefore has the right to rule them."

"As a Native-American, I can see why you

would think that's the worst possible evil, but what about genocide, or jihad, or terrorism?" she asked.

"Genocide, the idea that one race of people is so unimportant that another more superior race can exterminate them. Jihad, where one religion decides that it is superior to all others so they feel justified in killing people who do not believe as they do. Terrorism, where a splinter group of people feel unjustly treated by those who are claiming to be their superiors so they strike back the only way they know how, through treachery and deceit."

"Ok, you made your point. Everyone is inherently equal under the eyes of God." Tess said.

"Leave God out of it and you got it right."

Tess smiled toward Clyde's general direction. She was increasingly amazed by this man that was her adopted father. Actually he had her fairly convinced for the most part that he had been right to forgive Rivershade. But he had chosen the time and place for such forgiveness that put other people in harms way. She was about to bring this up when Kicky spoke.

"You know, Tess. You're right, what's done is done. We haven't had lunch yet, how about we go over to that restaurant downtown, the Verling, and get us an early dinner? Clyde will pay."

The entire room seemed to take a cleansing breath at once with this suggestion and it was agreed. A good meal just then would be a true comfort, especially with this nurturing family.

There was no more talk of religion or spiritual matters the rest of the day. Instead they shared a brilliant meal and several bottles of wine. This meal began at about 4:00 P.M. and lasted well past 8:00 P.M. The servers had never before had a party like this one and two college girls kept the family happy by making sure drinks were full and every new course was put down in front of them hot and with a flourish. They began with salads, and then ordered a combination of appetizers. Tess suggested that they eat in courses and ordered three entrees of baked white fish and rice pilaf to share among them. Then Tess ordered two plates of chicken cacciatore spooning it out onto their plates to try. After that she ordered six of the 8 oz. New York Strips in varying degrees of doneness. They topped off the meal with three slices of cheesecake, which everyone agreed they couldn't eat a single bite of, but yet somehow disappeared from the plates none the less. Tess was in her element. She took photos of all the dishes before doling them out and commenting on their flavors aloud so she would be able to remember what she and others said about each one.

After a long family argument over who was going to pick up the check Clyde finally sent one of the waitresses away with his credit card. When she returned he wrote a rounded up number that Tess couldn't read but it looked like he had tipped them about 100%. She just smiled.

They went back to Clyde's hotel room where they were confronted by several strongly worded messages from Marcus. He needed to talk with them. Tess called him back at once and calmed him down.

"What do you need?" she asked him.

"The DNA results came back. I pushed them through to the FBI lab and I just got the results. Your friend Rivershade had dog blood in him."

"Dog blood?" Tess said trying to sound dubious.

"Yes, he had certain markers in his blood that were canine. Furthermore, the samples that we got off one of his victims is a match. There is no doubt that Rivershade was the killer but the experts can't explain why he had genetic markers of dog in his blood. Can you?"

"I'm not a scientist. I don't have a clue . . ." Tess trailed off as she realized that Marcus was holding two different conversations, one with someone there in the room with him as well as her. The other person in the room was swearing that he had seen Rivershade change into a large dog.

"Tess," he said, and at once her attention was riveted. "I just want to make sure that you know what I'm dealing with here. There are people who are convinced that Rivershade changed shape. This confusion with Kit and Kicky and the name of your Wolf, I just want you to be very aware what I'm dealing with here. OK?"

"I think I know what you mean," She said.

"I don't want you or Kicky or Woofy to get hurt understand. So just do your job and lay low for a while, OK?"

"OK," Tess said.

"I mean, maybe you both should not allow Woofy to stray free. People are kind of nervous and might end up gunning him down. He's a nice animal and I wouldn't want that to happen, you know?"

"I know, I agree. I'll keep him in the RV until we leave."

"Good," he said. "I'll get in touch with you later." Without saying goodbye or indeed another thing, he severed the connection.

"You have to stay human for a while," she told Kicky. "Apparently anything looking like a wolf in these parts is going to be gunned down."

"It sounded like he knew I could change," Kicky said.

"For a second it did to me two. But I'm not so sure now. Mostly he was warning me that Woofy needs to stay under wraps."

"We can certainly handle that."

The next morning Tess woke in the RV and sneaked out of the bedroom leaving Kicky sprawled across the top of the covers. He was in human form but naked as usual. He had gone to bed the night before in his Wolf form. When she came out to the main room she could see that Ondag was not in his loft bed and there was fresh coffee. She grabbed a mug of it.

The laptop was on the table where she had left it the night before. She opened it to check her accounts and read her e-mail. She would have none from Dad, since he was here in town with her. Her finances were good. She still had enough in her account to pay her Visa bill and get them to the next town. She planned on going on up to copper country and visit some of the bars and restaurants depicted in that book that Ondag had found for her.

Upon checking her e-mail messages she found that she only had two. One was from her old pal Harry. She opened that one at once just hungry for news from him. He sounded just fine. He told her he was happy and had a new girlfriend and was really getting into school and learning new things. He didn't want her to worry about him and looked forward to seeing her when and if she ever got down that far. He was in Arizona going to school and she thought that maybe they could reach that part of the country before he graduated. She was certainly going to try. She immediately sent off a message to him telling him how good it was to hear from him and to give her more details about his new girlfriend, like starting with her name. She wrote a bit about Kicky and how happy she was with him, and her new circumstances with the RV and her brother Ondag driving her around in it. Lastly she chided him to please stay in touch. She needed to hear from him more often than once a year. After all, they were still friends, correct?

After she sent off this e-mail she felt a pang of guilt for not telling him about the abduction. She promised herself that she would tell him about it in her next e-mail. In fact she would begin it right now in the form of a journal entry. She pulled up Word and began typing. About two pages into it she stopped and realized that she hadn't read the rest of her e-mail. She went back to yahoo and opened her mail page.

The other e-mail she had gotten was from Rick Kraft.

It was a cryptic message which asked if she would contact him at once and gave his phone number. She checked the time, it was after 9:00 A.M. She called the number. Rick answered immediately.

"Hey Tess, Kit has something she says she has to tell you, and it's really important. She won't tell me what it is though so I hope I'm not wasting your time."

"Not at all," Tess said. "Anytime Kit has something to say to me, you just tell her to call me, OK?"

"Not a bit of it," Rick said. "She wanted to call you this morning at about 3:00 A.M. I told her you were asleep and had to wait until morning."

"Oh, I see, Ok, thank you for that."

"Here she is." Tess heard the phone being handed over to the girl.

"Tess?" came the high sharp voice of the child.

"Yeah, hon, what is it?"

"I had a dream last night and my mommy told me to tell you about it and to make sure you knew all about it, OK?"

"Your Mommy?" Tess asked.

"Yes, you know, Dawn, my Mom," Kit said.

"Yes, I met her. But she's passed away Kit. You know that. How could she tell you anything?"

"She told me, OK, listen. She came to me in this dream and she told me that I need to tell you about this dream. OK? So are you listening with your soul?"

"With my soul?"

"Yeah, she told me that you were supposed to listen with your soul."

"What did she say Kit?" Tess was getting upset about this whole topic of souls.

"She said that she was free now and that we weren't to worry about her any more. She's going to be OK, because now she's with her maker. Tess, what does that mean, exactly? She's with her maker?"

"It means that she's with God or Jesus. A lot of people think of God as the maker or the creator."

"Oh," Kit said and then there was a significant pause while she thought about this. "That explains it," she said cryptically.

"Explains what?" Tess asked without thinking.

"She said she was trapped, lost, alone and couldn't find her way home, but now she was home and fine."

"Really," Tess said.

"Yeah, and she ex-specially wanted me to tell you about it. She told me to tell you to believe it. Do you believe it, Tess?"

Tess thought about this. The easiest thing would be to tell Kit that she did indeed believe that Kit's mother was in heaven with her maker, but what about the rest of it? Did Tess believe that Dawn's soul was trapped in the spiritual equivalent of the stomach of a soul eater? She could not go that far. No one knew what happened to the soul after it leaves this plain. It could be that Dawn's soul had to wander for a time because of the violent way it had been taken. Tess could believe in ghosts because she believed in the survival of the soul after death. That would explain the feeling of being lost. But Kit had said "Trapped, lost, and alone." Tess didn't know what to make of it.

"Do you Tess? Do you believe it?" Kit was getting insistent on the phone. She could hear Rick in the background asking for the phone back.

"Kit," Tess said. "Calm down OK? Did she say anything else?"

"Yeah, but I didn't understand it."

"Can you remember it, word for word?"

"Yeah." Kit said then the other end of the phone went silent. Tess was about to ask the famous can-you-hear-me-now question that so many people who use cell phones ask. But Kit's voice came through clearly in the next second. "She said that you Tess have got to let go what other people tell you about spirit and go with what you know about spirit yourself."

Tess took in a sharp breath. Her mind went elsewhere for a few minutes.

That feeling of deja vu overtook her. She went back in time to a memory. She was waking up after a nightmare. The nightmare landscape had been a labyrinth of trees, bushes and underbrush. She had awakened with the sharp knowledge of a voice in her head. It was her dead mother's voice. "You have to let go of what the Priests tell you about spirit and go forward with the knowledge that you already know all there is to know about your spirit."

Kit was now shouting into the phone. She was saying something about another woman with her mother and the woman had hair like Tessa's and she even looked kind of like Tess.

"Do you know who she was?" Kit said. She repeated that last again as her father took the phone from her hand.

"Calm down Kit," he told her. Then into the phone he said, "Tess, I'm sorry about this. I had no idea she just wanted to tell you about her dream. I would have spared you that."

"No, Rick, it's fine. It's something that I needed to hear."

"Really?" He said. "Oh then."

"Rick," she stopped him.

"Yeah."

"Anytime Kit needs to speak with me or Kicky, you give her the phone and let her talk with us. OK?"

"Really? Anytime? She is going to take advantage of that you know."

"What she told me was important, Rick. It was information I needed."

"Really?" He sounded entirely dubious. But

he accepted it.

"Are you heading home today?" she asked him.

"Yeah, going back to my in-law's to get the baby and then we'll be heading home to Chicago."

"Well, keep in touch, I mean it," Tess said.

They hung up and Tess looked back over what she had been doing. She had been writing a journal entry about the abduction. She changed tacks and began writing what she remembered about the dream after her mother had died. She knew that the dream had been after her mother died but she couldn't remember how long after. She thought that it might have been a few weeks after her mother's death or maybe as long as a year. She couldn't remember.

But the message had been a strong one. She was to feel in her heart what the truth was, and not just take the word of a priest. So, at the tender age of fourteen, Tess began her spiritual quest to find out where her mother's spirit had gone. She had explored many of the major religions of the world, but when it all came down to it she felt that she had a pretty good idea that it was not like how any of the religions described it.

During college her spiritual seeking got sidetracked into her studies. And eventually went by the wayside entirely. So it was a shock to her system that she got this message again, right now, after her brush with death.

Kicky came out of the back room, he stood there naked and looked at her before he stepped into the bathroom. She loved the way he looked in the morning. She figured that was why he paused, so she could have a good look. A long drawn out thought came to her mind, "That's right!" it said.

She smiled and chuckled. When he came out he put on a pair of jeans and went outside to the fire where Ondag had been sitting with a book.

"You're up," Ondag said. Tess could hear his voice through the open door but couldn't hear Kicky's response after he closed it behind him. She could just hear the mumbled conversation of the two men.

In a little while they came in and told her they were hungry and asked if there was a place she wanted to try for brunch today.

"Sure," she said. "And then after brunch I want to go up to Ishpeming for dinner. I think it's high time we leave this wonderful city of Marquette. What do you both think?"

"I'm game," Kicky said.

"Whatever you say, sis, you're the boss," Ondag told her.

"Let's drive today," she said. "I'm not in the mood to walk."

"You got it sister," Ondag said. She turned her computer around so that it was facing forward in the RV. Then she sat down at it. Kicky sat next to her and soon she told Ondag the coordinates of the next restaurant. They were on their way.

Chapter 14

Blog Entry: Tessa's Travels
August 3, 2011

Results of the best pasty in the U.P. are in. The award for best overall Pasty in the whole of the U.P. Goes to Jean Kay Pasties in Marquette, Michigan. Their blend of potato and rutabaga and their fresh chopped steak was the perfection of filling. Their crusts were flaky and moist and melt in-your-mouth good. I have other awards going out to various other establishments around the U.P. as well, so to see the whole list, please contact my Agent, (my Dad) and buy the entire article. Also I've had the extended pleasure of staying in Marquette for the past few days and trying several very good restaurants in that area, including

Cocoa's, The Verling and a great Italian eatery on Third Street called Casa Calabria. I have individual reviews for each.

I've had quite the experience up here in the U.P. It's been amazing, but I am now ready to roll. I am now traveling in an RV belonging to my adopted brother, Ondag Stark. Kicky and I will still be setting off at times on foot. I can't just give up walking, not with everything I eat. I'd be fat within a year if I did. But having the RV is going to make life on the road a little simpler. I won't have to haul my tent everywhere, only where we want to hike through wilderness. I'll have Kicky with me and Woofy too. We plan to stay together. I'm going to write more travel articles as well as the restaurant reviews, so if you are a publisher interested in seeing some of my new articles please contact my Father, his digits are in the box to the right as usual. I'm heading up to the copper country next and then on to Northern Wisconsin, Minnesota and the Dakota's. Keep watch for when I'll be in your area. Until then, happy trails.

Tessa Gates

Heading next:

Negaunee
Ishpeming
L'Anse
Baraga
Houghton
Hancock
Gay
Lac La Belle
Copper Harbor
Mohawk
Calumet

Ironwood
Wisconsin
Minnesota
North Dakota
South Dakota

Chapter 15

Clyde felt strongly as the leader of his tribe that it was his personal duty to see to the remains of Talbot Rivershade, which is what lead to the request that the body be released to him as his nephew and nearest kinsman. A matter of hours after this request was submitted the morgue called him back. Clyde was still in Marquette in his room at the Ramada.

"Mr. Morrow?" the Morgue attendant asked after identifying himself. "I just got a request that the body be released to Rivershade's son in Minnesota. I know you gave us a request as his nephew. I just don't know what to do about this. He would be the closer relative."

"Rivershade had no son that I know of,"

Clyde said.

"Could he have a son that you don't know of?"

"He's never been married. But I guess that doesn't always preclude the other."

"Right," the man said chuckling, then his voice again became tenuous. "But, do I release it to him then?"

"Can you give me his name?"

"He said his name was Luca Campbell Rivershade, from Red Lake, Minnesota."

"Red Lake? Is he Ojibwa?"

"Um, I'm not sure, he looked more like an Irishman. Red hair, freckles, tall, very pail skin."

"Did he have any physical resemblance to the deceased?"

"Yes, he has the same facial structure, kind of high cheekbones and dark eyes. He looks a lot like him, I'd say."

"Is he there now?"

"Yes, sir, I asked him to wait while we get this straightened out."

"I'll be right there." Clyde hung up the phone before the guy could utter another word. He had to ask several people where to find the morgue. The desk clerk at the Ramada didn't know. But even with this delay he managed to get there in less than ten minutes.

When he entered the outer office of the morgue he was met with the sight of a man well over six feet tall. He had to look up to see this man's face even from several feet away. The man had light red hair clearly visible under his cap. He had on a blue uniform and the arm patch marked him as a tribal policeman. He did resemble Rivershade in the eyes and face a little. Clyde held out a hand to his kinsman.

"Clyde Morrow, I'm nephew to Talbot Rivershade."

The man was maybe only a few years younger than Clyde. He didn't seem to have inherited the agelessness of the Eagle Clan.

"Luca, my friends call me Howling Dog." Clyde knew this to be his Native name. He did indeed have Native blood if he had a name like Howling Dog.

"Nice to know you Luca," he said shaking the man's hand. "I didn't know I had any cousins in this branch of the family."

"I think Talbot did that on purpose," Luca admitted. "I would have liked to have known about you as well." Clyde heard a slight bitter tone in his voice and wished he had time to really get to know this man.

"I didn't want to step on your rights to bury your father. Of course it's your right."

"And I claim it. I want to make sure he gets in the ground personally. I still can't believe he is dead. I want to bury him next to my mother and all his other wives up on the Rez. How well did you know him?" Luca said and gave Clyde a look that spoke a whole manuscript.

"I didn't know him very well," Clyde admitted. "We were always afraid he would show up again on the rez. I always thought about what I would do to get rid of him."

Luca sucked in a long deep breath and nodded. "That's about how we felt too. I was raised by adopted relatives up in the Red Lake Reservation. My mother died about ten years ago giving birth to another of Talbot's children. These last twenty years or so, he seemed more and more bent on procreating. With whom, he didn't much care."

Clyde gave Luca a long look.

"I'm about to ask you a question, and you don't have to answer it if you don't want."

"What's that?" the man looked down his nose at his cousin.

"Are you Eagle Clan?"

"What do you mean?" he asked.

"You're name, Howling dog, do you change?"

Luca looked away, suddenly becoming interested in the sign posted on the doors to the left of him. He scratched his nose with the palm of his hand and then did his best to look bored before he turned his face back toward Clyde. "No. I haven't. Not in a long time. I took the cure."

"Cure?"

He shook his head. "So, do you want to let me bury him or not?" he asked abruptly, again looking at the signs on the door.

"You can have him. I only signed on thinking I was his closest relative."

Luca nodded again. He held out his hand. "Good to have met you."

Clyde took his hand reluctantly. "Keep in touch, won't you? We are relatives after all. You wouldn't ever hurt any of your relatives, would you?"

Luca turned without answering him and went into the morgue office.

Clyde stood for a moment contemplating the issues involved in questioning the man further. In the end he too just walked away. It was a problem for another day. But maybe, when Tess, Kicky and Ondag made their way up to Northern Minnesota, he might visit them and his distant relatives up there. He would tell Tess about a great restaurant up there that he went to one time. That might be enough to spur her in that direction. It would only be a suggestion after all.

Acknowledgements:

I want to thank all the readers who made it this far. I've enjoyed getting to know Tess, Kicky and Ondag as they've traveled through the Northwoods of Michigan. If you've enjoyed this story I just want you to know that it will be continuing. Tess has more to learn in the Northwoods!

Watch for more of the Northwoods series, Book 2, "Lost in the Woods." The first installment of which is available now for the Kindle.

I'd like to thank all of my supporters who have become my loyal readers. Especially those of you in RQK (you all know who you are!) and certain family members in Marquette and Traverse City. I'd also like to thank Adam Beach and Derek

J. Bailey for the models for Kicky and Ondag. My imagina uns away with me at times. Oh well.

Step King in some of his books describes a phenome alled "Toe-dash," which is how his characters n and out of different dimensions. I have ofter that this, more than any other, is a proper te or what happens with writers when they are e their own heads during the process of writin So I will add Stephen, my hero, my mentor, spirit guide, to the list of people to whom I gratitude. If ever I go back to school and get MFA in writing, my Master's Thesis will be led, "Extra Dimensional travel in the worlds tephen King."

, as Tess says, "Onward!" We have more food theeds to be tasted, more Northwoods to be documed, more questions to be answered! We will s ou again soon.

indy Koch-Krol, October 8, 2014

Made in the USA
Charleston, SC
03 December 2015